D0941909

Wild Rover No More

L. A. MEYER

Wild Rover No More

Being the Last Recorded Account of the
Life and Times of Jacky Faber

Houghton Mifflin Harcourt

Boston   *New York*

www.hmhco.com

Text set in Minion Pro

Library of Congress Cataloging-in-Publication Data
Meyer, L. A. (Louis A.), 1942–
Wild rover no more : being the last recorded account
of the life & times of Jacky Faber / by L.A. Meyer.
pages cm — (Bloody Jack adventures)
Summary: In 1809, just when it looks like Jacky Faber and her beloved
Jaimy will finally find their romance, Jacky is accused of treason and must
flee Boston while her friends attempt to clear her name. Of course that means
wild adventures for our fun-loving heroine, who manages to secure a job as a
governess — and run away with the circus. — Provided by publisher.
ISBN 978-0-544-21777-5 (hardback)
[1. Adventure and adventurers — Fiction. 2. Fugitives from justice — Fiction.
3. Love — Fiction.] I. Title.
PZ7.M57172Wi 2015
[Fic] — dc23
2014000739

Manufactured in the United States of America
DOC 10 9 8 7 6 5 4 3 2 1
4500502192

. . . and finally, just for Annetje

Prologue

Miss Clarissa Worthington Howe
The House of the Rising Sun
New Orleans, Louisiana, USA

My dearest Jacky,

It is my fondest hope that this letter finds you in the highest of spirits and in the very pink of condition, you sweet little thing, you.

You are surprised by my return address up there above? Well, dear, I felt it was a perfect place for me to go — my daddy will never find me here. Thank you for introducing me to Mademoiselle Claudelle de Bourbon on my previous visit here, for through her I find I have entry to a very sporting class of people. Mam'selle is well and great fun, of course, and sends her love and affection. And do not worry, I shall not again fall into dependence on those substances she is so eager to provide — no, I am older and far wiser now.

Is your Mr. Fletcher here by my side? Oh, you silly thing, don't you know that was an elaborate little joke? It was just a game. You do realize I had to pay you back for my loss of Randall, don't you? So now we're all even — Polly Von can have both Randall and my part in your little play. That was amusing, but time for me to move on.

And the very idea of me, Clarissa Worthington Howe, being married to a very junior British naval officer—oh my dear, it just could not be. Oh, I mean he was most pleasant company on our way down to New York. We had many fine promenades on the deck as night fell, but I did find him a bit gloomy. I suspect he is still mooning over the loss of his pwetty widdle Jacky Faber. Oh well, he'll get over that. But oh! Oh! Oh! If you could have just seen the look on your face when our ship pulled away from the dock and you came running down to find James looking out to sea and me with my arm around his waist. Joy! I must say my timing was perfect! It was as perfect as that scene you staged back at Dovecote when I pulled up in my coach to find you and Randall rolling around on the grass, Randall above and you below, with your skirts up around your waist. Turnabout is fair play, right, Jacky?

Anyway, dear, thank you for introducing me to New Orleans, as the place suits me. I have taken rooms here at the Rising Sun, as it seems to be the center of all activity in this city, and I have found employment as a singer. I did have to post a bond with Madame Babineau, considering my past behavior here at the Rising Sun, silly stuff that I can scarcely recall. Anyway, I gave her a check in the amount of $500, written on the account of Faber Shipping Worldwide, and she seemed pleased. You have probably noticed that one of your cunning little packets of checks is missing. Is it not the most wondrous thing, Jacky? I write out the amount and sign your name . . . I will try to be careful with it.

Thank you also for teaching me to play upon the guitar. With my good soprano voice and my beauty, of course, I am quite the hit. Could I be becoming you? Heaven forbid . . . but, possibly . . . a well-bred, cultured, and beautiful version of you, maybe. You have shown me the way, Jacky, and I thank you for it . . . and for the loan of your guitar. I'm sure you'll find another one soon.

As for my beauty, my fame is spreading. I am performing in several theatrical productions and do not lack for money nor notice. As a matter of fact, I am to be escorted to a grand ball tonight by a General Jackson — do you know him? He is friends with the Lafitte brothers, both of whom send their regards in hopes of seeing you again very soon. They were most emphatic on that.

And while we're on the subject of my beauty, if I were you, I would not go looking for the painting that Spanish boy did of you, as I have borrowed it, also. It has been beautifully framed and now hangs over the bar at the Rising Sun and is admired by all. The Lafitte brothers and I, together with Andrew, were just minutes ago standing in front of it, and all toasted you most warmly — the resemblance is simply amazing. I swear Mam'selle kneels in prayer before it every day. I cannot imagine why it upset your Mr. Fletcher so. After all, we have always known of your . . . exhibitionist tendencies.

Mr. Fletcher . . . Oh, yes, you will probably want to know about him. We parted at New York and he took ship for England, while I continued on to New Orleans. I believe he will try to regain his commission in the Royal Navy, and

I say good luck to him. Actually, I think he still loves you, poor man. I did, of course, intercept a letter to you that he had placed at the Pig, wherein he suggested a meeting of reconciliation between the two of you. Silly boy. I just could not allow that to happen. I enclose that letter with this one so that you might enjoy.

Your piratical friend Flaco Jimenez was in New Orleans last week. I believe he came because he had heard I was here, and he showed me an excellent time. The Lafittes do not know all of the low dives in this town, but Flaco is familiar with all of them. He asks after you, of course, but has invited me to go a-roving with him. He might even give me my own ship. I must say the offer is most enticing and I might do it someday . . . The dread Pirate Howe—it has a nice ring to it, don't you think?

The night is very pleasantly warm and the air is heavily laden with the perfume of tropical flowers, and, oh, I do believe Andrew is here to escort me to the ball.

Till later, Jacky. Keep well. I do love you, you know, in my own way. I used to think you were something nasty stuck to the bottom of my shoe, but I have changed my mind on that. Since you have come into my life, you have been ever so much fun.

Sincerely,
Clarissa Worthington Howe

PART I

Chapter 1

In the late summer of the year eighteen hundred and nine, we were just back from a fine Caribbean cruise on the *Nancy B. Alsop*, my lovely little two-masted Gloucester schooner — sixty-five feet in length, thirty feet in the beam — a fore-and-aft rig, and as sweet a sailor as ever did cleave an ocean wave. We angled in on a light, fair breeze toward our usual dockage on Boston's crowded waterfront. As we headed in, I noticed that the *Morning Star*, the larger of Faber Shipping's two dories, was not moored in her usual spot. Solomon Freeman probably had her out on the bay, hauling traps, but the *Evening Star* was tied to the floating dock.

I noticed also that the mighty British frigate HMS *Shannon* was moored alongside Broad Wharf. Well, fine. I am done with all that — the British Navy, British Intelligence, young British officers, be they navy, or cavalry dragoons, or whatever.

And that is for certain, as sure as my name is Jacky Faber. Though born in England, I sail under American colors, and my company, Faber Shipping Worldwide, is based in Boston, Massachusetts, USA. I am a free woman of nineteen years, and I owe no allegiance to any man, having vowed to live single all my life. My business thrives, and my many employees are happy with their lot, as I am with mine. I prosper and I am content.

After seeing the *Nancy B.* properly tied up, with her crew and passengers sent off to wives and sweethearts and other pursuits, I am headed back to the offices of Faber Shipping Worldwide to exchange reports of a business nature with my very able friend and lawyer Mr. Ezra Pickering. On the way there, I reflect on our latest cruise:

On this trip, I had taken along Joannie Nichols, my fourteen-year-old ward and fellow Cheapside orphan, and she purely reveled in every minute of it, knowing full well she would have to go back to the Lawson Peabody School for Young Girls upon our return. She is most unwilling to return to those hallowed halls, to be sure, much preferring a life on the open sea, as do I; but she has made many friends there now, so it will not be so hard on her this time.

I no longer permit Joannie to bundle with Daniel Prescott, another member of my crew and her long-time beau, as I perceive her to be now fully grown and capable of getting herself into trouble. No, she is kicked upstairs to sleep in my cabin with me, as I need the nighttime company to ward off the nightmares and she needs to watch herself, for Mistress Pimm accepts only certified maidens in her school. I should know, having been closely grilled by Mistress on that very topic more than a few times in the past. *Yes, Mistress, no longer your student but still a maiden, and I shall remain forever so.*

Davy Jones is also on this trip, as well as his dear wife, Annie. So, with Joannie, Jemimah, Annie, Dorothea, and me, this was quite the petticoat crew. But I don't care — it's my ship and I'll do what I want with her.

All in all, it has been an enjoyable cruise, and more and more each day, I am liking my new life free of males.

In addition to the others, I have my son, Ravi, by my side as ship's boy, both of us filled with joy at our reunion. After a few trips across the Big Salt on my brigantine *Lorelei Lee* — to prevent him from being retaken by the Boston authorities and tossed back into that wretched boys' reformatory — he pronounces himself "a true son of the sea, Memsahib, a sailor man skilled in many useful things. The clever Sinbad has not a single thing on sailor boy Ravi." He, too, must return to school soon, now that we've docked in Boston, but in the meantime delights in showing his fellow *Lorelei* ship's boys around the town. They are told they may eat and drink their fill at the Pig and Whistle, but are warned against visits to Mrs. Bodeen's fancy house. Don't tell me I don't know ship's boys, as I once was one.

Ah, yes, a lovely cruise, and one enjoyed to the fullest by Dorothea and Mr. Sackett, she being a former classmate of mine at the Lawson Peabody and he being a teacher at the same school. The two had been tossed out on their ears for the crime of marrying each other. Both are dedicated scientists and were in absolute glory over the richness of the fauna we had found in the warm waters of the Caribbean. Joannie and I delighted in getting back into our swimming suits and diving for specimens, as well as for dinner. Yes, plenty of lobsters, fish, and shrimp for our cook, Jemimah Moses, to work her magic on, but no more riches from the wreck of the *Santa Magdalena,* which had once yielded so much in the way of Spanish gold for the treasury of merry England . . . and for me. We look forward to more such voyages in the near future, and the Sacketts pronounce themselves delighted. I even plan a crossing of the Isthmus of Panama to explore the west coast of this continent. How I will accomplish that, I do not know. I do know, however, that I will *not* attempt to sail through Tierra del Fuego, down at the tip of South America, for I have heard too many stories of that fierce wind-blown passage. Plus, I do not like the cold.

Perhaps with the help of my leather-bound illustrations of their specimens, it is to be hoped that Mr. Sackett will finally gain a position on the faculty of the college in Cambridge, and maybe I will see some of the back rent they owe me, they being as poor as church mice. Hey, my illustrations worked for Dr. Sebastian back at the Royal Society in London; why not in New England? If not, the Sacketts will continue to travel with me, as I enjoy their company and their boundless enthusiasm for science and nature, and I have learned much from them as well. *Think of it as paying tuition, girl. You never know when it might come in handy.*

And so it is with no small measure of pride that I stride into the offices of Faber Shipping Worldwide. Long may it prosper.

Chapter 2

After I give an affectionate wave of greeting to Miss Chloe Cantrell, who sits at the reception desk poring over invoices and accounts, she shows me into the office of Ezra Pickering, Clerk of Faber Shipping Worldwide.

"So good to see you back, Jacky," says he, rising from his desk and holding out his hand. "I hope you had a pleasant journey." He is, of course, impeccably dressed and groomed, as well he should be, being a prosperous young attorney — made prosperous, in large part, because of the primarily legal business doings of Faber Shipping.

"Most pleasant, thank you, Ezra," I say, taking his hand and a chair. As usual after a cruise, I pass over to him my ship's log and any diplomatic pouches I might have been handed by foreign embassies. There is only one this time. From Havana.

He takes his own chair, and we begin our meeting.

"I perceive that you have been rather restless of late, Jacky. You have taken three trips to the southern waters," he says, picking up a sheaf of papers, "since —"

"Since I was bound to the courthouse whipping post,

my back bared, and administered twelve strokes of the rod for the joy of the mob? And you wonder why I prefer the sea to the land?"

"Well, I believe that situation could have gone much worse."

I reserve judgment on that with a solid *humph.*

"I hope that Amy Trevelyne is well?" I ask, with raised eyebrow. Ezra has been well-mannered in pursuit of the shy Miss Trevelyne for some time now, but she has proved elusive, saying only, "I am not yet ready for that sort of thing." She has forgiven me for some depredations against propriety and common sense on my part, and she is once again my dearest friend, in spite of the differences in our temperaments. I greatly enjoy my stays with her at dear old Dovecote between voyages.

"Yes, she is well," he says, and gives me his little half smile. "And she avidly looks forward to your next visit."

Then we get down to business in earnest.

"Ahem. Revenues are up. The fishing fleet is doing well, as are the Emerald Playhouse and the Pig and Whistle Inn. We were able to sell the cargoes of your last two cruises and expect no difficulty with this latest one. We must keep the rum distilleries supplied with ample molasses, mustn't we? Your fire brigade, the Shamrock Hose, Ladder, and Pump Company, under the able direction of Arthur McBride, are dashing about putting out fires and signing up new insurance subscribers every day. He has become quite the local hero."

"Hardly surprising," I murmur.

"And, since Pigger O'Toole's gang of scofflaws has been

cleared out of Skivareen's, all outstanding indentures for passage on the *Lorelei Lee* are now paid up, thanks largely to the fists of John Thomas and Smasher McGee."

"Good lads."

"And the *Lee* herself is due in with another load of passengers. The trouble between the rival gangs has quieted down, so there should be no trouble disembarking the Irish families."

"Wonderful news," I say. "I shall delight in seeing the rest of my friends yet again."

"Ahem. Well, on to expenses," he says briskly, handing me a bundle of bills covered with numbers, causing my eyes to cross in boredom. Seeing this, he goes on. "I'm pleased to report that all these annoying invoices have been paid, as has this check for five hundred dollars written on your account and made out to a Madame Babineau at the Rising Sun in New Orleans. I had to cover that, even though I did not recognize your signature. I did, however, close out that account so that no more withdrawals can be made from it. I hope I did right?"

"Yes, you did, Ezra, and thank you," I say, pulling out a letter from my vest and handing it to him. "This will explain." I flip Clarissa's New Orleans letter across his desk.

Never hide anything from your lawyer, I always say . . .

Ezra takes it and reads. When he is finished, he folds up the letter and looks off, plainly considering something.

"Very interesting and, indeed, it does explain much."

"It certainly explains why I have chosen to live single all of my life. If it does not, here is another letter that I received after that. It is one that certainly threw the latch on my heart for good and ever. It is from Cavalry Major Lord Richard Allen. When last I saw that gallant officer, he was being carried off the field at the Battle of Vimeiro, grievously wounded. I got it several weeks after Miss Howe's chatty little note."

I toss over the letter bearing the coat of arms of the Seventh Dragoons at the top. He takes it up and reads . . .

Major Lord Richard Allen
Seventh Dragoons
Kingston, Jamaica
August 28, 1809

Miss Jacky Faber
The Pig and Whistle
Boston, Massachusetts, USA

My dear Jacky,

Yes, Prettybottom, I am back from the dead and back on the line. I cannot thank you enough for seeing me into the care of the very competent Dr. Stephen Sebastian and his delightful family. I am quite sure I would now be bothering the imps of hell if not for your efforts.

You can see from my address that I am back in harness, and with a promotion to boot for showing "conspicuous bravery" in holding that breastwork at Vimeiro. I was also given a nice medal. I asked that you be awarded one, too, since you also were there, but they would hear none of that. Surprisingly, though, Old Nosey spoke up on that one, saying, "The girl was most valuable both in Portugal and Spain and certainly deserves something for her service," but nothing came of it. I think the only reward you will receive is being once again reassigned to his staff when he returns to Spain as Lord Wellington. Best lie low, Jacky, if you want to avoid that singular pleasure.

I have heard you are back in Boston, and I do hope you will meet up with your Lieutenant Fletcher, Royal Navy. That would be a good thing, as I found him a fine man and entirely worthy of you . . . should I ever let you slip from my grasp.

I myself have had a rather pleasant time of it — travel-, career-, and romance-wise. It went down like this:

Last month I was selected to lead a delegation of politicos to New Orleans to confer with American officials there to try to lessen the tensions that are growing between our two countries — maybe they thought a "Real British Lord" would impress the colonials; I don't know. But I certainly put on the Aristocratic and Arrogant Young Lord act for them, and I hope they appreciated it, and I further hope it did something to avoid a stupid war.

But if it comes down to a conflict, what will you be, Jacky — British or American? Hmmm . . . I hope you never have to choose.

But on to more pleasant things . . . much more pleasant things.

After the political business of the first day was done — thank God; dreadfully boring stuff — our party was shown to a very active gambling and sporting house for some pre-dinner drinks. We were standing at the bar and toasting kings and presidents and such, when the bell for four o'clock was chimed. Then one of the comely young things the place seemed to be full of advanced to a spot behind the bar where hung a silken cord that was attached to a set of velvet draperies, which apparently concealed something of interest to the crowd. I guessed this was a sort of ceremony that opened the night's festivities, and I was right.

The girl pulled the cord, the curtains parted, and a fine painting was revealed. The place gave a roar of approval.

Oh, my God, Princess, how you have gotten around!

Glasses were lifted and toasts were made to "*The Venus de New Orleans*," "*The Naked Maja*," and "*The Girl with the Blue Tattoo*," and I must say, Prettybottom, you may rest assured, your front is every bit as pretty as your back.

My gasp of astonishment was echoed even more forcefully by a young man who stood next to me. "*My God— Jacky!*" he said as his glass slipped from his hand and fell to the floor. I tore my gaze from the remarkably realistic painting of you, wearing nothing but a tattoo and a smile, to look upon him.

"Do you know her, Sir?" I asked. He is a newly minted Royal Navy Lieutenant named Raeburne, I believe.

"Y-yes, Sir," he replied. "W-we served together on HMS *Wolverine*."

"Ha! You dog!" I said, clapping him on the shoulder. "I have read that book. So you are the midshipman Robin Raeburne of that little epic and have seen that holy blue tattoo in the flesh, or, rather, *on* the flesh, as it were?"

He could only nod.

"Well, young fellow, my congratulations. It might interest you to know that she now has another tattoo stitched onto her lovely hide, it being a golden dragon, and it lies — "

I was interrupted on this discourse of your various comely parts and the decorations thereon by a very beautiful young woman who had come up beside me bearing a fresh glass of champagne, which she demurely offered to me, saying in a very soft and charming accent . . .

"Please accept this, Lord Allen," she murmured, her eyes modestly cast down, "for I know we share a mutual acquaintance with my very dear friend Jacky Faber, pictured so gloriously there. My name is Miss Clarissa Worthington Howe."

To make a long story short, Miss Howe and I have been enjoying each other's company for some weeks now. I get up to New Orleans when I can, and she has come down to visit me in Jamaica. I can tell you, my reputation has certainly been enhanced by squiring *that* one about Kingston. She does turn heads.

Clarissa's family — Clarissa's very rich and powerful family, from which she had been estranged — has made overtures concerning reconciliation, and she plans to go to Virginia in the spring and wishes me to be by her side. As a rather impoverished lord of a poor estate, I have little more to offer than my title and a rather nicely turned leg, but still, it seems to serve. So, having cleared it with my commanding officer, I intend to go and ride to the hounds in Olde Virginia. I shall show the colonials how it is done, by God.

Well, I must end this letter, as Clarissa and I are off to the races, and then to a play this evening in which she has a part. She lies, in fact, curled up next to me here in my rooms as I pen this and wishes me to tender her most warm regards as well as a heartfelt kiss. See, she has donned fresh lip rouge and leans over my lap to plant a kiss for you here on the letter itself. See, there it is. Then she places one on my cheek as well, which I find equally warm and welcome.

Before sealing up the letter, Clarissa has taken it from

me and taken up the pen. Between the impressions of her upper and lower lips, she has drawn a very sharp tooth.

Ah, the merry repartee between dear friends, how utterly charming.

I remain your dear friend and most ardent admirer,
Richard

"You can well imagine my reaction to *that* one, Ezra."

"Umm. The word *volcanic* comes to mind. And the letter is rather the worse for wear."

"Indeed."

I slip back into remembrance of that particular time . . .

"GODDAMITTOHELL, ANYHOW!" I bellowed as I crumpled up that letter and flung it against the wall. *"First she takes Jaimy, then Flaco, and now Richard! Must she have them all? I can't stand it, I just can't stand it!"*

"Now, Miss," said my good friend John Higgins, who was attending me in my state of towering fury and attempting to calm me. I stood quivering, with arms held to my sides, fists and teeth clenched, and face in a grimace of absolute rage. "Please sit down and let us discuss this situation. Please, Miss, you will injure your mind and bring on brain fever. You must be calm. Here, a glass of wine with you. There, that's better. Have another sip."

I did sit then, and attempted to quiet my heaving chest. "What I am going to do, Higgins," I said, more quietly now, "is outfit the *Nancy B.* for a cruise down the southern coast, deliver a cargo, then put in to New Orleans and kill that scheming bitch in the most gruesome way possible."

"Now, Miss, I know you do not mean that—"

"Yes, I do, Higgins," I retorted. "I befriended her, helped her out when she was in need, shared my bed with her, introduced her to my friends, gave her shelter from the storm, employed her in Faber Shipping Worldwide, and now I find I have clasped an asp to my bosom! And if Richard marries her, I shall have to call her Lady Allen! Oh, God, not that! I can't stand it. *I just can't stand it!*"

I stood and collected myself, then said to Higgins, "After that, I shall ready the *Nancy B.* for a cruise to the South Seas. Faber Shipping already has routes into the Oriental spice trade, and the *Lorelei Lee* is prospering in bringing Irish workers to New York and Boston. When I get back, I will load more armament on the *Lorelei Lee* and take her out on the broad ocean, and woe to any person, any company, any nation, and any vessel that dares to interfere with my trade. If need be, I shall turn pirate, and to hell with all of them!"

I paused for a shaky breath.

"And I will tell you this, Higgins," I continued, "I am done with love and the false love of young men. I will live single all my life, and this time I mean it. Do you know what love is, John? Do you? I will tell you: It is humbug . . . Humbug and nothing more! I have hardened my heart and will have nothing more to do with it, and I vow to become the most ruthless, heartless, determined businesswoman on this globe. Faber Shipping Worldwide will prosper and will cover the world, and I will rule that empire. We will sail in three days. If you want to go with me, you are most welcome. As for now, John, good day, as I want to be alone."

I seethed . . . I fumed . . .

HUMBUG!

"I sense you have suffered much, Jacky," says Ezra, putting down that letter and picking up Clarissa's again.

"You may rest assured that the readings of those letters were not high points in my life. I sense that Higgins accompanied me on the last cruise to make sure I did not carry out my threat to kill the divine Miss Howe. Trust me, the *Nancy B.* went nowhere near New Orleans or Kingston on our last jaunt. Furthermore, you may also trust me when I say I shall suffer no more in matters of love."

"Umm," he says, continuing to muse. Finally, he says, "There might be a complication here, a complication of an immediate . . . personal nature, Miss."

"How so? I believe I have my personal affairs in order." I sniff primly.

"Perhaps. May I direct your attention to a particular paragraph in Miss Howe's letter? Yes? Very well, to wit: 'Mr. Fletcher . . . Oh, yes, you will probably want to know about him. We parted at New York and he took ship for England, while I continued on to New Orleans. I believe he will try to regain his commission in the Royal Navy, and I say good luck to him. Actually, I think he still loves you, poor man.'"

"So? I do not care where he is or whom he loves. Good luck to him. He is out of my heart and out of my life."

"Perhaps you noticed on your way here that HMS *Shannon* is docked on Long Wharf?"

"Yes, I did, but I am done with the British Navy as well, and British Intelligence, too. I am now a simple Yankee trader and proud of it. John Bull has no more claim on Jacky Faber."

Ezra opens a drawer and pulls out a slim white envelope. He passes it over and I see that it has *Miss Jacky Faber* written on the front. Suspicious, I let it lie on the desktop and give him a questioning look.

He takes a deep breath, then says, "The newly reinstated Lieutenant James Fletcher is on the *Shannon* and requests an audience with you."

I shoot to my feet.

"Wot? How . . . ?"

"How did he get over to England and back in such a short time? My dear, you have been at sea various times over the past month or so, in, I believe, a state of high indignation. Ample time for him to go over and back if the winds were fair. As for his regaining his commission, he tells me he had help from a Dr. Sebastian and a Mr. Peel, who have influence with the First Lord of the Admiralty. His court-martial has been expunged from the record," says Ezra, refolding Clarissa's letter. "Powerful friends, indeed."

"I will not see him, and I will not read his lying words," I say, picking up the letter and flinging it back onto the desk.

"Perhaps if you knew that the *Shannon* is due to leave tomorrow for London, you might grant him his request. He is Second Mate, so he must go with her."

Damn! A complication . . .

"And it must be noted that he was very lucky to find you in port, given your rather peripatetic nature of late. Perhaps you could chalk it up to Fate? Serendipity, even," says Ezra, with a hopeful half smile. He is ever the skillful negotiator.

I seethe, I fume . . . and then I say, "Very well. Although I don't see the point of it, I will attend Mr. Fletcher in my rooms at the Pig and Whistle at five o'clock for what I promise will be a *very* short meeting. And tell him to leave his damned stick on the ship. You will take care of the diplomatic pouch? Thank you, Ezra. Will you be joining me when I go to visit Amy at Dovecote? Good, that will give me great pleasure. You may give those letters to her, as I have no further interest in them, and she will find them juicy grist for her literary mill. And give me his damned letter . . . Till later, then, Ezra. *Adieu.*"

He hands it over and I snatch it up, fuming, and head for the Pig and Whistle.

Damn!

Chapter 3

I breeze into the Pig and Whistle, outwardly bright and cheerful while inwardly in great turmoil, and merrily greet Maudie and Molly Malone, who are stocking the bar and getting ready for the night's business.

"Welcome back, Boss. Should be a good night," says Maudie, former owner of this pub and now my trusted manager of same. "The German American Friendship Society rented out the Playhouse for three days and has turned the place into a big beer garden for some sort of festival."

"Aye, Jacky," says Molly. "We've ordered an extra five kegs for those jolly burghers and their fräuleins, for they sure can put it away. I know we'll be right sick of polkas by the time we clear them out."

"Sounds like fun to me, Molly," I say, following with what I hope is a carefree laugh as I head for the stairs, seabag on shoulder. "I'm sure to be in the middle of it tonight. You know I'm always up for a party, and everyone knows I can polka with the best of 'em. Oh, and by the way, there will be a British naval officer coming to call at five o'clock. You may send him up to my rooms."

Molly cocks an appraising eye at me and asks, "I suppose I should be bringing up a tray of food and drink when he gets here?" Then she leers and says, "Or maybe I should be waitin' a half hour or so, and then go in with me eyes cast down?"

"No. Definitely not. Just send him up," I say, frost replacing merriment in my voice.

With that, I climb the stairs to my quarters to ready myself for this meeting that I really do not want to have.

Damn! I had this all settled in my mind, and now I do not. Damn!

I slide my desk, which usually sits next to my window so as to catch the light, across the room to sit three feet in front of the door, making the lack of welcome very evident. Then I look in the mirror, resolving to leave my face plain and free of makeup and further deciding to leave on my Lawson Peabody school dress, it being the least provocative of all my garments.

Then I sit and wait. I see by my brassbound ship's clock mounted on the wall that it is four forty-five, so I have some time. Well, waste not, want not, I always say. I have some correspondence to take care of, so I pull out inkwell, quill, and paper, and begin work on a letter to my grandfather, the Reverend Henry Alsop, headmaster of the London Home for Little Wanderers. That's the orphanage in Cheapside that I had set up with prize money and continue to maintain as a nod to my origins as a street urchin on the hard streets of that city. *Ah, to hell with it!* I toss the pen aside and rip open Mr. Fletcher's letter . . .

Lieutenant James Emerson Fletcher
Second Mate, HMS Shannon

Miss Jacky Faber
Faber Shipping Worldwide
Boston, Massachusetts, USA

Dearest Jacky,

Of the many star-crossed letters I have written to you, this one I know will get to you, for I watched you bring the Nancy B. *into Boston moments ago, so I know you are here. I have given this letter over to Ezra Pickering for delivery to your hand only. Believe me, Clarissa Howe shall not purloin this one.*

What is there to say, Jacky, after all this time? That I love you? That is true enough, but what of you? Have you hardened your heart against me forever and ever? I would not blame you if you had, but please agree to meet with me, Jacky, at least. The Shannon *leaves tomorrow and I must go with her. If you want me to leave you forever, I will do so, but I must see you before then.*

Yours,
Jaimy

FORGET IT! I'm sick of you, Jaimy. NO! I've taken enough from you. No!

I am stuffing the letter back into the envelope when I hear a tap on the door and, of course, it is a very discreet knock. *When will you ever learn, Jaimy?* I look up, and it is precisely five o'clock on the button. Ah, good old Royal Navy punctuality. *Not a moment to lose . . . but don't get there too early.*

I compose myself and say, "Come in."

The door opens and he stands before me. At last . . .

Oh, Jaimy, over the years, I had waited so long for a moment like this . . . When I was tossed into the Lawson Peabody and you were taken so far away from me, and then when I was trapped on the Bloodhound, *and all of those other times when we were worlds apart. Yet now you stand before me, oh so smart in your fine lieutenant's jacket of blue, with those cold gray-blue eyes drilling straight into mine. But NO! Not into my heart, for I shall not allow it. Know, Jaimy, that though you now stand before me, you are farther away from me than ever before.*

He gives a short bow, but I do not rise, saying only, "Mr. Fletcher," in my coldest voice. "You wished to see me?"

"Jacky, I — "

"Forgive the formality, Mr. Fletcher, but unless you are one of my close friends, which you are not, I prefer to be called Miss Faber. What is it you wish to discuss?"

He takes a deep breath and then answers, rather testily, "Miss Faber. I had hoped that by our meeting, we might possibly effect a reconciliation of the differences that have risen between us."

"Fancy talk, Mr. Fletcher," I retort. "Seeing as how the last time I had the pleasure of your company, I was forced to my knees and tied to the courthouse stake, my back bared, whereupon you inflicted on that poor back twelve lashes of your rod. The spectacle was well received by the mob, as I recall. Then when that particular nasty job was done, I was freed of my bonds in time for me to run down to the harbor only to see you sail off with Miss Clarissa Worthington Howe wrapped around you. You did not seem to mind her presence. I trust you and she had an enjoyable voyage."

"Ezra Pickering, Randall Trevelyne, and I all agreed that the proceeding at the courthouse was the best way out of that rather . . . tenuous situation. As for Miss Howe . . ."

"Pity I was not consulted concerning that beating, considering it was my body that was to suffer. As for Clarissa Howe, you can do what you want with her, as it is no concern to me. I have a business to run, so if you'll excuse me . . ."

"I attempted to lay on the blows gently, consistent with pleasing the court and the crowd as to the severity of the beating."

"The last lash wasn't all that gentle. It really hurt."

"For that I am sorry. My temper got the best of me. You see, I had seen that painting of you, and when you did not respond to the letter I had written you, suggesting we discuss matters that had come between us . . ."

"Ah, yes, the letter Clarissa so cunningly intercepted. Yes, she wrote me a letter of her own, from New Orleans, relating with great glee how she had pulled off that little trick. I was most amused," I say scornfully. "So you were displeased with me because of that painting and then you sat down and wrote me a nice letter," I say, my voice still dripping with contempt. "How very like you, Jaimy, to do things that way. Do you know that most gentlemen of my acquaintance would have simply grabbed me by the throat and put me up against a wall and demanded an explanation? Why didn't you do that, Jaimy? I would have gladly given you one, and either you would have accepted it or not and we could have gotten on with our lives, together or apart."

His lips are pursed tight, and he grows more and more red in the face as I continue.

"But you did not do that. Instead you donned a silly disguise and crept around as a hunchback. Why, Jaimy?"

"I . . . I had to know . . ."

Well steamed now, I get to my feet and say, "Had to know what, Jaimy? Had to know if Jacky Faber was still pure enough for James Emerson Fletcher to enter her chamber? That's it, isn't it?"

"I just—"

I don't let him answer. "You know what, Jaimy? I'm not going to tell you whether I am yet a maiden or not. And what's more, I'm *never* going to tell you. You and your demon will just have to live with that. I'm the same girl either way, but you will not understand that, will you?"

"But that picture—how can you . . ."

"Ah, that painting. Did you know Clarissa stole that particular piece of art and it now hangs over the bar at the House of the Rising Sun, where it is seen by hundreds of people every day? Did you know that, Jaimy? I can see by the expression on your face you did not know. And you know what else? I am glad of that, and I wish everyone who gazes upon it a measure of joy."

"I sent that unfortunate letter as a gesture of the lingering love that I, after all is said and done, still hold for you," he says. "Perhaps I should have been more direct in expressing my emotions. I am sorry I am not as direct as other of your male . . . friends."

"*Love*? If you love me, Jaimy, you certainly have a strange way of showing it." I snort. "First, you go and leave me all alone in America after I was kicked off the *Dolphin*; then you aim the *Wolverine*'s cannons and sink my lovely *Emerald;* then you run off and abandon me in the American wilderness at the mercy of Mike Fink, savage Indians, and slave hunters; then you almost break my jaw with your fist on Blackheath Road, while you're charging crazily about being the fine Black Highwayman; and, finally, you lay your stick upon my back and bottom here in Boston, causing me great pain and mortification. Strange way of showing your love, indeed. I do not know if I can survive much more of that so-called *love.*"

"You know, when you are thinking straight, Jacky," he says, his face growing more and more red above his tight collar, "which I know is damned seldom the case with you, you'd realize that all those instances were occasioned by the force of circumstance."

"Circumstances that seem to occur with alarming regularity," I say, my gaze unyielding in the face of his logic. Both our voices are increasing in volume.

"Come on, Jacky, what am I supposed to think? Nude paintings, lurid stories, your dalliances with various males laid out in penny-dreadful novels for all to see?"

"*My* dalliances?" I say, incredulous. That does it. I round the table and poke my finger in his chest and say, "Clementine Jukes."

He jerks a bit, then pokes his own stiff finger on my breastbone. "Lord Richard Allen."

"Bess, the landlord's daughter."

"Robin Raeburne." Another poke. "Randall Trevelyne."

"Sidrah."

"Joseph Jared."

I'm running out of young girls to fling at him, but he sure ain't runnin' out of young men.

"Arthur McBride. Jean-Paul de Valdon."

"Mai Ling!" I counter, grasping at straws. "Mai Jing!"

"Come on, Jacky, you can do better than that! Amadeo Romero!"

I am out of retorts and can only stand fuming. Seeing me bested, he reaches out and takes me by my shaking shoulders. Yes, I am beginning to cry.

"Take your hands off me, Jaimy!" I warn, my eyes streaming and my voice shaking. "I mean it!"

"You said that I should have put you up against a wall," he says, pushing me back against the wall next to my bed. "You mean like this?"

With that, he reaches around and grabs the hair on the back of my neck and holds it fast, putting his lips on my now open mouth.

He pulls back and says, "Is that how you like it, Jacky? Rough? Fine. Here's another. Is it rough enough for you?"

And again he brings his face to mine and *Oh, Jaimy . . . how I waited . . . No . . . No . . . Control yourself, girl, you can't fall into this again . . .*

I lift my hands and place my palms on his chest and push him away, my own breast heaving.

"No, Jaimy," I whisper. "I like it gentle . . . sweet and gentle like you have always been . . . but I need time . . . time to think . . . about things . . . about us . . . Can you imagine the shock I felt when I pulled into port and found you suddenly here, after all that has happened? Can you imagine that? I have put you out of my mind and out of my heart . . . No . . . I need some time . . ."

"Time?" he says, reaching out and lifting my chin. "Time is what we have plenty of, right now." He comes in for

26

a much gentler kiss. I . . . I let it come, but alas, he is wrong . . . Time is exactly what we do not have — not now, not ever, for I hear the cry of *"Jacky! Jacky! There's trouble!"* coming from the street.

I look at Jaimy, shocked. *Christ! What now?* We both go to the window and see Chloe Cantrell come running up the street, her long legs pumping for all she is worth. We catch but a glimpse of her as she disappears below and into the Pig. Her feet are instantly heard pounding up the stairs to my room.

She bursts into my room without knocking, her hair flying about her face.

"Jacky! Ezra says you've got to run!" She gasps, breathless. "That diplomatic pouch was a trap! There are incriminating papers in it! You're gonna be arrested for treason by the federal authorities! They've got warrants! Run!"

Jaimy rushes to the window and looks out.

"Damn! She's right! Here they come!" he shouts, clenching his fists in anger and frustration. "Go, Jacky, out the back! Meet me in the wardroom of the *Shannon*. I don't care who they are, they would not dare to force their way onto a British warship!"

Saying that, he whips out his sword and goes to the door. "I'll hold the blackguards off, by God! I'll make 'em eat every goddamned word of their warrant before they lay a hand on you! Go!" And he is gone down the stairs.

I think upon the wisdom of Jacky Faber climbing back aboard a British man-of-war for only a split second, then head out the back with my seabag on my shoulder, and I am gone into the back alleys of Boston.

Chapter 4

So I'm pounding down the alley behind the Pig — luckily the federals didn't know that Jacky Faber *always* has a back way out, by God — and head for Codman's Wharf as fast as I can. *Damn! The U.S. authorities are after me now! What next? Zulu warriors? Russian Cossacks?*

It doesn't take me long to realize I ain't makin' very good time in this rig I'm wearing — the skirt is too long. The Lawson Peabody dress, which I have always been proud to have on my back, is more suited for gentle tea parties and concert recitals than runnin' down side streets, evading ardent pursuers. I've hiked up the black skirt to my waist, to free my pumping legs, but it still won't serve. It's all much too conspicuous — a young girl running through the streets of blue-nosed Boston with her skirts hiked up, showing off her white petticoats and knickers. Nay, it will not serve.

Ha! There's a barn up ahead, with its door swinging open. I run to it and look inside. *Good, it's empty.* The cowherd must have taken his beasts up to the Common to graze. No tellin' when he'll be back, though, so I must hurry.

I toss my seabag on a bench and tear it open. Reaching

in, I pull out the old sailor togs I had made for myself back on the *Dolphin* — loose white duck trousers and middy top with back flap. So, off with the black dress, long drawers, petticoats, white blouse, and chemise, and on with my simple seaman gear. One good thing about not growing much is that my old clothes still fit — sort of. These pants are a bit tight. I fold the school dress and tuck it into the bag. My shoes, too, as I run better when I am barefoot.

Spying the floppy cap I had long ago made with HMS *Dolphin* stitched on the headband, I pull it out and cram it on my head, stuffing my hair up inside.

Seabag back on shoulder, I head back out, confront a herd of puzzled cows returning from pasture, then dart off to the side and continue running down to Codman's Wharf, where lies my little fleet of ships.

Arriving there, I see that the *Morning Star* is still out on the bay, fishing and pulling traps, so I pound down the pier and toss my bag onto the *Evening Star*, then follow it on myself. I'd rather have the *Morning Star* if I have to make yet another run for my life — because of the comfy little cabin — but the lesser *Star* will serve. Though a scant fourteen feet long, constructed by Jim Tanner, she has a watertight little cowling up forward, big enough to hold my seabag and my curled-up self if it ever comes to a real downpour . . . and it does, indeed, look like rain.

I pull up the gaff-rigged sail, tighten the downhaul, toss off the lines, put hand on tiller, and pull away from the dock.

As I go, I pass the *Nancy B. Alsop*, tied up, with Finn McGee onboard as petty officer of the watch.

"You ain't seen me, Smasher!" I call out as I pass the *Nancy*'s port side. "Got it?"

He raises his knuckle to his brow, smiling and shaking his head ruefully, as he has been with me a long time and knows me and my ways very well. "Got it, Skipper. You take care, now."

Rounding the end of the pier, I spy the mighty HMS *Shannon*, lying starboard side to Long Wharf. To my old military self, she is a glorious sight — a three-masted, thirty-eight-gun frigate, very similar to my dear old *Dolphin*, all neat and shipshape, sails furled and ready, flags flying — but I am done with all that now, being only an honest, peaceful, merchant seaman who wants nothing to do with war or warships, having seen enough awful carnage in that regard.

I see that the *Shannon*'s gangway seems to have rather more men clustered about it than usual — probably waiting for me to come prancing aboard. Well, if that's what they're waiting for, it ain't gonna happen. No way I'm placing myself in the not-too-gentle custody of the Royal British Navy yet again.

Instead, I point the *Star*'s nose to the north and sail across the *Shannon*'s bow, coming up on her outboard, starboard side, where no one seems to be watching, and . . . *yes* . . . there is a line dangling over the side — probably left over from a work party painting the hull. *All shipshape, two-blocked, and Bristol fashion, lads? I think not, but thanks, anyway.*

I steer for the line, tie up, then climb the very handy rope. When I reach the rail, I peek over the side and see that, indeed, all on the quarterdeck are looking over the starboard side, no doubt waiting for the arrival of one Lieutenant J. M. Faber. I wonder if she would be piped aboard with all honors . . . Somehow, I doubt it.

Seeing their inattention, I put a leg over the rail, pull myself over, and pad toward the open hatchway that I know will lead down to the gun deck. I get here unobserved and head below.

Sure enough, the officers' mess deck contains one long table with chairs pulled up, and officers' staterooms arrayed to either side. Very much like the *Dolphin,* the *Dauntless,* and, yes, even my doomed *Emerald* and my lovely *Lorelei Lee.* I go to make myself comfortable, when I notice I am not alone in this room — at the end of the table, under an open window to let in light and air, sits a small midshipman. In front of him are arrayed a book, a set of dividers, a chalk slate, and a chart.

He looks up, slightly perplexed at the interruption. I am dressed as a common seaman, after all.

"I say, my good fellow, if you are not here on a work detail, I must point out that this is an officers-only space," he says, not unkindly.

I ignore his words and go over and plunk down beside him.

"Don't worry yourself, lad," I say, "for I, too, am an officer in His Britannic Majesty's Royal Navy, sometimes willingly, most times not. I am Lieutenant Jacky Faber, and you are . . . ?"

His mouth drops open.

"M-Midshipman Peter Rees, Mum, at your service," he says, swallowing hard. It is plain my fame has once again preceded me.

"Well, good, Mr. Rees. I am glad to know you. Do you think you could order us up some food? I believe I am going to shortly be in need of some sustenance."

Unable to speak, he reaches behind him and pulls on a cord that hangs by the bulkhead. Presently, a white-coated steward appears. No, it is not the despicable Weasel — although nothing would surprise me anymore — but rather a pleasant-looking man of possibly Spanish origin . . . perhaps a Filipino.

"Ah . . . yes . . . Paraiso. Please bring a plate of food for our . . . guest here," the lad manages to say. I would place his age at about fourteen. Good cheekbones and jaw, fine brow. Some lord's son, I'll wager.

"And two glasses of wine. I believe Mr. Rees will take a drink with me." The lad nods eagerly as Paraiso bows and exits.

I look over at his work. "Studying your navigation, lad? Well, good. It will hold you in good stead, and maybe you won't run aground in the future. But look here . . ."

The chart turns out to be of New England waters, with an insert detailing Boston Harbor.

I point a stiff forefinger down on a line of symbols in a narrow part of the channel. "See that? These are my home waters, and I know them quite well, and that damned nun buoy right there has come adrift at least fifty times to my knowledge, so watch for it when the ship leaves. Some say it is patriotic American mermaids who pull up its anchor, hoping to lure British ships to the rocks on the other side of the channel, but I dunno . . . Ah, here's Paraiso with a lovely tray."

The steward places a plate in front of me, then a glass of red wine before each of us, and though the food looks wondrous good, I do not stick the Faber nose in it right away but instead raise my glass to my companion.

"Rule, Britannia! May she ever rule the waves."

"In-indeed." He gulps, downing about half his glass.

Then I tuck into the food — meat, cheese, sticky rice, and fresh bread, and all very good — while at the same time pointing out nautical points of interest on the chart. Presently, I hear a commotion at the door.

Ah, that must be Jaimy and Ezra. I have an evil urge to hop into Midshipman Rees's lap and give him a bit of a nuzzle as they enter — that'd settle Mr. Fletcher's jealousy issues right quick — but I don't. Instead I once again lift my glass to the bemused middy . . .

"To all pretty young midshipmen in the world," I say, putting my glass to his. "May their numbers increase."

"Goddammit, Ezra, I don't know where the hell she . . ." Jaimy is saying as he comes into the room and spies me at the table, sharing a toast with a handsome young midshipman.

". . . is," he finishes, with a scowl at me and my companion, who, of course, has shot to his feet, at the same time blushing mightily.

"Mr. Fletcher . . . Ezra . . . Come in," I say, by way of greeting, "and Higgins, too. How good of you to come. Here, seat yourselves and take some refreshment, and then we shall discuss our latest problem. Paraiso, a bottle of your best claret and three more glasses, please."

Paraiso looks over at Second Mate Fletcher for confirmation of this order, coming, as it is, from a commonly dressed unknown female who has already made bold inroads into the *Shannon*'s precious stores. Jaimy nods, and Paraiso produces the goods.

"You there, Rees," growls Jaimy, "get yourself gone."

"Aye, Sir," quavers Midshipman Peter Rees, but he does not immediately go. Instead, he risks punishment by reaching over and boldly grasping my glass, in which a half inch of red wine is left. He lifts it. There is a smear on the rim where my greedy lips have been, and he places his own lips on that spot and tosses back the remaining dram. "There," he announces to all within. "I can now state with full conviction that I have indeed shared a glass with Puss in Boots herself."

"Out!" roars Lieutenant Fletcher. "And keep your goddamn mouth shut about this!" And Midshipman Rees does indeed flee, barely evading Jaimy's booted foot on his way through the door. If it turns out that he is stretched over a gun and given a number of strokes of the Bo'sun's rod for his cheek, so be it. He will bear them gladly, for he will have a story to tell.

"Little blighter," grumbles Jaimy.

"Ah, Jaimy," I say, bouncing up and standing before him. I finger the hem of my blouse and look up at him from under the brim of my cap. "Forgive the lad. Remember when all the Brotherhood was dressed this way and our station in life was very similar to his?"

His face softens and he smiles. "Yes, when you made us all wear that thing. We hated you for it then, but I rejoice to see you in it now."

As he smiles, all my former resolve melts, and it is now quite plain that I have already taken him back into my heart and have forgiven him whatever has gone before. I place my hands upon his chest and look into his lovely gray-blue eyes and . . .

"Ahem. As pleased as I am to see the two of you reconciled, we still have a problem. A *big* problem," says Ezra Pickering. He does *not* wear his habitual secret smile.

Jaimy and I seat ourselves and are attentive.

"Very well," says Ezra. "Here is the situation. A pouch, brought to this city by you on the *Nancy B. Alsop* and addressed to the British embassy, was intercepted by U.S. authorities and found to contain highly incriminating material, to wit: detailed plans of Fort McHenry."

"Wot?" I exclaim. "That fort is high up in the Chesapeake Bay! I've never even been there! And besides, that was a diplomatic pouch — I am required by maritime law to convey such things!"

"That is true, if it were indeed a diplomatic pouch, which it was not."

"But it was sealed . . ."

"It was sealed all right, but not with the imprimatur of any legitimate government. The pouch was closed with the corporate seal of a small sugar plantation in Havana."

Damn! I thought those soldiers who delivered the pouch to me in Cuba looked damned seedy for Royal Marines. I should have checked!

"Furthermore," Ezra goes on relentlessly, "the packet containing the plans was addressed 'Agent J. M. Faber, State Street, Boston.'"

"But they can't be serious! The plans of an obscure fort —"

"Serious enough," murmurs Higgins, who has been musing on all this. "The same plan of the very same fort was what got the esteemed revolutionary General Benedict Arnold branded as a traitor and his confederate Major John André hanged as a spy."

As always, when the possibility of my being hanged is brought up, my hand goes to my throat.

"And," continues Mr. Pickering, "the packet is initialed 'Hon. H. F., British Intelligence.'"

That gets me to my feet.

"'H. F.'! It can be none other than Harry Goddamned Flashby!"

"Indeed," says Higgins. "He could have used any initials, but he chose to use his own. He plainly wanted you to know just who was doing this to you."

"I should have killed him when I had the chance!"

"A disagreeable solution, true, but one that might have been wise, in hindsight," agrees Higgins. "However, that is idle speculation."

"Yes," says Ezra. "But what is certainly true at this moment is that you must flee until this thing is cleared up."

"But why? This is obviously just a clumsy frame-up."

"True, but I'd rather try to rescue your reputation in absentia than from the foot of the gallows."

"Good point, Ezra," I agree, my hand once again to my throat. I reflect momentarily on its softness and vulnerability.

"Tell me, Mr. Fletcher, where is your captain?" asks Higgins.

"He and the First Officer are at the State House at the Governor's reception. I was invited but begged off."

"Would he offer our Miss Faber a ride back to England so that she might clear up this mess with the real Admiralty people?"

Jaimy shakes his head sadly. "I believe Captain Broke

would extend the invitation to the renowned Lieutenant Jacky Faber, but not to a fugitive from American justice." He pauses, takes a deep breath, and then says, "No, I shall return with my ship and then meet with your friends Dr. Sebastian and Mr. Peel to secure evidence of your innocence. I will return with it as fast as I can."

I put my hand on his arm. *Poor Jaimy, poor me, poor us.*

My eyes are beginning to leak, but I do not let them. Sniffing back the tears, I put my attention on the chart that Midshipman Rees has left on the table.

"So I must run and hide. The question is where."

"Dovecote?" ventures Higgins.

Ezra shakes his head. "First place they would look."

"New Orleans? Havana?"

"I couldn't get the *Nancy B.* manned and ready fast enough — the federals are probably out at the *Shannon*'s gangway right now. And in New Orleans, I would be arrested for the murder of Clarissa Howe."

New York would be good, but too far, I'm thinking. *New Bedford, yes, but, I've got no desire to round Cape Cod in this weather. Plus, I want to remain a bit closer, so as to stay on top of things. Hmmm . . . I know . . .*

I look around the room, then up at the small, opened windows, and announce, loud enough for any eavesdroppers to hear, "I will go to Provincetown. It is a large enough city so that I can easily hide there. Write to me, Ezra, under the name of Sarah Perkins, General Delivery."

Saying this, I put my finger to my lips and point to the windows. My companions sagely nod — we all remember how the good but naive Captain Hudson of HMS *Dolphin* blew our cover as simple sponge divers during the *Santa Magdalena* expedition by careless talk in his cabin. There are no secrets on a ship.

Having announced a fraudulent destination, I pick up Midshipman Rees's slate and chalk and write: *I'll go to Plymouth, under the name of A. H. Leigh.*

They nod and I take up my napkin and rub out the message — after all, Paraiso is still in the room, and who knows . . .

"How will you get there?" asks Higgins.

"Same way I got here — my small tender is tied up to the port rail."

"But the storm?" asks Ezra. It is, indeed, working up into a real gale out there.

"Don't worry, I'll be all right. But I will need a set of oilskins." My own set hangs in the closet back at the Pig. I did not have a chance to grab them.

"Paraiso," barks Jaimy. "Go to the midshipmen's berth and get Mr. Rees's oilskins. She is of a similar size and I'm sure he will be delighted to give them up."

Paraiso leaves and I pick up the slate again and on it write: *Thanks, Peter Rees, for your kind company and the use of your 'skins. Lt. Jacky Faber.* Under my name I draw Faber Shipping's fouled anchor emblem.

Jaimy, upon seeing it, says, "I, of course, am going to erase it in front of him, for his impertinence."

"You will do nothing of the sort, Mr. James Emerson Fletcher, as I know you for a good and kind man," I say, stretching up to place a kiss upon his cheek. "Ah, here's Paraiso with the gear."

"There are men at the gangway, Sir, arguing loudly

with the officer of the watch," says the steward, looking concerned.

"We'd best be out there to try to delay them," says Ezra. "Goodbye, Miss. Try to remain safe, and know we will be doing our best to clear your name."

"My sentiments exactly," echoes Higgins. "I regret I cannot accompany you."

"You will render me and Faber Shipping better service here, John, rather than out on the wild sea or some twisting highway or whatever road I will find myself upon. Farewell, both of you. Know that you are my dearest friends."

With bows, Ezra Pickering and John Higgins take their leave, and I cram myself into Mr. Rees's oilskins, which do, indeed, fit — first the trousers tied at the waist with draw-string, then the top, and finally the sou'wester hat with its under-the-chin tie. I am ready to go.

"You look like some child's toy," says Jaimy, taking me by the shoulders and gazing fondly down into my face. Then he looks out to the weather working up outside. "But I don't like this one bit."

"Don't worry, Jaimy," I say brightly. "It's just a little rain. Am I not rated Able? And what else can we do? Hide me in the *Shannon*'s chain locker till we get to England? Might be fun for a bit, me and you down there, but nay, it'd be damned uncomfortable after a while, and I'd be found out and you'd be in trouble. So no, I must flee. Be quiet and kiss me, Jaimy, if you truly love me, 'cause I gotta go."

And he does, long and long . . . and then I'm out the door and off and gone.

Chapter 5

For all my brave show in front of Jaimy on the *Shannon*, I really am just a cowardly fair-weather sailor, especially when a raging tempest can be avoided. I had hardly cleared Boston Harbor when the downpour increased twofold. The water in the hull of the *Star* was up around my ankles — my feet were turning blue — and I began looking around for some sort of shelter. The wind was beginning to slacken, but the rain showed no sign of abating as darkness descended.

When I finally left Massachusetts Bay behind me and crossed the mouth of the Neponset River only to see lights coming on in the great house of Dovecote, I lost all my former resolve. I had thought merely to pull up on a beach, tie to a rock, and cram myself into the tiny cowling and hope that the rising water didn't come up high enough to soak me down, but, nay. The sight of those lights meant one thing to me: shelter from the storm . . . that and the warm companionship of friends, food, and maybe a drink. It was enough for me to put the tiller over and head toward Dovecote's boathouse, and to hell with the risk . . . I would take precautions.

. . .

After tying the *Star* to the boathouse dock, I trudged up to the house and went in through the servants' entrance in back and renewed my acquaintance with the staff, all of whom knew me well — well enough not to wonder at me appearing unannounced and in dripping oilskins.

Before heading upstairs, I pulled a five-dollar gold piece from my money belt and singled out Edward Hoskins, former stable boy and now footman and hostler. "Eddie. Will you do this for me? Take a blanket and go up to the gatehouse and spend the night there. Take your horn and blow it loud and shrill if anyone you don't know approaches the gate. Here's five dollars for your trouble."

"You don't have to pay me for that, Miss," says Edward with a grin directed at the maid sitting next to him at the long dining table. "And I won't take a blanket. I'll just take Susie. She'll keep me warm enough."

There's laughter all around.

"I shall not go to the gatehouse with you, Edward Hoskins," says the girl named Susie, tossing her curls about and putting her nose in the air, "as I would fear for my maidenly virtue."

More laughter, leading me to suspect that she will, indeed, go to the gatehouse with the young hound. Ah well, I'm all for young love . . . and she's just seen him get the princely sum of five dollars, and maybe he might buy something nice for his little Susie, now, mightn't he?

"Who's upstairs for dinner?" I ask. "I shan't go up if there are too many people to offend with my presence."

"Only Miss Amy, and Master Randall and his mistress, Miss Polly Von," says Susie, with a bit of a prim sniff. "I don't think you'll offend any one of them." Count on the chambermaids in any household to know exactly who is sleeping with whom. "Dinner has already been served and cleared away."

Good, I'm thinking. *Randall being a First Lieutenant in the United States Marine Corps is a bit of a complication, as he would be honor bound to arrest me if he knew I was wanted by federal authorities, but I shall handle that by keeping the Faber mouth mostly shut on that matter.*

"Mind your manners, Susan," warns Blount, the butler. As befits his station, he is Head of Household, and when dinner is served, he sits at the head of the downstairs table. Susie buttons her lip and says no more.

He is about to carry up a silver tray, upon which sits a bottle of Portofino and three glasses, when I take it from him and add another glass from the overhead rack, saying, "Pray seat yourself, Mr. Blount, and enjoy your dinner. I shall take this up."

He yields up the tray with a bow, and I head topside.

Ah, yes, the grand dining room of Dovecote Manor, with its long polished table and glittering chandelier, where I had enjoyed one of my greatest triumphs, as well as one of my most inglorious downfalls. The triumph was in being seated, as a mere schoolgirl, at this same table with the high and mighty of New England and holding my own over Clarissa Worthington Howe's attempt to demean me because of my low origins. My downfall involved Clarissa's later, and very successful, attempt to get me stinking drunk by plying me with sweet bourbon whiskey, such that I was carried out of the ballroom in total and complete disgrace.

The three of them are seated midtable: Amy Trevelyne across from her brother, Randall, and by his side, my old friend and fellow member of the Rooster Charlie Gang of Cheapside Urchins, the beautiful Polly Von. All are startled by my sudden appearance in wet oilskins.

"Jacky!" exclaims Amy, rising in delight as I pull back my hood. Randall and Polly also get to their feet with similar exclamations of surprise at my entrance. "I did not know you were back!"

"I just brought the *Nancy B.* into Boston this morning, and believe me, Sister, my life has changed dramatically since then — some to the good, and some to the bad, too. But here, let me first pour the wine. Everybody sit."

I uncork the decanter and fill the four glasses. Then I raise mine and say, "Cheers!" and toss the sweet, musky wine down my throat. *Ah, that does warm the Faber belly!* Afterward I apologize, "Sorry for my rudeness, mates, but it was cold and wet out there."

Saying that, I strip off my oilskins, revealing myself in my mercifully dry sailor togs. Since everybody present has, at one time or another, seen me in my Natural State, as it were, I do not think I'm breaking any new, scandalous ground here, and, indeed, no expressions of shock are heard as I sit myself next to Amy and refill my glass. There is a tray of small dessert cakes on the table, and I dispatch a few of them down my throat. *Mmmm . . .*

"Perhaps now that you have refreshed yourself, Jacky," says Randall, in his usual languid fashion, taking another pull at his own wineglass, "you will tell us just why you were out on the sea in this maelstrom?" He is looking absolutely splendid in his blue–with–red–facings United States Marine Corps uniform.

I must admit, the very handsome but somewhat dissolute Randall Trevelyne and I have a bit of a past. Upon meeting me here at Dovecote several years ago, his main objective appeared to be getting my knickers down to my ankles — and the randy hound almost succeeded in that, me being so young and foolish at the time. My plan, on the other hand, was to play the flirtatious tease so as to break up his marriage engagement to Miss Clarissa Worthington Howe, of which union both Amy and I did not approve. I did succeed in that endeavor, to my delight at the time, but ultimately to my great chagrin, for she certainly paid me back in full for that ill-conceived little gambit. Oh yes, when Clarissa was quite through with me, the good ship *J. M. Faber* was indeed burned to the waterline.

"Well," I reply, after swallowing a mouthful of cake, "I am once again being pursued by the civil authorities, and this time I am completely innocent of any of the charges against me."

"That's what you say every time," says Amy with a bit of reproof in her voice. "What is the charge, and who is after you?'

"On the advice of my attorney," I say primly, "I am unable to say. However, Ezra will be here tomorrow, and all will be made plain to you then."

Amy visibly brightens on that news. Although she constantly protests "I am not ready for that sort of thing" whenever I bring up the subject of love and marriage in general—and Ezra Pickering, Esquire, in particular—I know she is pleased at the prospect of his arrival tomorrow.

"Probably involves some sort of larceny, if I know our Miss Faber," suggests Randall. He taps a fingernail on his wineglass, signaling that it needs refilling, and Polly reaches for the bottle to top it off. While Randall was at one time in hot pursuit of my somewhat puny self, he now has eyes only for his beautiful Polly Von.

"And what, may I ask, Lieutenant Trevelyne, are you doing here rather than performing your duty on your ship? I see her nowhere around. Where is she?" I ask, to change the subject. "Could you have already deserted your post?"

He laughs. "No, the noble *Chesapeake* is laid up in the yards in New York, undergoing repairs. There is scant use for a Marine sharpshooter there, so Captain Stephen Decatur has graciously granted me leave." He looks over at his consort and continues, "I begged my coy mistress here to join me in New York, but she refused. The willful thing would not agree to come. Can you imagine that?"

Polly speaks up. "We are mounting a production of the *Merchant of Venice* at your Emerald Playhouse, and I get to play Portia," she says, looking over at me. "Couldn't pass that up, now could I?"

Nay, Polly, you could not, and I am so proud of you for that — for is it not true that Shakespeare is forever, while it is equally possible that handsome young men are not?

"And, Randy," she continues, putting those radiant blue eyes on Randall and patting his hand, "the production closes in a month, and then I will join you there and we shall sample the joys of that grand city. All right, love?"

He nods reluctant assent, his hand gently on hers.

Then she brings those baby blues back to me.

"If what you have told us was the bad news, Jacky," says Polly in her whispery, breathy way, "then, what was the good?"

"Yes, please, Sister," echoes Amy.

"Ah," I say, with the happiness plain in my voice. "I am pleased to announce that Lieutenant James Emerson Fletcher and I have worked out our differences and have reconciled, and we intend to be married upon his return from England and certain . . . political problems have been resolved."

"Why, that is wonderful!" gushes Polly, and Amy chimes in with, "I am so glad for you, Sister! I know that has always been your fondest wish."

"I agree to the match," says Randall, nodding, as if his agreement were called for. "His steady composure should complement your impulsive nature quite nicely. Maybe he can keep a lid on your impetuosity when others have failed."

"How did this come about, dear?" asks Amy.

"I saw him today, upon my return from the Caribbean. He is Second Mate on HMS *Shannon,* which is moored at Long Wharf. With Ezra's connivance, a meeting was arranged and we . . . worked out our differences, and all is well between us."

"I imagine that little discussion was quite heated," murmurs Randall. "Considering . . ." Randall had witnessed Jaimy's caning of me at the courthouse.

"Yes, it was, but all was resolved to mutual satisfaction."

"The *Shannon,* eh?" says Randall, leaning back and

musing. "Hmmm . . . Me on USS *Chesapeake* as Commander of Marines, and James Fletcher as Second Mate on HMS *Shannon*. It is my profound hope that our two ships never meet in battle. Things are heating up between our two countries . . ."

"I pray that never happens," I manage to say, horrified at the very thought of my dearest friends being forced to kill each other in a senseless war.

"Yes, but it could . . ."

"Well, it isn't happening now," I reply. "The *Shannon* sets sail for England tomorrow, with Lieutenant Fletcher aboard with intentions to clear up my latest mess from that end. My good Higgins and Ezra will work on it here. I, of course, will be on the lam."

"But where will you go?" asks Polly.

"I'm thinking Rhode Island. They're pretty broad-minded there and might be a little more forgiving of my ways."

"But why not stay here? With me?" asks Amy.

I put my hand on hers and look into her sweet face. "Dear Amy, that would be my fondest wish, but it would be the first place they would look. Have you not heard of a certain series of books written about me and my wanton ways? Even police can read, you know."

"Oh," she says meekly, being the authoress of said potboilers.

"And in regard to that, if anyone comes looking for me here, please tell the truth: I came here today, stayed overnight, and then pushed off in my boat. You cannot afford to be caught in a lie, because I'm sure you realize that you could get in big trouble, all of you. Yes, the truth is best . . . You could even say that I had mentioned Providence, Rhode Island. It's a big town, and I could easily hide there till this ridiculous thing blows over."

"This 'ridiculous thing' you mention, Jacky," says Randall, "could the end of it result in a certain person being hanged by her delicate little neck? Hmmm?"

"Well, yes, Randall, it usually does, doesn't it?"

Both Amy and Polly gasp. Randall does not. He only looks into his empty glass. "Hmm . . . Then you must be very careful."

"I am always careful, Randall. You know that."

That gets me a good snort all around.

"Well, I am," I retort, slightly miffed. "But for now, let us forget idle troubles, and repair to the music room for some merriment and song! Let us banish all care!"

"Hear, hear!" is the answer from my companions as we all rise to go. I notice that Randall grabs the bottle on his way.

We belted out every song we each knew. Randall introduced us to some raunchy barracks ballads he had picked up from his time in the service of the U.S. Marine Corps. Polly blushed prettily at those tunes — in a very charming way — but I am sure she could produce those rosy cheeks on cue, as she is an excellent actress. I, too, did work up a blush, but it was difficult, my knowing that I knew a lot worse in the way of the vile and obscene.

But after all was sung and danced, it was time for bed, and Polly and Randall headed off for theirs, while Amy and I off to hers.

• • •

As we wash up before sleep, Amy offers me a nightshirt, but I demur, saying, "Nay, Sister, I'd best stay in these. There is not much of a chance, but we might have unfriendly visitors. Move over . . ." and soon we are wrapped around each other and falling into peaceful sleep — peaceful for her, anyway . . .

I dream I am on the back of my dear Mathilde, galloping across a large green meadow on a glorious, sunlit day without a cloud in the sky, and I am riding beside my beloved Jaimy Fletcher, dimly aware that we are on a fox hunt. He looks glorious in his lieutenant's jacket of blue, and I am supremely happy. Seeking to embrace him, I forget about the bloody fox hunt and urge Mathilde to the side of his mount and lean toward him . . .

But suddenly another rider comes up between us, forcing us apart . . . Wot . . . ?

I turn to my left and see that it is none other than Cavalry Major Lord Richard Allen, looking equally gorgeous in his deep scarlet regimentals, all red and gold and fine.

"Come, Princess!" he calls, his white teeth gleaming around a long black cheroot. "Can you not hear the huntsman's call?"

Indeed, I do . . . Arrrroooo! Loud and clear in the distance.

"They must have spied the fox! I'll race you to that hedgerow, Prettybottom! Away!"

Arrrooooo!

But then yet another comes up and slides between Lord Allen and me. It is Clarissa Worthington Howe, riding sidesaddle on her mighty horse Jupiter. She smiles upon the both of us.

"No, Richard," she says. "It is I whom you shall race to that row of trees. I am sure we will be the first upon the fox!"

Arrrrooooo!

"Tally-ho, then!" says Allen, spurring his horse forward and leaping ahead, not to be denied his place at the kill.

Arrrooooo!

Clarissa comes up beside me and leans over, holding up her left hand to me. On it is a large ring.

"Say it, Jacky, say it," she says, her cold blue eyes shining with a devilish light. "Say it."

"Never!" I cry. "Never shall I say that!"

"Oh, but someday you shall, darling Jacky," she says with a laugh as she spurs off to overtake Richard Allen. "Someday you most certainly shall!"

"Let them go," I say to my faithful Jaimy, who still rides by my side. "I'd rather be with you than anyone in the world. Come kiss me, love."

The day continues, lovely and quiet and warm, and Mathilde is changed in that way that dreams will into my dear gentle Gretchen from back at the Lawson Peabody. I lean over and nuzzle my nose into Jaimy's thick dark hair and prepare for his sweet kiss and . . .

Arrrooooo!

Then my eyes fly open and I suddenly realize that I have been nuzzling my nose into the hair behind the ear of Amy Trevelyne and not that of Jaimy Fletcher, and that sound of the hunter's horn is real! It is Edward's warning trumpet and I must fly!

I leap out of bed, gather up my oilskins — thanking God that I had slept in my sailor togs — plant a kiss on Amy's drowsy cheek, and say, "Goodbye, Sister," and I am through the door, down the stairs, and out the back, racing down the path to my waiting *Evening Star*.

There is the sound of galloping horses and shouting back at the great house, and I see torches being lit. Then someone yells, "There she goes!" and rifles are fired — *pok! pok! pok!* The dust behind me is pelted with angry bullets, but they don't hit me, for I am too far ahead. I manage to reach the boathouse unharmed and leap, breathless, into my *Star*. I throw off the lines, raise the sail, and grab the tiller.

A puff of welcome breeze and I am off to sea . . . *Let them shout and let them shoot; they can't catch me here . . .*

PART II

Chapter 6

Plymouth is a very pleasant, well laid-out port, with many places of business, nautical or otherwise, arrayed along Water Street, which runs along the ends of the wharves and piers that jut out into the harbor. I think I shall like it here.

Sailing in, I had found a good tie-up for the *Star*, in a nest of similar small working boats bobbing alongside a floating dock, so didn't have to pay anything for the mooring, which is good. I am wearing my money belt, but in my haste to leave Boston, I didn't have time to properly stuff it with coin of the local realm, and I expect it to grow even thinner as I go along. Oh, well, I do have my pennywhistle, if it comes to that.

Pulling my seabag out of the cowling, I stuff my ordinary seaman's cap inside and take out my midshipman's hat and cram it on my head, figuring I'll get a bit more respect than if sporting the cap of a common swab. My oilskins still cover the rest of me, and yes, it's still drizzling. So off I go in search of dry lodging and, ultimately, some worthy employment as a cover for my being here in this town as a single female.

Seabag on shoulder, I trudge up First Street, which takes its origin from Water Street and leads into the center of the town, glad to see up ahead the sign for the Tail and Spout Inn. It displays a blowing white whale against a blue background and words below that, promising food, drink, and lodging. Before I enter, I reach down and pick up a little mud with my forefinger and run it across the bridge of my nose, to show that I've run into some hard traveling on the way here, and for sure, I have seen that. Then I adjust my middy cap and go in.

It is a cheerful, welcoming place with maybe ten small tables and one big one running down the center, with a large fireplace at the end — unlit because it is the end of June and quite warm. A bar runs along the other end of the room, and a woman sure to be the landlady is doling out foaming tankards of suds to a chubby and cheerful serving girl, who carries them to the tables. There are quite a few customers in the place, too — a table with four seamen grouped around, and another with what look to be merchant officers. *Hmmm* — I notice some swarthy tattooed fellows off in a corner, their harpoons leaning against the wall. Most of the men are smoking their vile pipes, and there is a thick layer of smoke hovering next to the ceiling. Another table of four New England seamen is lustily singing "The Black Ball Line." You can tell they're Yankee sailors, 'cause their hair is cut short behind, unlike the Brits and Irish, who wear their hair long, in pigtails, like mine. Their rendition of the fine old song is met with approval from those within, as there are cheers and whistles when they end. I wish I could join in, but alas, I cannot, for I must lie low.

Well, the place seems right cozy to me, so I march my

sodden self up to the landlady and say in my deepest voice, "I'd like a room for the night, Missus. A single, if you please."

"A single it is, lad, and ain't you a fine-lookin' young sailor boy," she says, reaching back for one of the keys that hang on the wall behind her. "A half dollar a night, in advance."

These inns not only rent out single and double rooms, to those what can afford 'em, but also mere bed space — like in three or four blokes to a mattress — and there's no way I want that big Samoan harpooner over there throwing his heavy leg over me in the middle of the night. He must be three hundred pounds if he's an ounce.

I dig my finger under my oilskin and into my money belt and pull out the required coin, and she delivers the key. "Top o' stairs, first door to the right, number seven."

I shoulder my seabag and head up.

Number 7 is indeed a single — and not much more than that — a narrow bed and a washstand and room enough only to stand and turn around. But it sure looks like home to this weary traveler. The door opens inward, so I plant my wedges, peel off my 'skins and the rest of my damp sailor togs, and fall across the bed for a delicious afternoon nap . . . *Oh, yes* . . .

Later, I arise refreshed, then wash up and put on my midshipman's uniform — blue jacket, white trousers — my sword Esprit, snug in her harness, my cap back on head. "There," I pronounce, looking at myself in the washstand mirror, every inch a proud midshipman in His Majesty's Service. It's time to head back downstairs in search of some food, drink, and maybe some information.

On my way to an open table, I ask of the landlady, "Pardon, Missus, but where might I buy a newspaper?"

She looks me over yet again. "Royal Navy, eh? If'n I'd known that, I'd have charged you double for the room."

Startled, I stammer, "I-I'm sorry to cause you distress, Mum, but . . ."

She barks out a short laugh. "Nay, Old Gert's just foolin'. All sailors are welcome at the Whale. When the cruel water closes over a poor seaman's head for the last time, it don't matter what he is — Yankee, Blackamoor, Hottentot, or Royal Navy — it's all the same hard swallow. Sit yerself down, lad, and Bessie'll see to yer needs . . . and here's a paper some bloke left. It'll save you yer nickel."

Gratefully, I take up the rolled paper and head for my table. The aforementioned Bessie appears by my side and soon a mug of cool ale is in my fist. Careful not to look too ladylike by crossing my ankles demurely, I affect a male posture by crossing my legs, left foot resting on right knee, then lean back and open the paper.

I turn to the Help Wanted section and avidly read.

Hmmm . . . Plenty of ads for sailors — *can't do that, not now, too obvious.* Whalers, too — *but that's a nasty business, plus I'd be gone too long* — and for chambermaids . . . *well, if nothing else turns up, maybe.* The ropewalk, all quarter-mile of it, is hiring, but that's rougher work than I want right now . . . *Ha! Here's just the thing! I'll do it, by God, first thing in the morning, and . . .*

And dark shapes suddenly appear by my side. I look up to see two Royal Navy lieutenants in full rig — navy blue jackets with gold buttons and lace trim, blue trousers with sword belts strapped on, and fore-and-aft cocked hats. *Uh-oh . . .*

I shoot to my feet, case my eyes, and hit a brace. I stand there rigid with fear, my mind racing . . . *What the hell now? Damn!*

But I am somewhat relieved to feel a friendly hand on my shoulder as one of them says, "Nay, lad, let us not stand on ceremony here on terra firma. It is good to find a fellow member of our service here in goddamn Yankeeland." They both sit down, one to either side of me.

Even in my confusion, I know they are glad there are no United States naval officers in the room, because of the tensions building between our countries. Every officer wears a sword, even me, and one wrong word and . . .

"I am Lieutenant Mitchell," the older and obviously more senior of the two says, "and this is Mr. Tull, both of HMS *Endymion*, First and Third Officers. Tell us your name, boy, and sit down and let us enjoy what this inn has to offer. We'll all be back at sea soon enough."

Who shall I be? My mind searches about for a plausible lie. *Ah! Yes! He's got to be half a world away!*

"M-Midshipman Tom Wheeler," I stammer, signaling for Bessie to bring these worrisome gents some drink. She winks and nods. "If it pleases you, Sir."

"It pleases me well enough, Mr. Wheeler," says the older man. And as the tankards are placed on the table, he says, "And that pleases me even more. Thank you, lad . . ."

Long drafts are drunk, followed by heartfelt *ahhhhh*s, and then we fall into that old game that long-parted sailors have played since ancient mariners plowed the wine-dark Adriatic Sea . . . *Alexandrus! Apollo be praised! A glass of grappa with you! I haven't seen your dried-up carcass since the Siege of Syracuse! Vale Agrippa! Good to see you, and aye,* *what a mess that was — damned Greeks with their tricks! There I was, pulling my oar on the* Helena, *and the sail of our galley suddenly goes up in flame! Never again, I swear! Didn't pay me, neither, curse 'em all to Hades! Demetrius? No, ain't seen 'im since Troy . . . Hey, check out the amphorae on Athena over there . . . Athena, darling! Another round!*

"So, young Mr. Wheeler, tell us where last you have shipped and whom you have met," says Lieutenant Tull, signaling for another round.

"Well, Sir," I say, having had a bit of time to come up with a plausible lie, "I was lately billeted on the *Shannon,* but I was sent off by the Captain with a last-minute message to a person here in Plymouth —"

"Probably a letter to his American mistrius," mutters Mr. Mitchell.

"—and so missed her departure from Boston. I am to rejoin the ship in London, but since I knew there were no Royal Navy ships currently in Boston, I figured I'd take a coach to New York to see if I can catch a ride on one of our ships moored there, and so back to England."

"Put your mind at rest, Midshipman Wheeler," says Mr. Mitchell, "for you shall travel with us back to New York by coach in the morning. I am sure our captain, Simms, will offer you a berth for the return journey. After all, what's one squeaker, more or less. You certainly don't look like you eat much."

"No, Sir, I do not, and I thank you for your kind offer," I reply, never for a second intending to be on that coach in the morning.

Mr. Tull returns to the who-do-you-know game. "The *Shannon,* eh? Isn't Seth Parsons on her?"

"Yessir, he's First Officer. And do you know of a Lieutenant James Fletcher? He's Second," I venture.

Both consider, but it's Mr. Mitchell who says, "Fletcher, eh? Yes. I haven't met him in person, but I've heard he's a strong, silent type — knows his business as a sailor and a good man to have at your back in a fight. How about . . ."

It goes on and on, but it's no wonder, as there are not that many officers compared to the number of sailors, so, of course, we run into each other sometimes in the performance of our duties.

"Perhaps you have heard of a Mr. Joseph Jared, sailing master on HMS *Dolphin*? I served with him on the *Wolverine*, at Trafalgar."

"Ha!" cries Tull. "Joseph Jared! A fine man, indeed! A thoroughgoing seaman! Top notch! He is now a full lieutenant and Second Officer on our very ship. He will be delighted to see you when we return to the *Endymion*, I am sure."

I also am quite sure of that — but sorry, Joseph, it ain't gonna happen . . .

Later, after all the toasts toasted, drinks drunk, a fine meal eaten, and many sea stories told, I beg to be excused, with a promise to meet in the morning, and I retire, a bit unsteadily, to my chamber.

After I have made my ablutions, said my prayers, and climbed into bed, I let my mind wander and gleefully imagine the conversation that will surely happen in the officers' mess of HMS *Endymion* when Lieutenants Mitchell and Tull return . . .

"Midshipman Thomas Wheeler, you say?" asks Joseph Jared. "Of the Wolverine?"

"Why, yes, Joseph, he was quite clear on that," answers Lieutenant Mitchell, a bit nonplussed. "Strange that he did not show up this morning when we all boarded the coach."

"Odd, indeed," says Jared, his cocky grin beginning to spread across his face. "Perhaps, Jonathan, if you would describe this creature to me?"

"Well, he was very small but neat and thin of face. He had blue powder spray next to his right eye. I believe I spied a curious tattoo on his neck, under his pigtail, when it swung to the side. A dragon, I think. Why do you ask?"

Jared looks at his fellow officers with a widening smile.

"Because, gentlemen, I had the pleasure of seeing my former shipmate Midshipman Tom Wheeler not one month ago onboard HMS Regulus."

"B-but what . . . ?" stammers Lieutenant Tull. "But he said . . ."

"Have you gentlemen checked your purses since that little encounter?" asks Jared, with a questioning eyebrow raised.

Lieutenant Mitchell looks confused. "No, there was nothing untoward in that respect. However, we did play at cards, and the young lad, for all his fumbling inexperience, did come out the winner in the end."

"And he was most gracious about it — bought us our dinner, in fact," adds Tull.

"As well she should — for it was with your own money she bought it!"

"'She'?" they both mutter, aghast.

"The real Midshipman Wheeler is half a world away from here," says Jared, collapsing into helpless laughter. "Do you realize who it was you broke bread with? Ha! You're lucky you still have a penny in your pocket!"

"You don't mean . . . ?"

"Yes, I do, and by God, I would have gladly exchanged the contents of my own purse to have been in your place, right next to Puss in Boots herself!"

I think it would have gone something like that. *And I wish you the joy in the telling of it, Joseph. So, good night, you merry rogue . . .*

And good night, Jaimy, and Godspeed.

Chapter 7

The next morning, I pop up bright and early. I know the coach-and-four headed to New York and points south leaves at nine, so I've got to be out of here by eight if I don't want to continue to enjoy the company of Lieutenants Mitchell and Tull, well-meaning gents though they might be.

After washing the sleep out of my eyes and doing the necessaries, I don my Lawson Peabody School attire — long white drawers with flounces, black stockings, white chemise top, black silk dress over all that, with black pumps on feet.

I roll up the bottom of the dress and fasten it around my waist by tucking it under my money belt, then step into my oilskin trousers and tie up the drawstring. That secured, I don the oilskin jacket, put my midshipman cap back on my head, and pick up my seabag. *There. I will leave the Tail and Spout as I entered — as poor Jack the Sailor, a son of the sea, but now, alas, washed up on land.*

Down below, Gert stands wiping the bar in anticipation of the day's business, and good smells are coming from the kitchen door behind her. A quick glance reassures me that my Royal Navy friends are not yet in evidence, which is good.

"Good morning, lad," booms out landlady Gert upon seeing me ready to head out. "You'll not stay for breakfast? We're having eggs, bangers, and mash."

"Nay, Mum," says I, truly sorry to have to pass up the eggs, but especially the sausage along with the potatoes mashed with garlic and onions, "for I must be off. Time and tide wait for no lad. Thank you, Missus, for your kind hospitality."

And I am off into the light of day. Seeing the south-bound coach being loaded, I hurry up the street and out of sight, heading for the print shop. When I spot it, I dart back into a convenient alley, whip off my oilskin jacket, step out of the trousers, and release my skirt from its binding, letting it fall to my ankles. That done, I stuff the 'skins into my sea-bag, along with my midshipman's cap, and then pull out my black lace mantilla. Reaching back, I pull the blue ribbon that binds up my pigtail and untangle my hair, letting it fall over my shoulders. It is a mess, but I'll deal with it later. For now, I drape the mantilla over my head, letting one end hang down my front, and the other I whip around my neck. There. I have managed the transformation from sailor lad to young maiden, observed only by a yellow cat, who sits atop a garbage bin licking her paw, regarding me and my deceptions with profound indifference.

Breathing a bit more easily, I quit the alley and head up the street toward the print shop. On my way, I turn to glance back down the street — sure enough, there are Lieutenants

Mitchell and Tull, looking about in vain for the missing Midshipman Wheeler, and then shrugging and finally climbing into the coach. In a moment, both it and my Royal Navy friends are gone.

The newly reborn Miss A. H. Leigh — that's "A" for Annabelle, "H" for Hester, family name Leigh — goes into the shop, buys a newspaper, and asks directions to a nice teahouse where a young lady of good breeding, such as herself, might find refreshment, and I'm directed to "The White Rose Tearoom, Miss. You will find it to your liking. Just up the street on the left."

On my way to that establishment, I pass a schoolhouse, on the steps of which the school mistress is lustily ringing a hand-held bell, as the children file in for the day's instruction. The boys, dressed in uniform black short pants, matching jackets, and white shirts, tumble in the doorway, a riot of shouting and pushing and punching. The girls, of course, are more well-behaved, dressed in gingham dresses with white aprons over their fronts, white stockings, and sensible ankle-length lace-up shoes. As the door closes behind all, I look out on the schoolyard and notice swings, a seesaw, and a large playing field. *Very nice.* I would have liked to have gone there as a child . . . but, oh, well . . . I do know now, having run as a ragged orphan through the rough streets of London with the Rooster Charlie Gang, and later having gone to the finest of schools, that both places teach similar lessons in the ways of friendship, loyalty, bravery, and betrayal.

Moving right along, I pass a newly painted Congregational Church, a courthouse that I naturally shy away from, given my past experience with such places, and then, ah . . . the post office. I know that it is too early to expect a letter from Ezra Pickering concerning my latest troubles, so I do not go in, but it is good to know where it is. And, yes, right there is the First Mercantile Bank of Plymouth, Massachusetts, in all its austere glory.

As promised, the tearoom comes into sight. It is squeezed between two larger, more heavily timbered buildings, but still manages to look cheerful and even pretty. Over its varnished oaken door hangs a sign bearing a white rose painted on a lavender background with TEAROOM written below. I push open the door and go in, fully armed with the haughty Lawson Peabody "Look" firmly resting upon my countenance.

It is a pleasant room — well lit, with frilly white curtains and crisp linen on the tabletops — a bit fussy for my taste, but then, give me a rough-and-ready tavern anytime.

I am greeted civilly by a tidy young woman and then shown to a table on which are napkin-wrapped place settings and a vase with a single white rose in it. *A nice touch,* I'm thinking, as a delicate porcelain cup of hot tea is placed in front of me. It takes me back to teatime at the Lawson Peabody, without the tension of having to do everything just right under Mistress's unforgiving gaze. From a nicely lettered card placed on the table, I order toasted crumpets with butter and jam, take a ladylike sip of the excellent tea, and then open my paper to the Help Wanted section, hoping the advertisement I saw yesterday is still being run . . .

Yes! There it is . . .

WANTED :
Governess for Two
Small Children.
References Req.
Room and Board
and Remittance.
Apply In Person to
Mr. Polk at the
First Mercantile Bank
of Plymouth, during
Business Hours.

I know it's not the most exciting thing to do, but with my cover being already half blown by my chance meeting with those Royal Navy officers, I figure it's just the thing. Quiet, discreet, out of the public eye, and certainly not in any way nautical in case anybody comes looking for me in that direction. Yes, I shall apply.

A glance at the clock on the wall shows eight thirty, so I have a bit of time before the bank opens, which is convenient, for my breakfast has just arrived and looks good. Plus, I have some things I need to do.

As I pack away the toasted crumpet loaded with butter and jam, I notice a little girl peeking shyly at me around the corner of the kitchen door. She seems to be about five years old — plainly too young to go to school — and she holds a doll tightly to her chest. I give her a broad wink and she disappears. *Probably the landlady's child,* I reflect, as I knock off the rest of my breakfast, pat lips with napkin, and signal for the bill.

When the reckoning is brought on a little silver tray, I pay, leaving a nice tip, and receive a bright smile and directions to the privy. I rise and go to it.

As I had suspected, that particular room is very clean and well maintained — open window with filmy white curtains blowing in the slight breeze, sturdy wooden chair with white pot under, rack of clean towels, and washstand and mirror. It is the latter fixture that I need right now.

I dive into my seabag and pull out my brush, cosmetic kit, and Scots bonnet. My inclination is to comb my hair into a sensible bun, but that would expose my dragon tattoo, and we certainly can't have that in a would-be governess — *no, we can't* — so I merely fluff it up a bit and hope that it passes scrutiny. My bonnet, with the brim turned down, goes on next — after I've removed the gay feathered cockade from its headband. Then some light powder, to cover up the blue powder burns that radiate from my right eye. I do not have to worry about my troublesome white eyebrow, for my good Higgins has procured a permanent hair dye that matches my natural locks and fixed it up quite nicely. No more makeup for the cheeks, or rouge for the lips, no, not for this job interview. Must be as proper as can be managed, given the raw Faber material.

All that accomplished, I stride back into the street, mark again the still-closed bank, and spy a sundries store up ahead whose sign advertises it to be FILIBUSTER'S FINE EMPORIUM. I go in and look about. Sure enough, just about everything imaginable seems to be for sale here, from knives and forks, to leather goods, to sewing tools, to rolls of fabric. It even has a small counter, with fixed stools, that offers COLD, REFRESHING DRINKS, to wit: LEMON,

CHERRY, AND ORANGE SODA-WATERS. SAFE FOR THE LIT-
TLE ONES. NO ALCOHOL. *Hmmm . . .* I'll wager, though,
there's a goodly supply of something very akin to my good
old Captain Jack's Magic Elixer — that potion I had mixed
up, bottled, and sold on my journey down the Mississippi
several years ago, to the joy of all who purchased it —
under that pharmacy counter, for quick sale with a wink.
My own Cap'n Jack's had plenty of that forbidden liquid
substance in it, as well as a goodly dash of opium, and I
received very few complaints from my many satisfied customers. And I'll bet the friendly Mr. Filibuster did not
grow so sleek and prosperous solely by selling flavored
water to kids.

Mr. Filibuster himself is a very eager middle-aged man,
portly, and bald on top, with a fringe of white fluffy hair over
his ears and behind his neck. I look about at his ample stores,
seeking something that might make me somewhat more
presentable in the way of a governess, and yes, I find it.
While scanning the round reading spectacles, which I find
cumbersome and interfering with my so-far excellent eye-
sight, I discover a pair of pince-nez.

Perfect! They rest low on my nose, and I can peer out
over the top of them, and they have a black ribbon attached
with a clip, to affix to my front so they can be dropped anytime. Squinting into the mirror provided, I pronounce myself the perfect schoolmarm. Advancing to the counter, I
purchase writing paper, a small bottle of mucilage, and, of
course, an umbrella. Mr. Filibuster looks pleased as he totals
up my purchases, and he smiles even more at my promise to
return to sample more of his fine offerings.

After leaving Filibuster's Fine Emporium, Miss Annabelle H. Leigh walks up First Street, pauses a moment to adjust appearance, takes a deep breath, and enters the august portal of the First Mercantile Bank of Plymouth, Massachusetts, USA, to present herself for employment.

Chapter 8

The heavy oak doors to the First Mercantile Bank are open to let in what there is of a sultry summer breeze. I stride in with modified Lawson Peabody Look in place — chin up, lips together, teeth apart, eyes hooded. In this case, not overly haughty, but, it is to be hoped, just enough. I know the whole effect is slightly marred by the pince-nez that is clamped to my nose, but so be it.

Entering, I spy a central aisle that has on its right a female receptionist at a desk. A walkway to the left leads to several glassed-in private offices and terminates in a row of barred teller windows.

"May I help you?" inquires the person at the desk.

"Yes, thank you," I reply. "I wish to see a Mr. Polk."

"For what reason, may I ask? Mr. Polk is the President of this bank. You do have an appointment, I presume?"

This lowly employee I fry with my gaze. "I am here in answer to the advertisement the President has placed in the newspaper. For a governess."

"Ah, please have a seat over there, and I will inform him of your presence."

I see a bench aligned against a sidewall and go seat my-self on it to await an audience with the Great Man, while the receptionist, with a rustle of skirts, goes into the first office to tell him of my arrival. I hear the mumble of voices and she reemerges, saying, "He will see you in a few minutes. Please wait."

Waiting is something I am not very good at, but I sigh and resign myself, passing the time by looking about the place — the ceilings are high, and there is much dark oak in the furniture and moldings. There is a hush about the inte-rior of the bank — the hush of money, which, after all, must be respected. I chuckle to myself when I see that there is no armed guard.

Hell, me and my bully boys on the Emerald *could've knocked this place over in a moment. We'd just bring the ship up the harbor to the end of that street as far as she'd go, with her black Jolly Roger flag grinnin' at the masthead, and then all of us would leap over the sides and charge up the street, screaming horrible threats, waving cutlasses and shooting off pistols into the air, and generally scaring the populace away to the hills in terror. Yes, we'd put those timid-looking tellers over there on the floor right off, their money drawers stripped, the open safe over there emptied, as we went hallooing off with the loot.*

Like that time in the Spanish Port of Santo Domingo, on the Island of Hispaniola, which lay helpless before us on that day back in 1804 . . . I had burst into El Banco de Espania, a bank very much like this, with Arthur McBride on my left and Ian McConnaughey on my right, all of us armed to the teeth and screaming threats of bloody murder . . . Ah, and wasn't that indeed a time — heavy sigh — but that was then and this is now, and I have neither my beautiful Emerald *nor my brave bully boys by my side, and . . .*

. . . and there is the tinkle of a bell. "Mr. Polk will see you now," says the receptionist from her desk. I rise, pick up my seabag by the handles, between which rests my new umbrella, and walk in the door.

Mr. Polk is seated behind a grand mahogany desk that has several important-looking papers upon it. He is a thin man — well-dressed, hair combed back, slick with brilliantine — and is wearing a look of extreme reserve. He does, however, give me the courtesy of rising as I enter. There's that, at least.

"Miss Leigh, I presume? Please sit down." He gestures toward a chair, and I place myself in it, my bag by my side. "You are here to apply for the position of governess for my children. I assume you have references?"

"Yes, Sir," I say, removing my pince-nez and letting it dangle against my chest. "My full name is Annabelle Hester Leigh, and I am a graduate of the Lawson Peabody School for Young Girls in Boston. I am conversant in science, literature, and the classics. I am skilled in art and penmanship, and can speak both French and Spanish . . ."

I had purposely chosen that name, having remembered it from an embroidered sampler I had seen framed on the wall of the Lawson Peabody — the old Lawson Peabody, the one that had burned down with, it is to be hoped, all its student records. The real Miss A. H. Leigh would have graduated several years before I got there, and so I should be safe with that name.

" . . . and I was recently employed as tutor to several children of the Cabot family, but was let go after the lads

74

went into high school. I am sure they will give me an excellent recommendation."

"You have letters of reference with you?" He glances at my bag.

"Alas, no. They were in my other luggage, which has been delayed. However, I can write to a Mr. Pickering, an attorney who handles things of this nature for Mistress Pimm of the Lawson Peabody, and he will arrange to have the letters sent directly to you. They should arrive in a few days. That is, if I prove acceptable to you."

He leans back in his chair and puts his well-manicured fingertips together as he regards me.

"How old are you?"

"Nineteen."

"You don't look it."

"I have been told that, but I have indeed attained that age."

"Hmm . . . this is a bit irregular, no papers at all, and your young age . . ." He seems to come to a decision. "But, very well. You are hired as governess to my children. Here are the conditions: You shall be given room and board at my house. You will take your meals with the servants, but you will take tea in the evening with my wife and me, such that you will be able to report on the children's progress. You will be given a remittance of five dollars a week. Is that acceptable?"

"Yes, Sir. However, I must have one afternoon a week off to attend to personal matters. Fridays would be good."

"You realize you have no *personal* life when you live at my house and attend to my children," he says sternly.

By that I know he means "no men," and I set his mind at ease.

"I realize that, Sir. I need that bit of time to buy personal things — toiletries and sundry . . . female items . . ." I get a manly flush to his cheeks on that, as I knew I would. "And I will need to check my mail."

"Very well. However, I have some further rules concerning my family . . ."

I raise an eyebrow and listen.

"While my daughter, Catherine, will be no trouble to you, my son, Edgar, is very high-strung and, as such, must never be struck, nor shall he ever be spoken to in a harsh manner. Is that understood? It would be cause for immediate termination of your employment. I repeat, is that perfectly clear, Miss Leigh?"

"Perfectly, Sir," I say, with a look of rectitude on my face. "I have never raised my hand in anger to a child, and as for severe scoldings, I have other, gentler methods."

"That is very good to hear, Miss," he says, trying out what for him must be a rare smile and rising, signaling the interview is over. I also rise, and perform a medium, businesslike curtsy, which he returns with a slight bow.

"I shall inform my wife to expect you at . . . ?" He looks up at the clock that hangs on his wall. It is ten o'clock.

"I will need an hour or so to check out of my lodgings and write to Mr. Pickering for the references and will report at eleven thirty. Will that be all right?"

"Yes. I shall send a boy to inform Mrs. Polk of your imminent arrival. Good day to you, Miss Leigh."

I bid him a similar farewell, pick up my bag, and leave his office. On my way out of the bank, the receptionist asks of me, "Excuse me, Miss, and pardon me for asking, but did you get the position, such that I might tell any other applicants that the job is filled?"

I turn and say, "Why, yes, I did."

She smiles a very slight, knowing smile, then says, "Good luck."

Now, what could she mean by that?

Having no lodgings to check out of, I head directly for the post office to write to Ezra. Luckily, there is a writing platform built along one wall, with inkwell and pens and blotting paper provided, so I don't have to drag mine from my bag. I pull out my recently purchased paper and write . . .

> *Miss Annabelle H. Leigh*
> *General Delivery*
> *Plymouth, Mass.*

Ezra Pickering, Esq.
Union Street
Boston, Mass.

Dear Ezra,

I write in great haste, so bear with me, please. I have gained a position at the home of a Mr. Polk as governess to his two children, as I consider it to be excellent cover.

However, I will need the following sent to Mr. Polk, President, First Mercantile Bank of Plymouth:

Letters of recommendation from Mistress Pimm, stating my graduation in 1804, and from the Cabot family, me having been tutor to their children for several years. I realize that writing those would go against your professional ethics, so beg Higgins to do them. He is very good at that sort of thing, as you well know.

I believe that Higgins could write me directly at this address and under this alias, perhaps with word on Jaimy's efforts . . . Amy, too. I think it would be well for Miss Leigh to receive mail from various people, in case anyone is watching my mail.

Written in Great Haste,
J.

I blot the letter, take another piece of paper and fold it into an envelope, stuff the letter in, and glue it closed with my mucilage. I then pen addresses on the other side, blot that, and take it to the window, pay the Postmaster, exit, and head for the Polk residence.

Reaching the address given to me, I am pleased that the house is very near the harbor — in fact, on Water Street itself — which is good in case I have to make a hasty departure. It stands cheek to cheek with fine brick houses to either side, sharing walls and leaving no alleyways between. I climb the stone steps, lift the knocker, then let it fall.

The door is opened immediately by a very harried-looking woman. She is also very much with child and has the look of morning sickness all over her face. "Thank God you've come! Please, come in. Oh, God, I'm so sick."

If that was not bad enough as a welcome, there is the sound of a large racket coming from above. There is the pound of running feet and great shouts of rage. A maid comes into the hall, wiping her hands on a cloth.

"Midge, please take Miss Leigh up to the children. I can't, I just can't! I'm sorry, Miss Leigh. Please follow Midge . . . and please, Miss Leigh . . ."

She pauses to gasp out the last . . .

". . . please stay."

Midge opens the door at the top of the stairs, and I go in. It is a large, well-lighted room, with desks and books all around. It also has a very scared little girl cowering in a corner, clutching a little doll to her breast and looking up at me with wild, frightened eyes.

Also in the room is an older boy, in white shirt and short black pants. He is of a slim build, with brown hair parted on the right side and combed flat, and a curiously triangular face — broad forehead, narrow chin. But that is not his most striking feature — it is his enormous, dark eyes that slope downward at the outer ends. Most curious . . . On his head is a newspaper folded into a semblance of a cocked hat, and in his hand is a toy sword made of wood. He shakes the sword at me and snarls . . .

"Avast there! I am the pirate Edgar Allen Polk, and I am going to kill you like I have killed all the others, unworthy wretch!"

Chapter 9

No, young Edgar Allen Polk did not kill me, nor did he kill any of my unfortunate predecessors. No, it seems he merely scared most of them away within hours of the first day, and the rest left soon after. No wonder the elder Mr. Polk appeared ready to hire me on the spot, handy references or not, what with a wild child at home with his distraught wife and another child on the way. I'll wager he stays late at his office, too. Oh well, it's a good, safe kip for me, so I will see what I can do with all this . . .

Upon entering this room, designated as the children's classroom, I find, as stated, the place in complete chaos. Books and papers are scattered all around, some on the three desks that rest within, ignored, and some on the floor. There is a nice bookcase, but none of the books reside therein. There is a large blackboard with gory eyeballs and crude knives and swords drawn on it, all dripping with red chalk blood. Clothing, too, lies strewn about on the floor or thrown carelessly over chair backs, and in the middle of it all stands the defiant cause of the chaos.

Edgar looks at me with lordly disdain as Midge timidly says, "Children, this is your new governess, Miss Leer . . ."

With a slightly embarrassed aside to me, she continues, tapping her right ear, "You'll have to excuse me, Miss, but I am a bit hard of hearing."

And that must be a blessing on this job, I'm thinkin' as I gaze upon young Master Polk, who continues to lunge about, hooting and hollering and waving his sword, slamming it every now and then on an already much-scarred desktop.

"Thank you, Midge, I'll take it from here," I say, giving her arm a pat. "Oh, and before you go, do you have a handyman?"

"A *candyman?*" she asks, confused.

"No, dear, a *handyman,*" I say a bit louder, over Edgar's unceasing racket. "I will need some slight alterations to this classroom to make it a more restful learning environment for the children."

"Oh, yes," she says, brightening. "Our Mr. Olnutt. I'll send him right up." With that, she gratefully leaves, shaking her head over the thought of any learning going on up here with that little monster railing about.

As the door closes behind her, I turn to my young charges and clap my hands and begin introductions.

"Good morning, children," I say, with pince-nez back in place but with a pleasant look on my face. "I am your new teacher. You may call me Miss Leigh."

"I'll call you anything I want," snarls the boy, with a low glare straight into my eyes. "You will call me Captain Blood."

"Very well, Captain," I reply. "I have been told you will also answer to the name of Edgar."

"Doesn't matter." He snorts. "You'll be gone before dinner, just like the rest. You'll see. And you stink."

I turn and lean down to the little girl. "And you would be Catherine? What a lovely name. May I call you Cathy?"

She looks up over the head of her dolly and nods, a bit hopelessly, I believe, like she's seen all this before.

"You stink like all the others. Silly old maids . . . spinsters what couldn't find a decent husband, 'cause you're ugly, too. So, begone, foolish woman, and leave me be. I am the King around here, and I rule."

"I see that you do, indeed," I say, surveying the wreckage of the room.

"Yes, I do," he says smugly and seemingly pleased with my agreement to his terms, lifting his sword now as if it were a scepter. "And I know the rules: the King can be neither beaten nor touched, nor is he to be spoken to in a harsh manner. So you have no power over me; you can do nothing. So you may leave my presence."

I perceive that there is nothing wrong with this kid's vocabulary in spite of his shortcomings in the way of manners. We shall see . . .

I survey the chessboard that is laid out before me and decide that I shall not attack the King directly as he stands, all strong and powerful, at the end of the board, but rather from the weak side — from the side of the helpless pawn . . .

"Come, Cathy," I say all brisk to the cowering little girl. "Let us get you set up with a proper place of your own. But first, let us get some air in here . . ."

There are three large windows across the front of the room facing First Street, and two out the back, next to a door. I advance to the front and fling up the sashes, saying, "Ah, that's much better, is it not?"

Not waiting for a reply from either, I go to the back ones and open them as well. I am gratified to note that the door leads to steps, which go down to a back alley that ends on Water Street. And *yes!* I can even see the harbor where bobs the mast of my sweet little *Evening Star*! Good to know, in case quick escape is called for.

There is a tapping on the door, and a man steps in. He is thin of face, slightly stooped, and needs a shave, but he's a pleasant-enough-looking chap, all around. He wears a leather cap and tool belt from which dangle many useful-looking tools, and he appears competent. "Yes, Miss," he says, forefinger to cap. "Olnutt, here. How can I be helping you?"

"We need a little alcove built over here, so that Cathy might have a more private area in which to study." I give a significant look over my shoulder at the rampaging Edgar.

Mr. Olnutt nods grimly and mutters, "Give me five minutes with that little monster and —"

"Tut-tut, Mr. Olnutt," I say, waving a warning finger. "That would lose you your job, and we wouldn't want that. We both know of Mr. Polk's rules in regard to his gentle son, Edgar, do we not?"

He grunts in reluctant agreement and stands ready.

"Here, help me push this desk over to that nice window there," I say, laying my hand upon it. He comes over and we shove it about such that it faces the right-hand window, next to the wall. "That's it. Now we'll need a sturdy stool for our Cathy to sit upon. Ah, that will do. Up with you now, lass. Good."

She climbs up and sits, her eyes wide and mystified.

"Our Mr. Olnutt is going to make for you a fine little spot with a wall over here." I run an imaginary line across the floor with my finger so that the attentive Olnutt can take my meaning. "There will be a corner here, and a doorway right there. We'll be able to hang your pictures and drawings on the walls, and it'll be all yours. Won't that be fine?"

Again I get a dubious nod from the girl. She is a rather pretty little thing, all blue eyes and blond curls, but no kind of cheer rests upon her lovely face. She has not released her hold upon her doll, and her free thumb has gone into her mouth.

I turn to handyman Olnutt. "It does not have to be fancy, just some paneling below, and simple lath or lattice above. Doesn't have to go all the way to the ceiling, six feet high will do it. And we don't need an actual door, for I will rig a curtain across. Will you do it?"

He smiles and bows. "I'll get right to it, Miss, with pleasure." We both notice that the dread Pirate Edgar has fallen a bit silent, and we both know the reason. Someone else is getting all the attention he so desperately craves. Mr. Olnutt winks and leaves, and I believe I have found a worthy ally in this fight.

The young master recovers himself enough to sulkily say, "Don't bother with *her*. She's dumb and stupid."

Cathy doesn't say a word to that, but I know she is not too dumb and stupid to understand what he said, for her thumb is jammed farther into her mouth.

"Well, Your Majesty, we shall see about that. But as for this mess, we must see about cleaning—"

Just then a bell is rung from below.

"Ah. I believe we are being called to lunch. Shall we go?"

"About time," mutters Edgar, dropping sword or scepter to the floor and rushing out. I extend my hand to Cathy. She takes it, and I lead her downstairs.

The midday meal is served in the kitchen, at a table seating four. There are three steaming bowls at three places, with bread and milk at the side of two, a cup of tea at what I take to be mine. Midge is bustling about at her sink, but Mrs. Polk is nowhere to be seen—probably still sick and grateful for the rest my arrival has brought.

"Manners, everyone," I say as I sit and grab a spoon to dig in. It is very good, and I compliment the cook on her efforts. "Umm . . . This is quite good, Midge. Thanks."

"No, it isn't," sneers Edgar, tossing down his spoon and making a mess on the tablecloth. "It tastes like slop. And milk? Milk for a pirate king? Never! I should be served only the finest rum, so bring it over!"

"Drink your milk, Cathy, it is good for you," I say, and she does as she is told, leaving a milk mustache on her upper lip. Her spoon returns to her bowl of stew, and she finishes it up, as do I mine, sopping up the gravy at the bottom with my bread. *Yum!*

Master Edgar, however, does not attend to his portion, merely shoving it around with his spoon in a deep sulk. I know he is doing this to hold the rest of us up.

Well, we shall see . . .

I rise and ask, "You are not pleased with your repast, Sir?"

"Dammit, no, I'm not!" he shouts. "I'm—"

With that, I reach over and grab his bowl and go to the sink and dump it down the slop hole. "There! It's gone and shall no longer offend thee, my lord!"

"What? What did you do that for?" he sputters.

"A king should not have to eat what he does not want to eat. The food plainly displeased His Lordship, so I, as his loyal servant, got rid of it. Now, let us return to our duties upstairs. Cathy, your hand, please."

As we ascend the stairs, I hear Edgar mutter behind us as he follows, "My father shall hear of this, you may be sure."

I pause on the stair to look back down on him standing below. "Did I strike you, Edgar? Did I speak harshly to you?"

He does not reply, but merely glares at me with great dislike.

If you want to play this game, young man, you'd best sharpen up . . .

Once again in the classroom, I am pleased to see that Mr. Olnutt has already laid out the wall in chalk upon the floor, just where I wanted it. Good man.

"Now then, Cathy, let us set you up first, then Edgar and I will see about the mess in this place." That elicits a profound snort from the young master, who takes up sword again and says he has *absolutely* no intention of helping with anything I might have in mind.

I plunk Cathy back onto her stool, then rummage through the top desk drawer, where I find paper and crayons and place them in front of her. "Do you know how to spell your name, Cathy?"

She shakes her head.

"How about your ABCs?"

Again she shakes her head and looks about to cry.

"Told you she was stupid," comes from Edgar.

"Don't worry, Cathy," I say in my most soothing voice.

"You'll get it real quick, I just know it. I will teach you, you'll see. Here, I'll write out a few letters and you try to copy them. *A, B, C, D, E, F,* and I'll be back in a bit to help. All right?"

With that, I place a kiss on her cheek, and turn to her brother. At least she did look at the letters and pick up a crayon.

"Now, Edgar, let us clean up a bit, shall we, so that we might begin some serious study. How about we start by picking up around here?"

He goes to the blackboard and commences to draw a bloodshot eyeball with a stiletto run through it. "You do it. I am busy and not in the least bit interested in doing that."

"Very well, Majesty, I will do that," I say, bending down to scoop up a sheaf of carelessly tossed papers — more ghastly drawings. "But first you must answer me something."

"What?"

"Though you seem to be lacking any social graces, you are very well-spoken. How do you account for that?"

"I read books. I do not need any lousy teacher to teach me how to do that. I teach myself."

I look around at the books strewn on the floor. I see a science book and pick it up, placing it on the bookshelf. Another book appears to be on music theory; another is on mathematics. All look like they've never been opened. These I also put away. He says nothing to that.

Then I notice other kinds of books, down by my feet — books that look like they have been much more read, with folded-over pages and broken spines — and I look at the titles: *Dreadful Pirates of the South Seas . . . Cutthroats of the*

Caribbean ... and, good Lord, there's *Bloody Jack* ... and *Under the Jolly Roger*! *So that's where he's getting all that pirate stuff!*

I reach down and get a stack of those in my arms and go to one of the open back windows and toss them out.

"Hey!" he shouts. "What are you doing? Those are mine!" He drops the chalk, rushes to the window, and looks down at his pirate stash in horror.

"You treated those books as rubbish by throwing them on the floor, so I threw them out in the trash. I assumed, Captain Blood, that you would approve of my action. What needs a bold pirate of such silly books?"

"But ... but ... but ..."

"If you value them, Cap'n," I say, folding arms over chest, "then you'd best go down to get them, as it looks like it might rain."

One last glare of pure hatred, and then he rushes out the door and down the stairs, returning with the books cradled in his arms, his face red with anger.

"Put them on the bookshelves, or they will go out again; count on it, Blood."

"My father will hear of this," he warns. "*You* can count on that."

"I will be conferring with your parents tonight, after which you may discuss it with him," I say. "You will notice that I did not hit you, neither did I speak harshly to you. What will you report? That you nicely cleaned up the classroom, hmmm? I'm sure he will be delighted to hear it."

The books go on the shelf while my good Captain steams, and I beam in some satisfaction.

Chapter 10

I will not say my first afternoon with the Polk children was an absolute success, but it did have its bright spots. Cathy toiled away at her ABCs and even managed to draw an acceptable *C*, so we were able to get a start on her name. *See, Cathy, how your name starts out with a C and then goes to an* A *and then to a* T? *All by itself, it spells* CAT, *just like that cat right there, but when we add an* H *and a* Y *we get* CATHY, *and what a fine name it is! A fine name for a fine girl!*

And our skilled handyman, Mr. Olnutt, true to his word, managed to get Cathy's private space up in no time by bringing up the partitions in sections through the back door and fixing them in place with wood screws, such that they could be removed later. Smart man, for Mr. Polk might not like his new governess changing the floor plan of his fine house. At my request, Olnutt even threw together a simple easel out of scraps of wood he had in his tool shed. Yes, a very valuable man, indeed, is our Mr. Olnutt.

I did notice that, upon completion of the alcove, the

aforementioned black cat did not waste any time in quitting the greater classroom and planting herself on Cathy's desk, a perch from which she does not move. When Master Edgar appeared at the doorway to pronounce that all this was silly stuff, she lifted an unsheathed claw-clustered paw and bared her teeth and hissed loudly in his direction. Thus, I realized that Cathy was not the only victim . . . and that maybe the cat would be a possible ally in this battle as well.

For battle it certainly is. Young Mr. Polk, having realized, correctly, that he had lost the morning's fight, redoubled his nastiness, thrashing about outside the alcove in true piratical fury. *"Die, dog! Here's one in your filthy guts! Mercy? Never! Bow down, you scurvy knaves, bow down to Captain Blood!"*

Well, us knaves will see about that, *won't we?*

"Now, Cathy, I must go out to set your brother to some more productive work than what he is now doing, but first, tell me the name of your kitty. Blackie? Of course . . . And your dolly? Amy? What a nice name. Did you know that's the name of my very best friend? It's true. Now, why don't we sit Amy up here on your desk so that you might work a little more easily? There. See? She's watching you do your letters, and she's very proud of you. Later on, we'll play some music and I'll tell you a story, and maybe we'll do some drawing. All right? Good."

"Now, Captain," I say, confronting the little rotter. "Why don't you put down your mighty swift sword and sit at your desk, such that we might work on your math and science?"

"Won't do it. Can't make me, neither, *Governess,*" he pronounces firmly, point of sword on floor, hands on hilt, eyes daring me to say otherwise.

I put my hands out in gentle supplication and say, "It is true that I am but a poor, pitiable governess, but yet sweet reason says that a bold sea captain must know his math and science. For when his scalawags bring in helpless hostages for ransom, he must know what price to place on each head and how to count that ransom when it is paid. And when his men bring chests of treasure before him to divide up the spoils according to the Laws of the Pirate Brotherhood, he will have to know how to do it. Right?"

He looks dubious at that, but he does seem to brighten at the thought of helpless captives cringing before him. I go on.

"And that is math, of course. And as for science, surely that same bold sea pirate captain must know celestial navigation — the sun and the stars and the use of the sextant, so he will know where his ship is on that wild and trackless ocean. Otherwise, your fine ship might be cast away and lost on some cruel rocks."

He thinks on that while I press on.

"What is the name of your ship, by the way, Captain?" I just know he's picked one out.

"It is named *The Raven*," he replies. "And I can't wait till I have you tied to the mast, pleading for mercy. You shall receive none."

Hmmm. Not bad. I had expected something gory, but that has a bit of the poetic in it as well. The lad does have an imagination, that's for sure.

"So what do you say, Captain? Will you turn to your studies for the good of your ship and your loyal comrades, as a True Son of the Sea?"

He thinks, then shakes his head. "No. I already know enough of that stuff already."

Hmmm . . . But will you take a bribe, then, Captain Blood?

While he stands there, obstinate, I drag out a chair and climb up on it to intone, in my best theatrical manner . . .

"I am Señor Hernando de Castro, governor of this fine port of Santa Maria de Josa. When I arose this morning, I was happy and my people were happy. But then I looked out over my ramparts and saw, lying below in the harbor, *The Raven,* the ship of the dread Pirate Polk. His mighty guns were trained upon us while his bloodthirsty crew were hanging over her sides, screaming bloody murder!"

From my perch, I put hand to brow and feign looking out over a rampart, great distress upon my face.

"Oh, we are lost! They will land and burn our poor town and take all our riches! Whatever shall we do?"

Then I pretend a great thought has just occurred to me.

"I know! We'll offer him a bribe to go away!"

I lean over my imaginary battlement, cup my hands, and call down to him . . .

"Hullo, Captain Blood! Can you hear me?"

Edgar looks up and replies, "Hullo, yourself, and yes, I can hear you."

"Will you accept an honorable bribe as a token of our esteem and then take yourself and your ship to some other port?"

"Huh! What have you got to bribe me with?"

"If you consent to leave my harbor, and agree to attend to your nautical studies both this afternoon and tomorrow morning, I will take you and Cathy on an excursion tomorrow afternoon."

"An excursion?" he asks, a bit confused. "To where?"

"To Mr. Filibuster's Fine Emporium, where we shall sit at the counter and enjoy some of his fine and flavorful fizzy water. What say you, Captain?"

I see the prospect of getting out of here for an afternoon working slowly across his face.

"You can do that?"

"Of course I can!" I say in my most managerial tone, my finger in the air. "Am I not the governess of this colony! And do you not agree to the terms?"

"Oh, very well," he says, flinging down sword and seating himself at his desk. "But don't expect me to learn anything, because I shan't."

Oh, yes, you shall, young Edgar, I'm thinking as I pull the math book from the shelf and place it in front of him. *For I know exactly what a young boy should know in the way of math and science, for did I not go to school with five of the rascals on HMS* Dolphin? *And they were a helluva lot tougher than you, Master Polk.*

And so the afternoon at Maison Polk rolls on. Edgar grumbles, but he works on his long division — which I just knew he did not know — and Cathy is busy on her alphabet, humming away, seemingly happy.

To give them a break in the afternoon, I pull out my flageolet and give them a few tunes. Cathy claps her hands delightedly, while Edgar just grumbles about the noise.

At last there is the bell for dinner and we all go down.

We have a nice dinner, Midge, Nellie, Cathy, Edgar, and me. It's pork chops with stuffing and potatoes and gravy, with sweet cider on the side, and I tuck it away with piggish abandon. Edgar, of course, makes a great show of hating everything, but I notice, when I make another grab at his plate in order to dump it again, he lunges forward to prevent me doing that and then settles in to eating. Our eyes meet. We are beginning to understand each other.

After all have finished — and both Midge and Nellie turned out to be excellent company — the women turn to cleanup, while I take the children upstairs to get them ready for bed . . . and Presentation to the Parents.

Cathy, of course, is easy. She quickly doffs her clothes, does her business in the pot, lets me wash her in the warm, soapy water Nellie has provided, dries off with a fluffy towel, and then it's on with her white nightdress. She waits in the hall, Amy in hand, while I go to tackle Edgar.

"You will *not* enter this room when I am in here!" he shouts out to me.

Boys, I swear . . . Haven't I seen at least several hundred completely naked males?

"All right," I call back at him, "but you better come out clean! Believe me, I will check!"

Eventually, he comes out, dressed in his nightshirt and looking surly. I give a quick visual inspection, take a quick sniff of his hair — he will need a bath soon — and pronounce him presentable enough, for now. Then I take Cathy by the hand and lead them down the stairs.

Mr. and Mrs. Polk are seated at the grand table in the dining room, one at either end, when I bring in the children. I think both are surprised to see me still here. The missus is looking wan but a little better than when I saw her in the morning. It is plain that they have finished the main course and Mr. Polk is lingering over coffee. He lifts an eyebrow in question.

"Good evening, Mr. Polk, Mrs. Polk. I hope you had a pleasant day. I have worked with the children today and am generally pleased with the results. Cathy here has embarked upon her ABCs, and she is doing fine. See, she has drawn a C, the first letter in her name. Hold it up, dear."

Cathy holds up her paper to her father's gaze.

"That's fine," he says dismissively. "But what about the boy?"

Cathy drops the paper, and the thumb goes back in her mouth.

"Well, Sir, I can report that young Edgar is quite proficient in both history and English. However, he does need some work on math to bring him up to snuff, and we are on it. I am sure that you, as a banker, would approve of that?"

"Harrumph," says Mr. Polk, trapped into agreeing with his new governess. "That is so, I'd say. Were you happy with what went on today, Edgar?"

Here's your chance, Captain, to blow me away.

He does not take it. Instead he fixes a look of pure malice upon me and says, "Yes, Father, all went well. I hope you had a good day at the bank."

I notice that Edgar is much more polite in the presence of his father. He does not fear his mother, but he definitely is afraid of a stern word from his dad.

"That is good. Now off to bed with you," says Mr. Polk. "Miss Leigh, a word with you after you tuck in the children."

"Yessir," I say. "Come, children. Say good night, now."

They do and we trudge up the stairs.

"You don't have to tuck me in, Governess," sneers Edgar, going into his bedroom. "I can do it myself!" He slams the door shut behind him.

I take Cathy into her room, get her into bed, and tuck her in with Amy beside her. Planting a kiss upon her brow — *such a good little girl* — I pull the covers to her chin and wish her sweet dreams. She smiles and closes her eyes, and I go down to rejoin Mr. and Mrs. Polk.

Mr. Polk gestures to a place where a cup of tea has been placed, so I go and sit there.

"Well, Miss Leigh, we must say, we are most pleased with your performance so far" — even Mrs. Polk manages a wan smile at that — "and we hope that — "

All of a sudden, there is a loud rumpus from up above, in the direction of Edgar's room, of course. It sounds very much like he is pounding his feet on the floor.

Mrs. Polk's smile disappears and her hand goes to her mouth. "Oh, Lord, he is doing it again, and I so wished — "

Mr. Polk rises, as do I, my tea untasted. "Yes," he says. "It is a shame that our Edgar is so high-strung . . . so sensitive . . . but I imagine it goes with his fine breeding. Patience, I am sure you will go up and calm him down?"

Breeding, my Cockney ass! Why don't you just go up and kick the tar out of the little monster!

Mrs. Polk, the well-named Patience, nods in defeat as Mr. Polk takes his hat from the rack and announces, "I am off to my club to meet with some important business associates. Until later, then."

And I'll bet you go off every night when Edgar starts playing this tune, you coward, you.

As Mrs. Polk rises to go do her weary duty, I place a

restraining hand on her arm and bid her to stay. "Nay, Mistress, let me have a word with the lad. I believe I might be able to soothe his mind with a gentle bedtime story."

Putting on the full Lawson Peabody Look, I then turn to the departing Mr. Polk to say, "I believe, Mr. Polk, that you will not be disturbed in such a way ever again. Do have a pleasant evening."

With that, I turn and go to the stairs.

Although I made him promise to be good in class, I did not, however, tell him to lay off any other disturbance, and so we have this. He is a wily little bastard, I'll give him that . . . But I am wily, too . . . for I know that if there is one class of people more superstitious than sailors, it is little boys. *So stand by, Eddie, for some heavy weather.*

As it is growing dark, I grab a lamp from the hall, and then I burst into Edgar's room.

"Get out of here," he shouts, jumping back into bed. "You are not allowed in —"

I hold the lamp up to my face, revealing it to be a mask of pure terror. "Oh, Master Edgar, I am so sorry, but I fear for your very life! And it is all my fault!"

He begins to look concerned and pulls his sheet to his chin. "Why, what do you mean?"

"The Bed Monsters is what I mean! I heard them from below! They must have followed me here from the Cabots'! Oh, woe! How I hope they did not devour those poor, poor boys!"

"Nonsense," says Edgar stoutly. "There's no such thing as Bed Monsters."

"Get back there, you!" I cry, making a great show of stamping my foot on the floor. "Back!"

"What was that?" he asks, a trifle less stoutly.

"Nothing. Just a tentacle," I say, breathing hard. I kneel down and shout under the bed, "Now, you leave our Eddie alone! He's a good boy!"

I straighten up and say, "He . . . and the others . . . will stay back now . . . at least for a while. They'll mind me . . . up to a point. Now, let me tell you about Bed Monsters, for I know the buggers well."

"Still don't believe you," he says, his eyes wide now.

I crouch next to the bed, the lamp to my face, making me look right hideous, I know. Then I whisper . . .

"First of all, never let any of your bedclothes trail on the floor, 'cause they can crawl right up 'em and get you lyin' there all scared and helpless."

With that, I pick up the edge of a sheet and tuck it under the mattress.

"Second of all, they are blind, which is to our advantage," I continue. "How so? Why, that means that they can only find you *if you make a noise*. Watch this . . ."

Making a fist, I rap my knuckles on the floor, then quickly jerk my hand back to my chest, exclaiming, "Did you see that claw try to grab me when I made that sound?"

He tried to look, but I was too quick.

"Brrrr . . . that was close! You may be sure I won't try that again, and I advise you not to do it, either."

It is not likely he will try, for his covers are now up to his eyes. I stand to take my leave.

"So, Edgar, I am sorry I brought them here, but what is done is done. You know the rule: Make no noise and they will not be able to follow the sound of your voice and so find their prey."

I go to the door, but before I exit, I turn and say, "Please hearken to what I have said. I would hate to come up here in the morning and find an empty, bloody bed. What would I tell your poor mother? Sweet dreams, Edgar."

I close the door behind me and go down to rejoin Mrs. Polk for that cup of tea.

From above, all is silence.

Chapter 11

The Journal of Amy Trevelyne
Dovecote Farm
Quincy, Massachusetts
Begun September, 1809

Dear Reader,

I am beginning this journal to record what I know of the most recent peregrinations of my dear friend Jacky Faber. You might know of her earlier exploits from the biographical novels I have previously published concerning her wild adventures. The fact that I have no idea where she is right now and have no means of communicating with her are the reasons I have commenced this record. Another reason, I am loath to admit, is that I have a great sense of foreboding concerning the future well-being of my dearest friend — I am not superstitious, but she has tempted Fate far too many times, and I fear she may be brought to account this time. I feel I owe it to future generations to record what very well might be the final chapter in her life. Though I hope I am wrong.

I know that she is in serious trouble, for once not due to indiscretions on her part, but rather to machinations on the part of her many enemies. As to her whereabouts, I can only rely on the bits of information I am able to glean from conversations with Mr. Ezra Pickering, her friend and attorney.

Do not fear, gentle reader, that this journal will fall into the wrong hands, thereby leading to the capture of Miss Faber and causing her grievous injury, for I shall keep these pages in a secure casket under lock and key. I would never wish to cause her even the slightest injury, as I hold her in my heart and soul with all the love therein.

I pray for good news.

Entry dated September 19, 1809 — signed Amy Trevelyne

Chapter 12

The morning goes reasonably well. We have oatmeal for breakfast — a glop of hot cooked meal in the center of each bowl, surrounded by a moat of warm milk, and topped with a sprinkling of coarse brown sugar. Not bad, but it could be better. I make a note to buy some maple syrup later, when we go out into the town.

As soon as my charges and I tromp up to the classroom, Edgar corrals me in a state of high indignation.

"There ain't no such thing as Bed Monsters, you," he says, finger in my eye. "I looked this morning, and there wasn't nothing under my bed. So there!"

"Mind your grammar, Master Edgar," I say, pulling the math book from the shelf and placing it on his desk. "Everybody knows that at first light of dawn Bed Monsters slink away to their dank pools of slime, far below in the fuming cracks of the very earth itself. They rest up till darkness comes. Then once again they take up residence 'neath a poor boy's bed. Everybody knows that. Everyone who's still alive, that is. Now, let us attend to your math."

He remains unconvinced. "Then why don't they go after *her?*" he asks, gesturing toward his sister, who happily babbles away in her cubicle. I had lined out the rest of the alphabet for Cathy and she has mastered the first five letters, singing them as a song. She is a *very* bright little girl. I have also made a simple drawing of her cat, and she is enthusiastically copying it.

"*Because* . . ." I say, as if exasperated, "the Bed Monsters like only *boy* meat. Girl flesh is too soft for them . . . Gets stuck in their teeth, like."

"Still don't believe," he mutters, arms crossed in firm resolve.

Ah, yes, young man, it is easy to be so brave in the cold light of day, but tonight, when darkness comes creeping stealthily into your room like a black cat on quiet paws, well, we'll see then, won't we?

"Anyway, never mind that," I say brusquely. "We must now get to our math. 'Bout time we got into some geometry. Here . . ."

He looks at me warily. "You're not going to weasel out on it, are you? We are still going out this afternoon?"

"No, I am not . . . as long as you keep your part of the bargain. Now look at this. It is something that Captain Blood will find very interesting." I find a stray piece of paper on his desktop, and upon it I draw a right triangle.

"Bet he won't," retorts Edgar, all sullen.

"And I bet he'll find it very practical, Sir. It is called the Py-thag-gor-ean theorem, and it is just the most elegant thing. Ahem." And I recite: "*A* squared plus *B* squared equals *C* squared . . . or . . . the sum of the squares of the two sides is equal to the square of the hypotenuse, or the longest side."

"So?"

"So? Watch this."

With that, I label the legs of the triangle *A, B,* and *C.* Then I draw a boat's hull and sail at the end of the lower leg, a lump of land at the other end, and then, at the top of that leg, a crude cannon with a puff of smoke at its mouth.

"Now, suppose the dread pirate Captain Blood brings *The Raven*" — here I point to the boat — "up to this port" — here I point to the lump of land — "and intends to raid the town. But then he discovers that the port is not helpless, for here, at the top of a battlement, rests a mighty cannon that prevents him from entering the harbor." I point then at the smoking cannon.

"But Captain Blood is not dismayed, for he knows his math. He already knows the distance from *The Raven* to the land, as well as the height of the battlement, because of the chart he had earlier snatched from a helpless merchant captain who had knelt at his feet, begging for his life. The bold Captain Blood then takes pencil and paper and figures out not only the distance from his mightiest cannon to the gun that was annoying him, but also the very angle of elevation that his own cannon should be. To the amazement of all, he bellows, 'A triple charge of powder, me hearties, and crank 'er up to thirty-three degrees! Now, FIRE!' The cannonball flies and the shore gun disappears in a cloud of smoke and hot iron shards . . . Astounding! The legend of Captain Blood spreads even wider over the seagoing world, and *The Raven* is able to run right into the harbor to spread destruction all around: stealing booty, taking hostages, putting the town officials to the sword, and all the rest of that pirate stuff."

"Really?" asks Edgar, squinting at the formula.

"Really," says I, turning the pages of the math book to the proper spot. "Start here on how to take square roots. Then we'll get on to the fun stuff."

He picks up pencil and commences to work.

All goes well till noon, whereupon we have a nice lunch, after which I plunk round hat on my head, tuck umbrella under my arm, and take Cathy by the hand, and we lead Edgar out the front door.

Ah, it is good to get out in the sun and air again, plus I'll be able to check my mail. Tomorrow is my day off, so if I get any word from Ezra, I'll be able to write out a reply and get it right off. All is good.

"Master Edgar, get up here and walk with the rest of us," I order, to no avail. He has fallen about ten yards behind Cathy and me as he slouches along, head down, with hands jammed in pockets.

"Won't," he says. "Someone might see me."

"Wot? Who cares who sees you?"

"I do. Can't be seen walking with girls . . . or a governess."

His eyes are shifty in a way I have not seen them before. Then I follow one of his worried glances and realize just why he is concerned — up ahead, the boys of Plymouth School are out playing football.

Ah, that question of male honor again, even in one such as Edgar — all pretense aside, is one at heart a stout, brave lad, or merely a miserable coward?

"Well, it doesn't matter, for here we are at Mr. Filibuster's Fine Emporium. In with you both now." I shove them into the store, to Cathy's great delight at all the bright colors and fine things for sale, and to Edgar's obvious relief.

I arrange the children on stools to either side of me at the soda counter and order our drinks from the smiling Mr. Filibuster. "A cherry soda for our little princess here, and a blackberry one for me. Edgar, what will you have?"

"Rum," he answers firmly, back in character.

"I'm afraid we do not have that particular flavor, young man," says Mr. Phineas T. Filibuster, with a wink at me. "Not at this counter, anyway. Will a foaming glass of root beer do?"

Edgar grunts a grudging assent, and Phineas T. goes to make up the concoctions while I ask of Edgar, "How come you don't go to the regular school with the rest of the boys?"

"My father does not want me associating with ruffians is why." The lad sniffs. "And I agree with him on that. We Polks are a cut above." I know he is quoting his dad, but I don't know if he's fully convinced of its truth.

"Ah, here we are!" I exclaim as our sodas are brought and placed before us. "Aren't they lovely?"

They are indeed. Cathy looks in wonder at hers—all bright cherry red in its crystal glass, bubbles racing up the inside to pop at the top where floats a little piece of ice.

"Thank Mr. Filibuster, Cathy," I say, in true governess fashion.

"Thank you, Mr. Filly-buster," says Cathy.

Well! A complete sentence out of her! Bravo, Cathy!

Our host, from his side of the counter, notices that Cathy does not know quite what to do with her cherry soda.

There are no handles on the glass for her to grasp, but, curiously, there is a reed, of all things, stuck well down into the ruby liquid, its end sitting up at the top.

"Here, Missy," he says, leaning over and taking up the reed and holding it out to her. "Put your lips on the straw and suck up the soda through it. It'll work, you'll see. Why, it's all the rage in New York."

Her cheeks draw in and then puff out as her eyes widen in delight when the sweet soda hits her tongue. I believe a heartfelt *mmmmmm* is heard from the tyke.

"Not too fast, now, dearie; make it last," urges a beaming Mr. Filibuster. I apply the straw to the Faber lips and suck it up. *Oh, it is so wondrous good!* I exult to myself when the fizzy blackberry flavor hits the Faber mouth. Further study is *definitely* required.

No complaints from Edgar, either, I notice. Actually, when he is halfway through his root beer soda — I figure the "beer" part of the flavor appealed to his manly nature — he asked of our Mr. Filibuster, very politely, mind you, if he might keep the reed.

"Of course, young man," he pronounces grandly. "We use them only once here at our Fine Emporium."

I finish up my excellent drink with a loud slurp at the bottom, then stand to do some shopping while the children are finishing theirs. Mr. Filibuster follows me about as I choose my purchases.

"I'll need a pint bottle of paregoric . . ."

"Yes, some Mother's Little Helper," he murmurs, eyeing the restless Edgar and taking a brown bottle down from a shelf. "Perfectly understandable in your situation."

"And some maple syrup," I say, and a small gray crockery jug is added to the side countertop. "I'll also need a bottle of your excellent blackberry flavoring . . . and lastly, a packet of catnip, if you have it."

"I do," he says, with some satisfaction, putting a small brown packet on the pile.

"Oh, won't kitty have ever so much fun with that!" I exclaim, handing over my net shopping bag, into which he puts my purchases, then he starts totaling up my bill. "Oh, and three pieces of penny candy, please."

He nods and we go back to the children, whereupon he places upon the counter a clear glass gallon jar filled with brightly colored round candies and invites them to choose one each. Cathy, going with a proven winner, reaches in to take a red one and pops it into her mouth. Edgar the Bold goes for a black one, while I take green. *Yum, lime . . . for a true British Limey, even.*

With our cheeks distended from their sweet cargo, we take leave of Mr. Filibuster and head out into the day.

"I suppose we're going back home now," grumbles Edgar, kicking at a stone. The lads from the school are back safely inside now, so he does not have to worry about being seen by them.

"Not just yet, Captain," I say, pointing up the street with my umbrella. "First I wish to go to the post office to see if I have any mail."

"Humph!" he snorts. "Who would write to a dried-up old spinster like you?" It does not take him long to revert to form.

"I have two sisters, both dried-up old spinsters like me. We like to exchange embroidery patterns. It keeps our minds off the husbands we did not get."

As we walk and talk, we go by a kiosk selling news-papers. While I am buying one, Edgar walks to the back and calls out, "Hey, look at this!"

And there it is . . . pinned to the rough wooden wall . . .

WANTED FOR TREASON

The Notorious Pyrate

JACKY FABER

$500 Dollar

REWARD!

FOR INFORMATION LEADING TO HER ARREST AND CONVICTION ON CHARGES OF TREASON.

She is almost 5 ft. tall, has sandy hair,
often cropped short, and bears many Scars.
She is Considered to be armed and dangerous.

Do not Try to apprehend her. Contact local police.

"Now, that's somebody you should be like," sneers Edgar, pointing up at the damning sheet, "not like some silly governess, afraid of her own shadow."

Damn, they sure didn't waste any time, did they? Five hundred bucks, eh? They must really want my sorry butt.

I reach up to pull down the sheet and hand it to Edgar. "Here. If you like that Jacky Faber and her piratical ways so much, hang this on your wall, so you might admire it all day long."

"Gee, thanks," he says, eagerly folding the broadside and shoving it into his shirt front.

A bit concerned, I march forward to the post office, and the kids follow me in.

Hmmm . . . I notice another of those posters on the wall, but I can't do anything about that, other than ignore it. *Hey, I'm in deep disguise, so why should I worry?*

Advancing to the Postmaster's window, I demand, "The mail for Miss Annabelle Leigh, if you please."

He is a fussy little man, who wears spectacles low on his narrow nose, and pants pulled high by suspenders that rest on his thin shoulders. He turns and paws through a rack behind him. Presently, he chooses a thick packet and places it in front of me.

Hooray! I see that it is from Ezra!

As I reach for it, he pulls it back, saying in a prissy little voice, "This is highly irregular. A single young woman receiving messages from a man."

What? At first I am stunned. Then I grow angry and fix the little worm with my best Lawson Peabody Look, saying, "While it is true that Ezra Pickering is, indeed, a man, he is also an attorney who handles affairs for the school I attended. You will notice that I have been appointed the governess of these children. Their father, Mr. Polk, whom I am sure you know well" — *probably got you your goddamn job* — "requested that I write to him for my references, and I have done so. *That* is what is contained in this packet," I conclude through clenched teeth as I clamp my hand on the letter and bring it to me.

And mind your own business, Mr. Postmaster!

Steaming, I grab Cathy's hand and we exit the post office to head back to the House of Polk.

Chapter 13

"What are we going to do today?" asks Edgar, without much interest in the answer. "Besides wasting my time."

"'Scursion?" asks Cathy, hope writ large on her dear, open face. She has not forgotten her wonderful cherry soda.

"Afraid not, dear. This is my afternoon off, but your aunt Felicity is coming over to pick you up in her coach-and-four to take you both off for a nice ride in the country. That's an excursion, too, you know. And the fresh country air will do you both good. Won't that be nice?"

Edgar sighs and grunts, but Cathy claps her hands delightedly. I have met their aunt Felicity — she is a formidable old dame who scares Edgar into good behavior, but who dotes on Cathy. I believe she sort of approves of me, since I have lasted for a while, but she appears to be withholding judgment on that.

"So what are we going to do till then? Something boring, I'm sure." I note that he has that WANTED poster tacked up on the wall next to him. He has drawn some bloody cutlasses and severed heads in the margins.

"In addition to our usual studies, we are going to do some painting."

"Painting? That's stupid girly stuff," he says.

"No, it isn't," I say right back at him. "Wouldn't you like your picture to be up there on the hall wall with the rest of your illustrious ancestors, sword in hand, tricorn on head, looking every inch the bold sea captain?"

He snorts, but he does not say nay to that prospect.

I had noticed on my first evening here at Maison Polk that the walls of the long hall were, indeed, covered with framed portraits of some very stern-looking fore-bears. The pictures are easily separated by the era in which they were done — the early ones are dark, crudely painted on slabs of varnished wood, and are simply framed. They portray fierce, scowling men in black clerical garb with high tab collars, while the women look equally forbidding — neck-high dresses, black, of course, with what looks like white doilies tight about their thin, reedy necks. The more modern ones are on stretched canvas and are much more elegantly presented in highly carved gilded frames, and the people presented therein are more finely dressed — the steely-eyed men in grand uniforms of many colors, holding swords or spyglasses, or perhaps with their hands on globes and maps, and their women, beautiful in silks and satins and riding habits of every fit and hue. Then there are the portraits of little children. Curiously, though, through the years, it has been the custom that little boys, up to a certain age, are often portrayed in girl garb — dresses and ribbons and curls and all that. Even now, they still do it. There are a few of them on the Polk wall as well.

"So," I announce, taking two pieces of fine watercolor paper from my seabag, as well as my paints and brushes, "I shall start with Cathy first. Come, dear, sit over here in the light. That's it. Now tilt your head a little more that way. Perfect! And, yes, we will certainly put our Amy in the picture, too! Captain Blood, attend to your science, and I will be with you in a while."

People may say what they want about my skill in portraiture, but one thing I know: I am *fast*. The many times I have suffered with fidgety kids, bored men, and arrogant royalty have taught me to get the important stuff down quickly and accurately, or else forget about your fee, girl, 'cause you ain't gonna get it. One-Sitting Faber, I style myself, and I try to live up to that.

I quickly sketch in the shape of her head and the set of her shoulders, then come in with a wide brush laden with a wash of burnt sienna to lay in the planes of her face . . . now some raw umber, darker pigment on thinner brush to start delineating her features. I know what I have to get done now, while the model sits before me, and what I can save till later when I am working alone. It is good that Edgar is quietly studying, for a change, as I really need to concentrate.

As I work away, the door opens and Bert Olnutt comes in. I had asked him to stop by, as I had a small project for him. "Hello, be right with you . . ."

Now to the placement of the eyes — *and thank you, Maestro Goya, for your kind advice on how to do this* — and the dark line under the upper eyelid and . . .

YEEEEOUCH!

"Close the windows!" I screech, my cupped hand to my left ear. "I've been stung by a wasp!"

Damn, that hurts!

Mr. Olnutt slams the windows shut and comes over to me. I have dissolved into childish tears. *Oh, how I hate to be stung by a spiteful bee!*

"Here, lass, let me see. We should try to get the stinger out. That way it won't swell up so much."

I let his gentle hand remove mine from my poor ear. He looks for a moment, and then his gentle voice hardens as he says, "Ain't no stinger, Miss, and you wasn't stung by no wasp."

He crouches down and picks up something from the floor and shows it to me. It is small and round and hard. It is a common dried garden pea. Both Bert and I look at Edgar, who sits hunched over at his desk, for all appearances a scholar intent on his studies. Bert makes an angry move toward him, but I stay him with my arm across his chest.

"Nay, Bert, forbear," I say, going to stand over Edgar. "Let me handle this. It's not worth your job."

"That was very mean of you, Edgar." I sniff, wiping away a tear. "Very mean. You could have put out my eye."

Staring straight forward, he says nothing. Cathy, observing all this, has started quietly weeping.

"Hand it over, Edgar," I say, holding out my hand, palm up. "I don't want you hurting anyone else."

He still does not move, but Mr. Olnutt does. He pushes Edgar aside and pulls out the top middle desk drawer, shoving it roughly against Edgar's belly. Lying within is the reed Edgar had cadged from Mr. Filibuster's Emporium, as well as a handful of dried peas.

Bert Olnutt grabs the peashooter in his strong right hand and crushes it in front of Edgar's hot eyes.

"This job ain't worth puttin' up with a brat like you."

I put my hand on Bert's shoulder and take him back to the door before he follows his impulse to give Master Edgar Allen Polk the thrashing he so plainly deserves. On the way over, I take up my painting of Cathy.

"Here, Bert, is what I need: three frames to fit watercolor paintings of this size, ready to hang. With glass. Nothing fancy, mind you."

"Three?" he asks, looking over at the two kids.

"Three, Bert, and I'll need 'em tomorrow. I know it's short notice, but thanks; you're a dear." I plant a kiss upon his cheek and he leaves, his anger dissipated.

"Very well," I say, going back to my easel and seating myself before it. "Edgar. Sit in that chair there. Yes. Go do it now."

A bit mystified that I do not pursue his criminal use of the peashooter any further, he rises and does it.

I labor away at the portrait, extra working brushes held in teeth and hair, intent on getting only the face and head down right. After a bit, I fling the paper aside as if in exasperation, saying "Damn. That one wasn't working out. Can't win 'em all. Let's try again."

I go to my bag and pull out a fresh sheet of paper and start again, and this time I work over the whole painting, so that, during breaks, Edgar can see both the figure and the proud naval costume and sword evolve. I put a swirling flag in as background, and, perhaps emboldened by my timid response to his attack upon my poor ear, he orders, "Make sure that flag is *The Raven*'s own Jolly Roger," and I meekly nod assent.

Eventually, the chimes ring for lunch and I am free for

the afternoon. Edgar bolts off down the stairs, but Cathy lingers, her eyes all teary.

"What is it, dear?" I ask as I sit cleaning my brushes.

By way of answer, she comes around and puts a wet kiss on my wounded earlobe and says, "I don't want you to go away. Just because Edgar was mean. I love you, Governess."

"Aw, that is so sweet," I say, wrapping my arms around the dear little thing. "Don't worry, Cathy, I'm not going away. Not yet, anyway. So dry your tears and go down to lunch. Your aunt Felicity will be waiting. And yes, tomorrow we shall have an excursion. I promise."

I would like to run off to the Whale's Tale for a raucous afternoon of strong ale, bellowed sea songs, and the good company of my seagoing brethren, but alas, I can't do that. However, a nice quiet cup of tea at the White Rose doesn't sound too awfully bad, either.

Before I enter the Rose, I stop in at Mr. Filibuster's and purchase some candy — a large bag of the round multicolored treats — in fact, enough to satisfy any boy's craving for sweets.

That small task accomplished, I go into the White Rose and am warmly greeted by the landlady, who introduces herself as Mrs. Tibbetts, and I am seated by a window as I requested. There I have an excellent view of the street and the life thereon. Tea and cakes are brought, and I settle in to review my mail — both incoming and outgoing. First to Ezra's . . .

Ezra Pickering, Atty. at Law
Union Street, Boston, Massachusetts, USA

Miss Annabelle Leigh
General Delivery
Plymouth, Massachusetts

Dear Miss Leigh,

I hope this letter finds you safe and well. I trust you have received the letters of recommendation that you requested. Higgins hopes that they will suffice . . .

(Indeed they did — Master Forger Higgins has certainly not lost his touch. Mr. Polk accepted them without comment.)

. . . and assures you that we are doing everything possible from this end to clear you of that ridiculous charge.

To that I add my own assurances. I will tell you of our efforts in more detail later, but I wish to get this off as quickly as possible.

Your most respectful, etc.
Ezra

And then there was Amy Trevelyne's slightly more emotional letter . . .

Miss Amy Trevelyne
Dovecote Farm
Quincy, Massachusetts, USA

Miss Jacky Faber
Plymouth, Massachusetts

My dear Jacky,

You cannot know, dearest Sister, how distressed I was to hear of your current distress. Again I trouble the senseless heavens with my vain entreaties. Why, oh, why cannot your life, dearest Jacky, proceed in the orderly fashion usually ordained for those of our sex?

Yes, I know, in the past you have heard me rail against those strictures that bind us females, that relegate us to a secondary role in society, literature, science, and all worthy pursuits of the mind, but maybe, just maybe, in your case, they might be in order, if only to prevent what seems to be your headlong rush to disaster.

Oh, how I long for those halcyon days of yore, when we would lie about the hayloft at Dovecote, laughing and singing — you telling me tales of your travels and me writing them down. I know now that I was harsh in my judgment of your actions at times, and I bitterly regret my spiteful tongue — you are what you are, and I love you to the depths of my being.

My only comfort is that our very able Mr. Pickering is hard at work on the case and expects a happy result. Hoping the same, I have begun a journal detailing this woeful period in our lives.

Happy? Will I ever be happy again? I know I will not — not until you and I are reunited.

Your loving sister,
Amy

Geez, Amy, I'm thinking as I fold up her letter and put it in my handbag, *don't you know by now that a little of Jacky Faber goes a long way? Hope I'm worthy of your journal.*

Finishing up my tea, I withdraw from my bag my own letter of reply, which I intend to post today . . .

Miss Annabelle Leigh
General Delivery
Plymouth, Massachusetts, USA

Ezra Pickering, Esq.
Union Street
Boston, Massachusetts, USA

Dear Ezra,

Here's hoping all is well with you. Things are going well here, as well as can be expected. However, there is one worrisome hitch — we have here in Plymouth a very nosy postmaster who very forthrightly questioned me on the propriety of me, a single female, receiving letters from a male (you). I put the fussy little bugger straight right off, you may be sure, and I am equally sure he did not violate the sacred trust of his office by opening your letter, but . . . he is friendly with my employer, Mr. Polk, and seeks to curry favor with him, as Banker Polk is a very powerful man in this community.

That being the case, I think it would be wise if you would send all future correspondence to me, Annabelle Leigh, in packets under Amy's name. That will protect my good standing as spinster governess, as well as giving you a good excuse to visit Dovecote. Big wink on that . . . nudge . . . nudge . . .

On to the business of Faber Shipping in general and the Pig and Whistle in particular. I have run across a very interesting process called "carbonization," wherein plain water is made bubbly by pouring vitriolic acid over plain chalk and then adding the water to be so treated. Or something like that. Put our two staff (freeloading) scientists, Dorothea and Mr. Sackett, on it. See, the thing is, when carbonated water is mixed with fruit syrups, it makes the whole concoction much tastier. And having no alcohol in it makes it suitable for children, as well — and for bluenose churchgoers, too. We could close the Pig on Sunday mornings — some citizens have always hated us for selling booze then — and set up a stand outside. I'm sure we'd get the church crowd — Jemimah Moses's Story Hour, too ... Have Molly Malone set it up. If Ravi's back, send him out with baskets of wooden nickels. I am sure we would prosper with this, if only in a small way.

Anyway, tell Amy I miss her and will write at length but cannot right now due to press of events.

I know all of you are doing your best to get me out of my latest mess, and I hope you know how much I appreciate your efforts.

I am, your most devoted friend,
Annabelle

A movement outside my window catches my eye, and I quickly settle up with Mrs. Tibbetts, pick up my umbrella, and am off.

It is recess time at Plymouth Public School and the lads are playing rugby. I watch for a while, determining who is the head boy, and when there is a break in the action, I signal him over with my bumbershoot. We have a quick discussion, which is profitable to both sides.

After all, all boys love candy.

Chapter 14

"Today, for our excursion, we are going to the White Rose Tearoom," I say, planting my round hat on my head and picking up my umbrella. "Shall we go?"

"A *tearoom?*" sneers Edgar, who's been a perfect monster all morning. "What kind of girly excursion is that?"

"Don't worry, Captain, I just know you're going to have a fine afternoon. And yes, Cathy, you may bring Amy with you. Ready? First to the post office, then to the White Rose. Shall we go?"

We do, with two of us hand in hand, singing, and one of us hanging back, grumbling.

Yesterday afternoon, when I was at the post office, I had pointed out to Mr. Fussy Postmaster that the letter I was posting to Ezra was to thank him for getting my references. I added that he could check with Mr. Polk if he wanted, but he replied, "'Tweren't none of my business," and I agreed with him on that but did not say so. *Old busybodies, they're everywhere, sticking their pointy noses where they don't be-*

long. I went back to my room at Polk House and worked on my portraits of the children and soon had them done to my satisfaction. After they had dried, I handed them over to Bert Olnutt for framing.

Having some time to myself, I penned a quick letter to Amy Trevelyne, telling her once again not to worry about me. Intending to post it the next day, and it being a bit before dinnertime and the return of the children, I had then picked up my cosmetic kit and headed downstairs to see Mrs. Polk.

I found her in her bedroom, propped up in her bed, looking out the window, an unopened book of verse lying in her lap.

Unbidden, I entered and chirped, "Sit up, Missus, and let's have a bit of a go at you with a touch of the old powder and blush."

Surprised, she smiled wanly. "I don't think you should waste your time on me. Not with that sort of thing."

"Nonsense. All us women need a little fixing up every now and then. But first, take this."

"What is it?" she asked as I handed her a little glass of very dark purple liquid.

"A simple restorative, Ma'am, nothing more."

She swallowed it and said, "Umm. Like candy."

Others have said that, Missus . . .

It was, of course, a dose of Jacky's Little Helper, Tincture of Opium, cut with Mr. Filibuster's blackberry syrup. A bit of color had come into her cheeks.

"And now," I said, opening my kit and taking out the soft powder brush and applying it to her cheeks, "a touch of this to soften your excellent cheekbones a bit . . . and now just the slightest hint of rouge there, and on the lips . . ."

She let me do it, yet protested, "But, Miss, all your efforts will be in vain, for my husband no longer finds me . . . attractive."

I gave a good snort on that one. "He found you attractive enough to get you with child three times, didn't he? Now, hold still while I do your eyes." I ran my thin kohl brush through the tiny dish of dark brown paste and applied it to the lower edge of her upper eyelid — not too much; this is Plymouth and not Rangoon, after all — and then sat back to survey my handiwork.

"Good. Now a quick brush of your hair . . . Yes, let's pin it up a bit there, and let the curls hang by your face like that . . . and will you take a little dab of jasmine perfume? There, right behind your ears, and you may keep the bottle. Don't be silly, I've got tons of the stuff . . ."

Actually, I do have a lot of jasmine perfume — my ship, the *Lorelei Lee,* brought back an enormous amount of that essence on her return from the Orient. I know that unscrupulous members of my crew have tapped into Faber Shipping's supply of that heady scent to work their lusty way into the hearts — and beds — of many a wayward lass. I suspect that randy Arthur McBride has pilfered an entire cask for his own rascally use.

"There," I said, rising. "I believe I hear Miss Felicity's coach, and I must see to the children. If you feel up to it, you should rise and dress for dinner. I suggest the mauve dress with pink trim. You look just smashing in that."

Later, when presenting the children dressed for bed, I could see that she had taken my advice and worn the mauve.

If she did not look positively radiant, she certainly looked a lot better, and, I suspect, Mr. Polk did not go out to his club for the evening.

"Is it not a glorious day, children?" I enthuse as we emerge from the post office and head for the White Rose . . . *slowly* head for the Rose, as I want to time this just right. We are on a board walkway that runs along a low wall that, in turn, runs along the playground of Plymouth Public School.

"We shall have tea in just the finest little porcelain cups with pink roses around the rim," I say, prattling along in my most annoyingly female way. "And they have these cunning little cakes that I swear just melt in your mouth."

This bit of drivel is greeted with a squeeze of the hand from Cathy and with a groan from Edgar.

"But I don't want to go to a stupid teahouse," he grumbles as the doors of the schoolhouse open and the kids pour out, right on schedule.

"Oh, Edgar," I purr. "Do not worry, for *you* are not going to the Rose, just Cathy and I are."

"But what . . . ?"

Oh, you will see, you little worm, you will see . . .

Six of the schoolboys swarm over the low wall and come toward a very shocked Edgar Allen Polk.

"Hey, Eddie, we were lookin' for you!" says the grinning head boy, whose name I know is Roscoe. "We need another lad on the pitch! Come on!" Two of the other boys grab Edgar by his arms and haul him roughly over the wall. Roscoe gives me a broad wink, while Edgar fixes a look of the purest hatred upon me

For my part, I give him my little finger wave and say,

"Play nice, Edgar. We'll be over there at the White Rose when the game is over. Toodles."

Edgar disappears into the scrum, and Cathy and I slip into the Rose.

After the three of us are seated — Cathy, Amy, and I — Mrs. Tibbetts brings me a cup of strong tea, and a cup of sweet mint tea with grenadine syrup for Cathy, which she avidly slurps down. She makes short work of the cakes as well. I let her enjoy — we shall begin learning teatime manners at a later time.

As we enjoy the offerings, I notice the same shy little girl I had seen on my first visit peeking around the corner of the kitchen door, and make note of it as Mrs. Tibbetts approaches our table and asks if she might speak with me.

"Of course, Missus. Please, sit down."

She does, and gets to the point right off. "I know that you have taken on the task of being governess to the Polk children . . ." Here she cuts a glance at Cathy and continues, "And I cannot tell you how grateful I am that you have stayed with that thankless job. You see, Mrs. Polk was . . . is . . . a special friend to me, and I fear for both her health and her very life. You see . . ."

"Excuse me, Mrs. Tibbetts, for a moment," I say, turning to Cathy. "Cathy, would you like to take your doll and show her to that little girl over there? Her name is . . ."

"Chelsea," says the landlady.

Cathy glances over and then slides out of her chair, taking Amy over to visit with Chelsea. Cathy is small and young, but she does not lack for courage.

"Go on, Missus. Sorry to interrupt."

"The rudeness is all mine, Miss Leigh, and I am sorry to

intrude, but, you see, I am rather distraught over the decline of my dear friend Patience Polk," she says. "Oh, if you could have seen her when we were both younger! She was bright and gay and vivacious, the very flower of our society . . . Then she married Mr. Polk, who, as you well know, is the exact opposite of all that . . ."

"We both know that husbands can appear cold and distant to those outside the family. I do not believe he abuses her. And he provides well for her and the family."

"I know, I know. He is not the problem," she says, with a grim set to her mouth. "It is that *child*."

"I assume you mean Edgar?"

"Yes. He was born a year after the marriage, and things have gone downhill for her ever since. The boy, instead of being a joy to his loving mother, developed into a monster, completely breaking her spirit. Catherine was born three years after the boy, and though a perfect angel, the birth broke Patience's health as well. And now another is on the way. I just don't know what is going to happen to my dear friend . . ." A tear is working its way into the corner of her eye.

I put my hand on hers. "Do not despair, Mrs. Tibbetts, for there is hope. Only yesterday I attended to Mrs. Polk and . . ."

I describe to her my visit with Patience Polk, telling of how the sparkle returned in a small way to her eyes under my poor ministrations. I do not mention the dose of Jacky's Little Helper. That potion I had left in care of Midge, the housekeeper, with strict instructions to give Mrs. Polk a mere ounce, no more, each day at four o'clock, to improve her mood.

"Oh, if you could but stay! So many have come and gone because of that wretched boy!"

"I have no intentions of leaving, Missus, but who can presume to see the future?"

"If it is a question of money," she says, embarrassed, "I could supplement your income in a small way. I know your pay must be meager."

I have to smile at that, thinking about the state of my wealth and the holdings of Faber Shipping Worldwide on both the sea and land. I could buy and sell this woman and her pretty little teahouse ten times over. But then again, she is in her place of business, and I am not in mine, however rich I might be.

"Thank you, Missus, that is most kind," I say, putting my hand on hers once again. "But I have enough in that regard."

She nods, then looks around and says, "Where is the little beast, anyway?"

"I arranged for the local schoolboys to welcome him into their manly midst," I say, glancing in the direction of the schoolhouse. "He is there right now, enjoying a brisk game of rugby football."

"What! That little sissy? They'll eat him alive!" she says, incredulous.

"No, they won't," I murmur, with a sly smile. "I made sure they won't leave any marks on him — none that show, anyway. Actually, I expect him anytime now. I just heard the school bell ringing, to call the students back from recess."

Sure enough, a very disheveled and very angry Edgar Allen Polk bursts through the door. He is sweaty and dirty, with scuff marks everywhere — except for his face.

"Ahoy, Edgar," I crow. "Did you have a good scrum with

Roscoe and the lads? I bet you showed them what for, eh? Bully for you!"

"I will get you for that," he hisses. His normally carefully combed hair hangs lank and twisted against his furious face. "I will tell my father tonight, and he will send you packing, which he should have done when you first got here. I promise you—"

"Now, Edgar, mind your manners," I say, calmly rising and calling out for Cathy. "Come, Cathy, we must go. I am sure Chelsea will invite you back for another visit very soon. Adieu, Mrs. Tibbetts. I hope our little talk has set your mind somewhat at ease regarding your friend."

"It did, Miss Leigh, but—" says Mrs. Tibbetts, looking a bit worried at the fuming Edgar.

I take her meaning and laugh. "Do not worry. I have many arrows in my quiver. Till some other time, then. Cathy, Edgar, come along."

And along we do go, back to the House of Polk.

"You'd better be packed," warns Edgar, "'cause you're gonna be gone as soon as my father gets home. Count on it. I hope you have to sleep in the street tonight with the rest of the beggars."

"And you'd best get cleaned up for dinner, Edgar, as you are a bit of a mess," I say, unconcerned. "And as for my baggage, you know my seabag is always packed. See, there it is right there."

There is a light rap at the door and Bert Olnutt comes in, bearing framed pictures and a hammer.

"Ah, here's our Mr. Olnutt with your portraits ready to hang," I pipe. "Would you like to see them?"

Cathy nods in joyous anticipation.

I give Bert the signal and he turns her picture around. She yelps in delight at seeing herself painted all in ribbons and bows, with jolly daisies all around. She bounces over and plants a loving kiss on my cheek by way of thanks.

"Thank you, dear," I say. "Now let's see if Edgar gives me a kiss for his portrait."

He does not.

"It doesn't matter," sneers Edgar. "I'm still gonna see you gone. You, too, handyman, for busting my peashooter and calling me a brat and . . ."

Then his expression changes from one of righteous indignation to one of complete horror. Yes, I had done *two* portraits of the lad, one heroic, and the other, in keeping with the custom, picturing him as a girl. He is in a lovely yellow dress, with white petticoats, holding a bouquet of roses. His hair is curled with yellow and white ribbons entwined, and the top of his head is crowned with a big pink bow.

He is speechless, but I am not.

"Oh, your mother is going to just *love* that one," I chirp. "Mr. Olnutt, let's put them up in the entrance hallway, where all may admire them. And see, Edgar, so that there's no mistake in identifying you in years to come, I even put your whole name, Edgar Allen Polk, on your portrait. As a matter of fact, I invited Roscoe and the lads from the school over anytime they needed an extra lad on the rugby pitch. Surely they will want to see it. Bert, please put them up high enough such that no one can take them down.

"So what's it going to be, Eddie? You know the deal. This portrait or the other one? Hmmm?"

The shoulders of Edgar Allen Polk slump in absolute and total defeat.

That evening, as I present the children to their parents, freshly scrubbed and in their nightclothes, I relate the events of the day . . .

Cathy met and had a fine playtime with the daughter of your friend Mrs. Tibbetts, and bold Master Edgar here insisted on joining a group of the local boys for a fierce game of rugby and acquitted himself most admirably. He especially distinguished himself at goal, and the boys invited him back! Isn't that so, Master Edgar?

Master Edgar agreed that it was, indeed, so.

Chapter 15

Miss Annabelle Leigh
General Delivery
Plymouth, Massachusetts. USA
October 4, 1809

Miss Amy Trevelyne
Dovecote Farm
Quincy, Massachusetts

Dear Amy,

    Greetings and salutations from your wayward but loving sister!

    All continues to go reasonably well here at Polk House. It's been several weeks now since I fled Boston in some haste. Isn't it ironic, Amy? Way back when I first got to Beantown and the Trevelynes were in danger of losing Dovecote to heavy debts, remember when I asked you what you would do if you were kicked out and on your own? You replied that you'd have to leave the Lawson Peabody and take a dull post as a governess to somebody's children, and here wacky Jacky is the one who actually takes such a job! What a crazy world!

Anyway, an update: While the girl, Cathy, is a joy, the boy, Edgar, continues to be a monster. Every now and then I pull a trick that beats him down for a while, but he soon charges back, mean as ever. He is a worthy adversary; I've got to say that for the little beast. He has announced that he no longer fears the Bed Monsters, so I informed him that those demons sometimes had "familiars" — bats, cats, and such — that did their bidding when the monsters were otherwise occupied dismembering and devouring other naughty little boys. He scoffed at that, but I think it gave him something to think about in the dark of night.

It was about a week after I had brought him to heel with the double portrait threat that he was up to his old tricks again, but wait — I shall tell you how it happened . . .

I was down in the dining room with Mr. and Mrs. Polk, having a cup of tea with them after their dinner and relating the events of the day regarding their children's activities, when we heard a shuffling of feet on the floor above, one of Edgar's early tricks for disrupting the peace of the household.

"Ah, poor Edgar is a bit restless tonight," I said, rising. "I'll see to him and be right back."

I went up to his room and found him in bed, looking defiantly up at me, daring me to say anything. I said nothing as I sat down on the edge of his bed. Then I said, "*Tsk, tsk,* Captain, it appears you have been eating cookies in bed, as you have crumbs all over the front of your nightshirt. Here, let me brush them off. There. Now try to go to sleep. All right?"

With that, I went back downstairs. I was pleased to see Mr. Polk with his hand on his wife's, and she almost sparkled in her blue dress, with white trim at neck and wrists.

I had scarcely sat back down when from above came a horrified *SCREECH!* and *"NO! NO! GET OFF ME!"*

Once again I stand, saying, "Poor little man. He must be having a nightmare. He *is* so very high-strung . . ."

But Patience Polk rises, too. "I will go see to my son."

And so she does, and we hear no more from him this night.

Hearty chortle. What I had done was, early in the evening, I had put a heavy doorstop in front of Blackie's little cat door so she could not get out for her evening prowl. Then when I went up to see to Edgar, I spread catnip, not cookie crumbs, over his front. Later, when he closed his eyes for a moment, he felt a sudden weight on his chest. His eyes snapped open again only to find a large black cat sitting on his chest, claws holding him firm, and snarling, with white fangs bared; hence, the scream.

Yes, I am indeed the Nanny from Hell.

But enough of my battle with a little boy . . . (heavy sigh). One thing I do pine for is the male companionship of grown-up boys. Jaimy's off to London to try to save both my reputation and my neck, and Randall's all wrapped up with Polly Von. Lord Richard Allen is in Virginia, on Clarissa's plantation — damn her eyes — and Joseph Jared's down in New York, duty bound to another ship. It's not that I could see any of them, mind you, for it would blow my cover for sure, but still . . . another heavy, heavy sigh . . .

In that regard, I know that Ezra Pickering is bending all efforts to get me out of my current jam, and as I am on the run,

I cannot thank him enough in my usual fashion. Therefore, I officially delegate you, Amy Wemple Trevelyne, to be my proxy, and so you must do it. I order you to place a nice warm kiss upon his cheek the next time he comes to Dovecote. That, and enjoy a nice candlelight dinner, just the two of you. Do it for me.

Anyway, that's it for now. Regards and love to all,

Your loving sister,
Annabelle

This being my afternoon off, I seal up that missive to Amy and go to the post office to mail it, a lightness to my step and a song in my heart.

After posting my letter, I am delighted to find that I have a packet addressed to Annabelle Leigh from Amy herself. I can feel from the heft of it that it will contain something from Ezra, too.

Then, as I gaze upon it, my happiness fades and a sense of dread comes over me. An edge of the envelope has been lifted and is curled. It's as if it had been steamed open and a clumsy attempt had been made to reseal it. I look over at the Postmaster, but his face betrays nothing.

Now, wait, you. This could be nothing—a rough mail run from Boston to here—the weather has been damp, after all . . . But then again, Amy Trevelyne is as meticulous about small things as you are careless. She would never send a letter that was improperly secured. The blue seal with the letter T on the back is intact, but . . .

I may be acting overly careful, but so be it. In the past, my careless attitude has been my downfall many times, so I know I cannot let my guard down here.

I had planned to visit with Mrs. Tibbetts at the Rose for a nice cup of tea and conversation, but I quickly change plans. Instead I go to Mr. Filibuster's Emporium and purchase a tin of ship's biscuits, two bottles of good wine, another pint of paregoric, and several dry sausages.

"Planning a picnic, Miss Leigh?" asks Mr. Filibuster.

"Sort of," I reply, and leave to go back to my room to repack my seabag.

Yes, Mr. Filibuster, I hope it is for nothing more than a jolly picnic, but . . .

Chapter 16

It has been several days since my concern over the envelope, and nothing has happened, so maybe everything is all right. Maybe I was just worried about nothing. Maybe . . .

It is after lunch and we are back in the classroom, Cathy hard at work on her letters, Edgar drawing more bloody eyeballs. I sigh, pull out his math book, and make ready to force him into fractions, the multiplication thereof, when I notice a wagon being pulled up across the street. As it is rather cool today, the windows are closed. It is cool enough, in fact, for me to shed my Lawson Peabody dress in favor of my old serving-girl rig of loose white shirt, brown leather vest, and black skirt. It feels good, and my Lawson Peabody outfit could use a cleaning, for sure.

I look out, and the wagon seems to be a simple workman's cart, probably there to pick up trash. But then the driver steals a quick glance up at our window and I go rigid.

Uh-oh . . .

After a moment, a man in a dark suit comes up on

horseback, dismounts, and ties his horse to the wagon. He, too, looks up.

This is it, then. No mistake.

I force myself to be calm as I lift my seabag and put it on Edgar's desk.

"What are you doing?" he asks crossly.

"Never mind," I say. "Just stay out of the way."

I look out the window again and see that the man who had arrived on horseback is joined by several others, one of whom is the Postmaster, looking righteous and smug.

I tear open my seabag and pull out the two primed pistols that lie within, as well as the bandoleer, into which are inserted twenty small white charges. I put that around my neck and over one shoulder. Seeing me place the pistols on top of the bag, Edgar's eyes grow wide and his jaw drops.

I wait. I do not have to wait long.

The headman down below picks up a speaking trumpet and holds it to his lips. "I am Sheriff Williams and I have a warrant for your arrest. We know you are up there, Jacky Faber. So come down peacefully and no one will be hurt."

I pick up a pistol in each hand and shove their barrels through two of the windowpanes, the glass falling to the street below.

"You can cram that warrant up the Postmaster's bum, Sir!" I shout. "And how's this for peaceful?"

With that I fire my starboard gun — *wham!* — and the Postmaster's hat falls off his head. The reports are extremely loud in the enclosed classroom, and Edgar flinches at the sound. As for the postman, it was not my bullet that toppled his hat but his own fear, as my pistols were not loaded with ball. Good for the false bastard.

"She has killed me!" he shrieks, his hands to his unhurt head. Just to make sure there is no mistake about taking me easily, I fire my port pistol—*wham!* All down below take cover behind the wagon as I rip two charges from my bandoleer and reload—again with powder and cap only.

"Edgar! Pick up my bag and head for the back door! Now!"

"Wha-wha-what . . . ?"

I cram my right-hand pistol into my vest and grab him by the hair and shout into his face, "You wanted to join the pirate world? Well, you're in it now, kid! As a hostage! Now pick up that bag and get out that door, or I'll put a bullet in your brain right now! Move!"

Move he does, hastened along by my foot.

Before we go out the door, I spy Cathy standing with thumb back in mouth, and I do not blame her for that.

"Cathy! Go down to the bottom of the stairs and hold your arms out so the men can't get up the stairs!" The last I see of that sweet child is as she turns and goes down to do it.

I am at the top of the back stairs when I hear her small voice saying, "You can't go up there now. Governess is shooting."

"Faster, Eddie! Faster! They'll be on us in a moment!" I cry, pounding down the back street after him. "If you try to run away, I'll put one in your back! If you stumble and fall, I'll shoot you on the ground! Move!"

"Wh-where are we going?" he gasps.

"To my boat! It's right there on that pier! The one with the blue hull! When you get there, toss in the bag and get in yourself!"

"Why . . . why me?"

" 'Cause you're a goddamn hostage, is why! Move it!"

I hear the arresting party rounding the corner of First and Water streets with a great hue and cry, and I turn and give 'em something to really cry about. Turning and dropping to one knee, I get off my remaining shot, and they all duck away from a bullet that wasn't there.

That slows 'em down, for sure. Resuming my dash, I see Edgar has gained the pier and soon I put my foot on it as well.

"Yes! That one there! Get in!"

He throws in my seabag and, seeing my pistol trained on him, gets in as well. I cram both pistols into my vest, untie the *Evening Star,* and climb in after him. Grabbing an oar, I push us off the pier and pull up the sail, tighten the downhaul, and shout at Edgar, "Grab the tiller! Yes, that wooden stick next to you, and hold it amidships. Oh, just hold it straight, dammit!"

He does, and the *Star* moves out into the harbor as I reload my pistols. I rip off a white cartridge bag, feel for the bullet, bite it out, and hold it in my mouth. Then I pour the powder in the barrel, tamp it down with the ramrod, and place the percussion cap on the nipple. Now we're ready to fire. The same procedure goes for the other gun — bite ball, pour powder, spit bullet, tamp, and ready. I can reload a pistol four times a minute, and it has proved to be a very handy skill. I keep the two lead balls in the side of my mouth for disposal later.

The would-be arresting party has reached the pier, but they can do nothing to stop me. Although several of them have rifles, they cannot shoot at me for fear of hitting Edgar. Nay, all they can do is wave their arms and shout in vain.

Another man, however, has a much better idea, or so he thinks. He jumps into a handy boat — a fast-looking little sloop — and begins to rig it, planning to run me down on the water. I'll wager he has that reward in mind.

Oh, oh, how I wish I had the Lorelei Lee *or the* Nancy B. *and their bully crews here. I'd turn this puny little town to a pile of ashes in no time. But I have neither, so I must use what I've got.*

"Here's one in your boom," I shout at him. *Crack!* The man ducks, proving yet again that I am a very good shot with imaginary bullets. "The next one goes in your gut, Mate!"

He does not press the point, but only scrambles back out of the boat.

Reloading, I jam my pistols into my vest, twist around, and see that we are nearing the entrance to the harbor. "Edgar! Pull the tiller a few inches that way."

He does it, and the nose of the *Star* points down the center of the channel.

"That's it. Now rudder amidships again . . . good."

In another few minutes we are in the open sea. A few minutes more and we are out of sight of land and I begin to breathe easier . . .

They can't catch me now.

As the land disappears over the horizon, Edgar finds the courage to speak. "So . . . so you really are that girl pirate? The one on the poster? The one they are after?"

"You bet, Eddie," I say grandly, pulling out a pistol and waving it about. "The one and only Jacky Faber, Queen of the Ocean Sea, the Scourge of the Caribbean, and La Belle Jeune Fille Sans Merci!"

Squinting at the eastern horizon in search of shipping and finding none, I go on . . .

"And that last French bit means 'The Beautiful Young Girl Without Mercy.' You may discount the 'beautiful' part, but I'd advise you to pay attention to the 'without mercy' bit, for I have none of that particular quality, and would shoot you in a minute if you step out of line."

With that, I bring the barrel of my pistol around to bear on a point directly between his eyes, slowly pulling back the hammer — *click, click, click* — till it is at full cock.

"Do you take my meaning?"

He blanches and gulps. "So you mean to hold me for ransom, then?"

That sends me into gales of laughter. "*Ransom? You?* Who's gonna pay for you? You're the meanest kid alive! Nobody wants you back! Don't you know that? Oh, your poor mother will shed a few tears over you, but that's what mothers do. She'll get over it in a while. And your dad? Oh, Mr. Upright Polk will puff up and maintain that he will *not* pay tribute to filthy pirates, no matter what. Nay, Master Edgar, you have made your bed and you must lie in it! Or not lie in it, as I doubt you'll ever see that particular bed again."

I stick the pistol back in my vest. I know that while Edgar did notice that I had reloaded the guns, he did not notice that I did not load them completely. I had no wish to accidentally shoot the lad, nor did I want to lose the skin on my ribs due to a misfire. I also know that Edgar is thinking of his own dear bed with a renewed fondness.

Whatever the state of Edgar's mind, I need to change clothes. I open my seabag and pull out my sailor togs as well as my long glass. Standing and bracing myself against the mast, I unfasten the waistband of my skirt and take it off, revealing my long drawers with flounces. Well, we can't have that, can we?

"Close your eyes, Eddie, if you want to. I don't care." With that, I step out of the drawers and then into my canvas sailor pants. I leave my vest and shirt on, for it is likely to get a mite chilly out here on the bounding main, plus the vest is very handy for the stowage of pistols. I cram my *Dolphin* cap back on my head, and say, "Ta-da! Back to being Jack the Sailor Boy again, off at sea with his little brother, fishing for the family dinner!"

We are hitting some heavy rollers, but Eddie has not yet shown signs of seasickness, which is good. *Prolly too scared to be sick.*

If he did not close his eyes as I was changing, he has recovered enough from the sight of my bare nether regions to ask, without much hope in his voice, "So I shall walk the plank, then?" He looks over the side at the dark water surging by.

"Hmmm." I pretend to think on that for a bit, then say, "Nay. That's a common misapprehension about us pirates, that we do that sort of thing. Generally we don't. Y'see, if a captive is breathing, then he is worth some money, and that is what we really like — money. The hostage can be sold, if only as a slave. That's what I intend to do with you, as much as I'd enjoy seeing your face sinking in the old briney."

As he considers that, I pick up my long glass and train it on the horizon.

"What are you looking for?" asks Edgar.

"Some friends of mine in Boston have written me saying that an old piratical friend, Chopstick Charlie, is sailing

143

back to the Orient, probably today or tomorrow, and he's got to go right by here. He's sailing on a huge Chinese junk with at least four hundred Chinamen aboard. Bunch of Gurkhas, too. He'd be hard to miss. Hmm . . . nothing yet."

"But why do you want to find him?"

"Why? 'Tis plain. I'd trade him *you* for my passage back to Rangoon, and there I could lay low till the heat's off."

"But what would they do with me?"

I consider the question. "Hmmm . . . If you were bigger, they'd make you a galley slave and you'd spend the rest of your life chained to an oar. But you're much too small for that."

"So what would they do, then?"

"Prolly make you into a eunuch."

"What's that?"

"That's when they cut off your boy parts."

Although he is very young, he is old enough to react to that. Both his knees come quickly together.

"But why?" he asks, incredulous.

"So you won't grow up to be a man," I reply, the voice of reason. "That way you can guard their harems and the sultans won't worry about your messin' with them very pretty ladies, 'cause you won't be able to do anything with 'em, not havin' the proper equipment, like. The only thing you'll be able to do is to serve 'em their pommy-granites and figs and such, and to dry 'em off after their baths."

While he is digesting that rather ghastly bit of information, I take another scan of the horizon. "Damn! Nothing! Chops, where the hell are you?"

I know full well that Chopstick Charlie is back in Rangoon with his heathen horde, but I say, "Ah, well, we shall search again tomorrow. Have to find a proper berth for our hostage, don't we? Can't have him wondering about his future. But for now, we must find a place to spend the night, as evening is upon us."

I snap the long glass shut and say, "They'd expect me to go south, so I shall go north. Captain Blood, put your tiller to starboard . . . yes, to the right . . . watch out . . . duck now, the boom will be coming over your head. That's it. Done."

Actually, I set the *Star* on a westerly course, heading back in to shore, and it is not long till we see the loom of the land. And not long after that, I am able to pick out individual features on the beach . . . *and, yes! There it is!*

It is a small river — a wide brook, really — that cuts through a salt marsh that I had spotted on my way down from Boston. If I pull in there, we shall be well out of sight of any search party.

"Switch places, Cap'n. I'll take over the tiller now."

We scramble about and get it done, and I guide the *Star* into the mouth of the river and beach her on its southern bank. "There. That should do it. Crewman Polk, now take that small anchor, hop out, and put it up at the edge of the grass. That's it . . . push the flukes down into the mud so we don't drag anchor and float away in the night. Now come on back in and we'll see about some supper."

He does not have to be told twice about getting back to the safety of the boat. If this place looked creepy last time I saw it in broad daylight, it is doubly so now as a low fog descends upon us and dark night falls.

As I rummage about my seabag for the food, Edgar asks with some trepidation, "Where are we?"

Well, I happen to know, because of my knowledge of

New England charts, that we are at the mouth of the South River that runs through a salt marsh just below the town of Scituate, but that sounds too tame, so I improvise . . .

"I believe it is the River Ulaluma," I say, whipping out my shiv and cutting off a few inches of the sausage and a good chunk of cheese, and handing it all to Edgar, along with some of the crackers. "Eat up, Eddie. I can't deliver you to Gul Thampa half starved. He's the Gurkha in charge of Chopstick Charlie's captives, and he wouldn't like it. Best not to get on the wrong side of him."

Edgar eyes the gleaming blade of my shiv as he takes the food. I uncork a bottle of the wine, take a good slug, and continue . . .

"Anyway, the locals call that land off to the right the Region of Weir. They are a superstitious people and believe it to be haunted by ghouls."

"What are ghouls?" asks Edgar, dreading the answer.

"Demons that like to dig up graves and eat dead people," I answer, all matter-of-fact. "But it is said that they'll settle for live ones if their usual fare is unavailable . . ."

Edgar pauses midbite.

"And over there," I say, pointing to the banks on the south, "is the tarn-marked Land of Auber."

"And tarns are . . . ?"

"Pools of quicksand. If you got up and ran away through there, you wouldn't get five yards before you fell into one. I'd hear your cries, but I wouldn't be able to help you. One of my crew, a Snag Thompson, once saw a mate of his, Cut-Throttle Johnny, fall into one, and try as they might, they couldn't get him out. No, the last they saw of poor old Cut-

Throttle was the thick, black mud pouring into his mouth, then over his nose, then over his dead eyes."

Edgar casts a look about at our environs. We are surrounded by low banks with high marsh grass growing upon them, and the mud between the hummocks is thick and black. I do not think Master Edgar will be making a run for it.

"Well, time to go to sleep," I say, wiping off the blade of my shiv on my pant leg. "Tomorrow's bound to be a busy day. I'll be sleeping in the little cuddy. It's a bit cramped, but at least it's dry. G'night, Captain."

If I thought Edgar's big dark eyes could not get any larger, I was wrong. "You'll leave me alone out here?"

"Where else? You could go sleep up on the beach, but I don't advise it, considering where we are."

"But the — "

"The ghouls?" I ask, all impatient. "Look, if any come around here, just take this oar and whack it over what you think might be his head. That generally scares 'em off. Generally . . ."

Looo, looo, looo, looo, loooooooooooooooo . . .

The mournful call comes drifting over the marsh.

"What's that?" whispers Edgar.

"Prolly one of 'em," I say. "Sounds hungry, poor devil. Anyway, till morning. G'night."

With that, I toss my bag in the cuddy and go in after it. I latch the door shut, rutch around a bit, push some rope and tools aside, and, using my seabag as a pillow, settle in for sleep.

Looo, looo, looo, looo, loooooooooooooooo . . .

Again the weird, lonesome call floats across the marsh.

If Edgar were not a city boy, he would know that it was the plaintive call of the common loon, and not some fiend from hell. But, of course, he doesn't know that. I smile as I hear a light tapping at the hatch.

"Please, pleeeeeeese, Miss, please let me in with you, pleeeeeeze," whispers Captain Blood, his voice shaking with fear. *"Pleeeeeze . . ."*

"Go away, Edgar; you'll let in the ghouls."

"Pleeeeeze . . ."

I figure he has suffered enough. "All right, Eddie," I say, throwing the latch. "Get in here, but make it quick."

I do not have to say that, for he is in like a flash, clutching at me desperately. I make fast the door and say, "No, no, Edgar. Face away from me. That's it. We'll make like spoons, and that way we'll have more room. See? Calm down, now."

I can feel him trembling as I put my arm around him while I sing into his ear . . .

> *Go to sleep my fine young pirate,*
> *May your dreams be drenched in red.*
> *When you rise up in the morning,*
> *You'll find that all the ghosts*
> *Have turned and fled.*

With that, both my bold pirate and I drift off to sleep.

Chapter 17

Morning comes, as it always does, quite early. Groaning with stiffness, I kick open the hatch, and then I kick out Edgar.

"Let's go, lad," I say, squinting into the sun. "Lots to do today. Chopstick Charlie's sure to be by. Let's have a bit of breakfast, and then we'll shove off."

He says nothing to that, but merely gets out of the boat and goes behind a hummock to relieve himself. I do the same, warning, "Watch out for those tarns."

Apparently he does, for he soon returns.

"I'm afraid that breakfast is the same as yesterday's supper," I say, pulling out the sausage and cheese and handing him some. "But it will have to do. Let's sit on those rocks there . . . They look more comfortable than the boat."

Yes, I hand out the food, but I do not bring out the wine, declaring it much too early for that. Instead, I uncork the bottle of paregoric and pretend to drink from it. Then I hand it to him.

He takes it and drinks.

"Ummm. Like candy," he says.

"Yeah, right," I say, taking it back from him.

Again I pretend to drink from it, then I pass it back. "One more slug, and we must be off."

He does it, and I repack my bag, and watch him. Sure enough, his head begins to droop, and he settles back against a hummock. Smiling, I pull out my writing paper, pen, and ink, and write the lad a letter . . .

Dear Edgar,

Yes, Eddie, your head shall clear in a few moments, and while it does, I have some thoughts for you.

1.   *If you walk about five miles to the south, you will find yourself back in Plymouth. Stick to the beach. No tarns there.*

2.   *When you get there, be nice to your mother and father. Cathy, too. Tell them I appreciated their kindness toward me while I was in their home.*

3.   *I recommend that you petition your father to allow you to attend Plymouth Public School. It will do you a world of good and you will learn much — much more than any governess can teach you. You can be sure the students there will hang on your every word of your adventure with the dread Pirate Faber. Feel free to embellish your part in it.*

4.   *You are very good with words, so why don't you write up your own account of our days together? Maybe in poetry form, even.*

5.   *When, in the future, you play at pirates, make sure you don't run into a real one.*

That's it. Yo, ho, ho, and all that . . .
Cheers,

    Your own . . .
    Annabelle Leigh

I tuck the letter into his shirt front, plant a kiss on his forehead, and climb back into the *Star*.

I pull up the sail, fasten the downhaul, grab the tiller, and head out to sea, setting my course for Cape Cod, Massachusetts.

Farewell, Captain Blood. In spite of it all, I hope you have a good life.

PART III

Chapter 18

The Journal of Amy Trevelyne
Dovecote Farm
Quincy, Massachusetts

Dear Reader,

It was with the greatest distress that I learned of the recent attempt by the federal authorities to apprehend my friend and dear companion Jacky Faber, a misguided attempt, which mercifully did not succeed.

I learned of this unfortunate incident not from Mr. Pickering or any of our mutual friends, but rather from the local newspapers, which have been following the plight of Miss Faber most avidly. Apparently, scandal, violence, and other people's troubles are what sell their vile broadsides.

Boston journalists, knowing of my connection to Miss Faber, have been swarming all over Dovecote, hoping to glean information as to her whereabouts. I, of course, tell them nothing.

One man, a Mr. David Lawrence, Jr., who is held in high regard by his fellow hacks but whom I decline to call a gentleman, is a particularly persistent pest. His column in the *Boston Patriot* was most colorful in the use of language to describe the blaze of gunfire that enabled Miss Faber to make good her escape from Plymouth. I had him forcefully removed from the premises.

The legal fight to exonerate Miss F. continues. Ezra Pickering is optimistic. I am not. I am, however, desperate for news.

Entry dated October 12, 1809 — signed Amy Trevelyne

Chapter 19

There is an opening in the tent over my head, next to the center pole, which lets the sunlight shine in on me, standing on the highest platform. I lift my arms above my head in acknowledgment of the introduction and then bow deeply to the audience below. I am wearing a stiff sequin-covered corsetlike thing that extends rather tightly from my crotch to my upper chest, and over it a skirt that is full in back but is cut out in front to expose my legs. After all, I could not be expected to walk the wire in a full skirt, now, could I? No, matters of propriety must give way to practical concerns, and that is how we get away with it here in Puritan New England; otherwise, I would surely be arrested. Under the dress, I have on white stockings and ballet slippers. I had worn similar attire that time back in Paris, but that is another story.

All eyes are upon me as I step out on the wire. A hush falls on the crowd . . .

"Ladies and gentlemen!" roars out Ringmaster Generalissimo Pietro, through his speaking trumpet. "Your attention is directed high, *high* up in the very center of the tent, where stands, *direct* from the Royal Russian Circus of Moscow, performing *without* a net, our very own Princess Natasha Annasova Romanoff, death-defying Queen of the High Wire!"

Yes, I have joined the circus — the Montessori and Mattucci Grand Circus, to be exact. It seemed the safest place for me to go, but then again, if you can't hide out as a meek governess, where can you hide? I do not know, but we shall see.

After stranding young Master Edgar Allen Polk on that beach — older and, I think, far wiser now — the *Star* and I made straightaway for Provincetown on Cape Cod. Gaining the harbor of that town, I changed back into girl garb — long drawers, blue dress (yes, that rather scandalous thing, famous in legend and song, that I put on when I need to attract male notice), wig back on head, mantilla over all, and fake Russian accent on lips. Thus rigged, I headed for the big tent I had spotted on the outskirts of town and made application for employment.

My audition consisted mainly of lifting up my skirt to show my legs to Ringmaster Pietro, in whose estimation they apparently passed muster, and in doing my bit on the wire. After that, I was a member of the troupe, and glad of it.

I knew the circus would be there because of that circular I had spotted on the print shop's kiosk in Plymouth, right next to that annoying WANTED poster. In addition to having a fine engraving of a fierce tiger jumping through a flaming hoop, it handily listed their performance dates and locations, and so here I am, working the high wire.

Marcello Grimaldi, the trapeze artist whose act preceded mine, had just left the high platform, executing his signature finale, which is to swing out high on the trapeze bar, let go, tuck, do several flips, and then fall down into the net, landing on this back, always to great ovation.

Before he went off, Marcello said to me, "Be careful, my sweet little Russian sugar beet!" and I told him, "I am alvays care-ful, Mar-chell-o!"

After he climbed out of the net and took another bow, the net was unhooked from its fastenings and taken away. I picked up the balance bar and prepared to walk across.

The audience holds its collective breath.

I put my foot on the wire and look down into the yawning netless space. I mean, was there a net down there on the deck of the *Dolphin* to catch us sailors if we fell? No, there was not. There was only very hard oak planking, hard enough to crush the skull or snap the neck of any poor ship's boy who might misstep and fall from the rigging to land upon it. So this is nothing for me. Especially since I have this long balance bar to keep me straight. I have upon my feet shoes such as I wore back when I was a member of Les Petites Gamines de Paris, during my stay in that fine city, and believe me, the bottoms of the slippers are as well rosined as my fiddle's bow.

I step out onto the tightrope, and there is a sudden hush from the crowd. I go out for maybe fifteen feet, stop and turn around, and then proceed to the other high platform at the end of the wire. There I take a bow, acknowledge the applause, and then lay the balance bar aside. I unhook the skirt from about my waist and toss it carelessly away. Then I go back out into the air, this time *without* the balance bar. The audience gasps as I go forward, using only my arms as balance. Halfway across, I stumble and fake a fall, getting several real screams from the crowd, going over and catching the tightrope with my hands. Pulling myself up to my waist, I do several kips and then put my feet back on the wire. Hands over my head, I walk back to the platform to thunderous applause. I think part of the ovation is simple relief that I am not lying on the ground crumpled up dead, but I'll take it any way it comes.

I slide down a line next to the main tent pole, take another bow when I hit the ground, and exit the tent through a side entrance.

"Ladies and gentlemen, I now direct your attention to the center ring, where the world-famous Andalusian stallions, trained and ridden by the beauteous De Graff sisters, Gretchen and Heidi, will astound you with . . ."

I hear no more from our ringmaster as I plunge out into the bright light of day. As I go out, old Señora Elena, our costumer and seamstress, brings me a light robe with which to cover myself, my discarded skirt over her arm.

"I vonder, Señora," I say as I put on the robe and take the skirt from her. "How much ees my act skeel and how much *ees zee* striptease, eh?"

She laughs. "It is all the same, *chica*, as long as the applause is long and the money is good." And I have to agree with that.

Heading for the food wagon, I walk across the roped-off back lot where only circus people are allowed. On my way, I wave to the brightly dressed gang of clowns, harlequins, and dwarves heading for the stage entrance, getting many good-natured hoots and hellos in return, as well as a few honks of horns.

In the center of the back lot is a large cage, and in it is Balthazar, our magnificent African lion. He is lying next to the bars, so I reach in and begin scratching him behind his ears, which I know he loves.

"Poor old toothless Balthazar, does that feel good, baby? I know it does. Give us a bit of your roar now, please." He lifts his massive head and shakes it, rubbing himself against my hand. "Come on, Balthy, a good roar for your Natasha."

And he does it. He opens his mouth and lets out that deep, deep rumble of a growl that never fails to thrill me and send a shiver up my spine. I think it brings out the small, cowering beast in me.

"Goot boy," I say, in case anyone's listening, giving him a last pat on his head. I check to see if his cage is locked — it is — for old Antonio has been known to leave it unlatched. I know where the key is kept — on the inner hub of the left rear wheel — and I lock the cage whenever he forgets. Not that Balthazar has ever gotten out, for there is still a simple latch that holds the cage door shut. However, if some kid should sneak back here, well . . . toothless and with his claws clipped and dulled, Balthazar's still strong enough to do some real damage. Plus, we don't want him getting away, and then let some dumb yokel shoot him in a panic.

I go to the food wagon, which has flaps that open at the sides to form tables, about which are placed many high stools. Inside, Enrico, the cook, works at his stove. When we are moving from place to place, the flaps are latched up and the chairs hang from hooks on the sides.

We are quite a spectacle when we travel, especially when we parade through a town. There are fifteen brightly painted wagons drawn by plumed horses, led by the ringmaster, in red coat, white breeches, and black boots, on his fine, prancing white steed. The band is playing; me and Marcello in costume are standing on top of my wagon, striking elegant poses; the clowns are bouncing all around; Balthazar is roaring and pacing in his cage; and our elephant, Gargantina, is plodding along with little brown Makmud up top in turban and breechcloth. The arrogant Herr Udo von Arndt, our animal trainer, in full riding gear with whip curled up under his arm, rides the fine stallion Furio. In front of him is the cage holding Hans and Fritz, our two Bengal tigers. And I don't ever mess with that pair — they still have all their teeth and claws, and I haven't forgotten that beach on Sumatra when I almost ended up inside one of the beasts.

Of course, all the children of the town follow us, shrieking in delight. In each town there will be several boys who will try to run away with us.

The circus is in town! Hooray!

I hop up on a stool, nod a greeting to Makmud, who's shoveling his lunch into his heathen mouth across from me. Gregor, our hugely muscled circus strongman, sits next to him, making quite a contrasting pair. Little brown Makmud is clad only in a white nappy and always reminds me of my son, Ravi, who was dressed like that when first I laid eyes on that sweet soul back in Bombay. Gregor wears a costume made of animal skins that drape from one shoulder and extend to his thighs, tucked in at the waist with a broad, studded leather belt. His own dark hair extends to midforehead, as well as down his broad back, and though his looks are fearsome, he is actually quite shy and sweet — so shy, in fact, that he can barely bring himself to speak to me. I'm working on that.

At the other end sits Rigger O'Rourke, Head Roustabout, dressed in his usual tight red-striped shirt, dungaree trousers, and round bowler hat pushed back on his head. He and his crew are in charge of setting up the tents when we arrive in a town and bringing them down when we leave . . . and handling any trouble in between. He grins and brings his fingers to his hat brim. "Hiya, toots."

In keeping with my persona, I put aristocratic nose in air and do not acknowledge the greeting.

The food looks good, whatever it is. The day is warm, so I unfasten the robe and let it slip from my shoulders. There are only circus folk here, and we are a free and easy bunch.

"*Salute,* Enrico, dear one, and vhat ees for zee luncheon?" I ask. I have been picking up some Italian.

"*Stufato con salsiccia, mia cara,*" he says, putting a bowl of stew with several sausages in front of me, and a piece of bread as well.

"*Grazie,* Rico," I say, tucking into it. It is very good, and I tell him so.

Most of the people belonging to the Montessori and Mattucci Grand Circus extravaganza speak some English, since they have been over here in the States for some time, the wars in Europe not being kind to things like traveling shows. I maintain my disguise by speaking broken English and uttering sounds I think might sound Russian. If I ever do meet an actual Russian, I shall be sunk, but that hasn't happened yet.

I feel a mustachioed kiss on my bare right shoulder.

"*Nyet,* Marcello, you must not do zat," I say, shrugging him off my shoulder. "You know zat I am promised in marriage to Count Yakov Ivanillich Petrovsky, and I must remain pure of body for him. He vould kill you eef he knew you vere giving me attentions of love."

"I do not care, my beautiful little bowl of borscht. I will die happy," says the young man, taking his lips from my shoulder and plunging his nose into my neck hair. "Besides, he is not here."

"The Count dispatches his enemies by impaling zem, you know. Zey sit you on a sharpened pole and zen enjoy your struggles as zee pole vorks its vay up through you. It ees a very unpleasant vay to die. Vee Russians can be very cruel, you know."

"You are most cruel to me every moment you do not let me into your heart, into your bed, into your — "

"You vill stop zat now, Marcello, and come sit by my side and have some-zing to eat."

He slips onto the stool next to me. He is wearing the performance costume of the trapeze artist — skin-tight white pants and sleeveless shirt. He is, of course, given his trade, very well muscled — trim, though, not heavy. His hair is coal black and curly, as is the mustachio, of which he is very proud, having only recently been able to grow it, because of his youth. He is, by and large, a very handsome lad.

"I cannot eat when I am this close to a goddess," he says. "I will be content to watch you eat and take great pleasure in it." He puts his elbow on the table and his chin in his hand and proceeds to gaze upon me.

I reverse my spoon to dip forward into the stew in the

approved Lawson Peabody manner, lift it to my mouth, and take a sip.

"Such elegance of manner! Such perfection in the turn of lip, such delicacy! Oh my tiny little Volga River nymph, I cannot stand it, me being only a poor earthbound troll, in such a presence," he exults, while I try not to laugh and snort the stew out my delicate nose.

"I still do not believe that a goddess such as yourself, even though you are forced to be on this earth, must eat food like a mere mortal," he continues. This is, of course, a teasing game that has been going on between us since first we met, and we both find it fun. Up to a point, I realize, for should I weaken, I know he would be right there, ready for the Big Romp. And he is very, very charming, so I must be extremely careful — for the imaginary Count Petrovsky, as well as for the very real Lieutenant James Emerson Fletcher.

"Zere are man-ny things vee goddesses do zat vould surprise you," says I, deciding to be a bit wicked. I reach into my bowl with the fingers of my left hand and pull out a long, thin sausage, lock eyes with Marcello, and then bite the tip off with a loud *snap.*

"Yum," I say, which I know is a universal word, in Russia, Italy, or any language there is.

"*Arrrrghhh!* Oh, I am wounded to my very soul," he cries, hands thrust between his knees. "Cruel, cruel daughter of Siberian wolves, you have robbed me of my very manhood!"

He groans and buries his face in his hands. "Such torture, such exquisite torture, I can take it no longer." He lifts his face, his merry brown eyes round with delight. "But do it again, please."

I finish off my lunch and pat him on the back. "Very nice performance, Marcello, but I zink your manhood ees still very much intact." I look down at the very obvious codpiece that is part of his costume. "*Ciao*, dahlink, I vill see you later."

With that, I head back to my wagon to rest and get ready for the next show. I open the door, throw the latch, and kick off my shoes. It's another hour and a half till my next performance, so I flop back in my bed for a bit of a doze. If I fall asleep, Marcello will surely wake me when it's time, just as he has done so often before.

My seabag sits on the floor next to me. I had long ago pulled out the stitching that spelled out *J. M. Faber, Midshipman* and replaced it with *M. Natasha Romanoff*. Now I reach over, open it, and thrust in my hand. Feeling the very familiar shape of the frame, I pull out the miniature portrait of Jaimy I had painted all those years ago, and gaze upon his sweet face. As always, it brings tears to my eyes.

Oh, Jaimy, why must we be forever so star-crossed and at the whim of Fate?

Chapter 20

And so, life at the Montessori and Mattucci Grand Circus goes on . . .

They had done the top part of the Cape on their way to Provincetown, so now we will work the towns of the south shore—Chatham, Dennis, Barnstable, Falmouth, and then back to the mainland of New England. That means we will go back near Plymouth again and I must be careful. Even though it's been a good month since I left that town, and I'm assuming things have probably settled down as regards the pirate Jacky Faber, still . . . I'm relieved, however, to learn that the circus will not do Plymouth itself again, having already done it on their first swing through. No, we'll set up the Big Top in the town of Wareham, a bit to the south, where it should be safe. We'll do three days there and then pack up for Providence, Rhode Island. I'll breathe easier when we're out of this area, that's for sure.

Yes, both the ringmaster, Generalissimo Pietro, who actually owns the Montessori and Mattucci, and the dashing animal trainer, Udo von Arndt, with his whips and boots and tight white pants and open-collar hunter's shirt, had made it plain to me quite early that they would not mind slipping into the wagon of the fiery Russian aerialist for a bit of this and that. But by my hanging around with the somewhat more manageable Marcello, they hold off, assuming he is already ensconced in both my wagon and my bed.

And I do love my fine little wagon. It is gaily painted inside and out, and since I am one of the stars of the show — risking one's neck on a daily basis does bring some benefits — I do not have to share it with anyone. It reminds me of Zoltan's gypsy wagon when I had been taken in and had traveled with his band of Roma in Spain. 'Cept it's not quite so crowded with his daughters. And in my fine bower, I find I now have both the privacy and leisure to write a letter to my dear sister Amy.

Princess Natasha Annasova Romanoff, Aerialist
The Montessori and Mattucci Grand Circus
Wareham, Massachusetts

Miss Amy Trevelyne
Dovecote Farm
Quincy, Massachusetts

Dear Amy,

Yes, dear heart, I have joined the circus. It was inevitable, was it not? Come now, Amy, you know you are the biggest worrywart on Earth. All I really have to do is walk out on the high wire, do a few lame tricks, then retire to great applause. What could be easier?

I barely escaped Plymouth. That nosy postmaster I told

you about was actually reading our mail and so tipped off the local authorities. Can you imagine that? I know there is scant honor among thieves, but I didn't know it also applied to some politicians and those whom they appoint to trusted positions. Somehow I expected better.

No matter, what is done is done. Suffice it to say, on my last day at the Polk household, I was greeted with a fully armed posse intent on bringing me in to face their justice. I did manage to evade capture with the help of my pistols, but it was a close thing, believe me.

I have made up a sheer veil for myself to wear when wandering about on the grounds. Yes, the area for the circus people is well marked and guarded, but still, people can see in. Why am I being so careful? It's that I swear I heard Gully MacFarland's fiddle the other day, working the edge of the crowd. I didn't spot him, and I am sure he could not recognize me, veiled as I was . . . But still, nobody plays the fiddle as well he does. He's supposed to be at sea, but I don't know . . .

Don't bother writing back, for we will be long gone from this town by the time you get this letter. After we hit Philadelphia, the circus will head south for the winter, and I shall leave at that time and head back to Boston to see how things lie. You may tell Ezra that. You may also rest assured that I will be under heavy disguise. How about as a cloistered nun, spending my days mumbling prayers for the world's poor sinners? I haven't done that yet . . .

This time I will be a bit more careful and sign off, with all my love, as . . .

Your Russian cousin,
Natasha

I am sealing up the letter as I hear a knock on my door.

"Princess! We're on in fifteen minutes, my exquisite Russian rabbit!" shouts Marcello from outside, bringing me out of my reverie.

"Very vell, Marcello," I say, rising. I put my skirt back on, then check my face and hair in the mirror of my dressing table. I give my corselette a few tugs at the armpits to make it sit better on me before heading out into the sunlight.

"Let us go and entertain zee rabbles."

Chapter 21

Today I have a bit of a shock, make no mistake about that . . .

When I am high up on the wire, the faces of the crowd below tend to blend into a gray mass, but not today. Today, down below, I see broad swatches of color — like sports teams who sit together all decked out in their uniforms.

Sure enough, when I reach the ground, I see that I am right. But it is not adult teams that I spot. No, it is a tournament of local boys' football teams, and they have signs announcing who they are. There's Hyannis in green-and-blue jerseys, and over there is Falmouth, all proud in black and red, and there is — *Oh, God!* It's Plymouth in garnet and gold, and there, standing to the side, is one of their members. He has dark hair and dark eyes, and those eyes are trained right on me. He does not move.

I turn my head and pull my veil across my face as I hurry for the staff exit.

Damn! Did he recognize me? Am I undone?

Something has to be done, as I do not want to run from this kip just yet.

Marcello is waiting for me outside the tent, of course, ready to escort me to lunch. My first impulse is to run to my wagon to hide, but I cannot do that. I've got to fix this.

Marcello and I take our seats as usual at the food wagon and wait for Enrico to dish it out. Sure enough, a small figure in garnet and gold has appeared at the outside rope, looking in at me. *Damn!*

"May I say that you are even more beautiful today than when last my poor eyes gazed upon your glorious form," Marcello says, taking my hand in his and avidly kissing the back of it. "But why do you wear the veil today? To torture your poor Marcello by hiding some of your charms?"

"*Nyet*, Marcello," I say. "But you must help me vith some-zing, dear fool," I say, not looking over at the lad.

"You know I would lay down my very life for you, my sweet Russian potato," he says grandly. "You have only to name the task and I will do it."

"You see zat boy over zere?" I say, with a gesture of my head. "He has been bothering me. Looking at me funny. Make him go away, please."

Marcello leaps to his feet, full of manly resolve, and goes over to confront the boy.

"You, there! Go away!" he orders with a shooing motion. "This place is for performers only! Away with you!"

The boy does not move.

"You would presume to disturb the rest of the renowned Russian *artiste* Princess Natasha Romanoff, a member of the Russian Royal Family? Off with you, urchin, before I summon her palace guard. Away!"

I hide behind my veil and pretend to ignore the proceedings. A glass of wine is put in front of me, and I take an elegant, aristocratic sip.

The boy speaks up for the first time.

"Don't worry. I will not betray you."

When I look again, he is gone.

Damn, damn, damn, and double damn! But then, somehow, deep in my heart, I believe him.

Chapter 22

There's trouble. We all know that, for after the final show on our last day in Buzzards Bay, Massachusetts, the ringmaster does not direct the roustabouts to strike the tent, as he usually does. Instead he announces that the circus folk are to gather for a meeting under the Big Top.

Uh-oh . . . This can't be good.

It isn't, as we soon find out. We take seats in the bleachers usually reserved for paying customers and silently regard our plump little ringmaster, Pietro Mattucci, mournfully standing below, his head hung low. Marcello sits to my right, while Rigger O'Rourke sits to my left. I know Marcello wants to order Rigger to take a walk, but he cannot, for we are all equal here. Plus, my ardent Roman swain has seen the well-muscled roustabout in action. Last week we had some trouble with a pack of locals who thought they were tough. After the call of *Hey, rube!* rang out, thanks to the iron fists of Rigger O'Rourke and his lads, the yahoos went home, much wiser and minus a few teeth.

"It tears my heart out to say this, dear ones, but the Montessori and Mattucci Circus must close."

No!

There is much lamentation and expressions of great sorrow.

No! But why?

"There is no more money," says Mattucci, his head hanging, his mustaches drooping.

What will we do now? I hear asked in at least three languages, all of them sounding desperate. Marcello groans and grabs my hand, telling me I should not worry, for he will take care of his little Russian herring, which gets a snort from Rigger.

"Suppose you withhold our pay for a while? I'm sure all would agree to that."

There is a rumble of agreement, but . . .

"There is no money to pay you, *mi amici,* there is no money at all. I am sorry. We cannot even pay the next town its license fees."

Marcello's groans are echoed by many in the crowd. True, there are some who could just walk away from here and get another job — the laborers, the roustabouts, and me, for that matter — but for most, this is a disaster. What do you do with a lion? Or a cage full of tigers, for that matter? Some of these people can barely speak English! They are strangers in a strange land. What will happen to poor old Señora Elena? Where will she go?

"Why do we not do three shows a day, Maestro, instead of two?" calls out a hopeful voice. "That would bring in more money, no?"

The ringmaster sadly shakes his head. "Alas, I am sorry, but we tried that once and it did not work. It was too dark for the last show and the people would not come out at night."

There are no more helpful suggestions, only some sobs. *These good people were looking forward to some rest in their soft winter quarters down south, and so, frankly, was I . . . and Gargantina! What of her? And Balthazar?*

I spring to my feet and say, "Signor. Please. Your attentions. Ven zee pippils come to our circus, zey pay, zey vatch our show, and zen zey go home. *But zey still have moneys in zere pockets!* Vy do vee not sell zem some-zing different in zee dark time? Some-zing more suited to zat time of day, and maybe attract a different sort of customer?"

"Explain yourself, Princess Romanoff," says Signor Mattucci, and all eyes turn to me. I take a deep breath and begin.

"I haf traveled throughout Europe on my vay from Mother Russia to here, and I haf performed in many other circuses. Many of zem had places set off from zee Beeg Top for shows and games . . . and other kinds of performance. I saw zat zose places made a lot of money. In England it vas called zee midway. Zis circus does not haf such a midway, and—"

"If you mean freak shows like the Bearded Lady, the World's Fattest Man, Lizard Boy, never! Never shall the Montessori and Mattucci sink to that level!" He has enough of his innate dignity left to puff up in outrage.

"No, no, Maestro," I say, making placating motions with my hands. "Zere are other zings vee can do, eef I might explain?"

"Very well, come up here, and we will hear what you have to say," he says, yielding the floor, or rather the sawdust ring, to me.

I turn to my friends and say, "Vat vee vill do ees pull all

176

zee vagons into a circle on zee back lot, leaving zee loop open at one end for zee crowd to enter. No, zere vill be no admission charge, but each attraction costs a little. Enrico could set up his food vagon in zee center, selling his vonderful sausages, and tents stretched from zee sides of zee vagons vould shelter zee various . . . offerings."

"And what would these acts be?" I hear. "What can we do? We are circus people."

"Many zings," I reply. "Elephant and pony rides. Boys vill buy candy for zeir sweethearts and try to vin zem prizes at zee game tents. Zere vill be music and dancing and dramatic plays. Pipple may bring zeir children. Maybe zey don't vant zeir dahlinks to see Salome do zee Dance of zee Seven Veils, but zey can still enjoy zee antics of zee harlequins clowning about."

There is a low muttering as my proposal is discussed: "I could do the tarot and tell fortunes," and "I can make really good fudge."

I continue to press my case. "And zee Chuck-a-Luck Wheel . . . It ees zee roulette table for zee poor man, and a real moneymaker. Plus, eet does not require zat a circus *artiste* man zese booths. Rigger could handle zee wheel. Zee other roustabouts can handle zee rest of zee games. Zen, zere's our strongman, Gregor; he could challenge zee local bravos to match him in feats of strength — or wrestling. Or boxing! Vee could easily set up a ring for prize fights, set zee odds, take zee bets . . . and cockfights! Ta-da! Zee center ring ees just made for zat!"

"But . . . but . . . that smacks of gambling!" sputters Signor Mattucci. "The towns will not allow it!"

"Zey vill eef you clear it vith zem first. Send your most

clever man to negotiate zee price. You might be surprised," I retort.

"But who among us can do that? Neg-o-tiate?"

Good point, I'm thinkin' as I realize there is no one here who can actually do that. The ringmaster? No, those stiff-necked Yankees would see him as a rather silly little fat man . . . Von Arndt? . . . An arrogant foreigner. Me, a woman? Be serious. No, 'tis plain that none of us will do. But I know one who will.

"Maestro. Can vee stay vere vee are for three, four days? Do vee have enough food for us and zee animals?"

"*Sí*. Just barely."

"Goot. Now, who ees our fastest rider? Emilio? Very vell. I shall haf a letter for him to deliver to a man in Boston. He ees like my . . . protector. He vill come to me. He vill negotiate for us and he ees very good at it. Plus, he vill bring money. Vat do you say?"

The rumblings now sound more hopeful. From them, a voice speaks up. "You've told us what we all could do to make this work, Princess Romanoff, but tell us, what will you do?"

I may be mistaken, but I believe it is Rigger O'Rourke's voice that utters that question.

I strike a pose, hands clasped behind me and tucked into the small of my arched back, chin up, eyes looking off nobly into the distance at the top of the tent.

"To save our circus," I say, "I, Princess Natasha Annasova Romanoff, shall perform zee famous Dance of Zee Fans."

The motion carries.

Chapter 23

Princess Natasha Annasova Romanoff
The Montessori and Mattucci Grand Circus
Buzzards Bay, Massachusetts, USA

Mr. John Higgins
Faber Shipping Worldwide
Union Street
Boston, Massachusetts, USA

Dear John,

Yes, it's me again, Higgins. And yes, I have joined the circus, and I like it very much. However, this circus is in trouble and I need your help. If you can see your way clear, will you join me here? It is not far from Boston, and since I am in deep cover, it should be safe enough. We are in desperate need of some of your very special talents.

If you come, please ask the Shantyman to join you and to bring his fiddle and drum . . . and my Lady Gay, too.

Oh, yes, and bring as much money as Faber Shipping can spare. Here's the scam: I am the above Russian princess and you are my guardian who has been hired by the very possessive Count Yakov Ivanillich Petrovsky, to whom I am betrothed, to keep an eye on me. Being seventeen and headstrong, I had run away from you last month to join this circus, and you are somewhat miffed with me. Got it?

We shall be here in Buzzards Bay for four days. Please come, but only if you may safely do so.

Oh, how I long to see you and get the news from home!

Please excuse my haste, for you know that I count on you as my very best friend,

J.

Chapter 24

We are a hive of feverish activity.

The sides of the wagons must be repainted to reflect the games or shows that will be assigned to them, and canvas cut to form either full tents or half awnings, depending on the amount of shelter needed.

Me, I get a full tent, above which is lettered in black and gold TONDALAYO, QUEEN OF THE NAKED NILE. Over that is a picture of two large female eyes, all kohl rimmed and sultry, peering through exotic jungle plants. I painted this myself. Over the entrance is a sign reading *Admission $1 — Adults Only.*

Marcello is beside himself in anticipation of my first performance but is crushed when I inform him that no circus people will be permitted in my tent when I do my dance, except for Gregor, who will be my protection. That gets a blush from Gregor.

"*Cara mia,* you say you will allow the whole world to feast its eyes upon your heavenly form, but not your faithful and loving Marcello, whose heart I place at your feet? Oh tell me it is not true, Cruel Daughter of Siberian Wolves, that you would trust this hairy beast and not me?"

That gets a growl from Gregor.

I have to laugh fondly when Marcello puts on his sorrowful hangdog look. *Don't try that one on Jacky Faber, my boy, for she has been using that look for years.*

"Vell, maybe some night you shall see my poor performance, eef some night I drink too much vodka and fall victim to your charms, sweet Marcello, but not now, for zee goot of zee circus. Peace and no discord and fighting over zee vimmen, no?" Then I go into untranslatable Russian gobbledygook.

He accepts that with a great Mediterranean sigh and goes off with my light kiss on his cheek, so I am out of that . . . for the moment.

But while I am thinking about my promised dance, I take time amidst all the chaos to visit the wagon of our seamstress and costume designer, Señora Elena, to tell her of my needs.

"Of course, I have many feathers in many colors, Natasha. Is this not a circus? Two large fans, what color?"

"Vhite . . . or pink. As close to my skin color as possible so zat zee pipples vill not be able to tell vot ees feather and vot ees me. And, Señora, please make zee fans as large as you can, with goot, strong handles."

"*Sí, muchacha,*" she says, then smiles. "The show must go on, *verdad*? But you do know, don't you, how we all thank you for what you are trying to do?"

"Ees true, Señora," I say, acknowledging the traditional rallying call of circus folk and other theatrical people around the English-speaking world when trouble raises its head.

"Zee plan, I hope she works," I say with fingers crossed as I leave her to her task.

Now to the Chuck-a-Luck Wheel.

Rigger O'Rourke has that well in hand, having seen many such wheels at county fairs and even church picnics. It's funny. Lay the wheel down flat and you've got evil roulette, found in every godless gambling house, yet stand it upright and take it outside in the sun, and you're doing God's Work. Go figure . . .

We find that two more young boys have run away from their farms to join the circus. We get them all the time, at virtually every stop. Most such boys we kick back out to face angry fathers, but these we keep on my orders. They stand before me, hats in hand. Between them stands Gregor, the one who had caught them trying to crawl under the heavy canvas of the Big Top. He has a large hand wrapped around each of their necks. They are both astounded by the sight of me issuing orders while dressed in my aerialist costume.

"Your names?"

"Tad and Jerry, Miss," chokes out the less shy one. "Cousins."

"And joo both can ride? Do not lie, now," I warn. "You vill be put in lion cage eef you are found out."

"Yessum. Both bareback and saddle. Can handle a rig, too." They are loose-limbed and lanky, and are about fifteen years old.

"Do joo know all zee farms hereabout? Zee ones who raise and fight zee gamecocks?"

"Yessum."

"Goot. Report to Mr. O'Rourke — he ees zee beeg man over zere in zee round hat. He ees zee boss of zee roustabouts, of wheech you are now members," I say, watching their skinny chests rise and fall in joyful anticipation of a new and much more exciting life. "Zen go to Señora Elena's tent to get fitted for your red-striped shirts. Zen hop on two of our horses and ride to zee three nearest gamecock farms and tell zem of za center ring at our Beeg Top with eets fine and level sawdust. Zey shall never fight zere cocks in a finer arena, I promise eet. Three or four days from now, zey vill be informed. Prizes, too. Now go and do eet."

Do it they do, barely able to contain their excitement. "Boy howdy, Tad! New shirts!" I hear them exclaim as I head off for the next chore: the design and construction of the torches to light up all this stuff when night falls. A peek in our supplies reveals that we have some stout bamboo sticks that will serve. "Make it so, Mr. O'Rourke!" And so he does. He is a *most* valuable man . . . quite well constructed, too, I might add. *But never mind that, you. Ahem! There is work to be done here, girl, so go do it.*

The whole of the circus throws itself into the midway project, and that includes the *artistes*. The De Graff sisters, Gretchen and Heidi, both Germanic beauties, cheerfully set up for children's short rides on their magnificent stallions, and Mahmud decorated up Gargantina to her very best. There are many long strands of bright beads cascading from the edges of a small Persian carpet on her back as well as from a golden crown that rests on her head. She looks magnificent! And Señora Elena is ready to go with the tarot and the fortunetelling, and even my proud Marcello has agreed to man the simple throw-the-ball-and-knock-over-the-stuffed-cats game to win a prize for your lovely *ragazza*.

There is one who will not participate in all this, and that

is the animal trainer, Herr Udo von Arndt, pronouncing that it's beneath him. *Fine, Mr. von Arndt, just take care of your tigers and stay out of our way.* I am coming to profoundly dislike the man, a distaste that I find is shared by many around me.

But never mind that, for what should pull into the back lot but a coach-and-four. A door opens, and out steps my dear John Higgins. *Oh, joy!* And then the rear door swings wide and Enoch Lightner, the Shantyman, emerges, he of the deep baritone and vast knowledge of music and sound, and master of the fiddle, with his ever-present white cloth band drawn across his sightless eyes.

"Oh, John, thank you for coming! We have so much to discuss! And Enoch, so good of you to join us! And who's this?"

A dark-haired girl in her mid-twenties, as far as I can tell, tumbles out behind him, bearing a fiddle case and a bright smile.

"Eliza, Miss," she says, holding out her hand in a no-nonsense way. "Eliza Lightner."

"Welcome, Missus Lightner," I say, taking her hand and smiling back at her. "I thought our Mr. Lightner looked a good deal neater than when last I saw him." His coat is brushed, as is his unruly black hair.

He grins good-naturedly at the female sport being made of him. "She admired my singing of 'Captain Wedderburn's Courtship,' and so loved my rendition of 'Cuckoo's Nest' that she ended up in my bed that very night," he says, getting his own back at us.

"Aye, and we was married the next day," retorts this Eliza. "And now I've got to unpack." She goes to the trunk and begins to pull out luggage, which includes many music cases and, most prominently, a large drum. *Ah, yes, the Shantyman's trademark.*

I spot Mr. Barrow, a disagreeable dwarf who is also our wagon master.

"Meester Bar-row. Eef you please. Vee vill need accomadations for three — vun single vagon, vun double."

He casts me a surly look. "It don't please me none at all. But, well, I guess you're the boss of this mess, so I'll move some things around. Kick out a few clowns. Serve 'em right. Gimme an hour."

And he goes off, grumbling. *Oh well, I guess Rigger finds him useful . . .*

If I had thought the coach was empty of riders, I was wrong. The door on the other side slams, and who should come about to greet me, arms held wide, red hair blazing, but . . .

Mairead?

Chapter 25

If I thought I could just collapse into helpless joy at seeing my dear Irish companion and sometime Sister-in-Arms, I was wrong, for there is much to be done.

"Come, friends, into my wagon to refresh yourselves, and then we must talk business."

We pile into my wagon, and though it is a bit cramped, we all manage to get in. Mairead and I hop on my bed, with giggles and pokes; Eliza is given my chair at the dressing table, while Higgins and the Shantyman prefer to stand. Higgins, of course, opens and pours the wine. (Yes, I do tend to keep a stock of claret around to calm the Faber nerves at times.) And soon each hand has a glass of wine grasped in it — that is, after my fastidious friend has taken each glass, squinted at it, and then polished it to his satisfaction with an impeccable white handkerchief he pulls from his vest pocket, a piece of cloth that I know for sure has never been even close to his nose.

There is a knock on the open door's frame and our fine chef, Enrico, hands in a tray of cannolis. *Ah, grazie, Enrico,* and we lay to on those delicious treats.

"Interesting accommodations, Miss," Higgins says, lifting one of the pastries to his lips and his aforementioned nose to the breeze flowing through my open windows.

"Yes, John, somewhat like our digs on the *Belle of the Golden West* on our trip down the Mississippi. That was rather cramped as well, you might recall," I retort. "Do you like what I've done with it?"

"I recall that the Mississippi River smelled a good deal better than this," he retorts, without commenting on my decorating efforts.

"You'll get used to it, dear John. You have gotten used to a lot more than that in your unfortunate association with my poor wayward self."

I realize what an assault to his cultured nose the combination of tiger, lion, and elephant manure just might be. "But now I must put the entire situation before you, and here is the part you are to play. You must ride to our next town, which is Wareham, and meet with the town council there to renegotiate the original contract. They are expecting only the circus, and *not* the midway we are constructing outside, with its somewhat more . . . exotic offerings. In other words, we will need permission to operate the gaming wheel, the beer bar, the exotic music, and, er . . . dancing? Plus, you've got to take money to pay for the original two-hundred-dollar rent on their miserable patch of dusty ground. I assume you've got some money?"

He nods and taps his jacket pocket. "Fifteen hundred dollars. It's all Mr. Pickering could spare from Faber Shipping right now."

"Should cover us for a while, till we get the midway up

and running; that is, if we are allowed to run it. These stiff-necked Puritan Yankees, you know . . ."

"Yes, Miss," he says, dusting himself off and preparing to leave on his mission. "I know them well. 'Stiff necked,' yes, but also very . . . practical. I know what to do and say. And what shall be my official position at this . . . establishment?"

"I guess General Factotum of the Montessori and Mattucci Grand Circus should serve."

"Sounds impressive," he says, following with a sniff, visibly unimpressed. "Till later, then. Adieu."

After Higgins departs on his mission, I put the fake accent back on my lips and take the others on a tour of the grounds, introducing them to the circus folk, both human and animal, and pointing out what their duties will be — *music, lots of it, and loud!*

"We can handle that," says the Shantyman, grinning, and I know that to be true, having heard his drum and stentorian voice from one end of the *Lorelei Lee* to the other, all two hundred and ten feet of her.

I get Mairead to pet Balthazar's nose, but Eliza will have none of it. She does put a timorous hand on sweet Gargantina's trunk. I have brought along a sack of peanuts, and all delight in feeding her, feeling the gentle touch of her long nose on the palms of our hands as she gently picks the peanuts up and places them in her pink mouth.

We are not delighted, however, by the tiger cage and the two who stand next to it — Herr Udo von Arndt and his assistant, Emil Mussler. This Mussler is a slimy piece of work. He's not a roustabout or O'Rourke would have thrown him out long ago; no, his job is cleaning up after the big striped beasts and rounding up enough raw meat for them.

The tigers roar as we approach, making us each take a step back, which brings an arrogant smile to the thin lips of von Arndt. He suffers the introductions with ill grace, merely lifting his whip to his hat and then turning away.

"He doesn't feed them till just before the show, so they don't eat *him* when he steps into the cage. Pity, that, as I do not like the man," I mutter, and I especially don't like the way he looks at me . . . and now Mairead. "But come, I believe your wagon is ready, and you can settle in for a bit of well-needed rest."

They do not argue.

It goes without saying that Mairead will bunk with me. She has been, at odd times, a runaway from her father, a stowaway on my privateer *Emerald,* and a fellow convict on my *Lorelei Lee,* bound for a long stretch in an Australian prison. She is presently Matron of Women onboard the *Lee,* now a profitable passenger ship, having completed many safe crossings of the big salt twixt Ireland and the United States. Her often irate father, Liam Delaney, is now the Captain of the aforementioned *Lorelei Lee,* and her beloved husband, Ian McConnaughey, is now First Mate of her. The ship, not the lass, oh, no. No one is master of *her.*

Ensconced in my wagon, we joyously recount old times — *Back on an elly-phant again, Jacky! Just like that time in Bombay! I can't believe it!* — and we wait for Higgins's return.

We do not have to wait long. Soon after five in the afternoon, as we all settle down for a fine dinner at Enrico's newly expanded food cart, Higgins reappears, apparently somewhat pleased with himself.

"Well," he says, "it appears we shall be allowed to open our midway. Yes, on with the music, the silly carnival games, the animal rides, and the cockfighting — provided one of the councilor's cocks be allowed to enter without paying an entry fee. Yes, too, on the gambling, with the proviso that the First Congregational Church of Wareham will get ten percent of the profits from the Chuck-a-Luck Wheel. And I was informed that their constable will be present and keeping a stern eye on the proceedings, of that we might be sure. No, however, on the exotic dancing, but yes, surprisingly, on the liquid bar. All in all, an extra two hundred dollars."

I nod at this. A stiff tariff, yes, but it will allow us to open. In truth, I am somewhat relieved on the dancing thing because I haven't worked that out yet.

"Good work, John. Pray, seat yourself and have some of Enrico's excellent osso buco."

"In a moment, Miss," says Higgins. "But first, as factotum of this fine outfit, I must go visit the owner, to see if he can help out with some of this expense."

"Good luck with that." I snort. "But you can give it a try."

We are joined by Marcello Grimaldi, who gives his mustachio an extra twist while casting his eye on the two new girls, and we all fall to our delicious dinner.

Presently, Higgins returns, looking, I must say, a trifle nonplussed, which is rather unusual for him. He is holding a sheaf of papers. He shrugs and comes to stand before me. After a short formal bow, he says, "I believe I am addressing the new owner of the Montessori and Mattucci Grand Circus."

Wot . . . ?

"It is true, Miss. Signor Mattucci is an old man and he is tired of the financial worry. He will keep his old job of ringmaster, which he loves, but he has sold the rest of the circus to Faber Shipping Worldwide, for the sum of five hundred dollars."

Wot . . . ?

My fork falls in my plate. "The whole thing for five hundred dollars?"

"Yes, Miss."

"And Faber Shipping now owns an elephant?"

"I believe those will be the first words out of Attorney Pickering's astounded mouth," says Higgins. "However, Miss, there is not much to this organization in the way of assets — just some tents, horses, a stack of posters, ropes, supplies . . . and some considerable debts . . . payrolls and all, which we will have to assume. Many of the acts own their own wagons and equipment, so you see there is not much here."

"It is enough, and we will make it pay," I say, rising. "Shantyman. Muster the crew."

He stands and places a light hand on his wife's arm and she leads him over to the big drum that was set up in the center of the back lot. Eliza places the drumsticks in his palm, and he commences to pound, and it gets everybody's instant attention. Then he throws back his great head and roars . . .

"HEAR YE, HEAR YE! ALL HANDS TO QUARTERS! CAPTAIN'S CALL!"

If the circus people did not fully understand the nature of that order, they managed to get the gist of it, for soon they are all grouped around me, muttering among themselves and looking mighty quizzical — *Captain? What Captain?*

I flutter my hands, signaling for silence, and when they quiet down, I say, "I haf an announcement to make: I am now zee owner of zee Montessori and Mattucci Grand Circus . . ."

There is a gasp as I hold up the bill of sale and wave it about, but the noise subsides as I continue.

". . . and all vill remain in zeir jobs as before. Thees ees Meester John Higgins. He vill be taking over zee runnink of zee circus." Higgins gives a slight bow on that.

"What about this so-called midway we've been building?"

I look over to see that it was Rigger O'Rourke who spoke. He stands, arms crossed, my first challenge.

"Goot news, Rigger," I reply. "I haf just received news zat zee midway has been au-thor-iz-ed in Ware-ham. Ve vill break camp and move zere tomorrow and open zee next day! Shall vee haf a cheer?"

I get one, but it's pretty weak. Still, I continue . . .

". . . and as vee can plainly see, vee haf another few hours of daylight left, so shall vee all get back to vork?"

The next cheer is even weaker.

Later, as deep night falls, Mairead and I are snugged up in my bed, giggling away like any two schoolgirls.

After a while, we grow quiet and Mairead's eyes fall on my miniature portrait of Jaimy, which hangs on the wall next to my bunk.

"Have you done it yet?" she asks. "You and him, I mean?"

"Done what?"

"You know . . ." She gives me a nudge and a leer.

"Oh, that . . . well, no. Things got in the way, sort of . . ."

"You might give it a shot. It's rather fun, you know. People have been doing it for years."

"Makes babies, too, I hear . . ."

"Oh, yes, the Irish, especially. Can't grow potatoes? Grow babies instead. Lots of 'em. Ha! You watch, we micks'll cover the world someday!"

"Yes, about those babies . . ."

"Oh. The Queen of the Ocean Sea is scared of that?"

"No, but they might get in her way."

That gets me a shove. "You hard thing, you, to deny babies into this world just to satisfy your own selfish nature."

"'Tis a hard world. Why should the wee ones suffer? Especially in hanging around with someone like me for a mother. Huh! Wouldn't wish that on anyone."

"Och, Jacky, I don't think you'd be all that bad as a mum."

Eventually, the talk trails off and she falls asleep, with my nose buried in her red mane, but slumber does not come so easily for me, as it has been a very exciting day. My restless eyes fall on my picture of Jaimy . . .

Hello, Jaimy, I'm just lying here, thinking of you, and wondering what would have happened if I had I simply stowed away on the Shannon *that day in Boston instead of running off to Plymouth as I did. No, no, dear, not my usual way of getting aboard a ship, as a girl disguised as boy—I'd be discovered right off, as I've gone much too famous by now. No, I* mean as an actual stowaway, lurking about in the lower decks till we were gone far enough so that the Captain could not turn back . . . and then what would Lieutenant James Emerson Fletcher have found in his cabin about three days out? Could it be a small girl in her black burglar gear lying in his bed? What a delight to soothe the soul of a poor sailor when far away at sea! And maybe the Captain would agree to marry us, even. I would not mind being confined to quarters, that is, if they were your quarters, dear one. Ummmm . . . what a trip that would be, oh, yes! We'd blow the porthole out of your cabin, that's for sure.

Maybe your wicked girl could show you some new tricks, hmmm, Jaimy? Now, now, you be good, you. Jaimy is a gentleman, even though you ain't a lady, and you should go to sleep now. Enough of your silly fantasies. Big day tomorrow.

G'night, luv.

Chapter 26

Journal of Amy Trevelyne
Dovecote Farm
Quincy, Massachusetts

Dear Reader,

We have found that Miss Faber has now joined a circus as an aerialist — why I expected any less, I do not know.

Ezra feels that she is sufficiently deep in disguise, and so we might venture downstate to see the show. After all, Mr. Higgins and others have already joined her there at her request. I certainly hope she was wise in that decision — common sense is not one of her strong suits.

The war fever continues unabated in New England, the flames of war being relentlessly fanned by our so-called gentlemen of the press.

I count the days till I see my dear sister once again. I wait with bated breath.

Entry dated October 26, 1809 — signed Amy Trevelyne

Chapter 27

Wareham is a bigger town than what we have been visiting on Cape Cod of late, and that is good, for we need all the coin of this realm we can possibly haul in. Yesterday we had sent Eliza and Tad off to Boston in the buckboard, to buy candies and trinkets as prizes for the games, and they returned, successful but broke. The whole enterprise depends on that midway.

Our glorious circus parade rumbles through Wareham at noon, to the delight of the populace. Signor Mattucci, on his white horse, is in the lead, resplendent in his red ringmaster uniform, looking much happier now that a burden has been lifted from his shoulders. Mairead and I are on Gargantina, all three of us decked out in feathered finery, the two humans posing shamelessly, our dear elephant plodding along to the absolute delight of the children.

An Elly-phant! Look at that!

Behind us, we have set up a flatbed wagon, and on it stands, straight and tall, Enoch Lightner, the Shantyman of great renown, known from Bombay to the South China Sea, sawing away at his fiddle, while Eliza thunders away at the big drum. He bellows . . .

I am a jolly fiddleman, at fiddling I have been
For two-score years on this little isle of green.
I'm known from Boston down to the Bight
And everybody calls me Old Blind Light.

Sure, that's just "The Little Beggarman" tune reworked a little, but it works just fine here, so play on, Shantyman. Believe me, your mighty voice can be heard down to the end of any street or alley in this town.

Of all the trades a going, sure the fiddling is the best
For when a man is tired he can sit him down and rest.
He can play for his dinner, he has nothing else to do
But to sit at your table tapping his old fiddle bow.

After that, we have the De Graff sisters standing on the backs of their mighty stallions, waving to the crowd, and then the cat cages with their occupants roaring, and all along the route, clowns cavort and toss penny candies to the wildly excited kids.

Fresh paint is on the wagons, and we are as bright as a new penny. Shabby? Not at all. As a matter of fact, I'm rather proud of my brave little circus and the people who live in it and who make it come alive.

And, too, there is something about the traveling life that appeals to my restless nature. I often hark back fondly to my travels across Spain with King Zoltan and Bubya

Nadya Vadoma and their caravan of gaily painted Roma wagons, yes, and that trip down the Mississippi River on my keelboat, *Belle of the Golden West*. There was something new at every turn, and I liked that. I reflect that I could live like this. Hey, look — all around me, everybody's smiling and happy, and what's the matter with that, I want to know.

Tad and Jerry bring up the tail end of the parade and are kept busy putting up posters advertising the circus and its new offerings . . . that and sparking up the local girls, in their spanking new shirts and newfound sense of worldliness. Signor Mattucci had a stack of the sheets that had a space open at the bottom for the notation of times and dates, and other notes of interest. Into that spot I penned . . .

Come one, come all!
Wholesome entertainment at the Midway of the
Montessori and Mattucci Grand Circus!
Games of Skill, Games of Chance!
Much more! Come see!
Gather all ye hardy young men brave enough to
step up and challenge the Mighty Gregor in
bouts of wrestling. Big Prizes if you best him.
Cockfights begin under the Big Top at Nine.
Come see, come see!

Course I decorate any open space with arrows, exclamation points, and other embellishments, anything to catch the eye of the country boy or man.

• • •

The morning and afternoon acts under the Big Top went off without a hitch and the midway is up and ready to go . . . and night is falling. I cross my fingers in anticipation and hope. Many of the people who attended the afternoon show wandered over to the midway. *Good, good . . . Come on over . . . Stay.*

I am sweating it out, gnawing at my knuckles, and peeking anxiously through the curtains of my wagon. I have advised all the *artistes* to continue to wear their costumes when they circulate through the midway, whether they have a role to play or not. It adds exotic color, I figure, that the locals should appreciate — the kids, especially. In keeping with my own instructions, I still have my aerialist costume on, without the skirt. The veil, however, I will keep.

"Try to remain calm, Miss," urges Higgins, raising a square of chocolate to his lips. "Here. Try a piece of Heidi De Graff's fudge. It is quite good."

At any other time, the Faber jaws would have clamped down on the delicious brown morsel, but not this evening. No, I am too keyed up and too involved with grinding my poor tusks down to nubs.

Noticing my nervousness, Higgins attempts to settle me down. He takes a look out my window and says, "Regard, Miss. There are already a couple of lads at the bar right now, loosening up for the night's revels. You have once again made a profit on Demon Rum and Nancy Whiskey, two business associates of yours who have proved worthy of your attention in the past. Interesting, considering you yourself have forsworn the imbibing of said spirits."

Indeed, but since the Wareham town councilor who

owns the Boar's Head Tavern is requiring us to buy all the bar supplies from him, the profit will be scant.

Higgins is dressed in one of his many fine suits of clothes, a dark gray affair with a deep red cravat around his throat, all crowned with a top hat of the finest brushed beaver. Never let it be said that John Higgins, vice president of Faber Shipping Worldwide, was ever less than the height of male sartorial fashion. He will place himself at the entrance to welcome the crowd and watch for troublemakers. His velvet waistcoat does house two small but deadly pistols, after all, and he is not afraid to use them.

"Ummm," I say, with a doubting squint. "Just be sure they ain't none of our gang. No. It's all right; they're locals. Good. Drink up, lads."

Earlier, we had covered up the TONDALAYO, QUEEN OF THE NAKED NILE sign. There's no sense in promising them something they ain't gonna get. No, for that I will substitute a wild flamenco dance, and who should be my partner other than my ardent suitor Marcello Grimaldi? It doesn't take much for Señora Elena to deck him out in something that looks vaguely like a Majo from Madrid. As for me, I have my seabag and in it is stuffed my Maja rig: black dress that's heavy with embroidery, my ever-handy lace mantilla, and shiny castanets. As for the dancing, all he really has to do is stand there and look macho, while I do the rest. He does, however, protest mightily.

"Geet over here, you, my big sveet Italian sausage," I order. "Vee must practice."

"But I am trapeze artist, my slippery little Black Sea whitefish, not some foolish dancer."

"Eef you luf your Russian volfhound, you vill do it for me. Plus, I am now your boss as vell, so consider your sit-u-a-tion, woychik."

He sighs, relenting. "*Sí*. And that troubles my heart, too. I believe I shall go see Mairead, the flame-haired one, for comfort in this matter."

"Oh, faithless one, you vould abandon your sweet ba-bushka in her hour of need? Look, you stand zere and just stamp your heels in time to za music, clap your hands over your head, and look arro-gant. You can do zat! I vill do za rest. Besides, the beauteous Mairead ees a married lady who vill have nothing to do with Italian *ragazzi,* no matter how handsome and strong zey might be."

That, and the kiss I plant upon his brow, wins him over.

"Well, Miss, I believe it is time we hit the sawdust, as it were, and do our circus duty," says Higgins, rising and putting on his top hat, then taking up his gold-headed cane. "The smell of the greasepaint, the roar of the crowd, and all that."

There's a big gulp on my part and a simple clearing of the throat on the part of Higgins as we stride out into the midway.

Higgins, of course, takes to his new role as if he were born to it . . .

"*Ladies and gentlemen, step right up and walk right in! Welcome to the Montessori and Mattucci Grand Circus!*" He is every inch the proper English gent, with plummy accent to match, gesturing grandly with his cane. "*Yes, all you could wish for in wholesome and edifying entertainment for the entire family! Pony rides for your lovely children? To your right,*

Sir, and don't deny them the experience of riding our sweet Gargantina, who has come to you directly from the mysterious Orient. They will speak of it to the end of their days! And you, young Galahad! A prize for your beautiful lady? A stuffed toy to remind her of you when you are far away? Test your skill and win her love! To the shooting gallery, Sir, and you shall prevail and be uppermost in her heart! Ah! I believe I spy some sporting gents . . . am I right, gentlemen? There stands our wheel of fortune, and good fortune can be yours. Step right up!"*

Could it be that Higgins's close association with Lord Byron, back in London, has given his normally reserved character a certain flamboyance? One thing is sure, Higgins is always full of surprises.

I strut about and smile and wave at our lovely crowd. All my people are in place and ready. I wink at sturdy Eliza Lightner, tending the bar, brooking no nonsense from any patrons. The flatbed wagon will serve as a stage for my flamenco act later tonight, and now serves as a platform for Mairead and the Shantyman — she on pennywhistle; he on fiddle. If nothing else, we will have music; they are right now ripping through "Haste to the Wedding" in fine style.

Laughter and happiness are all around me. What was I worried about?

Rigger O'Rourke stands at the Chuck-a-Luck, with red ribbon garters on his sleeves and his top hat cocked on his head at a rakish angle. As I pass, Rigger gives me a knowing wink, reaches up, and gives the wheel a spin. "Lends a bit of dash, eh, Boss?" he remarks, and, indeed, it does.

"Round and round she goes, and where she stops, nobody knows . . ."

Chapter 28

"Rinse, please," says Higgins. Obediently, I duck my sudsy head 'neath the hot bathwater, and his strong fingers work at the roots of my unruly mop of hair.

"Ahhhh." I breathe as my face breaks the surface, eyes squeezed shut against the soap. "Nobody has hands like you, Higgins. I shall miss you."

We have visited two more towns since Wareham and are about to open in Taunton. We have been doing extremely well since the introduction of the midway, and I am most pleased. My people are happy and so am I. Higgins, alas, will leave us in New Bedford to return to Boston.

"The feeling is mutual, Miss, but I think that I shall be of more service to you there, in your current precarious legal situation, than continuing to act as an overpaid circus barker and following you and your circus down to your winter quarters to bask on some tropical shore, however attractive that prospect might sound. And Mr. O'Rourke has shown an aptitude for delicate negotiations with greedy town officials and should step into that role quite nicely."

'Tis true. Rigger cleans up real good in a new suit, hat,

shiny shoes, and spats. As his employer, I am pleased with his progress. Yes, well, more than pleased. I have always had room in my heart for a merry rogue, and he is certainly one of those.

"I suppose." I sigh. "But it is such a comfort having you near me, husband John."

He smiles at that, both of us recalling that time on the *Lorelei Lee* when we were briefly married and shared both a cabin and a bunk. Sort of married . . .

O'Rourke has shown himself to have quite the gift of gab. I have watched him at the wheel of fortune. He keeps up a flowing line of patter as he spins the wheel for the next round of betting. True, the odds are in the favor of the house, may it ever be so, but I think the success of that particular attraction lies in the subtle pressure of his knee applied to the bottom of the wheel as it slows to a stop . . .

"Number four! Alas, Sir! Only one off from your lucky number! Surely you will try again! See, the fine young fellow to your left has just won a handsome pot for his dear mother! The rent of their little cottage shall be paid! Won't his sweetheart be proud! Place your bets, gents. Here she goes again! Round and round . . ."

Of course, the "fine young fellow" is a shill, a roustabout who hasn't given his "dear mother" a dime since he ran off to join our merry band, and his sweetheart is Python Patty the Snake Charmer, but, hey, it's all entertainment, right?

Earlier this morning, I had met Higgins and O'Rourke on the midway just after they returned from a meeting with the town fathers of New Bedford. It went well, with an interesting twist.

"Yes, Miss. They agreed to everything," said Higgins, while Rigger stood by, smirking. "There are no restrictions. It is a seafaring town, after all, greedy and up for anything."

We all three had then looked up at the marquee above our heads, the one advertising TONDALAYO, QUEEN OF THE NAKED NILE, AND HER FAMOUS FAN DANCE.

A heavy sigh from me, and a "Will you do it?" from Higgins, as O'Rourke put fingertips to hat brim and went off to attend to his duties, leaving me standing slightly red-faced in the dust.

Why did I put myself in this situation? Why did I blurt out that I would do the exotic dance? It's because I know what sells in this world, count on it. My charming little play-let, *The Villain Pursues Constant Maiden,* or *Fair Virtue in Peril,* was a total flop until we added the bit with the torn-off dress. I want my circus to succeed so badly, and I want to do my part. And, hey, it's just another kind of show, and I do like to give one hundred percent when in performance.

"I said I would, so I will," I said, with chin in air, noble expression on face. "Everyone else is giving their all to ensure the survival of the Montessori and Mattucci Circus and so must I. The winter will be long, and even if we are resting up in sunny Georgia, there will be expenses."

"Very well, Miss," said Higgins. "Lady Godiva it is. For the good of the people and all . . ."

"Higgins . . ." I said, by way of warning. Perhaps I over-did the nobility thing a bit. "Surely you don't think I'll be doing it for my own enjoyment?"

"Of course not, Miss." Higgins tried unsuccessfully to suppress a smile. "I was merely thinking of your past experience in matters of *le striptease,* as the French so delicately put it. There were several times on the *Wolverine,* involving Mr. Raeburne and Mr. Fletcher, respectively, and then there were those times in the hold of the slaver *Bloodhound,* wherein you traded glimpses of your well-toned body in return for fresh water to ease the suffering of your sisters in captivity in the dark hold of that horrid craft. And then there were the many nude dips in the Mighty Mississippi, to say nothing of the naked dive off the pirate female Cheng Shih's mighty junk, *Divine Wind.* Oh, and there was the performance given before Lieutenant Harry Flashby that involved the careful unpeeling of an Oriental sari. And did I hear that you posed au naturel for the great artist Francisco Goya?"

Higgins often gave me advice as regards my personal safety but never on my conduct in the way of moral behavior. He may consider us fellow travelers, both sinners, and both outside the pale of the usual standards of conduct. We have been through a lot together.

"Thank you, Mr. Higgins, for that very complete summary of Jacky Faber's time in the buff, public-wise," I said. "And I must admit the truth of it — this poor hide of mine has, indeed, been around the block more than a few times, so one would think the novelty might have worn off, but apparently it hasn't. However, for your cheek in pointing it out, you may draw me a bath. The least I can do if they're gonna be squintin' at me bare bum is to make sure it's clean and presentable and my limbs are smoothly shorn."

He agreed, bless him, and it wasn't long before I was in a fine bath in the laundry tent, head to toe in wonderful sudsy hot water, with Higgins working his magic on my hair.

"But just wait till spring, Higgins, when we take the newly refurbished Montessori and Mattucci Grand Circus on the road again. We'll bring Fennel and Bean — "

"I'm sure those renowned . . . *thespians* . . . will prosper in this venue," says Higgins with a certain dryness. I know he chokes a bit on that word, preferring less kind descriptions — he and I have seen the *great* actors and actresses of our day on the London stage during our recent time in that fair city. "But then again, we all do strut and fret our hour on the stage, don't we, be we grand dame or poor ham actor . . . or impresario of a circus."

"Thanks for not calling it flea-bitten, Higgins," I say.

"Actually, I have been quite enjoying myself out here on the hustings, as it were, and have not been bitten by a single flea."

"They wouldn't dare," I venture. "What mere insect would presume to bite the hide of the redoubtable Higgins?"

"And I have grown quite fond of the smell of mildewed canvas."

The spread of canvas above my head is a bit spotty and exhibits none of the taut majesty of a sailing ship's mainsail, but still, it does its job.

"Oh, I have such plans for spring, John!" I say, exulting in both my lovely bath and my plans for the future. "Some monkeys, I think, and a dog act, and we'll hire a professional boxer to take some of the load off poor Gregor.

"And, hey!" I say, my feet propped up on the edge of the tub. "When we go by Clarissa's place on our way down through Virginia, maybe I'll drop in and see her. Old school chums and all that."

"I don't know if that would be wise, Miss."

"Umm. You're probably right," I agree. "Murder of one's hostess not being good form, eh wot? But do you know what would be really choice? If I were to procure from Chopstick Charlie a troupe of howler monkeys and let them loose on the Howe estate. They breed really fast, you know."

"While it is amusing to think of, I think that it is neither a particularly healthy nor profitable line of thought, Miss."

"Perhaps not, but the idea of Clarissa and Lord Richard Allen making like monkeys in her bedroom, with a cadre of howlers at the window laughing and hooting away at the amorous pair, is most satisfying to my vindictive mind."

"Perhaps it is lucky you cannot act upon that bit of vengeance."

"A pity, yes, but anyway, dear Higgins, back to next season: I think we'll add some more dramatics, such as short plays with Polly Von and the Emerald Players. We'll put on my *Villain Pursues Constant Maiden,* or *Fair Virtue in Peril...*"

"Good Lord, no," whispers Higgins in horror, his fingers slackening at their work.

Knowing in what low regard Higgins holds my past literary efforts, I press on with wicked delight. "... and I have started work on a new one. It's called *The Midshipman Stood on the Burning Deck.* Would you like to hear of it?"

Before he can reply, there is a scratching at the tent flap.

Higgins glances over and says, "I believe your ardent

admirer, Marcello Grimaldi, requests admittance. Shall I send him away?"

"No, bid him come in, John. In light of recent developments, I need to talk to him." The water is murky enough due to soap and my recently sloughed off layer of crud, so I sink down to my chin into its still-warm embrace, leaving my right foot hanging over the edge of the tub, as Marcello enters. He stares astounded at the scene before him, but his tongue does not fail him.

"Ah, behold! The Volga Princess in her fabled bath of the milk of many minks!" he exults, sinking to his knees tubside, mustache all a-quiver. "My eyes shall fall from my unworthy head."

He glances uncomprehendingly at Higgins placidly stropping his razor and preparing to relieve my lower limbs of the unsightly fur that persists in growing there. Higgins says nothing to relieve his mind, but I do say something that I hope will mollify the lad. Pointing a finger up at Higgins, I say, "You vill, of course, recall zee very jealous Count Yakov Petrovsky. Heem of zee horrible impalements?" I point to Higgins and draw my finger across my throat. "Meester Hee-gans here ees his man. *Capiche?*" Higgins nods in sage agreement to this. Marcello scowls, unmollified, as I continue. "Vee shall not dance zee flamenco tonight, Marcello."

"No, my sweet Russian wolfhound?" he says, still looking curiously from Higgins to me and not liking it much. "I was beginning to enjoy it."

He actually does a good job at it. Hey, stick the two of us in the proper garb, put a rose in my teeth and castanets on my fingers, and with the Shantyman strumming away on his guitar and Mairead beating on tambourine, you've got flamenco, rural-America style. All seem to enjoy it.

"No, sveet fool. Tonight my poob-blick demands zat Princess Natasha Annasova Romanoff dance her Famous Fan Dance, and she must bend as zee vill-ow and bow to zeir demands."

Marcello gasps and sucks in his breath.

"So you mus' prepare zee tent, *caro mio*," I continue. "Mairead and zee De Graff sisters vill assist me ven I am onstage. And Higgins, too."

"And your loving and faithful Marcello? What of him? Must he stand outside like a kicked dog?" He looks wounded.

"No, dear one, you shall sell tickets at zee entrance, and ven zee audience ees seated, my brave Marcello vill stand by to see zat no crude ruffian should rise up and give offense to my fragile self during zee performance."

At that, I lower the lashes and give him the big eyes. "You vill give protections to your poor Slavic rabbit, vill you not, my fine young *acrobato*?"

I guess that nails him, for he gets to his feet and bows, grasping my wet foot and lifting it to his lips.

"Yes, I shall. I swear by the ice water flowing through these lovely blue veins traced on this, the purest of white skin!" he exults as he places hot kisses on the heretofore quite unremarkable appendage, adding to the steam in the tent. "Yes, fear not, Princess. I shall defend you with my unworthy life! I live only for the coming of the night! *Addio!*"

"Zat ees possibly zee worst Russian accent I have ever heard," says Higgins after Marcello leaves, exhibiting a bit of uncharacteristic sarcasm.

I laugh. "It makes my jaw ache doing it. I'll be glad to stop after this is all over."

"Do you enjoy playing with him, Miss?"

"Oh, yes, he is ever so much fun, and cute — and handy, too. By letting it appear that he is my consort, the others stay away, and after all, I am promised in marriage to James Emerson Fletcher, and though Jaimy is nowhere nearly as ferocious as the fictional Count Petrovsky, I still think he'd be rather miffed if he returned from London only to find me knee-deep in amorous Italian males."

"I think Lieutenant Fletcher should be rather used to that by now."

That gets him a look, but I must admit the truth of what he says. Poor Jaimy. I lie back as Higgins's magic fingers continue to massage my scalp. *Ummmm.* But, eventually, it is over.

"Stand, please . . ."

Chapter 29

"*Le* trick in *le striptease,* Jac-qui," my good friend Zoe and fellow member of Les Petite Gamines de Paris dance troupe had said, "is never show them too much too quickly. And as for *le* fan dance, if the dancer is skillful, she never shows them anything at all, the fans covering her up just enough, at just the right time. The men will come together afterward and compare what they saw of her and her parts, and what they think they saw. *Oui, ma petite,* men are silly and stupid, but still we love them, no? Give them a bit of leg, a flash of derrière, they enjoy, so what's the harm?"

She and the other Gamines had been most kind in welcoming me into their company, teaching me the moves I would need for the performances, and I thoroughly enjoyed my time with them. What we did was what is generally known as the cancan. Not the classical ballet by any stretch, but still it was a lot of fun. Hey, ruffles shaking on the tail, or the bare tail shaking by itself, what's the difference?

Zoe had given me some advanced advice on the art of showing skin as we enjoyed a very fine aperitif at Café des

Deux Chats, my favorite restaurant during my stay in the City of Light.

"Come, little one," she said, dabbing her lips and rising, "to my place and I will show you. I have the proper fans."

Say, I wonder what Zoe and Giselle and the rest of the gang are doing now? Maybe they'd like a tour of America with the Montessori and Mattucci Circus in the spring. Oh, it would be so good to see them all! I shall write to Madame Pelletier posthaste, but right now Tondalayo must practice her night moves.

We have turned my wagon around such that the door faces into the back lot, allowing us to set up the stage and canvas right against it. That way, I can duck into the safety of my quarters between shows.

The stage has been constructed — about twenty feet wide and six feet deep — and along the front there hangs a red curtain. It will part to show me, standing, wearing nothing but my two strategically placed fans and a smile. There are benches in front to seat about thirty patrons of the arts. The bottom of the canvas tent is fastened down tightly to make sure no randy boys are peeking underneath. Don't mind 'em peeking; but not payin'? Nay, it goes against my nature.

We will have whale-oil torches for light . . . but not too much light — I don't want 'em countin' my ribs, that's for sure. If they could see what they were actually getting in the way of female pulchritude, well, they just might pass on it.

We have a dress rehearsal, where I do my bit in fans and underclothes, and it goes well, with laughter and giggles all around. Eliza regards me, and Mairead and the De Graff sisters — them all decked out in feathers, tights, and net stockings — and offers the opinion, "Sometimes, it is good that my husband is blind, lest his attention wander."

Mairead laughs, then says, "Don't worry, Eliza, our Enoch may be blind, but he can see us in his mind's eye, clear as day." The Shantyman says nothing to that but merely smiles and tunes up his fiddle.

So the stage is built and the posters are tacked on every tree in town. We are all excited and ready to go — except, perhaps, for the cowardly star of the show. Oh well, I've faced tougher crowds. We shall see. The worst that could happen is that I'd be laughed off the stage and people would demand their dollars back. *Shudder* . . .

"Come all ye good gentlemen who appreciate the finest in the art of dance! The Montessori and Mattucci Grand Circus presents Tondalayo, the Queen of the Naked Nile! She walks, she talks, she wiggles on her belly like a snake! All in the best of artistic taste! Just one dollar, gents. Step right up! Do not be shy! There are still a few seats available. Thank you, Sir! I promise you won't regret it! Step right up!"

For my part, in my wagon, I have stripped down to my skin with Higgins's help and then emerge covered in his heavy opera cloak. It has a high collar and a single button at the neck. I position myself in the center of the stage behind the closed curtain and listen to Rigger O'Rourke's patter and the murmur of the crowd. I know the skimpily dressed De Graff sisters are standing to either side of him while he is giving his spiel outside the tent, to get the randy gents in the proper mood, like. An excited Mairead stands next to me, offering encouragement.

"It'll be just fine, Jacky, you'll see."

"Easy for you to say, Mairead. I'm the one who's standing here all starkers. Prolly fall on my face and disgrace myself." I am teetering on a pair of high-heeled shoes. I thought they might lend me a little in the way of leggy grace, but I dunno . . .

"Nonsense. You'll do fine. Here, let me fix your headdress," she says as she fiddles with the feathered thing that I wear upon my head, causing the hanging beads attached to it to brush my face. "There. Oops. There's my cue . . ."

We hear the deep throb of Eliza on the big drum — *boom chucka boom, boom chucka boom* — over and over.

"Break a leg, Jacky."

With that, she exits through the curtain, and presently I hear her short opening remarks . . .

"Good evening, gentlemen. I hope you are comfortable and will enjoy our little show . . ."

I just know the shameless hussy is out there prancing back and forth in her own skimpy costume. Somehow that calms me, though, and I have to smile.

"Fresh from the cold steppes of Russia to the hot harems of Morocco, from performing before the crowned heads of Europe to dancing before you tonight . . ."

C'mon, Mairead, let's get on with it.

"Without further ado, I give you Tondalayo, Queen of the Naked Nile!"

Mairead puts pennywhistle to lips and warbles that timeless snake-charmer tune. Yes, it's that same old "There's a place in France where the women wear no pants" song, but it works for this sort of thing in any language, in any land. The Shantyman picks up the sinuous tune on his fiddle, while Eliza continues the relentless jungle rhythm on the drum.

That's my cue. Higgins removes the cloak and I get down on my knees and sit back on my haunches, and cover my forward-facing self with my fans. It will be my theme — an opening flower, like. It's best if a performance has a theme, I figure.

The De Graffs pull the curtain aside, and a hush falls over the crowd as I am revealed, kneeling, in the torch light.

With my heart in my throat, I bow my head behind my top fan, eyes peering over it. The torches are not so bright that I cannot see the audience, and what I see in their shining eyes is pure male lust. Well, all right. I can handle that.

Slowly, slowly, I begin to rise, coming off my haunches to rest fully onto my knees, my hips and shoulders swaying in time to the music, my kohl-lined eyes still looking over the top of my upper fan. I try to make them smolder with unspoken promise, but I don't know if I succeed. Still, I hear a few gasps and one *magnifico!,* which has to come from Marcello, but he's a pushover and doesn't count.

I continue working my sensuous way up till I am standing on my feet. Making sure that my right hand's fan covers me from chin to crotch, I put the left hand's fan behind me. Then I begin Right Fan's slow descent till its top edge gets close to revealing my chest. At the very last moment, I quickly whip around and reverse the position of the fans such that Left Fan now covers my bum, but not my bare back. I turn my head enough to smile wickedly at the audience. Then slowly, ever so slowly, I lower Left Fan, till I sense that the tops of the feathers are just about to drop below the crack of my bum, when I turn around quickly and reverse again the fans in a blur of white fluff.

The audience draws in a common breath.

See anything, fellas? I think not. But if you did, then you have something to dream on, and I wish you the joy of it.

It is then that I loudly whisper-sing, all hot and sultry...

There's a place in France
Ver zee vicked ladies dance,
And zee dance vee do
Vill make a man out of you!

I snake out a white arm from behind the wall of feathers and point a finger at various faces glowing in the torch light, saying ... *and you ... and you ... and you!*

They seem to appreciate the gesture, so I sing on ...

I come from Mandalay-o
And I have a leetle mango!
Eef you like congo mumbo jumbo
Zen listen to zee bongos,
Eef you vant to see my mango
Zen watch your Tondalayo ...

And I stretch out the *Tonda-laaaaaaay-oh!* to good effect, I think, as I hear some cheers and whistles from the mob. So, warming to my task, I give a little hip bump on each *oh! Be good now, boys.*

A big lascivious wink, and then I do a reversal of the routine, fans flying about and my bare self in the middle of it all, which ends with me back on my knees again, enveloped in my faithful fans, like any frail flower surrounded by the purest of white petals . . . and then, with a final roll of the drum, it is done.

The curtain closes and Higgins emerges from the wings and wraps me once again in his big, black opera cloak. He takes my fans and retreats as the curtain parts again and I take my bows, being careful to hold the front of the cloak shut as I am enveloped by the applause.

And Lord help me, I love it so!

Then the curtain falls again, and I retreat through my wagon's door, to collapse onto my bed, gasping.

"Well done, Miss," says Higgins. "A credit to the art of erotic dance — high in promise but low in actual delivery. Very crafty. A glass of wine for your surely dry throat?"

"It is, indeed, Higgins, and thank you," I answer, rising to a sitting position and taking the glass. As I raise it to my lips, I hear Rigger O'Rourke outside, taking up the chant yet again ". . . *she walks, she talks, she crawls on her belly . . .*" and I groan and stand.

"Break a leg, Miss? I believe that is the term."

"Tell 'em she died with her fans on, Higgins," I say, and head back out.

We had a decent crowd for that first performance, a full house for the second, and standing-room only for the third and subsequent shows.

The word does get around.

Chapter 30

We go to five shows a night, and the public comes from all around. We are a success!

The principals of the Montessori and Mattucci Financial Division are in my wagon, as is our usual habit after we close down for the night, all sitting around gloating over the take — three solid nights, five shows a night! To say nothing of the regular take from the circus acts and midway attractions. There must be two thousand dollars on the table, in coin or in paper money. Higgins, of course, counts the take and enters the amount into his ledger. Rigger O'Rourke sits by the door, a large pistol on his lap, taking some refreshment, his boots up on the frame of my bed, where Mairead and I sit in a state of high girlish hilarity. I have ceased putting on the Russian accent with Rigger, but not with dear Marcello, as it amuses me to do it, and he is not one to trust with a secret.

We are going to turn south, and Higgins will be heading north in the morning, taking Mairead with him. I will hate to see her go, so I am enjoying my last night with my wild Irish Sister.

I sit with cloak fastened at neck, hands clutching the front tightly closed, both of us giggling.

"I really think you enjoy doing that dance, Jacky," she teases.

"Well, I do like giving one hundred percent when in performance," I reply primly. "Besides, you don't seem to mind prancin' around on the wings, shaking your bum. Hey, maybe I'll have you do it next time, see how you like it. Surely you know the routine by now."

"Sure, and I know I'd do it better than you if I did."

I give her a shove. "You're too fat. They'd see too much. You'd get arrested."

"Aye, and you're skinny as a stick. They don't see enough. Don't know why they even bother squintin' at your scrawny tail."

"Ah, but if you trotted yourself out there and did your duty to this fine circus, then husband Ian would surely beat the living hell out of you when he discovered that his lovely wife had been doin' a little hoochy-koochy dancing on the side. Hmmm?"

"My Ian's never laid nothing but a lovin' hand on me," she says, shaking her red mop. "But my father would just as surely do the job for him. Right after he killed you for getting me into it in the first place."

"Ha! That he would! I can feel Liam Delaney's strong hand on my poor bottom right now! Him roaring 'I should have never had nothin' to do with that Jacky Faber back on that damned *Dolphin*! Nothin' but big sorrowful eyes and a whole pack of trouble!'"

I collapse backward, choking with laughter.

"Och, but wouldn't it've been Mr. James Fletcher's hand

that would be comin' down on that well-deserving British tail?" says Mairead.

I sit back up.

"Well, maybe it would . . ." I say, considering his past history in that regard. "But maybe it would not," I continue in a wicked sultry voice, "*after* I gave him a *private* performance. A very private one."

"If I might intrude on this charming display of schoolgirl merriment . . . I would feel much better, Miss," advises Higgins, "if you had a more secure place to keep the circus treasury." Rigger nods agreement, but I am not convinced as to the wisdom of that.

"Now, Higgins, I have traveled with a band of Roma, and took personal instruction from Queen Bubya Nadya Vadoma, bless her old Gypsy soul . . ."

He has separated the money into stacks of coins and paper money. He has at hand a properly sized leather bag into which he dumps the coins. The bills are placed in a separate wallet and then thrust into the same bag, the sturdy drawstring tightened and taut.

". . . And I know how to hide stuff. Find stuff, too."

However, I do not get to hide anything . . . including myself, as two shotgun barrels are thrust into the open door.

I gasp in astonishment. Wot?

"Is this a private party, or may we also attend? My small friend here thought we might not be velcome," hisses Herr Udo von Arndt, smiling through his teeth as he and Emil Mussler enter my wagon. "O'Rourke! Put the pistol on the floor. I see it is not cocked, so you can do nussing. However, one false move and I shall shoot that girl over there and her chest shall match her hair. Emil! Tie up the girl! No, not that one! The Russkie, idiot!"

"Yes, boss," says Mussler, von Arndt's slimy little underling, leaning his gun against the wall and advancing on me, a short length of rope in his fist.

"You. Russian bitch. Get up. You're coming with us."

"What?" protests Higgins. "What for? You've got the money! Why take the girl?"

I shrink back and try to disappear.

"Sit down, big man," he says, "or I shall blow your leg off." Higgins sits. "I vill explain to you as soon as my man has accomplished his simple task. Move, damn you!" Emil is hurried in said task by his master's boot.

Thus encouraged, Mussler puts down his shotgun and reaches over and grabs me by the throat and drags me forward. The dwarf is small, but his hands are huge and his arms are strong. I have no choice but to follow along. As he ties my hands in front of me, the front of the cloak falls open and I am exposed.

"Ha! The harlot has no clothes. Good. Nussing to dispose of if she goes to the tigers." Satisfied with the dwarf's progress, the obviously self-satisfied von Arndt goes on to explain.

"It is because I haf need of a hostage, and the so-called owner of this circus vill do," he continues. "You see, there are four roads leading out of here, and I could be taking any of them — to Boston, to Philadelphia, to New York, to Baltimore. I know your man O'Rourke here will attempt hot pursuit and I can't shoot you all, much as I would enjoy that. If he happens to choose the right road, I'll need a hostage. If

I notice anyone following me out of here now, I will kill her. My tigers are very hungry. Hear them roar? *Very* hungry, as they haf not been fed for several days. They will devour the wretch in a moment, with no trace, except for a bit of blood, which any investigator would assume was drippings from the horse meat the tigers usually eat. Except the drippings will have come from her. A lovely thought, hmm? And don't forget that both Mussler and I are well armed. I am telling you all this so you will think twice about following me. Understand?" He points the barrel of his shotgun at Rigger's forehead.

Rigger says nothing to that, but merely glares at the German, his eyes full of level rage. *This ain't over yet, you kraut-eating son of a bitch!*

Seeing that Emil Mussler has finished tying my hands, von Arndt growls, "Goot. Go out and bring the wagon to the door. Now."

As the little man sidles out the door, the German places his hand on the fat money bag — *And could we have made it any easier for the rat bastard?* — saying with a big smile, "Ah, *ja,* dis *gelt* vill hold me in very goot stead, wherever I go."

Having made his point, von Arndt waves his barrel around by way of emphasis, pointing it in each remaining face in my once safe and comforting little wagon.

He picks up the end of my tether and hauls my despairing self roughly out the door and into yet another dark and fearful night.

Udo von Arndt has planned well. The dwarf brings the tiger wagon neatly up to my door and I am thrown onto the driver's seat between him and the mastermind of this plot. Unlike the usual position of the low seat of a buckboard, these circus wagons have the seats placed up high so that the one sitting there can make sure that all below is secure. What I can see as I look back is a small, three-foot-square hatch, with latch, which I know is used to drop raw meat down to Hans and Fritz, 'cause no one wants to open one of the bottom doors to feed that angry pair.

Von Arndt takes the reins, and we are off.

It gives me a shiver to think of myself disappearing down that hole, but I've got other things to think about . . .

We have not rumbled more than five miles down the highway when we come to a crossroads and von Arndt takes the right turn, which I know leads to New York. The road is hard and the wagon will leave no tracks that can be traced.

Damn! If I could but leave a marker for those who will follow, but alas, I cannot, for I have nothing! I am helpless!

Helpless, yes, but not without work to do. Under cover of the cloak, I work away at the binding on my wrists with the unbound tips of my fingers. It would go better if I could bring my teeth to bear, but they would catch me at that, so I cannot. Still, I pick away with frantic fingernails at the loose knot that the hasty Emil had tied. No sailor he, that's for sure.

Another three miles down the road and von Arndt's head jerks up. He has heard something! Horses' hooves pounding! Riders shouting!

"Damn! They are right behind us!" he yells. "We've got to get rid of the girl! Shove her down the hatch! Now!"

"Yes, Boss," says Mussler, grabbing me and pinning my upper arms tightly to my chest. Then he notices. "Boss, her hands are loose!"

"Doesn't matter, fool! Just get her down to zem, and the cats vill take care of her. Meanwhile, I vill slow down those who dare follow!"

With that, he turns, reins wrapped around his left fist, and with his right hand, he gets off a blind shot behind us with his shotgun. I hear no cry of anguish from either horse nor man, so I perceive that no one was hit by the scatter shot. I do sense, though, that it has slowed down my gallant posse a bit.

Emil Mussler, however, is having a bit of trouble shoving me down that particular rabbit hole, now that my hands are free — my lower arms, anyway. He still has my upper arms pinned as he wrestles me toward that dreaded hatch.

In spite of my struggles, he manages to get my head and shoulders shoved into the hole. *Damn! So strong!* I feel the horrid swish of a tiger paw sweep past my cheek. *Another inch and he'll snag me and pull me down!*

Higgins's cloak flies out behind me, its button still firmly fastened to my neck, the dwarf still attached to me, and I can no longer prevent my descent into that hellhole. My fingers loosen and I fall to my doom . . .

But it is not in quite the way I imagined it, for Mussler, more terrified of his master than he is of the tigers, continues to hold me tight to him.

We do not fall to the floor of the cage, however, for on our desperate way down through the hatch, my heavy cloak has caught its hem on the hatch hinge and remains securely hooked up there.

As a consequence, both I and my clinging dwarf are brought to a swift halt in midair, dangling above two very hungry Bengal tigers; Mussler by his hands, me by my poor neck . . .

I can't breathe! Good God, I can't breathe! His . . . his arms are too strong!

But before I pass completely out of this world, finally hanged for all my crimes and depredations, I receive some unbidden aid from Hans and Fritz, who conveniently bury two pairs of merciless claws into the back of Emil Mussler, him being the one facing the beasts, thanks to the swinging of the cloak. He lets go of me with a scream of . . .

Boss! Boss! Help me! Help . . .

But he receives scant pity from his boss. The only reply we hear from von Arndt is the sound of the overhead trap door being kicked shut by his boot. That's one less to split the money with, I am sure he figures, and one to blame the whole stupid mess on should he be caught with my blood on his hands. Whatever the reason, that's as far as his under-ling gets in this world. I hear a final whimper and then the sounds of bones cracking.

But the fate of one miserable dwarf is the least of my worries right now, as I am still strangling in that cloak, legs kicking and flailing wildly in the air. Now that Mussler's arms have released mine, and my poor neck does not have to bear his weight, I am able to get my fingers to that very strong button. *Don't pass out now, girl! One more moment! There!* It's done, and I fall to the floor, gasping.

Well, I ain't gonna hang after all, but I've still got two very big problems, and one of them is looking right at me.

I carefully, *carefully,* scoot farther back in the corner and test the width of the space twixt the bars to see if I might fit through. Maybe a cage fit to hold massive beasts might not be designed to hold a skinny girl. Here goes. *Unngh!* The head barely fits, along with the top of the shoulders, but I know the rest of me ain't gonna get through. *Damn! What to do? Just wait for a grisly and very painful death? Is this where it all ends for Jacky Faber?*

The tiger, which has been casting its black eye upon my poor body, gets to a crouch and takes a tentative step toward me.

No! Think! What, what? Then, crazily, the deep voice of Jemimah Moses slips into my terrified mind. *"Come now, girl, you can't give up now. Think on that clever ole Brother Rabbit. When he find hisself in trouble, what he do? You said it before when you said 'rabbit hole.' Give you any ideas, Sister Girl?"*

Think! Think! Of course! Brother Rabbit! That tale Jemimah told on that last voyage of the Nancy B. *The rabbit was in jail and about to get hanged in the morning, but still he got out of it! How? By getting the Sheriff to grant him a whole pile of roasted peanuts as his last meal. But that crafty rabbit didn't eat those goobers. No, he crushed 'em up in a greasy pile and then rubbed the slop all over his body. He wriggled his slippery self right through those bars and went on his rabbity way!*

Course I ain't got no greasy goobers, and I don't think the cold sweat that covers my body is quite gonna do it . . . but I spy something that might . . .

Just outside the bars to my right spins the rear wheel, and on the inside of it is a big glob of axle grease. Frantic, I reach out and pick up a goodly hunk of it on my outstretched fingertips and haul it in, and begin to spread it over my chest. That done, I slap the remainder over my hipbones and tail. Then my greasy palms smear it over my chosen bars and I am ready to proceed.

Here goes . . . First the chest . . . *There!* Glad there's not too much of me there, and that part slips right through. *Now for the rest! Little bit more . . . shove! Ugh!* The buttocks bunch up and then . . . *Yes!* Bum and legs are through and I am out! I reach up to grab the bars on the outside and swing out. And just in time, for a large paw with wicked claws extended comes snaking out after me.

I look to the side of the road and see nothing but harsh gravel down there . . . *But wait!* There are some bushes coming up and they look a helluva lot softer than that crushed stone, so I send up a quick prayer and launch myself into the night.

I hit the rougher-than-they-looked shrubs with barely an *oof!* so I am reasonably sure von Arndt did not hear me depart, as his wagon clatters off down the road. Then all is silence as I contemplate my situation: I am naked, and have no tools to rectify that situation . . . except my bare hands . . .

. . . and with those hands I begin to rip branches off the bushes, hoping I have not landed in a patch of poison ivy. My plan? It is simply this: I shall cover my nakedness with fronds of the local flora, sleep as best I can through the night, and, at dawn, creep down to a neighboring farmhouse and beg the lady of the house for help.

Y'see, Mum, I'm in a bit of a pickle here, as you can plainly see, and iffen you could help me out, I'm sure you would be amply rewarded . . . But wait . . . Someone's coming . . .

There is a great hue and cry from my left, and a gang of men on horseback come roaring by. I crouch down as the riders surge past, led by a grimly determined Rigger O'Rourke. As soon as I recognize them as my own lads, I rise up. They do not notice me, in all the dust and turmoil of the chase, and charge on after their quarry. But how did Rigger know which road to take?

Oh, well, I'm thinkin', *I'll find out later. Back to plan A. At least I'm still alive, and that's something.* I tear at some more branches. But wait . . . *What's this?*

Presently, I'm hearing a much softer voice calling out in the night.

With joy in my heart, I recognize Higgins's voice. He is riding in the buckboard, stopping every twenty yards or so to call out, "Miss Faber? Are you there? Hello, Miss Faber?"

Hooray!

When he pulls abreast of my bushes, I leap out and crawl up beside him on the low seat.

"Good to see you, Higgins," I say, breathless.

"The feeling is mutual, Miss," he replies, unruffled as usual. "There is a blanket behind you, should you feel the need for it." The moon is out and it is apparent that I am definitely in need of such covering.

"Thanks, Higgins," I say, reaching back and gathering the woolly thing about myself. "I seem to constantly require additional cover as I stumble my way through this world, don't I?"

"Indeed, Miss, that does seem to be the case, if past experience is any guide," he says, and I know he is smiling at that. "And I figured that this case will not be all that different."

He is interrupted by the sound of shots and cries from far up the road. Obviously, the posse has caught up with von Arndt and the wagon full of tigers.

"I sure hope things go well up there," I say, shivering a bit under my welcome cover as we turn and head for home. Besides Rigger, I recognized Marcello and other dear friends in that mob of riders, and I fear for their safety — that evil shotgun of von Arndt's and all. "But how did you know this was the route the rotten bastard would take? And I know it was you, so don't deny it."

I lift a grease-streaked eyebrow in question at my rescuer.

"As factotum of the Montessori and Mattucci Circus, I receive all the mail. Before distributing the posts, I took the liberty of steaming open von Arndt's, believing him to be a security risk." Our ever-wise Higgins sniffs. "I noticed he had opened an account at a New York bank. I knew he would go there to process his ill-gotten gains. Stupid of him not to have thought of that."

"But very smart of you, dear Higgins," I say. "If I was not covered with axle grease, I would give you a mighty hug."

"Well, perhaps later, Miss, after a nice bath, we will . . ."

Presently, we hear riders behind us. Higgins stops the rig and pulls out his pistols and we wait, me with bated breath. I exhale when the leader of the riders comes into view. It is Rigger, holding up the bag of money and grinning in relief at seeing me safe and sound. "Hey, rube," he calls out triumphantly, "I lost the money but I got it back, just like I said I would."

"And so you did, Rigger, and we thank you for it," I say, the gratitude plain in my voice. "You saved the Montessori and Mattucci, for sure." Poking my head out of my protective blanket, I ask, "What's happening back there?"

"The boys are cleaning out the cage as best they can. We

stopped by a tidal stream up the road apiece. Buckets of fresh saltwater sloshed over the wagon floor should clean things up nicely." He laughs. "I'm sure Tad and Jerry had no idea of the jobs they would be doing when they signed up with us, but they are willing lads. The cats are very quiet now, having eaten their fill, so they will not bother them."

"And Herr Udo von Arndt, Wild Animal Trainer himself? Did he put up a fight?"

"A short one. He tried to outrun us, but he could not outrun our bullets. He shall train no more animals," Rigger says with a snort, "except maybe gangs of imps in hell. Here's his whip. He has no more use of it." He tosses the braided lariat in the back of the buckboard. "We shoved him down that hole in the top of the wagon and heard no more from him. I think he might have been still alive when he went in, but I don't know for sure. Don't care, neither."

Higgins chucks the horse, slapping the reins lightly on the horse's rump, to push on back to camp.

Somewhat chastened by my carelessness, which led to this whole wild night, I say quietly, "That was lucky, you know, Higgins. He could have gone in another direction."

"Yes, I know," says Higgins thoughtfully. "But if I was wrong, what was lost, after all? A wagon, two tigers, some money, and a very wayward and impulsive young woman — all easily replaced, except, perhaps, for the latter."

I reach over and hug him to me, grease be damned, and say . . .

"I know, Higgins. I love you, too."

Chapter 31

"The other arm, Miss, if you would," says Higgins as he soaps me up for what will surely be the last time on this trip. Come morn, he will head north to Boston with Mairead in tow, and I and the Montessori and Mattucci Grand Circus will go to New Bedford, set up the show, and then turn south toward warmer climes. He must consult with Ezra Pickering as to the status of that ridiculous charge against my name, and Mairead has to get back to her husband. And I have to let her go, however delightful I might find her company.

Soon the axle grease is history, as are thoughts of this awful night of blood and slaughter.

Ahhh . . .

Higgins, however, interrupts my reverie with a cautious observation while he works on my hair. "You know, Miss, in reviewing your past, I must make the following observation. Number one, there was the pirate Le Fievre who first laid a noose around your neck on that beach in South America. Then it was the demented Reverend Mather who was thwarted in his attempt to strangle the life out of you. That's two. After that, while we were abroad on the Mississippi, the slave hunters Pap Beam and sons had you mounted on back of that horse, with the cruel rope tight about your throat. Furthermore, when you were with Bonaparte in Germany, you were captured and stood up before a Prussian firing squad, from which you were miraculously delivered. That's four, I believe."

I think he is counting off on his fingers . . .

"And then there was that moray eel that attempted to end your life under the warm but dangerous waters of the Caribbean Sea. To say nothing about Professor Tilden's Diving Bell with its own peril, nitrogen narcosis, which did bend your poor body most cruelly, almost to the point of death. That's six, at least. Then, while on the *Lorelei Lee* and bound for the prison colony in New South Wales in Australia, you did kneel beneath the razor-sharp sword of Cheng Shih, the notorious female Chinese pirate, expecting nothing more than that your head should fall to her deck. I think that's seven, and then there was the terrible storm in the Straits of Malacca and the encounter with an earlier striped beast. That makes eight, and now the incident with the stubborn cloak makes nine."

He pauses to let that sink in, then continues, "Do you take my point, Miss Faber?"

"That I have used up all of my nine lives, Higgins?" I sniff. "Silly superstition, as I am not a cat."

"There are certain similarities, Miss, so I would be careful were I you, and stay away from any trouble that looks like it might lead to a noose. Better your luck stretched, rather than your neck."

Amen to that, Higgins, and believe me, I shall be most careful.

"Very well, up with you now. Time for bed."

Ah, yes, bed, delicious bed!

As I burrow down into the comforting covers into which Mairead has long since snuggled, my mind rejects the events of the night and turns to much warmer thoughts of one James Emerson Fletcher . . . oh, yes.

G'night, luv.

Chapter 32

Things were going well at the Montessori and Mattucci Grand Circus, and I was growing quite comfortable in my new role as circus impresario. After all, I got room and board, pleasant accommodations, good company, and the adulation of the crowd. What more could I want? Yes, put me at the center of attention, wherever I am, and I shall be happy. True, I itch to get back to Boston and await Jaimy's return, but this is all right for now. Food's good, too.

After seeing Higgins and Mairead off with promises of joining them again in the spring, if not sooner, we have moved on from Wareham and are set up at New Bedford, Massachusetts, and I am glad of that. Even though Edgar Polk had said he would not peach on me, I feel better being some distance from Plymouth.

I have appointed Rigger O'Rourke factotum, as he seems most qualified. Furthermore, he has been told he is to take over as manager in the event of my sudden departure. I have furnished him with the checkbook and the address of Faber Shipping Worldwide, and said that I expect the circus to pay. He nods and smiles, especially when I tell him he will receive ten percent off the top for his services.

When we do head south, I will drop the Fan Dance. There are too many Bible thumpers down there, so why take a chance for another dose of tar and feathers? I had enough of that the last time I was down in the slave states, that's for sure. I swear I'm still pulling black stuff out of my ears.

That's not to say we don't have our wicked fun at the old M and M. Sometimes when one of the local boys has a bit of a snootful at our bar and refuses to leave at closing time and then very inconveniently passes out blissfully on the back lot, we take up his limp form and toss him in old Balthazar's cage. It is my firm belief that we have converted many a worthless drunk into a teetotallin' Preacher of the Gospel overnight. I have personally seen the light of the Reborn sparkle in their rheumy eyes when they wake up in the morning and, instead of seeing pink elephants and such, find themselves in a locked cage containing a full-grown male African lion. Balthazar is kept well fed and doesn't mind a little human company, so sometimes a miscreant wakes up with a sunburn and massive leonine arm thrown over his chest. The awakening scream doesn't bother Balthazar a bit. He just yawns his mighty yawn, but we all get a real kick out of it.

I had been in New Bedford before, back in '03, right after I had fled the Lawson Peabody School for Young Girls in a panic, leaving it and a good deal of Boston in flames behind me. I wasn't here for long because it was in this seagoing town that I signed on as crew on the whaler *Pequod* to gain passage back to England. But that's another story . . .

• • •

It is on the second day of our stay in New Bedford, during the afternoon show, when — *Joy!*—from my aerialist perch high above the ring, I spy none other than the uplifted faces of Ezra Pickering and my dear friend Amy Trevelyne, who are sitting below to catch the show. What a fine holiday for them, and what an excellent opportunity for me to show off.

It warms my heart to see them together, and I plan to give them a really good show, with extra thrills and chills thrown in for their benefit.

Ha! And wait till Amy catches my Famous Fan Dance! Oh, won't that be grand? I can't wait!

And then, my eye catches something else out of the ordinary down below, something much more ominous, something that sends a chill up my spine and causes the hair on the back of my neck to stand up in warning. Thoughts of a joyful reunion with dear friends are now completely dashed . . .

A number of men in similar black suits and hats have mixed with the crowd. Although there's nothing remarkable in that, as most males who are not soldiers dress in somber colors these days, these men seem to have a singular concern in mind. They confer with one another, looking up at me when they do so. *Uh-oh* . . . And a pair of them have nonchalantly posted themselves at the exit. They are not being very subtle, which means they think they've got their quarry well in hand. *Damn.*

Marcello Grimaldi's feet land lightly on the platform next to me, his act over, while mine is about to begin.

"Marcello, if you luff me," I say, "you vill do some-zing for me . . ."

"Oh, I do love you, Anuschka, my little Russian pastry,

as I love my own life. Just name the deed and I will do it. You wish a triple somersault? Very well, even though it has never been done before and will cost me my life, I shall attempt it gladly. Goodbye, my love. I will see you in heaven." He takes my hand and kisses the back of it. Then he grabs the trapeze bar as it swings back to him, as if he is actually going to attempt the impossible trick.

"No foolink now, Marcello, beloved idiot," I say, putting my hand on his arm as he takes his bows and prepares to leave the platform. "Do not look down, but do you not see zose mens in dark suits at zee entrance and at zee foot of zee tent pole? And now zere are two at zee exit."

"*Sí, mi amore,* I do," he answers, glancing out of the corner of his eye.

"Zey mean to do me great harm, Marcello," I say. "Great harm to my person."

"Then I shall go down and kill them, my Flower of the Steppes."

"No, Marcello, you shall not do zat zing. Vat you mus' do is go down and get for me a goot horse. Get zat Furio. Yes, he is goot horse, and I vant zat you should put a saddle on him and tie on my bag, which is right next to my bed, to zee back of it. Zen lead him behind zee animal cages for ven I come down. Zen you must go avay from zere, for zey must not see you helping me. It vould cause you much trouble!"

"You will go away, Tsarina? I could not stand the pain—"

"Zey vill hurt me much more zan you can imagine. Zey mean to kill me, and zen I vill be of no use to you or anyone else. Please, *caro mio,* you must do as I ask. *Please.*"

He still looks doubtful, so I take his face in mine and say, "Vun kiss, Marcello, vun kiss to remember me by."

And I give him a kiss, full on the lips, a *real* kiss, something I have not yet done with him, to show him just how serious I am.

There is a quiet hum from the crowd upon viewing this unscheduled performance, but I can't care about that now.

I take my mouth from his and say, "Go now, and goodbye. I love you, *amico,* very much in my vay. *Addio, Marcello. Ricordati di me!*"

Stunned and amazed, he turns and grasps his trapeze bar. With one last look back at me, he swings out, releases, and does his landing in the net. He bounces up, takes a very quick bow, then heads for the stage exit. In a moment he is gone.

"Ladies and gentlemen!" roars out Ringmaster Generalissimo Pietro through his speaking trumpet. "Your attention is directed high, *high* up in the very center of the tent where stands, *direct* from the Royal Russian Circus of Moscow, performing *without* a net, our very own Princess Natasha Annasova Romanoff, death-defying Queen of the High Wire!"

Hearing Ringmaster Mattucci announce my act, I strike a pose, bow to the audience, and pick up the balance bar. Then I put my foot on the wire and head out.

I get halfway over before I steal another glance below. I see that two of the suspicious men are talking to the ringmaster at the side of the center ring. They all look up at me. Maestro Pietro angrily shakes his head *No!* and points his finger at the entrance, plainly telling them to get the hell out of our circus. But one of the men takes out some papers and shows them to him. I do not let on that I have noticed. I serenely look out over the crowd, elegantly posed, but actually I am anything but serene.

Good God, they have found me! But how? Edgar, did you . . . ?

No time for that now. Got to get away.

I do the first few tricks and then notice that Strongman Gregor, guarding the stage entrance, has been joined by several men, also in dark suits. These men, however, wear long white riding dusters over their clothing, like they intend to ride. Prolly with my poor self bound and thrown across the saddle. Gregor shoves them back, but they do not go away.

I get to the other platform, drop my bar, lift my arm, and bow for some applause. After I get it, I pull off my skirt, drawing the usual gasp from the crowd, and head back out on the wire — and, yes, I can see Amy has buried her face in her hands. I further notice that two of the men have gone to the foot of the main tent pole to stand exactly where I will have to come down.

I do my fake fall followed by several flips, regain my feet on the wire, and walk slowly to the end. I take my final bows, and I know they are the final ones, indeed. I put my hand on the main top rope, the one I usually slide down . . .

And I begin to climb *up*, up toward the light at the top of the tent.

There is a hush from the crowd, thinking this must be a further part of the performance, but the men below don't believe that. I hear cries of *"Look out!"* *"Get her!"* *"She's goin' out the top!"*

And indeed I am. This thick line extends to a pulley at the top of the tent, and is the rope that pulls the heavy canvas up. It takes twenty men and an elephant to do it, too, so the rope is as taut as a bowstring. It is easy to climb, for did I not grow up in the rigging of a very tall ship?

It takes me about thirty seconds to reach the hole in the top. Sticking my head out into the brilliant sun, I blink and look down the broad expanse of canvas lying below me.

Over on the back lot I see that Marcello has saddled up Furio, but instead of tying him up and fleeing as I told him, the lovely fool stands there holding the reins and waiting for me. Can he not see the hard-faced men on horseback who are encircling the back lot?

From below there is the sound of two pistol shots, one right after the other, and there is a *poof! poof!* as two round holes appear in the canvas, one on either side of me.

Damn! This sure ain't the British Admiralty wantin' me for some sort of questioning, or to stand trial for piracy. No, these people mean to take me either alive or stretched out dead in a wagon, and it doesn't seem to matter to them either way!

I pull myself out of the opening, do a somersault on the stiff canvas, lift my feet, and slide down on my rump, leaving, I am sure, more than a few bright sequins in my wake. I hit the edge of the tent, vault over, and land on my feet, then run toward my waiting horse, my only slim chance of escape.

And a forlorn hope it is, I realize with sinking heart, for there, all about, are mounted men, some of them in police uniform, but all of them very plainly armed with pistol and rifle. Even as I run, I see several pull out weapons from their saddle holsters.

Oh, dear God, is it all to end right here for Jacky Faber, to be shot down like a mad dog, to be left a limp rag of flesh and bone, bleeding out her life on this dusty piece of ground?

Not yet it ain't.

I run for Marcello and the horse, but as I sense the weapons aimed at me, I cut sharply to the right and dive under the lion's cage, grabbing the key on my way under. I hear several shots, and dust is kicked up next to me, but they serve nothing except to startle the beast within.

Picking up the wagon tongue, which lies tucked between the wheels, I give the bottom a few sharp raps to further alert Balthazar, and then roll the rest of the way to the front of the cage, shouting, *"Roar, Balthazar, roar!"*

And he does, oh, yes, he does. The deep rumbling that comes out of his throat, a sound that has terrified countless creatures for millions of years, is heard by the horses upon which my tormentors sit, and they start to whinny and shy, spoiling their riders' aim.

Then I open the cage, and mighty Balthazar, king once again of the land around him, leaps out, shakes his massive black mane, and gives out a truly magnificent roar.

All the horses shriek in terror, bucking and spilling their riders to the ground, and charging off in all directions, any direction, save the one anywhere near that awful lion. True, Balthazar has no teeth, but they do not know that.

I roll back under the cage, then quickly get up and run to Marcello and the horse he holds. Furio, being a circus horse, is familiar with Balthazar's scent and has heard his roar many times, so he is not as skittish as the others. Well, *almost* not as skittish, for his eyes roll about in his head as he eyes the loose lion. I am upon his back before he can flee without me.

"Goodbye again, Marcello," I say, the reins in my hand. "You should not have waited here, but I thank you for it anyway. Fare thee well, *compadre*."

"Circus people watch out for their own," he says simply, tears welling up in his big brown eyes, as well as in mine. *"Addio, Tsarina. Ti amo moltissima."*

He gives Furio a slap on his rump as I dig in my heels, and I am gone, leaping the back-lot rope and once again pounding across the American countryside . . .

. . . And I swear I hear, above all the tumult, Amy Trevelyne's voice crying out, "Oh, Jacky, no!" as she has so many times before.

Chapter 33

I know they're back there somewhere, probably only a half hour behind—that's how long I figure it would've taken them to recover their horses after Balthazar had spooked them. I hope they didn't hurt the poor old thing in getting him back into his cage. I didn't hear any gunshots, so maybe they didn't. I know I am so very hard on my friends, and I wish I were otherwise, but seldom am.

Luckily, I have not yet encountered anyone on this road, anyone who might think it strange that a young girl would be galloping along a country road wearing only a very small corset, white stockings, and ballet shoes. *So far, so good.*

Furio is a game horse and he pounds bravely on, but he is beginning to froth and sweat, so I must slow down to a walk for a bit, to give him a breather. Trouble is, the land around here is mostly open farmland and I have scant places to hide. My only hope is to outpace them till I can get to the sea, where I can buy or steal a small boat and so get away. The sea has always been my salvation, and I know it is only about twenty miles to the south of me.

It's so close, I can smell it.

I reach the top of a high hill and dismount, to let Furio graze and rest for a bit while I go into my seabag and pull out my long glass. There is a large boulder by the side of the road, and I climb up on it and put the glass to my eyes to look down on the road behind me. I am cheered when I see nothing . . . *But, wait* . . . Is that a cloud of dust behind that far hill? I squint and hope that it is not, but no, it is them.

Damn!

I jam the spyglass back in my bag and take up the reins again.

"C'mon, Furio, let's go!" I swing up on him and away we gallop. *If I can just make it to the sea!*

But we do not gallop for long. In a few minutes, I notice the horse's gait change. In another moment, I realize he is favoring his left rear leg. In yet another minute, he whinnies and pulls up lame.

I leap off him, then pull up his hoof, and see disaster written there. He has thrown a shoe. The nails have worked loose and the horseshoe barely clings to his bloody foot. It must be paining him awfully.

I look about me and see a small farm down the side of the hill to the left. I dive back into my bag to dig out my shiv, which I use to pry the shoe all the way off his foot. I fling the now useless piece of iron into the high grass next to the road, then strip the saddle and my seabag from the poor horse's back. I carry the saddle a few yards into the bushes and hide it. Going back to Furio, I tie the reins behind his neck and point his head at the barn down below.

"Go, Furio! Down there! They'll take care of you! Go!"

Then I give him the biggest hand swat on his hindquar-

ters that I can, and he grunts and starts limping down toward the farm, where I am sure he smells oats and warm hay
and others of his kind. And won't that farmer be delighted
to find a prime, ownerless horse in his barnyard?

*Enough of happy farmers, you. They're right behind you
and you've got to move on!*

I pick up my seabag, throw it over my shoulder, and
head across a field to the right. I see there is a fringe of forest
up there and it may be the beginning of yet a bigger growth
of trees. If I can make that, and there proves to be deeper
woods beyond, then I should be all right, for they will not be
able to follow me on horseback through dense forest.

To think I'm prolly only about thirty miles from dear
old Dovecote right now, forty-five from Boston and the Pig
and the Lawson Peabody, and from Amy and Ezra and
Clementine and Jim and Rebecca and Randall and all the
people I love in this world and those who love me and . . .
*Stop that, you! Stop your crying—it won't do you any good!
Push on, push on!*

As I hurry across the field, I am careful to close the
grass behind me, so as to leave no evidence of my passage. I
walk on rocky soil when I can, and when I can't, I make sure
to take a branch from a tree and rub out any footprints I
might leave.

The little stand of trees does prove to lead to a larger
forest, and for this I am profoundly grateful. *Thank you,
God, for this very great favor.*

When I am deep in the woods, I get my compass from
my seabag and set my course due south. I think about
changing clothes, but, no, I can run much better in this rig.

I do throw my ballet slippers into the bag, though, as they are already ragged. I have always run better on my bare feet, and I cannot risk a blister from shoes.

I'm off again, going south, ever south, except when I have to detour around brambles and deep ravines. My sea-bag grows heavy.

After about an hour of this, I discover a narrow road, just large enough for a single wagon, if that, cutting through the woods and heading south. Maybe it's an old Indian trail leading to the sea? Sure, they would often leave their inland encampments to fish and to gather clams, wouldn't they? I'm hoping it is just that.

I decide to follow it, at least for a while, 'cause I'll make better time on its smooth surface than I would back in the thick woods. I can hop back in the woods should I hear anyone coming, but all I hear now is the birds, which is very, very good.

The sun is beginning to set, so I must make plans for the night. I could try walking in the dark on the path, but I am dog-tired. It is spring and the day has been very long. Must be about nine o'clock, maybe later.

I decide to leave the road and strike out again into the woods. The path may be narrow, but men on horseback could easily travel on it, and travel fast — a lot faster than I.

It is much darker in the depths of the woods, and I stumble over branches several times. I've got to stop soon but . . .

Push on, girl, just a little farther!

Making myself trudge onward, I soon come upon a

babbling little brook, and a delightful sight it is. Giving thanks, I drop to my knees and drink deeply of the wondrously cool water. When my thirst is slaked, I look out across the brook. It is about twenty feet across, and shallow, which is good, there being nice, flat stones poking up through the surface all the way across. Picking up my bag, I easily cross to the other side.

There is a slight clearing here, and here I will stay the night. Opening my seabag, I put my compass back in it and pull out my cloak. I also get out my leather sheath that has my shiv in it and strap it around my forearm. Then, digging deeper, my hand finds the package of dried meat and pemmican I always keep there, a practice I picked up from my Indian friends.

I squat down cross-legged, the cloak over my shoulders, and eat, grateful for the food and thinking of Crow Jane, she who taught me how to salt and dry the meat so it would not spoil, and how to preserve the berries, rice, and other bits in thick tallow to make the pemmican.

Yes, dear, rough Crow Jane . . . are you still working the big river? Chee-a-quat, are you now a powerful chief? You should be. And Lightfoot and Katy Deere, where are you now? Have you gone across the mighty mountains and gazed upon the Pacific Ocean?

And where are you now, Tepeki, you who welcomed me into your tribe and named me Wah-chinga. Well, I, for one, Sister, am running like the crazy rabbit you named me after. I hope you have found a good man and that the rice harvest is plentiful and the hunting is good, and that you have peace and are happy . . .

Having eaten, I curl up in my cloak, using my seabag as a pillow yet again. It seems that the Jacky Faber luck is holding, at least for now. Tomorrow, the sea, and, it is to be hoped, salvation.

Good night, Jaimy. I pray you are safe. Please hurry back, as I am in much need of rescue.

Chapter 34

Ahhhwhoooooo! Ahhhhhwhooooooo! Ahhhhwhooooooo!

My eyelids fly open and I am on my feet. *Dogs! They've got dogs on me now!*

I shake the cobwebs from my mind. *Think, girl, think! If they catch you, they will kill you! Think!*

I'm guessing they're about a mile or two behind me now, and I gotta do something to throw them off my trail. Maybe the creek will save me.

Leaving my seabag on the bank, I run maybe a hundred yards away from the creek, deep into the woods. Then I stop at an open, rocky stretch and then retrace my steps, back to the stream, knowing the hounds will blindly follow my scent to that dead end, and be at a loss. *Where did she go, where did she go?* That's what they'll be thinking in their little doggie brains, snuffling about in the brush. The men with them know the dogs have lost the scent and will look up into the trees and point their guns there, thinking I might have taken that route, but no, I have not.

After getting back to the brook, turning over a few

rocks and breaking a few twigs in the upstream direction, I pick up my bag, turn, and wade downstream, careful not to dislodge any pebbles, touch any branches, or do anything that might leave my scent behind.

Downstream is the direction to the sea, and it is to the sea that I must go.

Wahwah-Whoooooo! Wahwah-Whooooooo! Ohhhh-whoooooooo!

They must be at the woodland road now, ready to plunge back into the woods, to the stream and, it is to be hoped, confusion.

I keep wading on down the center of the stream. Were it deeper, I could lie back and float with the current, but it never gets deeper than my knees. *Push on, push on!*

Wahwah-whooo! Wah-oooo! Wah . . . yap . . . yap . . . yap . . .

Aha! They have followed the false trail! I can hear the doubt in the dogs' voices. *Stay there, doggies! Be good and stay there! Push on, girl, push on!*

I wade as fast as I can, but the footing is not easy. Many times I go down, painfully, to hit my knees on the hard bottom, but still I press on. Suddenly, the stream widens, and then, just as quickly, the woods end and the brook pours out into an open field. I am startled by the bright light, so I stand blinking for a few moments, and then, *Oh, God, there is the sea! The beautiful sea!*

The sandy beach, the sparkling surface of the water, the gentle waves breaking on the shore lie not more than two miles away at the base of sloping fields of corn and wheat and rye. It's an easy run. I gallop joyfully down through the rows of corn toward the glorious ocean.

I am a good third of the way there when I hear a sound that chills me to the bone.

Bay-oooooooooo. Bay-oooooooo-ooooooooooo!

Damn! Sounds like one is still after me, still on my trail! How could he be back on me so fast?

I increase my speed, thinkin' that damned hound's got a different sound than the others. I stumble, fall, and get up again, to keep on running, and I —

Wooo-woooo-wha-hooooooooo! Yew got 'er now, boy! Git 'er ass!

He's gotta be clear of the woods, too, 'cause I can hear the dog's handler clear as day. I'm halfway to the sea now, and the air is ripping through my chest and it hurts, but *I can smell the salt! I gotta get there! I'll jump in and swim! I don't care if I drown, but I just gotta get there.* Then I do somethin' I ain't ever done before. I drop my seabag and run. *Just run, run for the shore! If I get there, I'll just swim out. I don't care anymore. I'll just swim out till I sink. I don't care! I'll take the swallow of salt 'cause I really don't care. Just leave me alone! Please leave me alone. Let me die if I have to, but, please, just leave me alone! Leave . . .*

Now I can hear hoofbeats behind me, and the sound of dog paws hitting the dirt. Then there is the panting of his breath, and he ain't howling no more 'cause he's got me in sight. Closer and closer, and now my ankle twists and I am down. I'm on hands and knees in the dirt, crawling for the shore. The dirt changes to sand 'neath my hands but the hot breath of the dog is upon me and I am down, down in the sand, not thirty yards from the water.

A heavy foot is clamped on my neck.

"Yew think that fake trail could fool ol' Jimbo, here?

Shee-it! He's chased down a whole passel of badasses a lot more cunnin' than you. Should've dipped down in that crick, girl, scrubbed the sweat offa yew, when yew had the chance. That's what ol' Jim Bob picked up on. He could smell your sweat and your fear. He caught it on the wind, not on the ground. Didn't know old Jim Bob could do that, did you, girlie? But you did it, didn't you, boy? Tha's right, you a good boy, Jimmy. You're the best, fer sure. Hee, hee . . . You 'member that next time, girl . . . 'Cept, from what I heard, there ain't gonna be no next time fer yew. Too bad 'cause yew run us a good'un, yew did."

Old Jimbo doesn't bite me. No, he licks the tears from my face and smiles his bloodhound smile, the game being over for him. But he has killed me all the same, sure as if I were a fox, a raccoon, or a possum up a tree.

There is a rattle of hoofbeats and rough hands are once again put upon me and I am pulled to my feet to be taken away.

And I know, with a cold, dread certainty deep in my soul, that this will be the last time I will ever be thus taken.

PART IV

Chapter 35

Journal of Amy Trevelyne
Plymouth, Massachusetts

They brought up my friend Jacky Faber from New Bedford, where she had been captured, to put her in jail next to the courthouse. It's in the town of Plymouth, which also functions as the seat of Plymouth County. This location had been decided by the state and federal authorities, who, Ezra Pickering believes, wanted to avoid riots in Boston instigated by firebrands in that city who take to the streets over any sensational trial—especially this one, for the newspapers have whipped the populace into a fine froth. The war fever runs high, and it is a frightening thing to witness—English and American blood will be spilled, to slake the thirst of the warmongers, and it will be spilled soon, I just know it, and I despair.

I was not yet in the town of Plymouth, but I heard later that Jacky's captors had paraded her through the intervening towns in an open wagon so that the populace could jeer at her on the way. Cries of "Traitor!" and "Murderer!" and

"Hang her!" were heard from the crowds. She was placed on a high seat with her hands bound behind her, and even though the agents who apprehended her were in possession of her seabag, she was not permitted to change into more modest clothing than what she was wearing at the time of her arrest. Thus, she was displayed, bare-shouldered and bare-limbed, in her scanty circus costume. There were reports that objects as well as insults were thrown. Such needless cruelty, I say. I have nothing but the deepest disgust for the majority of my fellow human beings.

It was also reported that she sat with what is described as a look of haughty arrogance upon her face while maintaining a composed silence throughout the disgraceful journey. Her composure was broken but one time, when a rock thrown by a boy caught her on the cheek. Then she did cry out in pain and despair and let her head fall forward for a time before she recovered her composure.

I came down to Plymouth by coach, while an enraged Randall rode on ahead. Since learning of her arrest, he has been sinking deeper into drink, and by the start of her trial had already torn up several local taverns. His engagement to his beloved Polly Von does not seem to have tempered his rage. She has pleaded with him, most eloquently, for calm, but to no avail; he seems a man possessed. I worry for her, as well as for him, and I long for our once calm and ordered world.

Upon arriving in the town, I went immediately to the jail where she was confined and met Mr. Pickering on his way out. He doffed his hat and greeted me most warmly.

"How is she?" I asked.

"She is bearing up quite well, considering, Miss Trevelyne, and we are both supremely confident that we will beat this false charge." Ezra's voice said those words, but his worried eyes told a far different story. He did not wear his usual merry smile.

"We must pray that it will be so, Mr. Pickering," I said. "I will go to see her now."

"And I will go to prepare our case. Good day to you, Miss Amy."

"Thank you, Ezra. Godspeed your efforts. Good day."

I was led into the prison by a Deputy Cole and introduced to Sheriff O. T. Williams, who then led me through a heavy outer door that he unlocked, then into a narrow corridor that held six cells, three to either side. Jacky Faber was in the second cage to the left. The Sheriff chose yet another key from the ring he wore at his waist and unlocked the door.

She was seated on a bed, her head down, obviously deep in thought. There is a tiny window near the ceiling, letting in just enough light so that she might read the Bible that lies beside her. She was wearing a drab gray prison dress, a smock really, and to see her so reduced and so confined nearly tore out my heart.

Upon looking up and seeing me, she gave out a cry of joy. "Oh, Sister, I am so glad to see you!" she exclaimed, and held out her arms and tried to stand to embrace me. Alas, she was thwarted by her ankle shackle, which was anchored by a heavy chain running to an iron ring set in the stone floor. I made as if to go to her, but was stopped by Sheriff Williams, who told me I must confine myself to the bench on the other side of the cell and not get near the prisoner. The Deputy would keep watch to make sure that all was kept proper.

I went to the bench and sat down, my heart in my throat.

Entry dated November 6, 1809 — signed by Amy Trevelyne

Chapter 36

"So how are you, Amy?" I ask, sitting up and giving her my best open-mouthed foxy smile, which I know she has despaired over so much in the past for its lack of ladylike demureness. I hope it will cheer her now, for I purely hate to see her like this.

"I am f-f-fine, Jacky. I—I—I . . . Oh, this is all just so horrible! I . . ."

She buries her face in her hands, her body wracked with sobs.

"Now, now, Sister, I have been in worse scrapes before and gotten out of them. Did Ezra not tell you how sure he was of winning the case?" I say brightly. "And with Jaimy Fletcher on his way over, with the evidence that will prove my innocence, why, there is nothing but good reason for hope. No more tears, now. Good. That's better." Amy folds her hands in her lap, twisting her fine embroidered handkerchief, I am sure, to shreds.

After a bit, she puts that abused piece of cloth to her eyes, and we fall into a brief silence.

"Does anyone know who betrayed me?" I ask after a bit.

"Ezra believes it was Gulliver MacFarland. He has fallen back into drunkenness again and is seen wandering about the city, with bottle in hand, mumbling constantly about making something or other 'right.' It is a pitiful sight, I am told."

"Hmmm . . . Ah, yes, it must have been Gully," I say, nodding. "One time, down near the Rhode Island border, I spotted him working the crowd outside the circus. I was in disguise . . . black wig and all — and he did not come into the tent, so I didn't think that he had seen me." I stop to think on this. "But I guess I was wrong. He must have, indeed, seen his 'Little Miss Moneymaker' and figured there was a bit more coin to be made from her."

Ah, yes, poor Gully, the finest of fiddlers but the worst of men, always prey to his worst instincts. But I am truly glad to think that it was not anyone at the Montessori and Mattucci Circus who had peached on me . . . or Edgar . . .

"But wh-why would he betray you? I thought you were friends again?"

I smile, shaking my head, thinking more in pity than in anger of the one who had brought me to this low state. "It is not too hard to figure: the American intelligence agents who were after me knew that Gully and I had been partners and friends at one time, so all they had to do was get him into a tavern, flatter him, appeal to his vanity, then get some drinks down his throat. That's all it would have taken for poor Gulliver MacFarland to tell all he knows — both truth and lies. Poor Gully."

More silence, then I say, "You know, I actually liked being in that circus. It really suited my nature, and I am sad to have left it."

Heavy sigh . . . *That and a lot of other things . . .*

"Did you know that Mr. Pickering and I attended the circus that day and watched your performance?" Amy manages to softly ask. "I was amazed and almost fainted when it looked as if you were going to fall. I so wanted to go see you after the show . . ."

"Yes, I saw you. Three rows up on the left side. You made a lovely couple."

She blushed at that. "No. Here we are talking about me. How are they treating you?"

"Quite well. The Sheriff is a decent man, and the Matron is a good soul. I believe they are quite nervous, the both of them. I don't think they have had to preside over an affair such as this before. The food is excellent, too. I think Mrs. Tibbetts is sending it over from the White Rose."

Again we fall silent for a few moments, and I know she is going to be asked to leave soon. Her comforting presence will be gone, and I shall be left alone, shackled in this bleak cell. Weakness of spirit overwhelms me and I whisper, "After all those fake falls I took up on the high wire . . . looks like I might die from a fall, after all," I say, putting my hand to my throat.

"Do not say that, Sister. I cannot bear the thought."

"I know," I say, bucking up. "I know. I'm sorry. No, no self-pity here. For am I not a Pimm's girl?" I force a brave smile. "So, how is bold, dashing Randall these days? He is well, I hope, and full of his usual rakehell bravado?"

"No, he's — "

"I'm sorry, Miss Trevelyne," says Sheriff Williams in a dolorous voice. He had just come back into the corridor. "Visiting time is over. The prisoner is due at court for

263

arraignment and the choosing of the jury. The trial will start tomorrow."

I rise to my feet and face my dearest friend, extending my shackled arms . . .

I can only move so far and I can only say . . . nothing, nothing at all.

Chapter 37

The next morning, at nine o'clock, I am led into Plymouth County Courtroom by Sheriff Williams, my hands shackled before me. I should be used to shackles, ropes, chains, and other bindings by now, but I find I am not. I look about in the dim light of the interior to find the high-windowed room packed with spectators, many of whom I take to be reporters, for they have pads and pencils well in hand. And why not, for is this not the story of the year, the dread pirate and accused foul traitor, Jacky Faber, at last brought to justice? Should sell lots of papers. *Hope all enjoy. Yeah, right* . . .

All eyes are on me, of course, as I am brought in, and I so wish I could present a better appearance. Alas, I am refused permission to don one of my better dresses and made to wear the gray prison dress, to emphasize my current status as the alleged criminal. My only adornment is a white mobcap I am given to cover my head.

Ezra Pickering is seated at a desk in front of the Judge's high bench, with a pile of documents in front of him. He rises in greeting me, and we both sit down. He is about to say something, but we are interrupted by a man in black, with short white wig, who is sure to be the Clerk of Court. He stands and intones, "This Circuit Court, in the County of Plymouth, State of Massachusetts, United States of America, is now in session, Judge Hiram Thwackham presiding. All will be upstanding."

Oh, no!

"Thwackham?" is all I can silently mouth to Ezra Pickering as I get to my feet and stand, astounded, to watch my old enemy mount the Bench, all clad in black robes, jowls waggling, eyes fixed on me.

"Be seated," orders the Clerk, and all do, except for the many standing at the back of the room.

"Yes, Jacky, he's back, The Mad Thwacker." Ezra sighs, sliding into his chair beside me and not at all pleased. "I found out only yesterday he's been assigned to this case. I was hoping for Judge Norquist, a more moderate jurist. Yes, you may read that 'moderate' to mean neither insane nor bloodthirsty, but there was a last-minute change. Politics, I am sure, and Boston politics to boot. But no matter, truth and justice are on our side."

Uh-huh . . . right, again, Ezra . . . But this is not a good omen.

The last I saw of Judge Hiram Thwackham, he was being escorted out of the Municipal Court in Boston, mumbling about purple baboons and his preference for wide female bottoms. I had heard he was banished from the Bench and sent to his country home to spend the rest of his days. Apparently, he did not agree to stay there.

"But how . . . ?"

"Well, it seems that the Honorable Judge Thwackham

recovered quite quickly after the Infamous Purple Incident, attributing it to a momentary aphasia, and he applied for his old spot on the Bench. However, while he was recovering from this brief lapse in acuity, the learned Judge Lemuel Tragg had moved into his place and was in no mind to give it up. I believe you are acquainted with this Judge Tragg?"

"You know darn well I am, Ezra." I sniff. "You were there when he ordered the original sentence of twelve lashes to be carried out. And I, for one, will never forget being tied to the stake in the open courtyard, my back bared to the entire populace, and given the twelve. My humiliation was total and complete."

"Umm. That is true," agrees Ezra, "but you must realize that it could have been much worse. Anyway, while Thwackham had friends and influence in Boston, Tragg did, too, so he was able to keep his post as Head Magistrate. And since Judge Thwackham exhibited no further signs of dementia, he was appointed to the Circuit Court. While it doesn't improve his disposition in any way, because the assignment requires the old buzzard to travel a bit, it does keep him in the game. Unfortunately . . ." Ezra pauses, and then continues, "although he acts normally, or what might be construed as normal for him, he does exhibit a curious aversion to the color purple and requires that any person wearing that color be removed from his court. Says it hurts his eyes." Ezra cuts a knowing glance at me.

I look down at my hands. I did have something to do with that . . . and I sure wish I had some of my Purple Passion Potion here right now, and the means to distribute it liberally. *But forget your tricks, girl, since you do not. It's all up to Ezra now.*

"Does he remember me?" I ask.

"I am afraid so. In spite of his annoyance at being relegated to the traveling Bench, I believe he rather relishes this particular case."

Needless to say, this is not a good development . . .

Again the Clerk of Court speaks. "This High Court is convened to sit in judgment of Mary Faber, aka Jacky Mary Faber, on a charge of high treason and various other crimes against the government and the people of the United States of America."

"Court is now in session," growls the Judge, bringing down his gavel loudly on his high podium. "Miss Faber. Stand up."

I do.

"How do you plead to these charges?"

"Not guilty, Your Honor."

"Very well. Please be seated so we may proceed. United States Attorney Anthony Belcher will lead the prosecution." Here he gestures to a very severe-looking man in wig and judicial robes standing to the right side of the Bench, next to the witness chair. "The accused will be represented by . . ."

Ezra gets to his feet and says, "Ezra Pickering, Attorney at Law, Your Honor."

Thwackham looks out over the half spectacles he habitually wears, and mutters, "Oh, yes, you again. Very well, let us get started. If you gentlemen have affidavits, dispositions, and other such papers, bring them up to me now. Clerk, impanel the jury."

Ezra gathers up his documents and whispers to me as he goes to approach the Bench, "This will take a bit of time, so please try to relax."

Relax. Right. Most of the people in this room would take great delight in seeing me dangle from a rope . . . especially those twelve hard-faced men being seated in the jury box. *No women, of course.*

I finger the gray prison garment I am dressed in. Might as well make the accused look as guilty as hell. Saves time, I guess. As I wait for things to start, I recall a picture of another person clad exactly as I now am, and in similar circumstances. It was back in Paris, beautiful Paris . . .

It was at the Louvre Museum, and I was on the arm of Jean-Paul de Valdon, as he was showing me about the place. I, of course, was most impressed by the fine work hanging on the walls and expressed admiration at one I thought was especially well done, a large painting of Napoleon Bonaparte on horseback, by an artist named Jacques-Louis David. Jean-Paul, a committed Royalist, grimaced and said, "Yes, very fine. Now let me show you another work by this David."

Saying that, he directed me to a small, rather crude pencil drawing hung around the corner. It depicted a woman dressed exactly as I am, sitting in a rude cart, her hands tied behind her and wearing a deep frown.

"It is a picture of the Queen being taken to her execution," explained Jean-Paul. "David was a fiery revolutionary who deeply hated the King and Queen, so much so that he drew this from a balcony as she was taken to her death. It is reported that, as she was being prepared on the scaffold, Her Majesty accidentally stepped on the executioner's foot and then asked his pardon for it."

The Executioner's reply was not recorded, only the fact that he did take the mobcap from her hair . . . one just like

mine . . . before he laid her down under that terrible ma-
chine . . . Moments later, the blade came hissing down and the
head of Marie Antoinette, Queen of France, lay at the bottom
of a common basket . . . I hope I will be as brave or as gracious
if that happens to me . . . but I doubt that I will . . .

Ah, Jean-Paul, those were wonderful days in spite of that
awful war, were they not? I hope you are happy now, my
bonny light horseman, you of the soft brown mustache, the
gentle manners . . . and our little white tent, there on the
battlefield of Jena . . .

I am shaken out of my reverie by Ezra's return to my side.
Enough of the troubles of French royalty, for now it's time to
focus on my own.

"They will take care of the smaller charges this morning," he reports, "then get to the serious business this afternoon."

"The small stuff?" I ask.

"Yes. Fleeing a warrant. Resisting arrest. Firing on an
officer of the law. Kidnapping of a small child."

"Oh," I say, in a rather small voice.

"They will start with the circumstances of your resisting arrest at the circus," Ezra goes on, "but I think you'll be
glad to hear this . . ."

"What?" I ask, grateful for any good news.

"The boy Edgar Allen Polk has refused to testify against
you, and without that, they have no charge of kidnapping."

"What?" I ask, incredulous.

"Yes. The lad maintains he went with you willingly. He
reports that for him to inform on you would be a violation
of some 'Brotherhood Code' or other."

Well, I'll be damned, Edgar. I guess you have some honest pirate in you after all. Good for you!

"I call to the stand Federal Marshall Orville Purvis," comes the sonorous call from United States Attorney Belcher, and a man attired in a black suit approaches the Bench. I recognize the outfit, if not the man, as one of my pursuers at the Montessori and Mattucci Grand Circus, which is where I wish I were right now, back in my snug little wagon.

"I will cross-examine some of these witnesses," Ezra goes on. "But I won't put you on the stand till this afternoon. Agreed?"

"Yes, Ezra," I say.

"And you will refrain from speaking out, no matter what is said about you?" he asks with a warning look.

"Yes, Ezra," I agree wearily. "I will try to keep the Faber trap shut."

"That would be very good. Ah, here we go."

Marshall Orville Purvis goes up to stand in front of Prosecutor Belcher, who has in his hand a Bible. He orders Purvis to place his hand upon it, and recites, "Do you, Orville Purvis, swear to tell the truth, the whole truth, and nothing but the truth, so help you God?"

"I do," replies Marshall Purvis.

"Please be seated."

Purvis places his bottom in the chair and waits to give his testimony.

"Mr. Purvis, you are a duly appointed Federal Marshall?"

"Yes, Sir, I am," says Purvis with a certain amount of righteous self-importance, his hands folded across his belly.

"Very well, Marshall," says Belcher. "Will you please tell us of the events of November fourth of this year?"

Purvis is about to answer, when Ezra gets to his feet and says, "Objection, Your Honor, for learned counsel is leading the witness. And furthermore, the question is irrelevant. This court has no interest in what Mr. Purvis had for breakfast on that particular day. Perhaps Counsel could be more specific in directing his questions?"

There are some titters in the room at this . . .

My good Mr. Pickering is plainly laying out his battle plan — to ridicule and confuse. Go get 'em, Ezra.

"Sustained," growls Judge Thwackham. "Let's get on with it, Counselor."

Attorney Belcher gives Ezra a glare, then continues. "Mr. Purvis, will you please give us a description of that day's events that concern the accused, Jacky Faber?"

"Yessir," replies Purvis. "Myself and nine other agents were sent to this circus in New Bedford to apprehend the criminal Jacky Faber — "

"Objection," says Ezra. "Miss Faber has not yet been convicted of any crime, the obvious hostility of this court notwithstanding."

"Sustained, but watch your mouth concerning the conduct of my court, Mr. Pickering," warns the Judge. "You seem to enjoy skirting the boundaries of contempt of court. Beware, Sir."

A somewhat steamed Prosecutor Belcher returns to Purvis. "Go on, Marshall Purvis. Please be specific."

"Harrumph. Yes, Sir," answers a now red-faced Orville Purvis. "Anyway, we were sent to arrest a certain fugitive from the law named Jacky Faber, at the circus where she was employed. We had the proper warrant for that arrest."

"And did you accomplish that arrest?"

"Yessir."

"And, accomplishing that task, did you bring her back here to face these charges?"

"Yessir, we did."

"Thank you, Mr. Purvis. No further questions. Do you wish to cross-examine, Counselor?" asks Belcher with a look to Ezra.

Purvis has his ample butt halfway out of the witness chair when Ezra replies, "Indeed, I do." The Marshall sinks back, a wary look on his face as Ezra clasps his hands behind him and begins the destruction of U.S. Marshall Orville Purvis.

"Mr. Purvis, ten of you were sent to apprehend the suspect on that day. Did you accomplish the arrest on that day?"

"No, Sir," replies Purvis, digging his finger into his collar, which seems to have grown quite tight. "It was on the next day that we nabbed her."

"You mean ten full-grown officers of the law could not seize that one small female right there on the day in question? What was the problem?"

Here Ezra points at me, and I put on the full big-eyed helpless-waif look, the best one I've got.

"Well, Sir, she sort of escaped, like."

"And how did she do that?"

"When we arrived, she was doing her act high up in the tent, Sir."

"Did you serve her with the warrant when you entered the tent?"

"No, Sir. She was too high up to do that."

"How did she get out of the tent?"

"Through a hole in the top, Sir."

"Did you fire bullets at her fleeing form?"

"Yessir."

"Did she fire any at you?"

"No, but she did —"

"Please answer just *yes* or *no*, Mr. Purvis. Those are the rules."

"No."

It is growing quite hot in here, but the witness seems to be growing even hotter under his collar.

"So just how did she effect this miraculous escape from all you big, strong, and well-armed men, all of whom seemed perfectly willing to shoot her down like a dog?"

"She slid down the back of the tent and took off on a horse."

"You did not pursue? You had mounts, I assume? You did not arrive on the scene barefoot?"

"Yessir, we did. But you see, she set the lion on us."

"The *lion?*" exclaims Ezra, holding his arms out to the court and affecting complete astonishment. "What *lion?*"

There is a gasp from the courtroom at that.

"Ahem. Well, there was a fearsome African lion in this cage and she set it loose on us. A fearsome beast it was, too, Sir. It scared the hell out of the horses."

"And their brave riders, as well," says Ezra, his voice dripping with contempt. He gets a good laugh from the audience on that. "I have it on good authority from the

Montessori and Mattucci Circus that old Balthazar is both toothless and harmless."

"Didn't look harmless to us, it—"

"Never mind," says Ezra, cutting him off. "So when and how did you finally run down this suspect?"

"The next day, Sir . . . with dogs."

"Ah, my congratulations to the dogs, if not to our rather timorous Marshall Service. Now, after this creature led you on that merry chase, what did you do with her?"

"Why, we brought her back here to face justice, Sir."

"In an open wagon, was it not? And exhibited to the scorn of the crowds that lined the route to here?"

"Yes, but—"

"How was she dressed?"

"Why, in her circus costume."

"Describe, please."

"A very skimpy white corselette. Quite scandalous, it was."

"If it was so scandalous, why did you not allow her to change into better clothing for the journey here, as she re-quested? You did have custody of her baggage, did you not?"

"Yes, but . . ."

Here I hear some hissing from the crowd . . . probably from the women. *Sure wish I had a few of them on that jury, for they would know how I felt during that ride.*

"Yes, but you did not want to grant her even one shred of dignity, isn't that true? Isn't it true that you did not—?"

"Objection!" shouts Prosecutor Belcher. "That calls for a conclusion on the part of the witness!"

"Very well," says Ezra. "I withdraw the question. I have no further queries of this witness. He may step down."

A much relieved Mr. Purvis leaves the chair and heads for the exit, mopping his brow with his handkerchief, while Ezra goes to stand before Judge Thwackham.

"Your Honor, I move that the charge of resisting arrest against my client be dismissed on the grounds that —"

"Motion denied," states Judge Thwackham. "We'll let the jury decide that. Call the next witness . . ."

And so it drones on till noon, when Thwackham brings down his gavel and says, "This court is adjourned for lunch till one o'clock. When we come back, we will conclude this trial."

The Honorable Judge is not kidding, because in America trials are swift, nearly always concluded in one day, whether that day be eight, twenty-four, or forty-eight hours long. And Thwackham shows no inclination whatsoever to prolong these proceedings. It is plain he wants my neck in a noose, and he wants it there soon.

Yes, I will know my fate this afternoon, that is for sure . . .

And God help me . . .

Chapter 38

Needless to say, the rest of my trial did not go at all well . . .

Oh, Ezra, of course, did his level best, popping up every time Prosecutor Belcher opened his mouth to make a point, to object to whatever he said, bringing laughter from the court on many occasions. Restraining me was his biggest challenge.

And yes, Sheriff Williams was called to the stand and had to admit that, yes indeed, I had fired live rounds at him and his posse. He also confirmed the fact that he had served the warrant for my arrest at the Polk residence, so I could not slide out of that charge of resisting arrest quite so easily. The kidnapping of Edgar Polk was given a try, but that was all small change, compared to the Big One . . .

"The next and final charge being brought against the defendant, Jacky Mary Faber, is one of high treason against the people of the United States of America," intones Judge Thwackham, bestowing upon me a satisfied smile from his high perch. He fairly licks his ample chops. "Mr. Belcher, you may commence your case."

Attorney Belcher fairly leaps to his feet in anticipation. I know what he is thinking, *A capital crime! How this will enhance my résumé! What joy! When she swings, a judgeship for sure!*

He bounds to a table set up before Thwackham's elevated bench and says, "Your Honor, the Government offers this pouch as evidence and requests that it be marked Exhibit A."

"Very well. Explain."

"It is a so-called diplomatic pouch that was taken from the defendant's schooner, the *Nancy B. Alsop,* in Boston Harbor on August twentieth of this year."

"Is it a true diplomatic pouch?"

"No, Your Honor, it is not. It is a facsimile and was crudely sealed with a fraudulent wax stamp."

"Did the Defendant sign for that pouch?"

"Yessir, right there on the manifest list on the outside. Her signature, authenticated."

"What does it contain?"

The Prosecutor reaches into the pouch and pulls out some papers and says, "I enter into evidence Exhibit B, a letter written on official Royal Navy stationery, addressed to the Defendant."

"Very well, so entered. Please read it and then hand it up to me."

Belcher clears his throat, then reads:

Office of the Admiralty
Naval Intelligence

British Royal Navy
Admiralty Court
London, England

To:

Agent J. M. Faber
Faber Shipping Worldwide
Boston, Massachusetts, USA

Miss Faber:

You will see that the enclosed documents are delivered without fail to our operatives in the United States, as they are of the utmost importance.

H. F.

There is a rumble in the courtroom as Belcher passes the letter up to the Judge, saying, "It is believed that the letter is from a Lieutenant Harry Flashby, a known British Intelligence agent."

"Damn, Flashby!" I hiss to Ezra, grasping his arm in helpless fury. "I should have killed him when I had the chance!"

"Perhaps," says Ezra Pickering. "But calmness, now. Let it be, Jacky. We will have our turn."

After reading the note, Judge Thwackham asks, "And what else might be in that pouch?"

"Entered now as evidence, Prosecution Exhibit C."

"Which is . . ."

"A complete and accurate plan of the fortifications at Fort McHenry on Chesapeake Bay, the fort that guards our nation's capital in Washington, D.C.," announces Attorney Belcher in triumph, tossing the bundle on the table.

There is a common gasp from the courtroom. They recall, all too well, that it was British Major André's carrying very similar plans for the fort at West Point that got General Benedict Arnold branded a traitor. So now, I'm branded a traitor, too.

The Judge brings down his gavel hard on his bench. "Order! Order in my court! Or I'll throw out the lot of you!"

The crowd settles down and waits, the scratching of the reporters' pencils being the only sound in the room.

"That's better," grumbles the Mad Thwacker. "Mr. Belcher, do you have anything else to offer in evidence?"

"No, Your Honor."

"Any more witnesses?"

"No, Your Honor. The Prosecution rests."

"Counsel for the Defense, do you wish to examine the evidence?"

"No, Sir," says Ezra, rising to his feet. "I call to the stand Miss Jacky Mary Faber."

As I get to my feet and advance to the stand, Ezra whispers, "Keep it simple, Jacky. Let me ask the questions."

The clerk directs me to put my hand on the Bible and swears me in.

"Do you, Jacky Mary Faber, swear to tell the truth, the whole truth, and nothing but the truth, so help you God?"

"I do."

"Please be seated."

I settle in for the fight of my life, as Ezra comes up before me.

"Miss Faber, have you seen the evidence against you?"

"Yes, Sir, I have."

"And your answer as to the veracity thereof?"

"Lies, all lies," I reply. "I am but an honest merchant seaman, caught up in a web of lies woven by my enemies, and —"

I catch Ezra's warning glance and shut up.

"Have you, at any time, raised your hand or caused harm to the United States of America?"

"No, Sir, I have not."

Ezra nods approvingly.

"Or have had anything at all to do with the evidence presented?"

"No. I have nothing but love and respect for the United States of America. My own company, Faber Shipping World-wide, is based in Boston and my ships are home-ported there. I —"

"Thank you, Miss," says Ezra. It is plain he does not want me to go on about my holdings, they being much greater than those of many in this room. I can see glances between several members of the jury. *Just who does this twit of a girl think she is?*

"I have no further questions, Your Honor," says Ezra, going back to his chair. "You may cross-examine, Mr. Belcher."

I am shocked by this turn of events, but I did know that if Ezra put me on the stand, then the Prosecution could have a shot at me, too. I get ready for it, and it comes on fast.

"Miss Faber," asks Mr. Belcher with a certain amount of relish, "have you ever been a member of British Intelligence?"

"Yes, but it was against my —"

"Please answer *yes* or *no*, Miss Faber."

"Yes," I say, through clenched teeth.

"Are you a member of British Intelligence at this time?"

"No, Sir. I am not."

"Oh? The letter from Agent H. F. seems to contradict that statement."

"I don't care. Harry Flashby is a bounder and a liar. I was given my discharge from that service last year. By a Mr. Peel, an *honest* member of British Intelligence."

"You have proof of that?"

"Yes, Sir, I do . . . or will. My fiancé, Lieutenant James Emerson Fletcher, has gone to England to procure proof of that."

Attorney Belcher gives out a short snort. "I hope for your sake, Miss Faber, he gets back here in time." He does not sound like he really means it. "Mr. Pickering, do you wish to redirect?"

He does, and stands before me and asks, very plainly, "Miss Faber, do you deny all the charges laid against you in the matter of high treason?"

"Yes, Sir, I do," I reply as firmly as I am able.

"Very well," says Judge Thwackham. "Closing arguments, then. Attorney Belcher, you may proceed."

And proceed he does, mainly just lining up all the evidence against me, for really, that's all he has to do. I see the men in the jury hanging on his every word.

"Mr. Pickering, your summation, if you please," requests the Judge, glancing at the clock high up on the wall.

• • •

Yes, Ezra was most eloquent . . . "This poor young girl, cast about by the winds of Fate, forced to obey the orders of men much more powerful than she . . . From the war-torn fields of France, to the dangers of the undersea world, to those of Spain, too . . ."

But all to no avail. Judge Hiram Thwackham charges the jury, then leaves the Bench while they deliberate in an anteroom. In an indecently short time, both Judge and jury are back.

"Gentlemen of the jury, have you reached your verdicts?"

"Yes, Your Honor, we have," says the foreman of the twelve good men, holding a slip of paper.

"Then read them, please."

"First count of resisting arrest, not guilty," he announces. "Second count of resisting arrest, guilty. Charge of the kidnapping of Master Edgar Polk, not guilty."

Here he pauses, then says, "On the charge of high treason, we find the Defendant guilty as charged."

My head falls to my chest as Judge Thwackham smiles and passes sentence upon me.

"Jacky Mary Faber, you have been charged with the crime of treasonous acts against the United States of America and found guilty by a jury of your peers," rumbles the Judge from his podium high above me. "Do you have anything to say before I pronounce sentence upon you?"

I shake my head. "I am innocent of all the charges, and God knows that. Do what you will to me."

"Very well," intones Judge Thwackham. "It is the

judgment of this court that you, Jacky Mary Faber, be taken out three days from now, on the morning of November the tenth, to be hanged by the neck until you are dead. May God have mercy upon your soul."

I certainly hope he does . . .

Chapter 39

Carpenters have started building my scaffold.
Conveniently, they are constructing it in the courtyard so that I might enjoy its progress when I take my daily exercise walks. The carpenters have set the sturdy eight-by-eight piers in the ground in a rectangle roughly ten feet by twelve. The posts are about twelve feet high and will support the gallows platform that will equal the same area. Midway on the short side, two additional eight-by-eight piers thrust upward for another eight feet. These, I know, will support the crossbeam that, in turn, will support the Executioner's rope. I am sure it will support my weight. I believe they will attach the joints and begin laying the platform boards soon.

Yes, I am given an hour a day to walk about the little yard that lies between the jail and the courthouse, such that I might take the air, for we must keep the condemned healthy, mustn't we? We surely wouldn't want her to die of some wasting disease before the Big Show. I am shackled with my hands tied behind me, and I'm under the watchful eye of the Matron, so there is no hope of my making a run for it. Plus, Deputy Cole and his cohorts stand fully armed inside the rope they have stretched to mark off my area and keep all others out, including any of my military friends who might want to spring me.

A crowd does generally gather to watch me at my exercise. Morbid curiosity, I suppose. *Hey, let's watch the Dead Girl Walking.*

"Miss Faber, it is time to go in now," announces Matron, and she leads me back to my cell. "I believe your lawyer is here."

"Jacky, you must not give up hope," urges Ezra from his place on the bench opposite me. "I know that it is only two more days, but much can still happen. I have appeals pending in both the state and federal courts. You have friends in the city and they are doing their utmost to stay the . . . date of the . . . event. My cousin Senator Timothy Pickering is a member of Congress and is using all of his considerable influence in Washington. A delay could be in the offing. And your Mr. Fletcher is expected at any moment with the exonerating evidence from the British Admiralty, and — "

"Thank you, Ezra," I say, looking up at the tiny window above me, through which comes the sound of more sawing and hammering. "Your words do bring me comfort, and I know you are doing your very best for me." He follows my eyes up to the little window and grimaces. "But you do not have to mince words. The date is the tenth and the 'event' is my execution by hanging."

"Well, yes," says Ezra, looking down at his hands and not at me. "And there is some further information on that . . . topic." He clears his throat and continues. "I have been informed that the state and federal officials have sent a state marshall to oversee the . . . procedure. And they have sent a professional executioner, as well."

My hand goes to my throat. I cannot help it. In a moment, I am able to respond, "That is good. I don't want an amateur, and I do not want to suffer any more than necessary. I have never really been very brave."

"Please, Jacky, we must believe it won't come to that."

"Your news is good, too, Ezra, because it will relieve Sheriff Williams of a sad duty, one that I know he did not want to perform. He is a good man, and this will ease his mind."

Ezra gets to his feet. "I must leave you now, Jacky. I have to get back to the city to keep pushing on the appeals." He glances over at Deputy Cole to see if he is listening. Actually, he seems to be dozing. Ezra again speaks to me. "But know this, Jacky: You have friends in places you would not expect them to be. Higgins sends his regards and regrets that he cannot visit with you. That's all I can say. Adieu, Jacky."

"Goodbye, Ezra. You have always been the best of friends."

After another doleful visit from Amy, I am greeted this day by the Plymouth Ladies Aid Society, come to bring me some comfort. There are three older women and two younger. They also bring fabric — black, of course — with which to sew me a proper dress. Must be a lady, of course, even if one is being hanged. They give me a prayer book, too, and offer spiritual advice, but I have already made my peace . . .

I also received a letter from Mistress Pimm of the Lawson Peabody School for Young Girls. The Sheriff gave me the opened letter, satisfied that there was no knife or saw concealed within, and I pulled it out and read it.

Miss Miranda Pimm
Mistress of the Lawson Peabody School for Young Girls
Beacon Street, Boston, Massachusetts
November 8, 1809

Miss Jacky Faber
The Plymouth County Jail
Plymouth, Massachusetts

Dear Miss Faber,

I hope this letter finds you as well as you can be, given the circumstances.

I make no judgment as to your guilt or innocence of the charges against you. I write only to remind you that a Pimm's girl is a Pimm's girl to the last. While you are the first of my girls to be executed, you are not the first to die. It is expected of you that you will conduct yourself in such a manner as to be a credit to the school. You have before you the example of Lady Jane Grey and Anne Boleyn and Marie Antoinette, ladies all, who faced their brutal ends with grace and dignity. I expect nothing less of you.

I know you to be a young lady of spirit and solid character, and I am confident that you will bear up under this ultimate tribulation.

Pray to God, child. He will either spare you or He will take you to Him and, either way, it will be His will, and for the best.

Yrs. Respectfully, and etc.,
Miranda Pimm

Great. Thanks, Mistress. Stiff upper lip and all that, and keep the Lawson Peabody Look upon your face till they put the hood over your head.

And yes, Mistress, I will try to comply.

I fold up the letter and slide it under my pillow for Amy to put in my seabag tomorrow with the rest of my personal effects.

I sigh and look about me. I have thought of nothing except escape since they first brought me in here, but all those thoughts have been in vain. There is a lock on my shackle, a lock on the cell door, and yet another on the entrance to the corridor. I have no metal with which to fashion a key, and the Deputy and Sheriff keep too close an eye on me for any of my visitors to pass such a thing to me. No, I am truly lost. This is one cage that Jacky Faber will not get out of . . . until, that is, they take me out for the final time. Yes, I am truly —

I am startled, not so much by a sound, but by the sudden lack of any noise, and I realize what has happened. Outside my window, there is no more hammering or sawing . . .

"All right, boys, let's give 'er a try," I hear one of the carpenters say, and there is the rasp of a lever being thrown, and the sound of something falling with a *whump!*

They have completed the gallows and are testing the trap, the platform that will fall from beneath my feet.

I crawl into the bed and pull my knees to my chin, my ankle chain rattling on the bedstead as I do it. I put the pillow over my head and squeeze my eyes shut.

Oh, was I ever so bad as to deserve this?

Chapter 40

The gallows is ready.

It looms up against the sky, and seems all right and proper. It has the required thirteen steps from the ground up to the platform on the right, and the noose is in place, looped over the center of the crossbeam. The edges of the trap are plainly visible at the front of the platform, the trap lever off the right. The carpenters have done a workman-like job.

When I am let out for my airing today, I am chilled to find that both the newly arrived Federal Marshall Overseer and the Hangman himself are up on the scaffold. The two are attired in somber suits, and the Marshall wears a round black hat. The Hangman is hatless, but a tight leather hood covers his upper face. Both of the men wear thick beards that go from neck to eyes, the Marshall's being black laced with gray, and the Hangman's a bristly brown. The former is a large man while the latter is a hunchback, very small. But hey, how big do you have to be to merely sling a rope?

The Hangman is up there, testing the trap on the brand-spanking-new gallows over and over and over again. It is a hinged piece of the platform that lies level with the rest; that is, until the long lever over to the right is pulled. Then it swings smoothly down. Good job. Too bad this rig will be used only once, for it is very well made. He has rigged up a sandbag approximating my weight, around which he puts the noose. I hear a *twang* from the rope after each fall of the trap and look up to see the bag descend quickly and then jerk to a halt with another *twang*.

Well, at least they are being professional, and I trust they will not botch the job. I do not want to suffer. I certainly hope that I will be able to make a good show of it and not shame my friends. But I have never been very brave, not really, and I fear I will quail at the end. I hope I will not . . .

After I watch a few of those tests, I can't look anymore, so I turn away to gaze over the harbor and out to the sea. I think of the many things I have seen and done, and the many wonderful people I have met upon my way . . . Then I think on Jemimah Moses. I know she has heard of my troubles and taken them to her great heart, and I also know what she would say . . . *"Now, you know, child, that Brother Rabbit never give up, even when he hangin' over a pot of boilin' oil; no, he didn't. So he don't expect you to give up, neither, girl, not till you're singin' in that Heavenly Choir. That rabbit had lots of tricks up his sleeve, he did, but so do you, Sister Girl. Don't forget that you be the trickiest one of the bunch."*

I shake my head and smile ruefully at that. *Sister Girl done run out of tricks, Jemimah. No more cheating at cards, no more purple potions, no more Jacky's Little Helper, no more deceptions. No more anything, 'cept that gallows looming above. That's gonna put a stop to all my tricks, for sure.*

As I am looking out to sea, there is a sudden commotion

behind me! I turn and look. Someone has breached the rope! Is it Ganju Thapa and his Gurkhas? Is it Randall Trevelyne and the U.S. Marines? Is it Cavalry Captain Lord Richard Allen and his lads?

No, it is not. It is merely one very small boy, standing there before me.

"Edgar! You are not allowed, you—"

"I hate what is going to happen to you. It is not right." His big dark eyes smolder as he looks up at the gallows.

"Hey, Captain Polk, how else is a pirate supposed to end up?" I ask, trying to keep things light.

"I want you to know that I did not tell on you."

"You don't have to say that, Edgar. We both know that pirates don't peach on each other." I spy a frantic Mrs. Polk ducking under the rope and heading our way.

"I have a knife up my sleeve. I will pass it—"

I force a laugh at that. "Spoken like a comrade in arms, Captain Blood!" I say. "But you see my hands are bound, so I couldn't grab it. The two of us would get caught, and then we'd be in deep trouble."

Mrs. Polk is almost upon us.

"Nay, Edgar Allen Polk, the best thing you can do for me is to go on and live your life. Be the best you can be. I was so proud to see you in your school's football team uniform, I—"

Mrs. Polk takes her son by the shoulders and turns him away.

"I—I'm . . . sorry, Miss," she whispers.

"Don't be, Madam. You have a fine young son there," I say, then I bid farewell to the lad. "Goodbye, Captain Blood."

He turns for a last look. "Goodbye, Annabelle Leigh."

A tear comes to my eye as they walk off . . . *And please, Missus, don't let him watch . . .*

Matron takes me back to my cell. This will be my last exercise period, as things need to be put in train.

All my appeals have been exhausted; all my hope of pardon is gone. Ezra Pickering is back in Boston, trying with all his very considerable abilities for a last-minute stay of execution, but there is little or no hope of that. The war fever between England and the United States has grown so intense that no politician would risk his political life by trying to save a mere girl who was caught with damning evidence of high treason.

There has been no sign of Jaimy.

Oh, well . . . I have lived more adventures and seen more things than I could have ever thought possible back when I was Little Mary Faber running the streets of London with Charlie and the gang. All that time at sea when many about me died and I didn't — "a girl what's meant for hangin' ain't likely to be drowned" . . . or hit by a cannonball or run through with a sword. No, I always sort of knew I would wind up on the end of a rope, 'cause it was what I feared most. And now here it is. Tomorrow morning, I will . . . *Enough of that, you.* They have given me quill and paper and I shall write my last letter to Jaimy, and thus calm my raging mind.

Jacky Mary Faber
Plymouth, Massachusetts
November 9, 1809

Dearest Jaimy,

Tomorrow, as you will find when you reach this place, I will be at my final rest. Please, Beloved, think of me not as the cold clay that will be lying in the ground but as the young girl you knew on the dear old Dolphin. *Think of you and me swinging in our hammock, our wonderful secret known only to us two. I have known true bliss in my day, and I assure you, Jaimy, that was one of the best of times for me.*

I set out on a life of adventure and I got it — but this is the other side of that coin. Sometimes you do adventure, and sometimes the adventure does you. So I ain't complaining about how it all ended.

It is time for you to be getting on with the rest of your life, and I mean that, Jaimy. I want you to have a fine life out on the ocean, and I want you to join with a good young woman and have a fine family with her. Perhaps, if your wife doesn't mind too much, you could name one of the kids after me . . . it doesn't matter, boy or girl, as "Jacky" works both ways. Ha, ha. It gives me comfort to think there might yet be a Jacky Fletcher abroad in the land, even though it didn't turn out to be me.

Please excuse the shaky handwriting and the tears that have fallen on the page. Know, Jaimy, that my last thoughts were of you.

Yours through eternity,
Jacky

Chapter 41

It is the night before . . .

I sit on my bed and await Amy's arrival. It is six o'clock in the evening, and she will be my last visitor. I shall give the letter to her, and she will see that Jaimy gets it.

Earlier in the day, I had received another visit from Reverend Milton, he who will be carrying out his clerical duties tomorrow on the scaffold. He is a kind man and we have spent many hours in the past two days reading Scripture and discussing theology. We prayed for a while, and then he patted my hand and left.

Next, in trooped the members of the local Ladies Aid Society. They, too, have been kind, reading me passages of the gospel and rendering what solace they can.

Presently, they leave, and Amy is let in. The door is left open behind her, but little good that will do me, shackled as I am.

"Hullo, Sister, it is good to see you," I greet her as she enters and sits down upon the visitors' bench. "You've met the ladies of the Aid Society?" I ask, trying desperately for a note of cheer to what is sure to be our final visit.

"Yes," she says. "I hope they have been a comfort to you."

"Oh, yes, they have," I answer as brightly as I can. "They have sat with me for great amounts of time, brought me good things to eat, have read me even more Scripture, and prayed with me for hours on end — or so it seems. And they have sewn for me a dress to wear on . . . well, you know when . . . It's all prim and proper — black, of course — and covers me all the way to my . . . neck. But, *ahem!* Can you believe that two of the younger women are both Lawson Peabody girls? Yes, it's true, and we have shared humorous stories of the dear old school and Mistress Pimm. But the lady who brings me the most cheer is old Missus Milford, who is convinced, in her dotage, that I am to be *married* tomorrow and not . . . the other. She gaily prattles on, oblivious to the others' protestations, giving me the most outrageous advice on how to conduct myself on the wedding bed! You would . . ."

But Amy will not be cheered. I want to say something like, "Don't worry, Sister, the reprieve will come through, and soon we'll be back in your room at dear old Dovecote," or something like that, but I can't, for we both know it would be a lie.

Instead I say, "Will you take my nightdress out of my seabag, Amy? I will dress for bed."

She nods and goes to my bag to pull out the nightdress, which I knew to be right on top. She hands it to me, and I pull off the Lawson Peabody dress I had been wearing and give it to her. Deputy Cole has the good grace to look away. She folds it and places it in the bag.

"Deputy Cole, will you see that my seabag goes with

Miss Trevelyne when she leaves, as I want her to have it? Thanks so much."

It is warm, so I don't get into the nightdress right away, but instead sit back down on the edge of the cot in my underclothes.

Another sad silence falls upon us, but finally I suck in a breath and say, "Have you got a place to put me?"

"Yes," she says quietly. "Up on Daisy Hill."

"Has it been dug?"

"Yes."

There is silence for a while. Then . . .

"Will you see me put right? Straighten out my legs and cross my hands upon my breast?" I know my voice is beginning to tremble, but I can't help it. "I don't want anyone touching me but you," I manage to whisper.

She nods. "I will do that."

"Daisy Hill," I say, collecting myself and taking a deep breath. "That very same hill where we first rode together at Dovecote, with Millie the dog bounding about . . . chasing butterflies and geese. Yes, that is a fine and wonderful place, with the sea close at hand. Thank you, Sister. I shall rest easy there, and I hope you will bring your children up to visit me some . . . times and tell them about me and how we were friends and maybe tell them I . . . I wasn't really so bad . . ." I begin to choke on my words.

"There will be no children. None of mine, anyway," she says, all calm and collected.

"What . . . what do you mean by that? That you intend to live single all — "

"No. I do not mean that at all. I mean that I intend to cross over with you."

I shoot to my feet, all thoughts of tomorrow swept from my mind. "You cannot mean that, Sister! It will be a double tragedy! It's against God's laws!"

"I cannot live in such a cruel world," she says, quietly folding her hands on her lap, "nor worship a god who would allow this to happen . . ."

"Promise me you will not do that, Sister! Please promise me that!"

"I hear you, Sister."

"That is *not* an answer! Swear to me that you — "

There is a sudden commotion near the cell door . . .

"Sir! You cannot go in there! Stop!" shouts Deputy Cole.

"Like hell I can't! Get your hands off me!"

Wot? Who? Randall?

"Get him out of here!" roars the Sheriff.

"He's Colonel Trevelyne's son! *You* get him out!"

I look to the door of the cell and there stands Randall Trevelyne, coatless, in a shirt that is stained with whiskey and vomit. He is unsteady on his feet and has to lean against the bars of the cell to prevent his falling to the floor.

Wonderful. The final joke. I pray to God for deliverance and he sends me a drunk.

"Randall," I cry out to him. "You must talk to Amy! I'm afraid she is going to — "

"To hell with . . . *hic!* Amy, to hell with ever'thin'," he says, slurring his words. "Here. Put this on."

I see that what he holds in his hand is an article of clothing.

"The Ladies Aid Society sent this. Finished it thish afternoon. Thought you should be . . . hanged . . . in something modest. Ha. You. Modest." He probably took it from the Ladies Aid Society as they were bringing it to the jail. They must have been quite shocked.

He flings the dress across the cell and it lands on the floor, out of my reach.

"Here! Out with you now," shouts Sheriff Williams. "Let the girl have some peace and dignity in her last hours!" Deputies Cole and Asquith manage to get Randall by the arms and are dragging him out when a sudden hush falls upon the jail.

A small, stooped man has entered the corridor. He is a hunchback, and he wears a leather hood over his upper face, into which two eyeholes have been cut. The hood comes down to cover his nose, and beneath it there is a bristly brown beard.

It is the Hangman.

Randall stops struggling and Amy stands up in horror. My own legs turn to jelly, and I start trembling. *Oh, God, help me!*

"Get everybody out," rasps the Hangman in a whispery voice. "I must take my final measurements." He sees the dress and bends over to pick it up. He runs the garment through his hands, as if feeling for knives or anything else that might be concealed therein. He has yet to look upon me directly.

Sheriff Williams takes Amy by the arm and leads her out of the cell, saying, "Come, Miss, it is time to go. Quiet, now." He nods to the pair of deputies, and they drag Randall down the corridor and Amy follows them out.

I am left alone in the cell with the Hangman.

Apparently satisfied that the dress contains no weapons, he turns and hands it to me.

"Put it on, girl. Cover yourself."

It is then that I look through the slits in the mask and into the cold, dead eyes of the man who will take me out in the morning and hang me from the gallows tree . . .

Chapter 42

The Journal of Amy Trevelyne, continued . . .
The day of November 10, 1809
The day Jacky Faber was hanged

This will be the last of my chronicles concerning the life and death of my dearest friend, Jacky Faber. There will be no more of her, nor of me, either.

On the morning of that awful day, I awoke from a fitful slumber, and for a moment, my mind was confused. *Where am I? What is happening? Why am I here, wrapped in my cloak, lying on these rough boards?*

But then the awful realization of the horror that was to come this day swept over me. I did not think I would have fallen asleep last night, but I did. I awoke in this wagon with the sun in my eyes, in the shadow of that horrid gallows and next to the coffin that was soon to receive the dead body of Jacky Faber. I sat up, looked about, and realized it was a shout from the huge crowd that had gathered to witness the execution that had awakened me. I looked around me in amazement. People were all about, held back from the foot of the gallows by a rope strung on makeshift poles around it and guarded every few yards by the Sheriff's men. Aside from them, we in our wagon — our hearse, rather — were the only ones allowed in the enclosure.

People had come in from far around, families even, on horseback and by buckboard and even some in coaches, vying for the best viewing spots. They spread blankets and set up picnics. Boys and girls frolicked about, playing tag as if this were a country fair and not the horror that it was. Peddlers were selling miniature nooses as souvenirs of the event. I gagged and lurched to the side and threw up what little I had in my stomach.

How could I have even slept? My only memory of last evening was the drunken Randall forcing me to drink something to calm my hysteria after both of us had been forcefully ejected from the cell in which she was held. I shook the cobwebs from my brain and looked wildly about me. I saw Randall next to me, sitting on the coffin, his head down and his hair hanging in his face. Plainly, he was still filthy drunk, his shirt stained brown with whiskey and vomit. He swayed back and forth, a bottle clutched in his hand. I twisted around and saw George Swindow, our head stable man, sitting up forward on the driver's seat, the reins of two horses in his hands. Jim Tanner sat beside him, slumped over, his shoulders shaking.

"We have done all we can, Sister. I had hoped you would have slept through it, but it will all be over soon," said Randall softly, his eyes bleary with the drink. "All over."

Aghast, I looked up at the gallows, and there stood the masked Hangman, the end of the rope in his hands, the noose dangling over the trap upon which she will soon stand. Sickened again, I realized what was going to be done. They will bring her out, kill her, and then when the Marshall pronounces her dead, George will back the wagon under the gallows, the coffin will be opened, the rope slacked, and her body lowered into it. Then we will go back to Dovecote and bury her and that will be that. Efficient, so damned, damned efficient.

Then, with another sickening lurch to both my reeling mind and my belly, I realized what the shout from the crowd that awakened me had meant. They were bringing her out.

Twisting about again, I looked to the jailhouse door. Coming forward was a party of six: two guards, the Sheriff, the Marshall, the Matron, and in the midst of them, my dearest friend, Jacky, looking pitifully thin and small, dressed in black, with her hair pinned up under a white mobcap. Ah, yes, so as not to interfere with the work of the noose, my oh-so-orderly-and-analytical mind surmised, even at that dreadful moment.

She walked steadily enough, her head up, yes, steady enough, till she looked up at the gallows, and then a look of complete horror came over her features and she stumbled and had to be supported by the Sheriff.

"There, now, Miss. Steady on," I heard the Sheriff say, not unkindly.

She nodded and composed herself as best she could. I could see that she was weeping but could not lift her hands to wipe the tears from her eyes, for her hands were bound before her and fastened to a rope around her waist. After a moment, she continued on her journey to the gallows.

The Sheriff allowed her to pause as she came up next to Randall and me, and looking upon each of us, she simply said, "You'll visit me sometimes up on Daisy Hill, won't you? I will be there in spirit, if not in life."

I was unable to speak and could only look into her eyes one last time. Randall could only nod and hang his head.

She looked at the coffin, and at a nudge from the Marshall, she turned her gaze away and walked to the gallows stairs, hesitated, took a deep breath, and started to climb. Only Jacky and the Marshall joined the Hangman on the platform, while the rest remained below, with the Preacher at the foot of the stairs, giving her his final blessing.

There was a great roar from the crowd as she reached the top and turned to gaze out over them. As she did so, a look came over her features . . . head up as if balancing a book, eyes hooded, teeth apart and lips together. It was the Lawson Peabody School for Young Girls Look, and I wished I could have been able to put it on my own face, but I could not.

The crowd grew suddenly quiet as the Hangman now took firm control of her, guiding her feet to the very center of the trap. Reaching out for the noose, he brought it over her head to fall about her thin neck. It lay there for a moment like some grim parody of a necklace before he then drew it snug, placing the huge, coiled knot under her left ear. The Marshall stood off to the side, his hand on the lever.

"You should not watch this, Sister," said Randall. "Turn around. I'll tell you when it's over."

But I could not . . . I could only sit speechless and watch in horror.

The Marshall stepped forward and read from a paper held in his hand, his voice booming out over the crowd. "By order of the Government of the United States of America, you, Jacky Mary Faber, have been sentenced to death by hanging for the crimes of treason and sedition. Do you have any last words before the sentence is carried out?"

"I do, Sir," she said, lifting her chin from the rope that lay about her neck. "You are killing an innocent girl here today, and I hope you remember that, those of you who condemned me falsely, as well as those of you who have come here to enjoy this cruel spectacle. I fear not any judgment that may be placed on me in the next world, for I have never done any real wrong to others. Maybe it is to a better place I am going, I don't know, but as I look out and see that many of you have brought your children to watch this murder, I know it has to be a better place than this." She took a deep breath and said, "That's all. Get on with it."

The Hangman pulled a piece of cloth from his pocket, which I knew to be the hood he would place over her head so the more sensitive in the crowd would be spared the sight of her contorted features as she was slowly strangled to death. The crowd remained silent, expectant, hushed.

"Wait!" came a cry from the edge of the throng. "Hold on!"

It was a man on horseback, followed by two others, and all eyes turned to him as he charged through the assembled people. As he grew closer, I could see that he wore the uniform of a British Naval Officer. Oh, great hope! Maybe it is her reprieve. Maybe it is James Fletcher with the proof of her innocence, maybe, maybe . . . *Oh, please, God!*

"Hangman, slack your rope a while," said the Marshall.

"We'll see what he has to say." The rope was slacked and it fell over her back. She let out her breath, and her legs began to tremble. She looked over at the approaching officer, and I could see that she recognized him. She shook her head and again looked straight ahead into eternity, all hopes for earthly deliverance gone.

What? Surely there is still hope, I thought as the man pulled his horse up next to the restraining rope barrier and dismounted, handing the reins to a boy standing by. But then all hope was most cruelly dashed.

"Do you bring reprieve from the Governor, Sir? Do you bring proof of her innocence? What do you bring?" demanded the Marshall.

The officer dismounted and smiled up at the condemned. "I bring nothing, Sir," he said, taking out a long cigar and placing it between his teeth. He grinned. "My name is Lieutenant Harry Flashby, His Majesty's Royal Navy, Intelligence Branch. I bring nothing but a burning desire to see this bitch hang, for she cost me two weeks in the mosquito-infested interior of this country, a month in Newgate Prison, and many other indignities to both my career and my person. String her up.

"Remember those alligators, Jacky dear, hmmmm? I certainly do. And too bad poor Blifill isn't here to enjoy this, hey?"

"Executioner, carry on," said the Marshall, turning away, and the Hangman again tightened the noose about her neck.

"I'm glad to see that you colonials have not yet adopted the long drop in the way of hangings as has our enlightened

Britain," said Flashby, plainly enjoying the effect of his discourse upon those standing next to him. "A snapped neck is much too quick and no fun at all to watch, don't you think? It will be a pleasure to watch her kick. I say, can't a man get a drink around here? I intend to enjoy this thoroughly."

A man with a large jug on his shoulder and little tin cups dangling from his belt answered his call. He filled one of them and handed it to Flashby, saying, "Here ya go, Gov'nor. That'll be two bits."

"Ah, thank you, my good man." He took a sip. "Ah, yes, excellent whiskey. You Yankees could show those damned Scots something about making whiskey. Let's have a bumper for each of my men," he said, flipping the man a coin. His two fellow officers dismounted and, smiling, took up their cups.

My stomach bucked and I thought I would be sick again, but I had nothing left, nothing but the sourness in my stomach to throw up.

"Stiff upper lip, there, girl," said Flashby to the condemned, his drink in hand, his cigar lit. "Let's take one in the neck for old Mother England now, shall we? Duty and all, you know." His friends chuckled in appreciation of his wit.

Jacky took her eyes off the horizon and looked down at him. "I'll see you in hell, Flashby," she said in an even tone. "Count on it." Then she looked back off again.

"Probably, my dear, but you're guaranteed to beat me there. Be sure to save me a spot by the fire. Perhaps in the flames of hell, we'll have that little romp that has so long been denied me . . . fornicating amongst the flames, hey?

Sounds festive. Hello, what's this?" He turned and looked back over his shoulder.

Again there was a tumult from the edge of the crowd, but this time it was accompanied by raucous and derisive laughter. I looked and beheld the sight of an obviously drunken man riding a sway-backed old mule and swinging a rusty old sword over his head, plowing through the crowd. It was, I saw, Gulliver MacFarland, ragged and drunk, with his fiddle case bouncing on his back.

"Let her go, goddamn it! Can't you see I'm here to make things right? Out of my way!" he shouted, coming relentlessly on and on.

"Good God!" exclaimed the Sheriff. "Get back there, you! Stand off! Men, arrest that man!"

"Gully! Stop!" exclaimed Jacky, shaking her head vehemently at her would-be rescuer. "Stop! It ain't gonna do no good!"

The crowd parted in front of the demented man, everyone scurrying out of his way as he approached the rope barrier. Everyone, that is, except the vile Lieutenant Flashby, who stood there alone, with his men backing him.

"Go away, fool," said Flashby contemptuosly as Gully and his mule pulled up in front of him.

"I will not! I am Gulliver MacFarland, the Hero of Culloden Moor, and I will yield to no damned Englishman! You will stand aside, you rotten bastard! You're the one who made this happen!"

With that, he lifted his sword over Flashby's head. Flashby calmly transferred his tumbler of whiskey from his right hand to his left, and with that same right hand pulled a pistol from out of his jacket, quickly aimed, and shot Gully MacFarland in the middle of his chest.

A small bloom of red blossomed on the front of Gully's shirt, right above his ragged tartan sash. Gully looked down at the wound. He tried to take a breath, but could not. He could only gasp, blood streaming from his torn chest and bubbling out of his open mouth. His arm, which still held the sword aloft, fell to his side and the sword clattered to the ground. And then Gulliver MacFarland, Master Fiddler, fell backward out of the saddle, taking his fiddle with him. The case popped open with the shock of the fall, and the violin inside bounced over to land near Flashby's feet. He looked down at the delicate, reddish brown instrument lying in the dirt, lifted his boot, and crushed the fiddle beneath his heel, its wood splintering, its ruptured strings giving out one last mournful sound. One of Gully's feet was still caught in the stirrup, and the mule, terrified by all the noise and blood, ran off screaming, dragging Gully's lifeless body through the dust and away from the crowd. Incredibly, many people laughed.

"Oh, Gully, no . . . no . . ." I heard Jacky sob from up on high.

"I have over a hundred witnesses to the fact that that was an act of self-defense," said Flashby, having a sip of his drink and bowing to the crowd. "Do I not?" Many in the crowd shouted their approval. "This day is turning out even better than I expected," he crowed, exultant, turning his attention once more to the condemned.

"Well, my dear," said Flashby, sending a puff of smoke up in her direction. "I imagine you have no further hope of rescue now, do you? So we might as well get on with it, hmmm?"

Jacky did not give him the satisfaction of an answer. Instead she faced forward again and put on the Look, her eyes fixed on the sky.

The Marshall went to her side and asked, "Are you ready?"

She gave a short nod.

The Marshall, in turn, nodded to the Hangman, who again whipped out the hood and, this time, pulled it over her head. The crowd went silent.

Oh, no, I shall see her face no more. Oh, God, this is all happening too fast, too fast. Stop, please stop, please, God!

The Hangman took some time fastening the drawstring at the bottom of the hood, adjusted the noose again, and then took a thick black belt from a hook on the gallows brace and wrapped it around her at the knees. It is put there to prevent her dress from flying up when she is dropped, for modesty's sake, and to prevent her from kicking too violently in the throes of her suffering. *Oh, the awful banality of death, of evil! Everything is just so precise, just so ritualized, just so awful, and the end of it all is death!*

I could see the fabric of the hood draw in toward her face as she breathed, I could see the rise and fall of her chest, and then I saw the Hangman walk away from her and go to a long lever that I knew would spring the trap and send her off. *No! No! Not yet! Stop this thing! Stop!* The Hangman looked to the Marshall, and Randall grabbed my arm. *Sister, do not watch!* But I must, I must . . . and the Marshall nodded and the Hangman pulled the lever and there was a creaking sound and the trap fell out from under her . . .

And she fell. She fell as far as the cruel rope about her neck would let her fall and then . . . *Twang!* She was jerked to a halt.

I believe I screamed, but I don't know . . . The sound of any scream I might have made would have been drowned out in the roar from the crowd.

The fall was not sufficient to break her neck. No, of course, she must be made to suffer. Her head snapped to the side, but still she twisted and turned, her bound legs kicking and kicking in the air, her hands trying in vain to reach up for the awful choking rope. I watched as the shoe on her right foot fell off, to land in the dust below. On and on it went *and on and on and kicking and twisting, kicking and twisting. Oh, please . . .*

"Put her out of her misery, for the love of God!" roared Randall, standing beside me and brandishing a pistol. "She's too light to hang! Put her out of it or I will!"

The Hangman looked down through the open trap at her struggling form, and roared, "Be still, Sir! It will be over in a minute!"

And sure enough, it was. There was one final spasm as her knees drew up, and then suddenly, her legs fell straight and her hands fell to her sides. She hung limp, no longer struggling, her head to the side, with a slight tremor in her unshod right foot the only evidence she had ever been alive. And then even that ceased.

Jacky Faber was dead.

Chapter 43

The Journal of Amy Trevelyne, continued . . .
Plymouth, Massachusetts

But the grim spectacle at the gallows was not yet over.

I saw the Marshall look at his watch and then walk down the stairs, to stand next to the body. He put his hands behind him, to wait. I knew they would let her hang there for twenty minutes, because that's the way these things are done. To make sure she was dead and all. I looked up on the hill and saw that the black flag had been raised, telling the reporters in their swift cutters that the execution had been carried out and they could hurry off to Boston and report to their newspapers. Several men, trusting horses more than boats, galloped off as soon as they saw the deed done. Either way, the papers were sure to be on the streets before noon.

Very well, that's all done. The time for tears is over. Time to tidy up now. There are things to do.

Dimly, I heard the sound of families being loaded back into buckboards and the wagons going off, silent and subdued now, the ghastly show being over. But not all the people left, oh, no, for there was a rush to the rope barrier, a throng of souvenir sellers and necromancers and would-be witches, shouting out offers. "Sir, ten dollars for the rope!" "To hell with that, I'll give fifteen; no, twenty!" "Two dollars for her shoes. She don't need 'em now. Come on, Sir!" "Fifty cents for a good thick lock of her hair! Come now, Sir . . ."

Randall lurched to the side of the cart and pulled the whip from its holder and began to swing it at the mob that was pressing ever harder at the restraining rope.

"Back, damn you to hell!" he shouted. "Back to the holes from which you crawled!" He cracked the whip and one man shrieked and fell back, his cheek laid open by the tip of the lash. "Miserable swine, get back!" Randall raised the whip again, and the rest of them retreated out of range. All, that is, except for the three Royal Navy officers.

Lieutenant Flashby leaned an arm on a barrier post and affected a posture of pure gloating insolence. I do not believe I have ever hated a human being more than I hated that man at that moment.

"Why, do not despair, my entrepreneurial friends," said he, gesturing grandly at the hanging body, which a breeze had started swinging ever so slightly. "After they cut that piece of dead meat down, they'll dump it in some ditch and you'll be able to take what you want off of it. Although she was small when she lived, I'm sure there'll be enough of her corpse to go around." He blew a puff of smoke in Randall's direction.

Randall, his eyes wild, faced Flashby and was about to speak, when Sheriff Williams spoke up in warning, "Be careful, Sir. He is a Trevelyne . . ."

"Trevelynes be damned," said Flashby, looking into

Randall's unfocused eyes and sneering. "I've been to their house and seen what they are. Bunch of filthy rebel pig farmers, is what. Heard they can't tell their daughters or wives from their sows, and make no distinction between them when it's time for bed. Here's what I think of the Trevelynes," he said, and he spat in the dirt in front of Randall.

"Sir!" protested the Sheriff, but it was too late.

Randall rose in righteous, drunken anger, and though he swayed, his words were firm: "The honor of my family and the honor of the one who hangs there in the gallows have been stained. I demand satisfaction. James Tanner, you will second me."

"Gladly, Sir," said Jim, standing up in the wagon. It was the first time he had had to look at the poor, pathetic thing on the gallows swinging slightly in the breeze, and he blanched but managed to stand upright behind Randall. I, for one, could not take my eyes off that tiny white-stockinged foot. Why that more than anything else right then should strike me to the quick, I did not know . . . but let us be done with all this!

"Please, Lieutenant, the man is obviously drunk," pleaded the Sheriff. "It will hardly be a contest."

"Honor must be served. Mine has been impugned by this insolent puppy. We go back a long way, she and I and he and I, and it's time that old scores were settled. The score has been settled with her, and now it's his turn." Flashby smiled and drew his sword. "Mr. Winfield, you will be my second?"

"Of course, Sir. It will be a pleasure." The toady smirked behind him, with a slight bow.

"As I must be off to serve his Britannic Majesty, I cannot wait for a dawn meeting. This thing will have to be settled now, and as I have been the one challenged, I have the choice of weapons. Since I have already discharged my weapon into the gut of that meddling fiddler, I choose swords. I see you have one hanging by your side. Agreed?"

Of course not pistols, said what was left of my mind. *Even a drunk can get off a lucky shot . . .*

Randall reached down and took another long drink out of the bottle, and then said, "Agreed."

And with great deliberation, he corked the bottle and tossed it aside. He drew his sword and jumped to the ground, and though he landed on his feet, he lost his balance. Lurching to the side, he fell down in the dust, his sword falling from his hand.

Oh, God, no! To watch my dearest friend die and now my brother . . . How much horror can I stand today before I go stark raving mad? Randall managed to crawl over to his sword, pick it up, and get back on his feet. He stood there weaving, waiting . . .

"You there," said Flashby to the Marshall. "Will you act as duel master?"

"I suppose," said the Marshall, shaking his head as he came down from the gallows. "A sad day, a sad, sad day," he lamented, going to take his place between Randall and Flashby. "I assume honor will be satisfied at first blood?"

"No, Sir, not at all. This fight will be to the death," said Flashby, barely able to suppress a grin.

Randall nodded with all the gravity of a drunkard and lifted his sword. "To the . . . *hic* . . . death."

"I cannot persuade you gentlemen otherwise? Surely you can reconcile your differences?" Both of the so-called gentlemen shook their heads. "No?" The Marshall stepped back. "Then, en garde."

The two sword points crossed and the opponents assumed the stance, Flashby much more steadily than poor doomed Randall. Today I watched my friend die, and now I will see my brother needlessly butchered. But, really, it doesn't matter now . . . nothing matters . . . anymore.

"Engage!" cried the Marshall, and the blades clashed.

Flashby, supremely confident, tried a casual thrust at Randall's chest, but Randall just managed to turn the blade aside and stagger back.

"Running away, are we, boy? You can run and hide, you know. Go ahead, I shan't stop you," sneered Flashby, advancing, point forward. He tried a feint at Randall's sword arm, and then reversed and slashed at his head. Randall clumsily lifted his blade to ward off the blow, but not quite quick enough. A cut showed on Randall's forehead, and then a trickle of blood ran down the side of his face. There was a shout from what was left of the spectators.

"Surely, Sirs, that's enough!" said the Marshall, stepping between the swordsmen.

"No," said Flashby.

"No," said Randall, wiping the blood from his eye with the back of his hand.

"Very well," replied the Marshall, stepping back out of the way. "Such a waste . . . but proceed."

Flashby, breathing a bit harder now, had obviously planned to end this thing quickly, but that was not to be. He came at Randall hard, charging and slashing with his blade, but somehow Randall was able to parry each thrust and evade, however clumsily, each slash of Flashby's sword.

Now fear was beginning to show in Flashby's eyes. Sweat appeared on his brow. The drunken boy had managed to somehow fend off his attack, and he discovered that his easy opponent now stood much straighter, his eyes focused and unblinking, his blade beginning to get under Flashby's guard, to snick in close to his now heaving chest.

Flashby redoubled his attack, swinging his sword cavalry style, in an arc, at Randall's neck. Randall stepped aside, slipped his sword under Flashby's, and enveloped it, sending it harmlessly off to the side. Then he put the point of his own sword on Flashby's belly, just below his breastbone, and drove it home, all the way to the hilt.

"It seems you will be the one saving that place by the hellfire, Mr. Flashby, and not her," said Randall, giving the blade a hard, sharp twist.

Flashby looked down, wide-eyed, unable to comprehend either the sight of the sword that had pierced his body or the flow of his life's blood pouring down the blood gutter of Randall's sword. Randall twisted the blade again, then pulled it out. Flashby stood for a moment, staring at his blood puddling on the ground, and then his eyes rolled back in his head and he fell backward into the dirt.

The Marshall knelt down by him and put his ear to Flashby's chest. Then he took up his hand and felt for a pulse. Shaking his head and getting to his feet, he said, "This man is dead. You may take your fellow officer away, gentlemen. You may tell your comrades that honor was, indeed, served." The two stunned subalterns managed to pick up their suddenly deceased senior officer and drape his body across the saddle of his horse. After tying it down, they rode slowly off and were seen no more.

Shaking his head, the Marshall wearily walked back over to the body hanging under the gallows. Again he put his ear to a now still chest, again he lifted a dead hand and felt for a pulse. Again he shook his head.

"You may take her down, Mr. Trevelyne. Sheriff, I will now sign the death certificate. Justice has been done."

Randall climbed back into the wagon, his bloody sword still in hand, and signaled to George Swindow to back up under the gallows. When Jacky's body hung directly over the coffin, he said, "Stop."

I could not take my eyes off the little stockinged foot that now pointed down at the coffin that would soon contain it and the rest of her. *Soon, now, Sister. Soon . . .*

Jim Tanner, who had leaped down to retrieve her shoe, to the great disappointment of the necromancers, was again back in the wagon.

"Open it up," said Randall, and Jim, his face red with fury, lifted the lid of the coffin.

I looked in. There was a bit of silk cushioning, a small pillow, and to the side rested her pennywhistle. How touching. *Well, this will serve,* I thought.

"I'll have my rope back, if you please," said the Executioner from on high.

"You'll get some of it back, Hangman, but not all," answered Randall. He put his left arm around the waist of the hanged girl, and with the sword that was still in his right hand, slashed at the tight rope, severing it. He dropped his sword as the body slumped in his arms, and as gently as he could, he laid his burden in the coffin. "But you shall have this back."

Randall untied the drawstring of the hood, gently drawing the hateful thing off her head and flinging it away.

I felt I could not bring myself to look upon her then, but I did. Her face was pale and her head lay to the side, her neck at a sharp angle, the thick rope concealing the marks that were sure to be on her throat. Her mouth was open, as it so often was in life when she smiled that vulpine grin, but now that mouth was slack, devoid of any mirth or joy. Her eyes, half-closed, stared out at nothing.

I could not stand seeing that. I reached out my left hand, and with my fingers, closed her eyes. Then, because I had promised, I began to put her body right.

"Jim. Your knife, if you please," I said, and put out my hand. The blade was put in it and I leaned down and cut her hands free of the bonds. First I cut the rope that went around her waist, then slid the knife next to her wrists and cut the ropes that bound her hands. Then I tried to loosen the noose's knot, but I could not, so I slipped the blade between her neck and the rope and began sawing away, but Randall appeared next to me and said, "Let me do that." He took the knife from me and flung it back to Jim and put his fingers between her neck and the rope that had choked off her life and pulled on the knot and so was able to loosen it and take it off, her head bouncing senseless off the silk pillow as he did so. He threw the thing at the Executioner, but the wind caught it and it fell among what remained of the ghoulish crowd, which swarmed over the prize like flies on carrion.

I moved her body a little so she would lie flat on her

back. I straightened her legs, putting her feet together. I took off her other shoe. Then I placed the pennywhistle on her chest and picked up her hands and crossed them on it. *There, it is all done, Jacky. Almost all done.*

"Forgive me, Lord, for what I am about to do," I said as I climbed into the coffin and knelt over her remains, my knees just outside of hers in the narrow space. "Wait for me, Sister. I am coming with you," I said as I drew out the loaded pistol I had concealed beneath my cloak the night before and held the barrel to my temple. "One grave will suffice for the two of us." I closed my eyes and pulled the trigger.

I believed I heard Jim Tanner cry, "No, Miss, don't!" just before the hammer came down and the flint struck the steel that would ignite the powder charge, which would take me out of this woeful life.

But I felt not the shock of a cleansing bullet going through my brain, nor did I see the flash of divine light that would mean heaven was nigh, nor feel the soft comforting blackness of the Void. I saw not the hand of my friend extended toward me in the brightness at heaven's gate, smiling her foxy grin and waiting for me to take that hand and cross over with her to the other side. No, I was rewarded only with a click and a dull pop, and when I opened my eyes, I saw only the still body of my friend lying below me and I knew that the pistol had misfired and that I yet remained in this wretched world.

I looked at the pistol and cocked the hammer again, then thrust the barrel in my mouth and fired again, and again, ramming the barrel against the back of my throat, tears of frustration pouring out of my eyes. But nothing . . .

no, nothing but the smell of wet powder, and I knew the truth of it: Randall had found the pistol when I slept last night and had wet the powder.

My friend had gone over to the other side and I was left behind in this vale of tears, and there was no catching up with her now.

I fell down upon her body and wailed out my despair.

Then I felt hands upon me, and I was pulled from the coffin by Randall and Jim and put down on the floor of the wagon.

Oh, God, if you won't let me go with her, at least take my mind and wipe it clean. Let me be a mindless lunatic, anything but this . . .

"The lid, Jim," I heard Randall say. "Let's get it on. There. Hand me the hammer." Then I heard the sound of pounding, which went on for a while and then stopped.

Randall, having driven in the last coffin nail, took the hammer and hurled it out into the crowd. He threw it with all the strength and rage that was in him, shouting, "Here, scum, see if there's any black magic in that! The very hammer that nailed the coffin on Jacky Faber! May you all rot!" There was a yelp of pain when it landed, but again there was a struggle to gain the prize.

"Mr. Swindow, let us be gone," said Randall, sheathing his sword and sitting down next to my crumpled form. He said something to Jim Tanner, who nodded and jumped out of the wagon.

George flicked the reins over the backs of the horses, and the cortege, small as it was, began the journey back to Dovecote, bearing its sad burden. I felt Randall's hand on my shoulder as we left that horrid ground, and it did give me some small measure of comfort, in spite of it all.

We traveled in silence for quite some time, a silence broken only by the snorts of the horses and the sound of their hooves on the road; that, and the steady sound of my own weeping. Randall rooted around and found the rum bottle he had been drinking out of earlier and took a long swig from it.

Presently, we rounded a curve in the road and I found that we had left the town entirely behind us. There was only countryside all around us now.

"Sit up, Sister," said Randall. "Come, now, look about you. Do you not see the growing things all around?"

I sat and looked out on the green, growing fields.

"Yes," I managed to say.

"There will be a harvest here in the fall. There will be one at Dovecote as well. Will you be there to see it brought in?"

I noticed that a troop of horsemen had come up and closed in around us. They wore the colors of Randall's militia unit, but I cared little for that.

"Will you, Sister?"

"It is so hard," I whimpered, "to keep going on."

"She would want you to keep on. Certainly you know that."

"I know, but . . ."

"We will abide, Sister, through this season and the next, and the ones after that, too. Will you be with those who love you, Sister, and see those harvests in?"

Exhausted, I bowed my head and nodded.

"I will abide," I whispered.

"Good," said Randall, putting the bottle to my lips and tipping it up. "Here, have a drink of this. It will refresh you."

The liquid hit my mouth, spilling out, and I expected the harsh bite of rum on my tongue, but . . . what? Sassafras? Root beer? What?

"Would that the unfortunate Lieutenant Flashby had known what was in the bottle, eh?" Randall laughed. He leaned back and rapped sharply with his knuckles on the coffin. "How's it going in there?"

"It is gettin' a mite stuffy in here," said a voice from inside the box. "Could you possibly pop the top a wee bit?"

Randall picked up a crowbar from beneath the wagon's seat and inserted it under the lid of the coffin and pried it up a few inches.

Instantly, a nose and a pair of lips appeared at the opening and noisily sucked in the cool outside air. In my astonishment, I was reminded of a time when I was a young girl being taken by Randall on a winter walk along the shore of the frozen bay and we saw the nose of a young seal come up to an opening in the thick winter ice, to draw a life-giving breath.

Then I fell backward in a dead faint.

Chapter 44

THE BOSTON PATRIOT

Nov. 10, 1809—Special Edition

NOTORIOUS PYRATE AND BRITISH SPY JACKY FABER HANGED

THE CONDEMNED SHOWED NO REMORSE AT END OF LIFE

Your Correspondent on the Scene, Mr. David Lawrence, reporting on the Events of the Day:

Protesting her Innocence to the last, the Criminal Jacky Faber, also known as Bloody Jack, the Scourge of the Caribbean; La Belle Jeune Fille Sans Merci; the Lily of the West; and the Belle of Botany Bay, was hanged today at 9:38 in the morning by Order of the State of Massachusetts, County of Plymouth, having been Convicted of High Treason against the United States. Incriminating Documents concerning detailed plans of the Fortifications at Fort McHenry had been found in her possession.

Other charges laid against her in the past include Piracy, Murder, Arson, Inciting to Riot, & Robbery.

The Condemned was brought out of the jailhouse at 9 o'clock and escorted to the Gallows by the local Sheriff, his Deputies, along with the Reverend Milton and the Federal Marshall. She appeared calm, but had to be steadied when she caught sight of the Gallows.

Recovering herself, she mounted the stairs and seemed ready to meet her Fate. She spoke some last words concerning her Innocence, and was led by the Executioner to stand upon the trap. The noose was put in place about her neck, and the Marshall had his hand on the lever that would spring the trap, when there were several interruptions. Those resolved, the trap was sprung, and she fell to her death. The crowd, which was considerable, was at the end sympathetic to her. For while they expected to find a shrill harridan being hanged, instead they found a very slight and pitiable young girl. A great mournful sigh was heard from the assembled when she was let off.

She suffered much and her struggles were long,

but she was finally pronounced Dead at 9:58. Her body was claimed by friends for the burial at the Dovecote Estate, in Quincy.

More on this in our Regular Edition.

David Lawrence, Jr.

Chapter 45

James Fletcher
On the road to Dovecote Farm
Quincy, Massachusetts

My dearest Jacky, lost forever,

Now I truly write to a ghost. When I hurried off the ship that bore me to Boston, with the papers that would have exonerated you under my arm, I was joyful and full of anxious hope, but all that was cruelly dashed when I heard the hawker's call and grabbed the hateful broadsheet to read the awful words. I was too late. Too late, dear God, always too late . . . My heart turned to lead, and so it shall remain.

I was too shattered by the terrible news to seek out any of your friends with whom to share our mutual grief and rage over the monstrous act that took your life. No, instead I hired a horse and am traveling alone to the place where they have buried you, so I may stand next to you one last time.

You might think, Jacky, wherever you may be in this universe — and I know you are somewhere — that I would stop these messages of the mind from me to you, but I know now that I will not. I will talk to you in this way to the end of my days, for you will always be with me, you, my brown-eyed sailor.

I am approaching Dovecote now, and, oh, what a sad, sad throng it must contain, and I must go to join them.

But I will contain myself, so as not to add to their woe. I'm sure you would ask that of me.

There's the gatepost now.

With ashes in my mouth, and no joy in my heart, I say goodbye, Jacky, for now.

Always,
Jaimy

Chapter 46

"So, Miss Faber, it seems that at last you have consented to play Cordelia, as I knew you someday would!" crows Mr. Fennel, still in disguise as the Federal Marshall.

"And played her very well, I must say," adds Mr. Bean, late the Humpbacked Hangman, who had by this time taken off the hump, along with the Executioner's hood and the false whiskers he had worn beneath the thing. "The suffering portrayed, the nobility, the agony... My lips cannot frame the words, except to say, 'a toast to our Cordelia!'"

"Hear, hear!" There are roars all around as glasses are lifted in my direction. This is a *very* festive gathering.

"It was not hard, since that harness hurt like hell," I retort, rubbing my armpits, which had taken most of the punishment from the drop. The Cordelia dress also had straps that went about the waist and between the legs, so I was a bit sore in those places as well. "The worst thing was having to hang there, perfectly still, hardly breathing, with the hood over my head and quite blind to what was going on all around me. There I was trying to guess . . . not knowing if the trick was working, nor able to watch what was happening twixt poor Randall and that Flashby."

"And, oh! The bit with the shoe, such a nice touch!" enthuses Mr. Fennell. "Pure tragic poetry!"

"Really, my dear friends, I did nothing," I protest, exhausted from the events of the day. "It was you who saved my poor unworthy self, and I mean that. Thank you from the bottom of my heart and soul."

"Well, then a toast to the master plotter, the one who set the whole game afoot, our own Mr. John Higgins!"

"Hear, hear! John Higgins!"

"Please," says Higgins, in all modesty, shaking his head in refusal of the honor. "I merely helped design the plot, but the deed could not have been accomplished without the help of all those involved." He lifts his glass. "A toast to the Grand Conspirators!"

"Hear, hear!"

All, or almost all, of the conspirators are seated in riotous celebration, not in the grand dining room at Dovecote but at a long table in a side room, a room with many windows so we can watch for the arrival of anyone who might question the proceedings of the morning in Plymouth. Although I have been saved once again by my loving friends, I am not yet exonerated of the false charges against my name. We wait for nightfall, when I will go onboard the Nancy B. *and be spirited away to safety somewhere in this world, as I cannot remain here long. Jim Tanner had brought the schooner down from Boston, and she is now anchored off the beach at Dovecote. Where I will go, I do not know, but I ain't thinking about that now. I'm just glad to be still alive and with my friends.*

It was Higgins who opened the coffin after the wagon, surrounded by a company of soldiers, was pulled around to a side door of Dovecote's main house.

He reached in, lifted me out, and carried me up to Amy's room, with her following right behind. It might have been a bit of a shock to him, for I had fallen sound asleep in there, having had no sleep the night before. I must have looked the perfect hanged corpse — especially with that old neck welt I had long ago gotten courtesy of the pirate Le Fievre, all flared up and red, as it always became during times of stress. When I awoke to see his dear face above me, I cried, "Oh, Higgins, I . . . I . . . can't tell you . . ."

"There, there, Miss. A change of clothes and a little rest and you'll be your old self again." I could say nothing, I could only sob and bury my face in his neck as I was carried in.

"And Mr. Trevelyne, what a great performance!" continues Mr. Fennell, quaffing yet another glass of wine. He is plainly in a congratulatory mood, and I fear for the Trevelyne wine cellar as I see glasses being filled and refilled around the table. "The pitiful drunkard who turns into the hero who saves the day!" Randall lifts his glass in acknowledgment of the praise.

"You all saved the day, and I cannot thank you enough," says I, meaning it to the depth of my being and about to break into tears again.

"It was nothing, my dear," exults Mr. Bean. "Fooling a bunch of country bumpkins, why, we do it all the time. Given the opportunity, we could have convinced them I was the King of Spain and Mr. Fennell was Madame Du Barry!" Much laughter and more toasts.

"But, Sirs, surely there was a real Marshall and a real Hangman?" I say, sniffing back a sob. "I mean, the Sheriff and the court at Plymouth would not simply have accepted you on your word that you were sent to officiate at my hanging!"

"Indeed, there were," answers Higgins. He sits at my left side, while Amy sits, fuming, to my right. "It was Mr. Pickering who found out in court who had been assigned the task. He also found out when they would be leaving Boston and what route they would take. It was then an easy matter to waylay them, confine them, and take their papers. And it was Mistress Pimm who contacted two of 'her girls' in Plymouth to join the Ladies Aid Society, to effect the exchange of dresses, and Mr. Trevelyne who, with his superb act as a drunkard, managed to deliver the Cordelia dress to the cell without its being examined by the Sheriff."

"What I do not understand is why I was not let in on the plot?" demands Amy, arms crossed, eyes narrowed, and lower lip out in a pout, very much as I would have been had I been in her place. She is *not* laughing and carousing with the rest.

"Ah, dear sister Amy," says Randall. "We thought you would give a much more convincing performance if you were kept in the dark. And you did, oh, yes, you did!"

"Yes, please forgive us, Miss Trevelyne," says Mr. Fennell. "But the fewer people who know a secret, the better. As our Dr. Franklin once said, 'Three people may keep a secret if two of them are dead.'"

"After all, Miss, you are a lady and not a trained actress," purrs Polly Von. "And Randy thought it best."

"Oh, *Randy*, is it, now?" snarls Amy, who is about to say more, when I step into the breach.

I put my hand upon Amy's arm. "I myself didn't know until last night, when Randall brought in the Cordelia dress and I recognized the dreaded Hangman as dear Mr. Bean. You and Randall were tossed out, so I could not tell you. As I put the dress on and Mr. Bean adjusted the straps, he whispered details of the plot and how I was to play my part in it. You see?"

Amy nods, and then smiles at me. "I know I should still be angry, but the joy of the outcome of this day overwhelms all other feelings."

And you, Sister, I think, *so willing to follow me over to the other side . . . tsk! And when you climbed into the coffin with me, you put your knee in my belly and I almost let out an ooof, which would have ruined everything. If you ever try something like that again, I will shoot you myself. But, yes, let the joy of this day banish all else.*

Then a thought occurs to me. "What about that open grave up on Daisy Hill? Suppose someone looks and finds me not there? Should I not be laid out in the parlor or something?"

"We have put Gulliver MacFarland in it. It is a fresh grave," replies Amy. "No one will be suspicious."

I nod, still too exhausted to do any more crying. *Poor Gully. You did try to make things right, Gully, at the end, you did.*

Blount refills my glass, and I shake off sad thoughts of magic fiddlers and say to Higgins, "Did you think me not alive when you opened the coffin and looked in on me, my eyes closed and looking dead to the world?" I tease, the wine beginning to warm me and make me bold.

"No, Miss, I did not, as I heard you lustily snoring in there before I lifted the lid," he says right back at me to great laughter and applause all around. "But it was a very delicate, quite ladylike sort of snore, Miss, you may rest assured." More guffaws at my expense.

I give him my best I'll-get-you-for-that look and turn to Randall. "A very picturesque wound you have there, Lieutenant Trevelyne. You wear it well. The fact that you received it while defending what was left of my good name, as well as that of your family, makes me doubly grateful to you." I lift my glass to him. "Having to hang silently there, not knowing what was happening to you, hearing only the words spoken and the clash of swords, was one of the worst tortures I have ever endured."

Randall lifts his glass to me. Polly has cleansed his wound and tied a white bandage around his brow, and he somehow manages to look all the more roguish for it. A spot of red has appeared on it, but the blood flow seems to have stopped. "A mere trifle, my dear, one that will hardly be noted in the annals of great moments in the history of love and war."

I don't know about war, but as for love, I do know that Polly is right at his side, looking up at him with those great glorious blue eyes fairly brimming with tears of love and admiration. I know that Amy thinks it's all an act on her part, but I don't. I've known Pretty Polly since she was six, and I believe I know her quite well, her faults as well as her virtues. Randall's arm is carelessly thrown around Polly's shoulders but, I perceive, not all that carelessly. I see his fingers gently stroking her cheek as he banters with me and the rest of the company.

"Can you not see Mr. Trevelyne trodding the boards as Prince Hal in *Henry the Fifth*?" asks Mr. Bean. "Or as the bold Hotspur?"

"Oh, indeed, Mr. Bean," retorts Mr. Fennell. "After the recent contretemps, it could not be much of a stretch for him."

As the accolades shift from me to others, I signal to Blount and ask of him a piece of paper and a pen. It is immediately supplied.

"How about as Romeo opposite our Jacky as Juliet?" counters Randall, grinning widely, as he gets a mock glare and a poke from the real actress who sits close beside him. "Excuse me. I meant, of course, my dear Polly. How could I have . . ."

As they all laugh, I pen my quick note. While I put an address on the outside, I do not bother with any on the letter itself. Instead I draw my grinning skull and crossbones up at the top and write . . .

Dear Captain Blood,

Never, ever write me off till you see me actually hanging in a gibbet.

And if ever we shall meet on the High Seas, Edgar, I shall blow you out of the water. Count on it.

Yo, ho, ho.

La Belle Dame Sans Merci

I blow on the note to dry the ink, then fold it up and hand it to Blount with a request to see to it that the letter is delivered. I purposely did not date it, so that Edgar will have to wonder whether I wrote it *before* or *after* the execution. Serves him right, and maybe it will stimulate his very active imagination.

The talk rambles on till there is the rattle of hooves and a commotion outside the door. It is roughly shoved open, and before anyone can react, an officer in full uniform enters. Higgins, the first to recover, gets to his feet and says, "May I present the Commander of the company of infantry that captured the unfortunate Marshall and Hangman, Captain Clarissa Worthington Howe."

I shoot to my feet and gasp in wonder.

Clarissa? Captain Howe?

She is dressed in a fine red riding habit cut in the military style, with white turnouts and gold braid, a gay red bonnet on her head, and, of course, looks splendid. On her shoulders rest the epaulets of a cavalry captain. In her hand is her riding crop, which she slaps into her palm as she gazes into my eyes.

"So it worked," she says, turning about to cast a queenly look down her aristocratic nose at the assembly. "Good." She turns to Randall. "I assume I can release those two awful men now and take my company back to Virginia?"

"Best wait a few days, Captain," says Randall, leaning back languidly in his chair and looking not overly impressed with the new arrival. Virtually everyone here shares some sort of history with Clarissa Worthington Howe. "Till we can get her safely away."

"Well, good," she says as a chair is pulled out for her and

she settles her perfect body into it. "It is very pleasant to once again enjoy the hospitality of dear old Dovecote . . . and the pleasure of Miss Jacky Faber's sparkling company. How good to see you, and so glad that my men and I have been able to be of service to you, Jacky, dear."

All the pent-up rage I have ever felt for Clarissa, my great enemy and sometimes friend, comes bubbling up in me and I clench my fists in helpless fury. However, now I owe her a lot, and so I seethe and I fume. Then all I say is . . .

"*Captain?* Clarissa? How . . . ?"

She looks off, bemused. "Daddy promised me a company of militia if I would agree to leave New Orleans and come back home. And so I did. And here they are, armed and ready."

"Was there anything left of New Orleans," I ask, "when they threw your skinny ass out?"

"They will recover." She sniffs.

"But what if there is trouble with the federal government over this?" I persist.

"Who cares? If they want to start a civil war, let it begin here," she replies with a toss of her blond curls. "Oh, and Blount, two glasses," she says as the butler puts a glass in front or her.

"My husband will be in directly," she says to me with a slight smirk. "He's seeing to his men."

It is then that I notice the ornate gold ring that rests on the third finger of her left hand.

Clarissa is married!

Amy notices at the same time and we exchange looks. *Oh, the poor man, who could — ?*

The door opens and Cavalry Major Lord Richard Allen strides in, resplendent in his scarlet regimentals.

"Cheerio, all!"

Richard!

I leap up and throw myself upon him. *Oh, Richard, I am so glad to see you, so glad . . .*

"Princess!" he exults, gathering me to him and swinging me around.

I poke around at the site of the wound he had received at Vimeiro, weeping and asking, "Are you all right? You have completely recovered? But . . . but . . . what are you doing here?"

"Well, Sergeant Bailey and the lads and I thought we might like a little respite from the heat down in Jamaica, so we took up Clarissa's invitation to come north for a bit. Quite bracing, I must say. And then we found that Prettybottom had gotten that same bottom in a bit of a mess — her ass in a sling, as it were — so we were glad to come up to help out. And do some other things."

It is then that I reach for his hand, his left hand, and am about to hold it to my breast, when I feel something on his finger and realize in an instant that I must step back, I must forever step back from my gallant Cavalry Major Lord Richard Allen.

It is a wedding ring.

As I release him, Clarissa holds up her own ringed hand and waves it so that there is no mistake. She wears a wide smile.

"Everybody," I say, in as calm a tone as I am able, "may I introduce Lord Richard Allen, a very dear friend of mine?"

Bows and curtsies all around, except from Clarissa and me. We rise and face each other.

"Say it," she says, her eyes level with mine.

"Thank you, Clarissa, for helping to save me," I dutifully say.

An imperceptible shake of her head signals that that is not enough for her. I know what she wants, and I sigh and give it to her.

I give a low curtsy, come up, and say, "Thank you . . . Lady Allen."

Though it sticks in my throat, that will apparently do.

"You all know my wife, Clarissa, of course. Isn't she beautiful?" Lord Allen whips off her hat and ruffles her hair. "What a pistol! You should've seen her poke that vile Boston hangman with the point of her sword. He was on his knees, crying like a baby and begging for his miserable life! Ha!"

Again Amy and I look at each other. *Ruffling the Queen's hair? We've never seen anyone do that before! Finally, could our proud Clarissa be tamed?* Well, if any male could do it, it would be Richard Allen, and I wish them both the best.

"A true feather in my cap, I must say," he continues proudly. "And please, all of you, join us for the hunting season in Virginia. I am sure our Clarissa would agree."

"Yes, do," says our Clarissa. "Perhaps I shall teach you how to ride properly, Jacky."

"Well, we must be off. Archie and the lads send regards. I am sure they are well into their plans to knock up at least half of Dovecote's domestic staff and I must set them straight. Come, Clarissa, let us go. I do outrank you, so you must obey. Cheerio, all."

He extends his hand to his recent bride, and she dutifully rises. As he hustles her out the door, he gives me a big wink. Then he turns back and, with a final clutch around my waist, whispers in my ear, "You've got to come, Prettybottom. I can't spend all that Howe money by myself! It's enormous! And now, one last kiss, Jacky, for old time's sake."

"Nay, you rascal," I say, turning my face from his. "I don't have many scruples, but one of them concerns kissing married men. Go now, you beautiful rogue. We will meet again, I know."

I put a modest kiss on his cheek, and he is gone.

I settle back down with my friends and heave a sigh for a certain bold dragoon. I have scarcely taken a breath when there is yet another commotion outside.

Oh, no! Another alarm! There is a knock on the door and everyone suddenly falls silent. Amy is closest, and she jumps up to look out the tiny window set in the door.

"It is Sergeant Matthews," she says, opening the door to one of the militiamen.

The soldier enters and says, "Pardon, Miss, but someone on horseback is coming. It's a British officer," reports the soldier. "Navy, I think. Should I let him through?"

A shot of fear sends me to my feet. "I'll not be taken alive again, I won't! Higgins, my pistols! My friends, you've done all you can for me, please, save your—"

Amy pulls the curtain away from a window and peers out. "Save your concern, Sister, and come look," she says, smiling as broadly as I have ever seen her smile. "Yes, Sergeant, please lead the Lieutenant to the front entrance, if you will."

The militiaman salutes and leaves, while I go to the window to look out.

Oh, my God!

Chapter 47

The Journal of Amy Trevelyne, continued . . .
Dovecote Farm
Quincy, Massachusetts

"Good Lord," gasped Jacky in open-mouthed wonder as she clutched her clasped hands to her breast. "It's Jaimy! My Jaimy Fletcher! Oh, my joy!"

I stood with her at the window on that wonderful day and looked out over her trembling shoulder. It was, indeed, a very pale and drawn Mr. Fletcher out there, tying the reins of his mount to the hitching post. After doing so, he commenced to walk slowly to the front door. He had a packet of some sort under his arm.

I watched to see what my friend would do at this point, the culmination of all her dreams and aspirations. I would certainly have expected her to rush out and fling herself in his arms, but instead, she turned, her face radiant with happiness, and said, "Polly! Go meet him at the front door! You are a serving girl full of grief over my being strung up! Keep him there until you are given a signal, then send him up the hill. I need to change!" And with that, she ran out of the room. I knew Jacky was headed for my bedroom, as her sea-bag rested there on the floor, and I thought I knew what she had in mind.

Polly put her hands to her face and said, "All right. Give me a moment to get in character." She took a deep, theatrical breath, then said, "There. I've got it." She put her hands together in front of her face, and I swear a tear trick-led out of each eye. We heard the expected knock on the front door and Polly exited, stage left, as it were, to go an-swer it.

I did not immediately follow my friend up to my room, but instead stayed back to find out what would be said in the entrance hall so that I could record it here.

"Good d-d-day to you, Sir," stammers Polly tearfully, upon seeing James Fletcher in the doorway. "Please do come in."

"Thank you, Miss. My . . . my name is James Fletcher and . . ."

"Oh, Mr. Fletcher!" wails Polly, falling to her knees be-fore him and covering her face with her hands. "I know who you are, and I must tell you that the most awful thing has happened!"

A bit overly theatrical for my taste, but I let it go. Actors will be actors.

"I . . . know," he says softly. "I saw the newspapers when I landed in Boston. I have here with me the evidence that would have spared her" — it's plain he is trying to control his emotions — "but too late . . . always too late."

Polly rises from the floor with the utmost grace, of course, and puts her hands lightly on Mr. Fletcher's arm. She looks up at him with those huge, teary, baby-blue eyes and says, "Oh, Sir, her last words were spoken of you . . ."

I turn and hurry to my room. Jacky had best hurry or Polly will have him a total wreck.

"Why, Sister, do you wish to prolong his agony?" I ask as I enter the room where she is hurriedly undressing. "Why did you not just fly into his arms?"

"Because, Sister, I want him and me to reunite, for what I hope will be the final time, *alone,* and not in front of a roomful of people. It would not be fair to him to show myself then. It would have been a blow to his pride if he were to seem unmanly in front of others. Believe me, I know a lot about male pride. No, Amy, I want to do it this way."

"Perhaps, dear, you could wait until we have the Preacher here before you and him . . ." I suggest as my friend strips off her clothes.

"Nay, Sister, I have waited long enough, and so has he," she says, peeling off her black Lawson Peabody school dress and stepping out of it. "If I hesitate for even a moment, I'm sure a troop of Royal Marines will appear up over that hill with orders for him to return to his ship to sail away forever. Or Professor Tilly will show up with one of his silly kites to send me aloft again . . . or legions of black-robed Men of God will take me and hand me over to black-hooded hangmen waving their nooses . . . or Naval Intelligence will want me to spy again, or . . . *Damn!*"

Her foot gets caught on the waistband of her drawers and she falls over on the floor in her haste to get them off. Accomplishing that task, she gets back to her feet and whips her undershirt off over her head. She lunges to her seabag and rummages impatiently through it and at last says "Ha!"

as she draws out some sort of faded . . . *Aha!* I see that it is indeed the fabled Kingston dress . . .

". . . Or a Mike Fink, or a Constable Wiggins, or a Captain Scroggs, or the Spanish Inquisition, or Napoleon Bonaparte himself, or any of hundreds of others who want to be done with me for good and ever. No, Sister, I must go now."

She puts her arms through the short, puffy sleeves and flips the flimsy dress over her head. It slips over her body, covering her nakedness . . . well, at least it covers her from bottom of breastbone to top of knees.

She fluffs up her hair and sticks a leg out the open window, then turns to face me. "You see, Sister," she says, "I gave my vows long ago in a goldsmith's shop in Kingston, Jamaica, and I have kept those vows, in my way. Give me a moment's head start and then tell Polly to send him up. And if you will be so good as to do me a great favor, Amy, I'd like you to keep everyone out of the barn for a good long while, as we'll be needin' the hayloft."

Then she grins that oh-so-familiar open-mouthed, foxy grin of hers, and is out the window.

I go to the window and watch my dearest friend race up Daisy Hill, her hair loose and blowing in the breeze, her legs flashing under the hem of that ridiculous rag of a dress. In less than a moment she is gone from my sight.

I heave a great sigh and go back to the parlor and give the nod to Polly. She catches my eye and says, "Yes, Sir, it's at the top of the hill. In a very pretty place, I . . . I think you'll take much comfort there."

She stifles a sob and takes her hands from Mr. Fletcher's arm, puts those same hands to her face, and collapses in tears into a nearby chair. It's a bit overdone, Gentle Reader, you will agree, but let it go, for it is just such a joyous time and all can be forgiven their excesses. Mr. Fletcher's back is to me, so I am able to slip out of the parlor and back to my room, unseen. I go again to my window and look out. In a few moments, I see the poor, bereft Lieutenant James Fletcher trudging up the hill, a world of sadness on his shoulders. He will come down from that hill a much happier man, and I wish him the total and absolute joy of this day.

Well, *ahem!* There are things that must be done. First, I must go back down to see that a basket of bread and cheeses and cold meats is prepared, which will be discreetly set at the foot of the ladder to the hayloft. Several bottles of wine, too, are added, as those two will need more sustenance than just love and love only.

I'll go outside to the place where the barn is missing a few boards, the same spot where she and I, snug in the hay, used to lie side by side and look out on the green fields of late summer to dream our dreams, and I will softly call up to her that there is refreshment below. No, no, Gentle Reader, do not think me forward. I know her, and I know her appetites, and I know she will not mind that slight invasion of their privacy.

Some thin sheets and blankets will be provided, too, for the night might turn chilly, and it is entirely possible that they will not emerge till morning. Although they will be wrapped up in each other's warmth and buried deep in the hay, their cuddling might not be enough to serve them comfortable, on this, their wedding night . . . or almost wedding night.

Oh, I expect the lovers will come out tomorrow morning, sated with love, for the time being, at least. They will be disheveled, with straw poking out of their clothes, leaning into each other as they walk down the path to the house. We will take her from him to clean her up and get her into the wedding dress, and we will prepare for the ceremony and the wedding banquet. She will sparkle and be gay, but all will know that what she really wants the most is to run off to the hayloft with her Jaimy again. After all is said and done, we will let them go.

Ah, but I am getting ahead of myself. There are more things to do, for we have this wedding to plan on very short notice.

First, I must send a boy to fetch Reverend Sturgis to perform the ceremony. Though it will be a day or two late, I'm sure that even in our strict society she should still be permitted to wear white, as the act of marriage was close enough in time to the legal contract of marriage. Not that she would care one whit whether the dress be white or scarlet, but she would care very much if they succeed in putting a baby in her belly this day — and it is very possible that they will. She'll want the child to bear the father's name, no matter what she says now. So I must have our Dovecote girls put together a white gown and veil. It will be simple, with a high neck, straight front, and gathered back, I think. She may protest, but I will be firm. She will *not* be married in that Kingston rag, not in my house she won't.

I ring my little bell, and when the girl knocks and is told to come in, I say, "Charity, please tell Mrs. Grubbs that we'll be putting together a wedding and reception for, maybe, fifty . . . no, sixty people, tomorrow or the next day. Yes, we'll need all the fatted geese and turkeys, so make preparations.

Yes, dear, it will, indeed, be a grand time for all. Off with you now . . ."

Oh, yes, and a man must be sent immediately on horseback to Boston to inform her friends that they will be going to her wedding and not to her funeral, which news I know will be received most joyfully. I have been informed that the *Lorelei Lee* has made port in Boston, and I am sure she will be loaded with all her Boston friends, to be brought here to Dovecote for the celebration: Peg Mooney, Sylvie and Henry Hoffman, Annie Jones, and Betsey and Ephraim Fyffe; and, of course, Joannie Nichols and the entire student body of the Lawson Peabody School for Young Girls. Rebecca Adams is still in attendance and it's entirely possible she could persuade former President and Mrs. Adams to join us in that happy celebration, as they live not far away. I know old John still enjoys a good party. And Chloe Cantrell and Solomon Freeman and Daniel Prescott and the rest of her various crews. I can just imagine the introductions . . . *Mr. President, may I present John Thomas and Smasher McGee, both able-bodied Yankee seamen.*

Oh, and Maudie and her man Bob from the Pig and Whistle, can't forget them, and Jemimah Moses, too, as well as many, many others. I know that Jacky will be overjoyed to see each and every one of them. In fact, I don't expect her eyes to be dry for days, as she is famous for crying most copiously during times of great happiness.

Bridesmaids? Mairead McConnaughey, of course. And Joanie and Rebecca and Annie and Betsey, and yes, Molly Malone; and it is to her that I wager Jacky will throw the bridal bouquet.

Ringbearer? That will be little Ravi, for sure. Turban and all.

And that other master plotter, Mistress Pimm — she with her Underground Network of Pimm's Girls and the Cordelia dress switch they accomplished — shall be Matron of Honor, and well she should be, having taken on Jacky Faber, who was, without doubt, the Lawson Peabody's most difficult student, and having succeeded in both her education and her refinement.

Best Man? I am sure that James Fletcher will choose John Higgins, and I am equally sure that Liam Delaney, Jacky's old sea dad on the *Dolphin,* will be glad to act as father of the bride and will joyously give her away, in probably vain hopes that she will finally settle down.

And as for the groomsmen, well, there are Davy and Tink, the present members of the Dread Brotherhood of Ship's Boys of HMS *Dolphin,* plus Jim Tanner, Ian McConnaughey, James Fletcher's First Mate on the *Cereberus* . . . and let's be a little evil here, shall we? How about Arthur McBride, Mr. Fletcher's constant thorn-in-side? *Hmm* . . . ? Or Cavalry Major Lord Richard Allen? I'm sure he will be good for a few ribald jabs in regard to his Princess Prettybottom . . . There will be enough from those two to keep Mr. Fletcher very red-faced in his effort to keep his emotions under control. Maybe some of Jacky's wickedness is rubbing off on me.

My wedding present to her, and to Jaimy, will be that little piece of land that adjoins Dovecote to the west. It is on the river, and she will appreciate that, I think, always having a connection to the sea. The land was left to me by a great-aunt, and I have little use for it. They will have a cottage built there, with green fields and red roses all about. Whether Mr. Fletcher will be able to keep her in it is quite another thing, but at least it will be a place for her to rest between voyages.

The Reader will have noted that I did not mention either Brother Randall or myself, in any capacity, as we might well be otherwise occupied during the coming festivities. Who knows, Dovecote may have more than one wedding this week. And maybe more than two.

Ah, Dear Reader, I know my mind rambles and my pen wanders aimlessly over the page, but I hope you will forgive me, as I am in a state of complete and utter joy.

Well, there goes Edward off to Boston in a rattle of hoofbeats and a cloud of dust to spread the great good news. Tucked in his vest is a special letter that I had quickly penned and given him to deliver. It is addressed to my dear Mr. Pickering, and in it I inform him that Miss Amy Trevelyne will be most glad to wait on him upon his arrival, as I am now ready for that sort of thing.

All is in train — the riders dispatched, the preparations begun. The *Nancy B.* lies out on the bay, waiting to take the two lovers off to wherever in this world they wish to go, no longer star-crossed. Of course, I do not know for sure that this is what is going to happen, but I do not think I will be proven so very far from wrong.

However, Dear Reader, if you are a person of a doubting nature, fear not, for you shall know the truth of it in the following way: If you find no further entries in this journal by my hand, then you will know that my predictions were found to be perfectly and absolutely correct.

Researcher's Note:

The above is the last page in a recently found journal "An Account of the Life and Times of the Adventurer Miss Jacky Faber, Otherwise Known as Bloody Jack," which is stored in the archives of Radcliffe College, Cambridge, Massachusetts, and was used extensively in the doctoral thesis of Rebecca Byrnes Adams, PhD, "Early Eighteenth-Century Women Poets and Their Times," published by University Press in 2004. The journal was found, carefully bound in black ribbon, in a chest in the attic of Trevelyne House in Quincy, Massachusetts, now a National Historical Site, and bequeathed by the Adams family to Radcliffe College, along with many other invaluable notes and papers. Dr. Adams is a direct descendant of the author. The manuscript is signed, "Mrs. Amy Trevelyne Pickering, in Her Own Hand, November 10, Eighteen Hundred and Nine."

Chapter 48

I run up the path to Daisy Hill, then slow to a walk next to the fresh grave there at the top. I put my hand on the simple board that someone had put at the head of the grave and that bears the words... SHE WILL PLAY THE WILD ROVER NO MORE.

Poor Gully. I know you meant well and I do hope there really is a place called Fiddler's Green and you are there now and happy. And I'll wager there's some fiddle repairman there who can put the Lady Lenore back together — maybe the same old Italian who made her in the first place will do her up again. Wouldn't that be something? Shall I sing you a verse or two before my Jaimy comes up here to join me?

And I sing in a soft voice...

> I've traveled this wide world over
> And now to another I go.
> And I know that good quarters are waiting
> To welcome Old Rosin the Beau...

Here's the verse you always liked to bellow out, Gully...

My race on this world is now over.
And up to Heaven I'll go.
Send up a hogshead of whiskey,
To welcome Old Rosin the Beau!

And I hope you are, indeed, welcome, wherever you are, Gully, and . . . *Uh-oh! He's coming!*

I dive into the bushes that grow at the crest of the hill, to hide and to wait.

I do not have to wait long, for soon my dear James Emerson Fletcher comes along, his shoulders slumped, his face a mask of sorrow and pain. I part the high grass to watch what he does. *Oh, Jaimy, it's been so long, and I'm sorry, but I just want to savor this moment so that I can remember it forever. I'm sorry, but it's my nature, and I do want to do it this way. It's wrong of me, but just a little longer, a little bit longer, Jaimy. You'll see, you'll see.*

Jaimy walks up to the crest of the hill and goes to the grave. I see him read the simple epitaph on the rough board that was put up at the head of it.

He shakes his head and then bends down and kneels on the grass next to the freshly turned earth and begins to talk to me.

"I'm sorry, Jacky, I . . . I . . . was too late," he whispers, his voice shaking. "I was always just a little too late for you, always a step behind, never able to catch and hold you and protect you and . . ." He stops talking and simply stares down at the head of the grave for many moments and then finally says, "I hope and pray you are in a better place and looking down upon me now."

Oh, I am looking down upon you, Jaimy, with all the love

I have in me. And as for that better place, well, the hayloft will have to do, my dear, and I think we will find it just the finest of bowers.

Then he reaches his hand into his jacket . . .

Uh-oh! I have already seen this day someone willing to follow me into the next world. No, Jaimy, not you, too . . .

But it is not a pistol that he brings out, it is a ring — a match to the one I wear on a chain about my neck. They are the rings we placed on each other's fingers that wonderful day in Kingston, all those years ago.

I part the bushes and step out into the light and stand next to the marker at the head of the grave. Startled, he turns his head at the sound of my footfall on the grass. My Kingston dress blows about my knees and I put my hands behind my back and I say to him what I said on that same day in Jamaica. "Hullo, Jaimy . . . So what do you think of your saucy sailor girl now?"

His eyes widen and his mouth drops open. I *do* love astounding this dear boy.

"Jacky . . . No, it can't be you . . . It can't be . . . They killed you . . . I must be seeing a . . .

"No, Jaimy, I'm not a ghost from our past. My good friends came in the nick of time to save my poor self, as they have done so many times before. Stand up, Jaimy, and hold me. You're gonna see that I'm quite real."

And I'm trying not to cry, Jaimy, at this, my happiest of moments, but I feel the tears coming anyway. Unbidden as they are, they are tears of joy, pure joy.

"Please, Jaimy, come hold me . . ."

For I am alive and the blood still flows in my veins and the love of my life has come to join me . . .

"There's nobody here to keep us apart anymore, love, no, and there won't be, not ever again. So come put your ring on my finger, and we will be wed."

He rises to his feet and he opens his arms.

Oh, Jaimy, you are so splendid, so beautiful . . .

"Come kiss me, Jaimy, if you love me . . ."

And he does! Oh, yes, he does . . .

Author's Note

And so little Jacky Faber sails off into the sunset, her fondest wishes now come true—well, most of them, anyway—but is our wild girl finally done roving? Is this the last of our impetuous little lass? If it is, I will miss her, for I assure you I enjoyed every minute I spent recording her wild adventures. Gone for good? Well, she does have a way of popping back up, you know . . .

She did get her Bombay Rat and her Cathay Cat, and yes, she saw her Kangaroo, and all that, *but wait . . . what's that up there? Can't you see it? Just around the curve of the winding road, the bend of the river, just over the edge of the horizon, there . . .*

Sail on, sailor girl.